ISLE OF THE DEAD

Also by Julia Gray

ICE MAGE
FIRE MUSIC

ISLE OF
THE
DEAD

JULIA GRAY

ORBIT

An *Orbit* Book

First published in Great Britain by Orbit 2000

A CIP catalogue record for this book
is available from the British Library.

ISBN 1 85723 978 4

Typeset by Solidus (Bristol) Ltd, Bristol
Printed and bound in Great Britain by
Mackays of Chatham plc, Chatham, Kent

Orbit
A Division of
Little, Brown and Company (UK)
Brettenham House
Lancaster Place
London WC2E 7EN

With thanks, as always, to Meg Davis and Don Maass for their help and encouragement.

PROLOGUE

Lanzar had been waiting eight years for this moment, and now that it had arrived he was as unprepared as a new-born baby – and as helpless. Ever since his wife had given birth to twins, he had been sure the soldiers would come one day but, as the years passed, he had begun to hope that the daydreamers might have overlooked his remote mountain village. Perhaps the inevitable rumours about his children's talent might not have reached Qara. He realized now that he should have known better. Hope made a poor shield.

Although the soldiers approached at a leisurely pace, their horses were thoroughbreds, reared for stamina and speed, and there was no point in trying to outrun them. Even in terrain that Lanzar knew so well, flight would be futile. Given a few days' notice, he could have hidden his family away in one of the upland caves, where they would have survived for a few miserable months until winter came, but such thoughts were irrelevant now. With the early morning sun bright on the loose fitting white uniforms of the soldiers – who were suddenly so close that the jingle of their mounts' harness was clearly audible – Lanzar could only wait and prepare to lie, plead and, in the end, fight. He stood alone in the central clearing between the straggle of village huts. His neighbours knew better than to be drawn into this confrontation and, even in his bitterness, he could not blame them. Many of them had wanted him to take Sayer and Aphra to the authorities, to confirm or refute the suggestion that they possessed special abilities. Lanzar had been unable to accept this advice, knowing that he might well lose his children for good that way. Now it seemed that he was going to lose them anyway.

Behind him, obeying his command, Elta remained in their cabin with the twins. Like the rest of the village, they were silent as the cavalcade came to a halt. The patrol captain reined in his mount a few paces from Lanzar but did not dismount, merely looking down with a deceptive smile on his sun-hardened face.

'Welcome to our village, Captain. How may we assist you?'

'I think you know, Lanzar.'

The man's use of his name almost jolted the twins' father out of the last remnants of his composure, but he tried not to reveal the depths of his dread.

'There's no one here—'

'Your children,' the captain stated bluntly.

'I have none. The twins died as infants more than six years ago, and my wife and I have been barren since then.' The second part was true at least.

'You're lying,' the soldier replied contemptuously. 'The Eyes of Qara have seen them. They are needed for sacred work. The gods honour you.'

'The gods know . . .' Bile rose in Lanzar's throat and he could not complete the sentence.

A moment later all pretence became meaningless. A shrill cry sounded from the hut, and Lanzar turned in horror to see Aphra elude her mother's despairing grasp and run forward to join him. In her hands she carried his staff, the length of smooth wood dwarfing her eight-year-old frame. Moments later Sayer also emerged, moving more slowly, his frightened eyes locked on the soldiers but, as always, seeming to look into other worlds. Not for the first time, the boy was silently cursing the strange, inexplicable part of his mind that marked him as different from others and which had finally brought about this disaster.

The captain smiled again.

'A miracle!' he cried, mocking. 'Your children have returned from the dead.'

'Go away,' Aphra told him.

The soldier only laughed.

'I'm not scared of you,' she added defiantly.

'There's no reason why you should be.'

'And I'm not going with you.'

'In that you're wrong,' he replied calmly. 'You and Sayer are needed.'

'Please,' Lanzar put in. 'They're only children. What use—'

'The decision is made,' the captain stated, cutting off the protest. 'And we are wasting time.' He made a gesture with his hand, and a number of his men dismounted smoothly.

'I won't go!' Aphra screamed, trying to brandish the staff and almost overbalancing.

Lanzar caught her, took the staff and held it ready for combat. There was a whispering of steel as some of the guards drew their swords.

'You are no match for us,' the captain pointed out. 'Bloodshed would be pointless.'

Elta came out into the open then, her eyes wild and her hands fluttering like wounded birds.

'If they must go,' she cried in a terrified voice, 'then let us come too! They are all the family we have.'

'We have no use for talentless peasants. You all know the law. From this day, Sayer and Aphra are under the protection of the Archivects' Council. That is all the family they will need.' He waved his men forward.

'No. Have mercy. Please!' Elta ran forward to put herself between Aphra and the nearest of the advancing soldiers, and Lanzar saw the knife in his wife's hand for the first time. Her inexpert lunge was turned aside with disdainful ease and then the man clubbed her to the ground with his forearm. It all happened so quickly that Lanzar hardly had time to react, but Aphra moved faster, springing at her mother's assailant like an enraged wildcat, spitting and scratching. Already tasting defeat, Lanzar went to her aid but the soldier's companions intercepted him, and although he fought with the bravery born of desperation and landed a few telling blows, he was soon disarmed and forced to his knees. In the end, his opponents merely used the flat sides of their blades to batter him into a bloody, unconscious heap on the ground. His last thought was to wish that they had been given the necessary dispensation, and could do the job properly and kill him. The oblivion of death would have been a welcome escape.

The twins' own resistance was quickly overpowered and they were hoisted up to ride in front of two soldiers. As the cavalcade moved off, Sayer could see that Aphra was still squirming and struggling – and even managed to bite the wrist of her captor – but he slapped her hard and she subsided into tears of rage and misery.

No less heartbroken but more practical than his sister, Sayer went into exile in calmer, almost docile fashion, knowing he had no choice. Twisting round he saw, through eyes misted with his own tears, his mother crawl over to her husband, as a few of the other villagers slowly emerged from hiding. Elta's desolate wailing was the only sound that carried over the noise of the wind and the clatter of the horses' hooves, and the scene was imprinted on the boy's memory. It was the last time he would ever see his home – or his parents.

CHAPTER ONE

'The wall that divides us from heaven is at its thinnest
here. Rebuild my towers that we may hear the voices
of the gods once more.'

From *The Oracles of Zavanaiu*

This was the part of his job that Sayer hated. The main element of his task had been completed. The stone had been located, identified beyond doubt and registered in the legal tally by his scribe. Now it was up to the artisans and the silk to retrieve it.

It was Sayer's most important find to date; the cornerstone of the arch of the seventh door to the Ancestors' Shrine, one of the most significant structures within the Great Temple of Qara. He had been excited ever since the daydreamer's vision had indicated the relic's approximate location and he had been assigned the task of tracking it down. The journey had been long and sometimes arduous, but everything had gone smoothly and this should have been his moment of triumph. But as he watched the merchant grovel, he found it difficult to take much pleasure in the success, and just wanted the next stage to be over.

'Please, don't take the stone. You will ruin my home, my business, all of our lives.' The merchant waved an arm to indicate his wife and three young children. 'I beg of you—'

5

'Silence!' Captain Nazeri's white uniform was stained and dusty from travelling, but his badges of rank and natural air of authority lent weight to his command. 'Save your miserable breath, dung-eater. The stone is claimed. There is nothing more to say.'

For a moment Sayer thought the merchant might fall on his knees in supplication, but the man retained the last vestiges of his dignity even in the face of the soldier's insults.

'Then at least let me call the masons,' he pleaded. 'Perhaps we can save—'

'You should have thought of that when you bought a house containing a sacred relic,' Nazeri cut in, his expression unyielding. 'You know the law.'

'But there was no mention of it in the deeds. How was I to know?' The man's desperation was becoming embarrassing, and Sayer wished he would shut up.

'Then the deeds were forgeries,' the captain replied. 'You should not have been so eager for a bargain.'

The merchant had no answer to this, and his silence spoke volumes.

'It was cheap, no?' Nazeri went on, not bothering to hide his contempt. 'Because the man who sold it to you knew this day would come – and you are a greedy and gullible fool.'

By now a sullen but inquisitive crowd had gathered to watch the drama unfold. Sayer knew that the merchant was likely to receive scant sympathy. Until now he had been one of the lucky ones, rich enough to own a fine stone-built house, to eat well – his girth testified to that – and to raise a healthy looking family. Only a small proportion of the Tirokian population could say as much. Nevertheless the family clearly had some support, judging by the dismay and pity on the faces of some of the onlookers. Perhaps the merchant – whose name Sayer had been careful not to learn – was a good man and generous to his neighbours. Even so, they would not come to his aid, being held at bay by the presence of the soldiers and their natural awe of authority – and by the mysterious powers that had brought the visitors there. My powers, Sayer thought with a flash of pride. My magic.

The stone's unique resonance had drawn him to its location, and now it was as plain to him as the face of a friend. Asked to explain how this had happened, he would have fumbled for words, trying to describe a sense that was not sight, not hearing, not touch or taste or smell, but something of all of these and more. It was a sensation he experienced inside his head, with the whole of his being, and was a record of the past, an echo of history absorbed by the stone itself and available now only to those with rare talent. That the cornerstone had once been part of the Temple of Qara was something Sayer had already known – that was why they had come, after all – but now he knew, without conscious thought, how it had been stolen in the aftermath of the earthquake and how its long journey had eventually led to this provincial town far to the east, within a few leagues of the border with Khorasan. He had sensed earlier events too; from the distant past when the stone had been quarried, then shaped by mason and sculptor, their craft turning mere rock into an offering to the gods. It was one of many such histories now lodged in his brain, testament to his achievements as a seeker, and to his small part in the great task.

The merchant tried one last time to salvage something from the calamity that had befallen him.

'At least let me retrieve some of my stock, my tools. Grant me that small mercy.'

Nazeri spat on the ground.

'Be thankful we did not bring the house crashing down around your head,' he said. 'As it is I could arrest you, but you're not worth the trouble. Stand aside or suffer the consequences. You know the law.'

In earlier times, before The Decree, a relic such as the merchant's cornerstone would have *added* to the value of a dwelling. But now it was a liability. The wilful blindness of such people still astonished Sayer. How could they ever think they could avoid discovery? It made no sense. Although superficial attempts had been made to hide or disguise the stone – enough to fool a casual observer – there was no escape from his own elusive craft. And now the man's family were paying the price. At least the superstition surrounding the Temple had prevented any deliberate defacement of the stone – and it was just as well for the merchant that it had. The penalties for such sacrilege were harsh, sometimes including imprisonment or even exile.

Sayer could see now that Nazeri was reaching the end of his patience.

'It will only take a few moments,' the merchant pleaded. 'Surely—?'

'You'll have plenty of time to search for your trinkets when we've gone,' the captain stated harshly, then beckoned to two of his men who came forward briskly and dragged the man away. Although he struggled briefly, he soon capitulated, accepting his fate while his wife looked on, her face pale, and his children began to cry again.

'May we begin?' Nazeri asked, glancing at Sayer. His request was simply a formality. As seeker, Sayer had ultimate authority in the party but both he and the captain knew that, at this stage of the operation, the real power lay in military hands.

'Go ahead,' Sayer replied, keeping his expression neutral. 'We will prepare the silk.' He turned to look for Damaris and found the small man close behind him, his dark eyes already half glazed in readiness.

Without further prompting Damaris moved in front of the seeker and sat down cross-legged on the dusty flagstones facing the building.

'Give me its shape,' he said, the formal words sounding flat and unnatural as he approached his trance state.

Sayer placed his right hand on the top of Damaris's head and let the thoughts flow. When he had first learnt to do this, the process had been unsettling and arduous but now, especially with a silk with whom he had worked often, it was a natural and relatively simple transfer of knowledge. The trick, he had learned, was to keep the information to a minimum, excluding everything that was unnecessary. All the silk needed was the physical location and shape of the stone, nothing more.

'Do you have it?'

'It's clear,' Damaris replied, his voice dreamy and almost rapturous.

'Then go ahead,' Sayer said, removing his hand.

For a few moments everything was quite still and silent, and then a murmuring grew among the watching crowd, a mixture of wonder and fear as they saw the first glimmer of the protective shield appear around the cornerstone. The shield took the visible form of a softly glowing violet light which spread over the outward surface, but which Sayer knew also extended inside the wall to enclose their prize completely. While it lasted, no matter what happened to the rest of the building, no harm would come to the relic contained within.

While this was happening, the first artisans had gone forward into the house and taken up their positions in readiness. Damaris would only be able to maintain the magical position for a short time and it was essential that the removal be completed before it faded. The light grew in brightness.

'Complete,' Damaris murmured, his eyes closed now.

'Go!' Nazeri yelled, and the demolition began.

To the uninitiated it might seem like random destruction, but to Sayer's eyes there was a pattern to the violence as sledgehammers swung, wedges were driven in and masonry

crashed to the ground. The spectators muttered but kept
their distance, under the watchful eyes of the soldiers. After
an astonishingly short time, the final preparations were made.
A temporary wooden brace was set between the side pillars
of the archway, while nearby four men held a net in readiness. At a signal from the leader of the artisans, the last
blows were struck and the shimmering prize was freed.

There were gasps from the crowd as, instead of falling to
the ground with the other debris, the cornerstone floated
gently down and was deftly caught in the net – which was
then carefully carried out over the rubble into the open.
Damaris sighed deeply and slumped to the ground as the
violet light faded. Stretcher bearers came quickly and lifted
the now exhausted and almost comatose man onto his litter,
while Sayer stepped forward to examine his trophy. The artisans cleared the building, and as the last of them emerged,
he gave the brace an almost casual swipe with his hammer.
Moments later, the wood creaked, buckled and then
splintered. Lacking a cornerstone, the archway immediately
collapsed inwards and – like a house built of children's playing slates – the entire structure seemed to fold in upon itself.
When the dust settled, all that was left was a pile of rubble
with only a few sad remnants of the ground floor walls still
standing. What had once been a fine house was now a worthless ruin. Most of the onlookers were astonished at the scale
of the destruction, but Sayer had seen such things before.
Because of its significance the Temple stone had been
crucial to the design of the entire house, not just one doorway. The builders had no doubt considered this to be an
omen of good luck . . .

Nazeri regarded their handiwork with evident satisfaction, and even Sayer could not help thinking that their
point had been made very effectively. He did not look at the
distraught family as he supervised the porters in packing

the cornerstone for transport, and the entire party left the scene of devastation without a backward glance.

It was very quiet in Sayer's lodgings that night. In the next room Damaris lay sound asleep, and would probably remain so for a full day. As a silk – so-called because they produced a protective film like the silk used as the innermost layer of covering in more mundane circumstances – his talent was used only sporadically, but the intensity of the magic was such that its mental and physical aftermath was utterly draining. An average silk could work only once every seven or eight days; the best – of which Damaris was one – every four days at most, and their recovery time was always long. By contrast, Sayer himself felt invigorated and, as always after a successful hunt, he was impatient to move on to the next project. Instead, he faced the long journey back to Qara and the enforced inactivity that implied.

The room on the other side of Sayer's was occupied by Kebir, his assigned scribe and lore-master. He was by nature a quiet, withdrawn man, older than Sayer by more than two decades and dedicated only to his painstaking job of recording the details of the seeker's finds. Documentation played an important part in the great task. Kebir had once displayed some magical skills of his own, but his abilities had faded over the years until he had been forced to play a secondary role to younger talents. Even so, he was the closest thing Sayer had to a friend among the men and women he worked with.

He wished now that his sister could be there to share his triumph, but knew she was over a hundred leagues away. He drank a toast to her in the excellent wine that had been provided with his evening meal. Then he summoned servants to bring him hot water and took a long scented bath before retiring to his bed.

CHAPTER TWO

'Men have venerated water since life first came to this
land. The lakes, rivers and springs of Tirok are the
pantheon's greatest gift to us.'
    From the preface to *Balak's Codex of Water Rituals*

The Lake of Souls lay at the geographical centre of Tirok
and was large enough to be called an inland sea, extending
for fifty leagues from east to west and almost twenty from
north to south. It was the country's foremost natural resource,
and more than half the population lived within an hour's
walk of its shoreline. Qara, Tirok's only major city, lay near
the middle of its southern coast, and all the major trading
routes by both land and water passed through the area.

The main road from the east, along which Sayer and his
party were riding, came right down to the water's edge for
the last part of its journey to the capital. On the travellers'
left lay the squalid shantytown dwellings that had spread out
from the old walled city like a fungal growth around the bole
of a tree. On their right lay water, its smooth surface broken
only in one place, where a single island rose from the lake. In
the changing light of dusk this island appeared as no more
than a hazy smudge on the northern horizon, and was so far
away that even in full sunlight it would have been impossible

to make out any details. In any case Sayer did not even glance that way. Like most people he would have preferred the island to be completely invisible. He rode on, looking straight ahead, anticipating his homecoming and trying to ignore his surroundings.

Before long the pale stone walls of the old city came into view, and as soon as they had passed through Souls' Gate, Sayer relaxed. Within the ancient defences Qara was just as crowded, but there was an air of comparative calm, of space and air and prosperity. As night drew in, the caravan threaded its way through the bustling streets, heading for the southwestern part of the city, which was commonly referred to as the Magicians' Quarter. Once there they went first to the Treasury, where Sayer and Kebir completed the necessary formalities for the cornerstone to be placed in safekeeping. Had they arrived earlier in the day Sayer would have been tempted to take it straight to the Temple itself and hand it over to the rebuilders, but in the hours of darkness the holy site would be deserted. Night was when the gods walked on the earth, and the strange lights and sounds that were sometimes witnessed coming from the site were enough to persuade anyone to stay well away. Then it was a forbidden realm, inhabited only by the kyars, the sacred cats who were the embodiment of lost spirits. As it was there would be plenty of time for the rededication of the stone the next day, and Sayer was anxious to return to his own quarters and see Aphra again.

Their home was only a short distance from the Treasury, so he left his horse with one of the soldiers and walked through the narrow alleyways, feeling weary but content. However, as he reached the steps that ran up the side of the whitewashed building to their first floor apartments, his mood changed abruptly. The door at the top opened and although from where he stood he could not see inside, he heard Aphra's voice.

'Go on now. You can't stay here any longer. You know that.'

Sayer looked up, wondering who could be visiting his sister while he was away, and saw a bedraggled figure emerge into the twilight. He came out backwards, almost stumbling, and for a moment Sayer thought he might be going to fall. There was no rail protecting the stairway and the drop from the landing might even have been fatal, but the man recovered his balance and stood swaying slightly, still looking back into the doorway and unaware that he was being observed from below. If Sayer had not recognized who it was he might have thought that the visitor was drunk, but the dishevelled clothes, spiky hair and unhealthy white skin could only belong to one person. This was the last thing he had expected to spoil his return and his anger began to rise.

'What are you doing here, Tump?' He had meant to keep his voice level but the words came out harshly.

Startled, the unkempt figure turned to look down. His movements were jerky and erratic, like those of a nervous bird, and Sayer could not help recalling a time when the visitor had possessed the languorous grace of a kyar. Tump's pallid face registered surprise, then fear and finally a kind of bewildered hope. His mouth opened but no sound came out.

'You're not supposed to be here. Remember?' Sayer added, his tone more gentle now.

'I . . . I . . . I . . .' Tump swallowed hard. 'You . . . you away.'

'Yes, well, I'm back now.'

'I go.'

In a sudden burst of energy Tump ran down the stairs, lurching from side to side in an alarming manner but moving with remarkable speed. He veered round Sayer and, without another word, careered off down the alleyway, soon vanishing into the darkness. Still feeling unsettled by the encounter, Sayer watched him until he was out of sight, then looked back up to the top of the stairs. Aphra was standing there, a slight smile upon her face.

As always, the sight of his twin gladdened his heart and made him feel both admiring and protective. She was beautiful, like a work of art, and even though her clothes were generally plain, as befitted her status, she carried them on her slim frame with a natural grace that he could only hope to emulate. Her oval face, a more delicate version of his own, was marked by flawless, sun-gilded skin and unusually deep blue eyes that – like Sayer's own – could shine like gemstones or seem empty and almost black, depending on the light and her mood. She was quite short and slender, and often seemed frail. Sayer was also of light build, but he was taller and his levels of fitness and strength were greater than his sister's, in part because of his importance to his masters. They ensured that he remained healthy, supervising his exercise regime and his diet, and providing whatever medical assistance or advice he needed. In contrast, Aphra, who was plagued by frequent and debilitating headaches, was left to her own devices. At such times Sayer did his best to help her, acquiring herbal remedies when he could and hating the fact that he could not relieve her pain instantly. He had frequently offered to see whether he could help control it mind to mind, hoping that his magical talent could be turned to healing. Others were apparently able to do this, and his experience with the silks had given him some insight into communicating telepathically with another person. However, Aphra had always firmly refused, saying that his talent was too important to waste in that way. He admired her stoicism, but hated to see her suffering.

'It's good to have you back,' she said now.

'It's good to be back,' he replied as he began to climb the

stairs. At the top he kissed both her cheeks and, after a brief embrace, they went inside.

'Have you eaten?' she asked, after they had given thanks at the household shrine for his safe return. 'Would you like some wine?'

'I'm fine. What was Tump doing here?'

'He just wanted to talk.'

'You know he's not supposed to enter the quarter now, don't you?'

'Yes, but—'

'Then why encourage him?'

'He used to be your friend,' she pointed out defensively.

'I know, but he can't be now,' Sayer replied. 'He no longer has the Council's approval and besides, he's mad!'

'And whose fault is that?'

'It doesn't do any good to talk like that,' he said quietly.

'If they'd let him recover, instead of forcing him to keep working like that—'

'Be quiet,' he cut in, with more heat.

Aphra looked as if she were about to say something more, then evidently thought better of it.

'Daydreamers know the risks they take,' Sayer went on. 'Talent brings its own obligations.'

'I know,' she admitted, 'but he didn't have much choice, did he? And don't you think he deserves better than to be cast aside now that his usefulness is over?'

'He was weak.'

'Not everyone can be strong all the time.'

'Stay away from him,' Sayer warned. 'He's addled. He could be dangerous.'

'He's harmless,' Aphra replied with a touch of scorn. 'Even I can see that.'

'Just do as I say. I don't want him in this house.'

'All right.' Her concession was grudging, but Sayer knew she would keep her word.

'I don't want to argue,' he said, touching her arm lightly and finding the strength to smile.

'Me neither,' she replied. 'Was your trip successful?'

'Oh, yes,' Sayer answered, pushing aside the fading memory of the merchant's distress. 'Completely successful.'

CHAPTER THREE

'The black-hearted robbers came to the tomb at night, but the gods saw and fooled them. They did not find the treasure they were hoping for – and left with more than they had bargained for.'

From *The Chronicle of a Barbarous Time*
(Author unknown)

By the time Sayer got to the Temple the following morning his mood had been soured by a succession of unfortunate events, and he found it difficult to summon up much enthusiasm for the ceremonial to come. When he had woken, he had felt the lingering effects of several uneasy dreams, although the only image his conscious mind retained was a vision of a man falling from the top of the steps outside his home. At first he'd thought it was Tump, but then the point of view of the dream had changed with an inexplicable lurch so that it was Sayer himself who had been pushed over the edge. He had woken as he hit the ground.

Although nothing else remained from his dreams, the disquiet they had induced made him cautious and irritable. He wondered whether he had somehow unwittingly displeased the gods, and so spent longer than usual at his morning devotions – without receiving much comfort or reassurance.

He knew that omens came in many forms but this day should have been marked for celebration, not doubt, and that made his discomfort doubly unwelcome.

He would ordinarily have taken pleasure in dressing in his best clothes rather than the travelling garb of recent days. But the smooth material felt awkward and would not sit right, so that he fidgeted constantly, and when he came to tie his headband – whose bright red colour denoted his rank as a seeker – his fingers were incapable of tying the knot correctly. In frustration he went to find Aphra.

Although he had risen early, his sister – as always – was up before him, looking cool and elegant in a long white shift. As she moved, the light cloth seemed to float about her brown legs and bare feet. She calmly tied his headband, readjusted his shirt so that it was instantly more comfortable, and presented him with the breakfast she had already prepared. Sayer ate to please her, though he had no real appetite, while she busied herself with other chores. Her quiet competence lessened his anxiety but did not eliminate it.

'You will come to the rededication, won't you?'

'Of course,' she replied. 'I'll see you at the shrine.'

Sayer nodded. He had wanted her to say that she would come with him, join in all the facets of the ritual, but he could not blame her for deciding to attend only its culmination. The placement of such an important stone was a delicate business, and there was much to be done before the masons could even begin their work. The whole process would take several hours, most of them under the glare of the midsummer sun.

'Wish me luck then,' he said, rising and taking her hands in his own.

'Good luck,' Aphra replied obediently. 'Although you won't need it. Your achievements speak for themselves.'

Sayer knew that she had recognized his state of mind and

was trying to soothe his nerves, but he would have been happier if she had not qualified her wish.

'You mean more to me than anyone,' he told her quietly.

Aphra smiled but did not respond.

'What are you thinking?'

'Nothing.'

'Liar,' he accused, laughing. 'You can't hide anything from me, you know that. Tell me.'

'I was wondering whether I'll still mean as much to you when you're married.'

Sayer stared at her for a few moments, his thoughts whirling in confusion.

'What makes you think . . . ? Have you heard something?'

'No, but it's only a matter of time. Halion won't want to waste your bloodline.'

'There's no guarantee . . . Even brothers don't always . . .'

'I know that,' she agreed softly. 'Even twins.'

'I'm sorry. I didn't mean . . .' he said awkwardly. 'In any case, I've no intention of marrying. And even if I did, you'd still always be first in my heart.'

'It may not be your heart a wife would be most interested in,' Aphra commented, grinning.

Sayer was slow to realize what she meant, and blushed furiously when he did. His life had been too full, its progress too single-minded, to allow any thought of romance, and sex was a mystery to him.

'Your face is almost the colour of your headband,' Aphra teased, enjoying his discomfort.

Sayer laughed with her eventually, but even after he'd left the house his cheeks still burned with embarrassment, and another layer of unease had been added to the day. On his way to the Treasury he could not help wondering what would happen if Halion did choose to force a wife upon him. Would the apartment be big enough for three? And what about children? He had never even considered the prospect until this morning, and did not really want to think about it now.

His thoughts were distracted then, but not in a way he would have wished. The scene before him was far from unique, but rare in the Magicians' Quarter. Elsewhere in Qara, especially in the poorer areas outside the city walls, it was a common occurrence. Two soldiers, with cloths tied over their mouths and noses, were half carrying a man out of an open doorway. Their charge appeared weak, his legs buckling beneath him, and on his face and hands there were the dark, telltale swellings of the contagion. The man's eyes were wild and he struggled feebly, even though it was obvious he could not match the guards' strength. Behind them came another man, whose dress marked him as a physician, and a woman who was crying hysterically and clutching at the doctor's sleeve.

'It's just an infection. He'll be better soon. You can't—'

'The contagion is deadly, Sara.' He spoke firmly but not without compassion. 'There's no saving him now, and he must leave so others do not suffer.'

'No!' she wailed helplessly, but Sayer could see that she was beginning to crumple under the weight of the inevitable. The soldiers were already some distance away, and every moment took her husband further from her. Before long he would be aboard one of the plague boats on his way to the Isle of the Dead, whence no one ever returned. Sayer shivered at the thought, instinctively covering his mouth with a hand.

The physician caught the woman by her arms and held her fast.

'You did all you could.'

'Then let me go with him,' she pleaded.

'You cannot,' he replied sadly. 'You know the law. Go

back inside. Mourn for him, then begin a new life.'

The woman sagged, weeping again, all hope gone. After one last despairing glance at the retreating figure, she allowed herself to be led back inside the house.

Sayer hurried past, turning down a side street as soon as he was able, so that he would leave the horrible scene behind. The contagion was a fact of life and could strike anywhere. Better living conditions and food helped make some more resistant, but no one was immune. The plague had reputedly originated from a recess in one of the ancient tombs in the Temple. The story went that grave robbers had broken in, in the days before The Decree, and the gods had released the pestilence to punish the sacrilegious act. Sayer knew that others doubted the truth of this tale, but it seemed logical enough to him. What *was* certain was that the infection had become more prevalent in recent years – which was taken as a sign that the progress of the great task was not fast enough for the gods' liking. There was no cure, and because no one really knew how the illness was passed from one person to another, the only remedy was to try to isolate the victims as quickly as possible on Jazireh in the Lake of Souls, now universally known as the Isle of the Dead.

The seeker had to force himself not to run the last part of the way to the Treasury, and he walked so fast that he was breathless when he arrived. Kebir was already there, draped in a black robe and with a twisted headband of the same colour tied round his forehead. He only wore the official garb of a scribe on ceremonial occasions, complaining that it absorbed too much heat, and although the day was still young he was already sweating.

The paperwork had been completed and Kebir had arranged for bearers to carry the cornerstone, so that all Sayer had to do was wait until the relic was fetched from the vaults so that he could formally identify it. Once that was done, the procession set off at a dignified pace, heading first for the city wall and Temple Gate. There the guards saluted as they passed through and other citizens made signs of reverence, touching their fingertips initially to their foreheads and then over their hearts. Sayer accepted this homage as his due, knowing that seekers were venerated and that an important relic would always inspire feelings of awe. The cornerstone was still wrapped in its protective coverings, but the onlookers had no need of Sayer's special power to realize that it was a significant find.

The Causeway, which led from the city gate to the Temple itself, was a wide paved thoroughfare that ran in a southwesterly direction with open scrubland to either side. Although various craftsmen and traders set up their stalls here, no permanent structures were allowed this close to the sacred site. Directly ahead of Sayer's party was the famous Kyar Arch. Even though it was more than a thousand paces away it was an imposing sight, formed as it was of two gigantic statues sculpted from a single honey-coloured rock. Each portrayed a kyar, its forelegs stretched out as they leapt forward so that the two sets of claws interlocked, and together they formed a giant gateway. They were so massive that neither earthquake nor the efforts of mankind had affected them during the centuries since they had been carved from the earth itself. Immovable and enduring, they had nevertheless been eroded by time and weather so that outlines had softened and the more detailed features had blurred. Even so, the archway was unquestionably impressive and when, during major festivals, it was used by processions of colourfully robed officials, it made a suitably grand entrance.

The last part of the Causeway leading up to the Kyar Arch was a gently rising staircase, lined on either side by more decorative statuary. The entire Temple site was raised above the level of the surrounding land and marked by a perimeter bank that was built of huge but perfectly fitted blocks of stone. These too had survived the depredations of the years, their size and weight making the original construction seem an almost unimaginable undertaking.

By the time Sayer and his companions reached the base of the steps, the sun was already quite high and Kebir was not the only one who was perspiring freely. Sayer called a halt, intending to allow them to rest while he said the necessary prayers before entering the Temple, but he was immediately distracted by an argument among a nearby group of men. One of them, a woodcarver by trade, was obviously very angry about something, but he was opposed by a reconstruction overseer flanked by two intimidating guards.

'You have to let me in!' the woodcarver shouted. 'I've paid all the fees, and if my work isn't completed today the contract is null and void. I won't get paid for what I've already done!'

'You should have seen to it that your paperwork was in order,' the overseer replied evenly, waving a document in the air.

'But it is!' his adversary protested. 'It is!'

'Well, I've never seen wording like this before.'

'It was good enough for all the others.'

'But not me,' the overseer replied implacably. 'I'd not be doing my job properly if—'

'What will it take?' the woodcarver demanded resignedly. 'How much do you want?'

'Are you offering me a bribe?' the official asked, pretending to be affronted. 'In front of these guardians of the law?'

One of the soldiers grinned for a moment, then became sternly impassive once more.

Sayer turned away, regarding the encounter with distaste. The woodcarver should not have made such a fuss. His work was to pay homage to the gods; that honour should be payment enough. And if some officials took advantage of his avarice, then it would teach him a valuable lesson.

'Think of it as a votive offering,' the overseer remarked as money changed hands.

The woodcarver went on his way, almost running up the steps, and Sayer tried to put the incident out of his mind in order to concentrate on his devotions. He found it difficult, however, especially coming on top of the events of the morning. It was some time before he was ready to move on.

By now others were moving in and out of the Temple site, including some people that Sayer knew would be attending the rededication of his cornerstone, but the overseer and the guards made no attempt to stop any of them. They obviously picked their targets carefully. On occasions Sayer had heard various craftsmen grumbling about official corruption, wondering out loud why the archivects and their servants did nothing to stamp it out, but he believed that this was none of his concern. His eyes were fixed on higher goals – and besides, he had always been treated with perfect respect and honesty by everyone from Halion down.

'Come on,' he said to Kebir and the porters. 'We're falling behind schedule.'

The bearers stooped to lift the handles of the wooden pallet, and then followed the seeker up the steps. As Sayer passed under the golden archway he felt again a familiar sense of wonder. For him, the Great Temple of Qara was the most inspiring place in the world.

CHAPTER FOUR

'Henceforth we pledge ourselves and all the people of Tirok to this great undertaking. We will not rest, nor spare any effort or expense until the glory that was Qara has been restored.'

From The Decree

The Temple of Qara was vast, covering an area as big as the walled city itself. However, whereas the city was roughly circular, the Temple was built upon a rectangle whose sides were perfectly straight except at the rounded corners. Each of the long sides had been measured at over a league, and the ends were half of that so even a fast walker would take two hours to make a complete circuit of the perimeter. As well as the Kyar Arch, there were some fifteen other entrances where steps ran up the steep bank to give access to the interior. Although these stairways were irregularly spaced, all those who worked within the site soon discovered which was best for them; walking inside the Temple was like trying to find your way through a labyrinth. The internal layout was so complicated that visitors unfamiliar with their way around were either accompanied by guides or given maps showing their own particular routes. Even so, people regularly became lost, disorientated by the peculiar twists and turns of the alleyways between half-completed buildings. Even for those with greater experience of this strange man-made landscape, it was possible for quite a short journey to take a long time as it was often necessary to double back on oneself, and most routes were anything but straightforward.

The exception to this rule was the Penitents' Way. This relatively wide road ran down the long axis of the rectangle like a tree trunk, with smaller paths branching off to either side. It was a continuation of the Causeway, running from the Kyar Arch in a southwesterly direction, and was arrow straight except where it split into two to circle around each of the four most sacred structures in Qara. The first and largest of these, positioned at the exact centre of the Temple, was the Tower of Clouds, so called because it was built of a milky-white stone that was almost translucent. Unlike most of the buildings on the site the Tower was almost complete, pointing a pale finger high into the sky, and it was the most easily recognizable landmark for leagues around. Beyond that, in decreasing order of size, were the serpentine coils of the Oracle's Tomb, the black sepulchre known as the Raven's Dome, and the exquisitely proportioned Sanctuary. Much of the early reconstruction work had been concentrated on these four buildings, and as a result they had all been restored to something near their former glory. Greater activity was now focused elsewhere.

By day the entire site was a scene of constant animation, with builders, craftsmen and officials discussing and organizing every detail of their painstaking tasks, while scribes recorded their progress and checked it against the archive records. These dated from the Temple's heyday, before the earthquake that had wrecked it centuries earlier, but most visitors with any sense of imagination needed no historical evidence to realize that it must have been a wondrous place when it was whole.

The restoration had been prompted by a prophecy. A seer named Zavanaiu had seen a great vision, predicting two futures. In the first, the Temple of Qara still lay in ruins and Tirok was destroyed utterly by a succession of natural disasters – earthquakes, hurricanes, fire spurting from the earth, drought and famine. In the other, the Temple had been rebuilt and none of these catastrophic events took place, allowing the people to live in peace and prosperity. After a time these auguries were accepted by the ruling Council and, in the belief that the gods must be placated, the rebuilding was set in motion. Meydan had issued The Decree, in the name of all the Council. The great task had begun.

In the chaotic period that followed the earthquake, the Temple had been plundered. Many of its treasures had been spirited away – some even transported to other lands – and this made their recovery all the more difficult. However, the archivects were prepared to use whatever means necessary to pursue their obsession, and spared neither expense nor resource in the effort. Other, seemingly less significant pieces of the Temple had not strayed so far from Qara. Many stones had since been used in other buildings, but it was decreed that these too must be returned. Even if this meant demolishing entire houses to retrieve one stone, it was done without a second thought.

For a few years progress was rapid, but as the recovery of the more widely dispersed relics became necessary, the rebuilding took on a different character and new techniques were required. As a result, magical talent had become so important that it was now central to everything done in the name of The Decree. In the minds of most people, magic had become synonymous with the Temple.

Walking down the Penitents' Way, Sayer felt himself surrounded by history. He had to shut down much of his seeker's ability, narrowing his mental focus to the stone being carried before him; his senses would otherwise have been overwhelmed, so great was the concentration of echoes from the past. The site was so enormous and so complex that no one man could hope to know it all intimately, but Sayer was aware of the general layout – and proudly conscious of every one of his finds. If asked he could have gone directly to each of them, locating the relics by the same unique resonances that had led him to them in the first place.

Looking about, Sayer felt himself to be part of an extraordinary enterprise, one that would almost certainly not be completed in his lifetime, but – as he had known for a long time – that was not the point. It was important to feel that his existence had meaning, and the great task gave him that. Even if the pessimists were right and the Temple could *never* be fully rebuilt, that did not invalidate the effort involved. The gods would surely recognize that the people of Tirok had *tried*.

The further they went towards the heart of the Temple, the more Sayer's pride swelled and the day's earlier tribulations paled into insignificance. He began to feel far from penitent and smiled to himself, knowing that he would be forgiven such thoughts. He was a seeker! One of the best. History would remember him!

Even when a train of mules was led out from one of the side alleys, delaying their progress for a short while, Sayer watched benevolently. Beasts of burden were allowed within the site to fetch and carry for the artisans, but no man, not even Halion, was permitted to ride inside the Temple perimeter. Everyone walked, out of piety, on an equal footing, and this seemed only proper to Sayer. His world was putting itself to rights.

After some time they reached the point where the Penitents' Way divided to circle round the Tower of Clouds. The turning to the Ancestors' Shrine was one of a large number of streets that radiated outward from this circle. As they reached the junction, the entrance they wanted was no more than forty paces to the left, but Sayer and his party automatically turned right and went round the far greater distance in the other direction. It was customary to travel withershins round each of the four loops in the Penitents' Way, so as not to be presumptuous and emulate the passage of the sun.

A short while later they reached their destination at last. The Ancestors' Shrine was an octagonal structure, built upon a circular granite plinth. Although it had no roof, six of the walls were almost complete. Of the remaining two, one was merely a pile of unmatched stones and one rose to only half the height of the others. It was the cornerstone to the door of this partly built wall that Sayer was bringing with him. Many other component parts had already been retrieved, but until his find there had been no way to put them together.

As soon as they arrived, the stretcher was descended upon by masons, scribes and other artisans, all eager to see what had been brought to them. The protective coverings were removed and the relic was examined for damage and wear, measured and remeasured, and its characteristics compared with the stones with which it would be fitted. Records were checked – with unnecessary thoroughness as far as Sayer was concerned – and various incantations spoken by one of the lore-masters present. Only then could the real work be allowed to begin.

Sayer felt a slight pang of loss as he handed the cornerstone over, but watched the ensuing activity with pleasure and satisfaction. It was already obvious that his contribution would make possible a good deal of progress. As the rest of the ceremony's participants began to gather nearby, the masons worked with astonishing skill and dexterity under the direction of one of the senior overseers. This grizzled old man, his thick hands scarred and gnarled from a lifetime's work, obviously knew the plans by heart. He only referred to his scribe occasionally as a succession of new blocks were added to the wall and the outer parts of the door arch were carefully put into place and held steady.

At last all was ready, and Sayer watched as the cornerstone was brought forward. Although he would have no role in the ritual that was to follow, he felt part of it nonetheless. Looking around, he saw that Halion was among the spectators – basking in the reflected glory of his seeker's find – together with several other archivects and many other men of dignity and renown. The fact that it had attracted such a distinguished gathering was testament to the importance of Sayer's achievement. Kebir, Damaris and Nazeri were also present, together with Akar, the daydreamer whose vision had first indicated the general location of the cornerstone. He stood alone, not joining in any of the conversations, his pale-blue headband tied above pale-blue eyes.

At a signal from the overseer, Halion stepped forward. He too wore a ceremonial headband, but his was a mark of rank, rather than denoting any magical talent. It was dyed yellow, like all the archivects', with gold and blue threads woven into the cloth to specify his clan. Unlike most of the onlookers, his robes were also brightly coloured, a sign of his exalted status.

There had been no priests as such in Tirok for more than two centuries, but their role as spiritual leaders had been undertaken by the archivects. Halion touched head and heart, waited while the others repeated the gesture, then raised his arms to the sky. As he did so, the musicians began to play a soft, rhythmic tune whose exact nature had been determined by the time of sunrise that morning, the phase of the moon, and by the precise requirements of the ritual of rededication. Over this, Halion spoke in the old tongue, words that would have meant nothing to most of the citizens of Tirok but which to Sayer were a source of joy and wisdom. They told of the longing of stone to be returned to its rightful place, of the evil that had taken it far away, and of the heroic efforts that had been made to retrieve it. They asked the gods for forgiveness of past sins and for a blessing now that honour was restored, and finally they spoke to the stone itself, asking for strength and good fortune for the newly recreated shrine.

When Halion had finished, a brazier was brought forward and the kindling within lit by a candle handed to him by a servant. Several items were burnt – aromatic bark, some dried herbs, a little oil – and the varied scents spread with the smoke as the musicians played another wordless incantation. Then eight goblets of wine were passed round, with each of those present taking a sip before all were returned to Halion and three of his fellow archivects, who doused the last of the flames with the remaining wine. As steam and smoke rose into the air, everyone looked upwards, waiting to see whether there were to be any omens in the fluid, translucent shapes. Sayer could see nothing of any significance, but Akar cried out suddenly.

'A serpent! See! A serpent.'

Others took up the cry, pointing at the smoke as it dispersed on the breeze. A snake could be an omen for either good or ill, but Akar had sounded pleased and the others took their lead from him. When Sayer looked down again he, along with all his companions, saw another sign which could only be interpreted as auspicious. A kyar, its nose twitching at the unfamiliar smells and its green eyes gazing around inquisitively, had arrived unseen in their midst. It stalked silently across the granite, its long tail held high. As the onlookers watched breathlessly, it leapt gracefully and landed on top of the cornerstone where it stood, eyeing its audience with a regal air. This display was greeted with delight, even some laughter and applause, and Sayer knew beyond doubt that their enterprise had met with the gods' approval.

After the kyar deigned to step down again, the long-awaited restoration began. As if by sorcery the archway was suddenly complete, and the rest of the wall grew around it until it too was perfect once more. Sayer looked on, feeling a sense of achievement and also a camaraderie with all seekers, past and present. He was glad that the cornerstone would remain in view of all who came this way, even now that it was incorporated into the shrine. One of the legendary seekers of an earlier decade had returned to Qara with a beautiful statuette of a water nymph, only for it to be walled up inside a hidden niche within the Sanctuary where no one could ever see it. This was done because that was how it had been before the earthquake – no one knew why – and although Sayer recognized that it had been the correct thing to do, he could not help feeling a little regret on behalf of his fellow seeker that such a prize had been placed out of sight for ever.

The crowd began to drift away once the final prayer had been said, and Sayer belatedly looked round to see whether Aphra was there. There were several women present, each demurely hooded as custom demanded, but he could tell at a glance that none of them was his twin. He was just beginning to worry about why she had broken her promise when he became aware of Halion bearing down upon him. Contact with his master was usually made through intermediaries, but on this occasion Sayer knew that he should have expected to be granted an audience. Even so he instantly felt nervous, despite the wholly positive outcome of the ceremony.

'A happy day, Sayer.'

'Yes, my lord,' he answered, bowing his head in greeting. 'The gods have been generous.'

'Indeed,' Halion said affably. 'And I too may be in a position to be generous before long. Come to my house this afternoon, an hour before sunset.'

'To your estate?' Sayer queried in surprise. He had only been to the archivect's home a handful of times, and then in the company of many other servants.

'Yes. And don't look so worried. I think you'll like what I have to say.'

'Of course, my lord,' the seeker replied, trying his best to return his master's smile.

Halion nodded, turned and strode away, leaving Sayer to wonder what was so important that it could not be discussed then and there.

CHAPTER FIVE

'The eye that looks inward sees all.'
From the 'blue' fragment of The Plan
(Archive reference CT711)

Most of the archivects and their families lived on large estates to the west of the walled city, on the northern side of the Gold Road – which separated them from the Temple site. Each of the estates was surrounded by high walls and guarded by soldiers, but inside they were havens of beauty and peace. The carefully tended gardens, made green and luxuriant by irrigation, were filled with colourful flowers and unusual trees where exotic birds sang exquisitely. Fountains, streams, waterfalls and artificial ponds added their sparkling light to the artfully contrived vistas, and the archivects' mansions were sited to take advantage of the landscaping. Lesser buildings – housing servants, stores and equipment – were placed discreetly in hollows, surrounded by vegetation, or in unobtrusive locations on the periphery of the estate. The mansions themselves were usually built on a vast scale, incorporating every amenity that almost limitless wealth could buy.

Sayer was still feeling apprehensive as he was admitted to Halion's estate. His master's earlier assurances, and his own success that morning, were not enough to overcome his nervousness in such surroundings. Although the seeker's apartment was luxurious compared to most dwellings in Tirok, it was an insignificant hovel compared to even the least grand of the archivects' homes. Naturally enough, Halion's house was the most palatial of them all, a sprawling expanse of domes and turrets, courtyards, halls and countless smaller rooms. Sayer could see part of it now at the end of the long avenue, as his somewhat reluctant footsteps took him closer to his appointment. The building glowed in the late afternoon sunlight, like a jewelled mirage.

Even though he was preoccupied with speculation about the meeting, Sayer could not help marvelling over everything around him. As well as the abundant flowers and verdant foliage, the gardens were decorated with statues of stone and gilded wood. Many of those lining the avenue were representations of various gods, and each was a work of art created by one of the country's foremost sculptors. There was silver-tongued Ailor, the breath of clouds, many-fanged Durak, the drinker of blood, blind Yma, the goddess of prophecy and fire, as well as the Snake of the Sun and a number of the lesser divinities. As he passed them, Sayer repeated the appropriate prayers, bowed his head or averted his eyes as custom demanded, and touched head and heart in greeting and reverence. He sometimes found it hard to understand why such statuary was an acceptable tribute to the gods when there were almost none elsewhere – even in the Temple. It was against the law for ordinary citizens to own such idols, and it was also forbidden for the archivects – or anyone else – to build their homes within a direct line of sight of the Temple. This taboo was strictly observed, even to the point where huge banks of earth had been erected to screen off any possible view. Such intimations of humble piety sat oddly beside the ostentation that allowed the entire pantheon to be on display within the walls of the archivect's estate. It was as though Halion were claiming a special familiarity with the gods; even if his status justified such a claim, it still made Sayer feel uneasy.

Reaching the house itself at last, he turned towards the side entrance he had used before, only to be called back by a grey-robed servant.

'This way, Seeker.' He indicated the grand gateway to the main entrance hall.

Sayer did as he was told, looking about in awe. The sides of the hall were lined with golden pillars, five times the height of a tall man, and the elegantly curved roof was decorated with brightly painted carvings of birds, dolphins and flowers. Sunlight from high windows slanted down, striping the marble floor so that he passed through alternate bands of shade and rose pink, until he came to a heavy wooden door at the far end. Its panels were decorated with scenes of war, hunting and fable, but Sayer had no time to study them. As he approached, the doors swung back, revealing a much more intimate chamber beyond.

Even though he had never seen it before, Sayer knew that this was Halion's formal reception room, and when another servant silently beckoned him on he felt his sense of awe increase. This was truly an honour. The furnishings were rich and colourful without being ornate; whoever was responsible was clearly a man of taste as well as having had access to considerable wealth. The contrast between such opulence and the sordid conditions in which many of the citizens of Qara existed did not seem objectionable – or even strange – to Sayer. It was just part of the natural order of things.

'Greetings, Sayer,' Halion said as he strode into the room. 'Prompt as always, I see.'

The seeker merely bowed his head in acknowledgement. His anxiety had returned in full measure. Whatever had prompted this invitation was obviously important, but he had no idea what it could be.

'Sit, please. Will you join me in some wine?'

Sayer hesitated. Although he would very much have liked a drink, he also wanted to keep a clear head.

'It's from Khorasan,' Halion added, 'and it's actually very good. I know you have a nose for a fine vintage.'

'Thank you, my lord,' Sayer replied. He did indeed enjoy wine, but he had never tasted any from the country that lay beyond Tirok's eastern border. Such wine was rare and very expensive.

A servant poured the wine into two goblets, then left his master and his guest alone. Halion sprawled on one of the cushioned couches and indicated that Sayer, who was still standing, should occupy another.

'To the gods,' the archivect said, raising his glass.

Sayer repeated the toast and sipped gingerly. The wine was indeed excellent, and he savoured it with his entire mouth. Seeing his evident pleasure, Halion smiled but said nothing for a few moments. Sayer wanted to ask why he had been summoned, but to do so would have been discourteous and so he forced himself to wait. To cover his uneasiness he drank again, swallowing rather more than he intended.

'There are two matters I wish to discuss with you,' Halion said at last. 'Are you ready to get down to business?'

'Of course, my lord.'

'I recently acquired the services of a new daydreamer,' the archivect began. 'She is still very young and her talent is unformed, but the power is there for all to see. No one can remember anyone scoring so highly in the standard tests, and when she was given a fragment of The Plan she went into a spontaneous trance.'

'The Plan' was the name given to the original designs for the Temple, which had been recorded on various scrolls

and stone tablets in diagrams and coded text. Not all of
these had survived, of course, and the remaining fragments
were therefore the most sacred of all the Qarian artefacts.
They were the object of the most intense and never-ending
scrutiny.

'How long had she been without sleep?' Sayer asked, his
reticence fading now that the discussion was underway.

'Only two days.'

Sayer was impressed. Daydreamers usually had to be
kept from sleeping for at least four days before prophetic
hallucinations could be induced.

'Were her visions genuine?'

'I believe so, and I am not alone in this,' Halion replied.
'But there are others who do not think she is reliable yet.'

The seeker thought for a few moments. He knew that there
were some who believed it was not wise to trust women
when it came to magic – but he was not one of them.

'Did she see something you want me to find?' he asked,
drawing the obvious conclusion from the conversation.

Halion nodded.

'She did.' His black eyes glittered, and beneath his loose-
fitting silk robes the archivect's body was tense with sup-
pressed excitement.

'Was the interpretation clear?' Sayer asked, eager now.
'Do the lore-masters know what she saw?'

'Oh, yes. The Eye of Clouds.'

Sayer's eyes widened and his jaw dropped. This had to be
a dream. The Eye was one of the few missing stones from
the Tower of Clouds – and by far the most important. It was
small enough to fit into a man's hand, and crafted from the
same distinctive milky stone as the rest of the building. What
made it unique was the fact that the legendary stonemason
who had designed and built the tower had inscribed its
surface. As well as his own signature marking of a star, he

had carved the symbol of Ailor – the never-sleeping eye. According to archive records, the stone had originally been set high inside the topmost spire of the structure, where no one would ever see it, but it had disappeared after the earthquake and was believed to have been stolen. There had been no sign of it since then, and it had been gone so long now that some experts had even begun to doubt its existence.

'You're certain?' Sayer managed to whisper.

'Yes. If the vision has any merit at all, it's the Eye.'

'And you want *me* . . . ?' If he was indeed able to find such a priceless relic, his name would join the ranks of the immortals.

'You're the best seeker we have,' Halion answered. 'If you can't find it, no one will.'

Sayer felt his pride swell at his master's words, but knew that they were ominous too. This was clearly not destined to be an easy mission.

'Where is it?'

'Somewhere beyond the Rivash Canyon.'

Sayer's premonition was confirmed. The Rivash Canyon was a vast natural gulf, so big that it could have swallowed whole mountains. Moreover, its depths formed a generally impassable border between Tirok and the barbaric land of Mazandaran to the north. Sayer had never left his own country – few Tirokians ever did – and to cross or circumvent the Rivash Canyon would be a huge challenge in itself. Even the journey to its southern rim would be arduous – but all that paled into insignificance when he considered the possible rewards.

'Was there anything else?'

'I'm afraid so. Apparently the Eye is buried deep underground, but there are no further details to help you locate it.'

Sayer thought that it was no wonder there had been no sign of the relic for so long. If it was indeed buried in such a remote and inhospitable place, beyond the boundaries of the country, then it would take a remarkable talent even to catch a glimpse of it. However, he had no doubt that he would be able to pick up its trail.

'Can I talk to the daydreamer?' he asked, unable to conceal his excitement.

'No. That's not possible.'

'Why not?' Sayer demanded, then cringed inwardly. He must be mad to speak to his master in that tone.

'Because, in trying to get her to confirm her vision, her tutors pushed too hard,' Halion explained, apparently unconcerned by the seeker's lack of tact. 'She's been in a coma for three days and can't be roused. Some of the physicians think she may never wake again.'

Sayer was disappointed but not overly surprised. Such occurrences were not uncommon with daydreamers. These mystical creatures were usually too gentle and unworldly to be able to withstand much stress, and many lost their usefulness while still quite young.

'How soon can you be ready to leave?'

'Tomorrow,' Sayer answered promptly.

'I assume you'll want to take your usual team?'

'Damaris and Kebir certainly. We work well together.'

'What about a second seeker to assist you?'

Pride and common sense opposed each other. Although Sayer had no wish to share the glory with another talent, he knew that another seeker might well be an extremely valuable member of his party. Common sense eventually won.

'That would probably be a good idea. I'll think tonight about who it should be.'

'Fair enough. Captain Nazeri will accompany you again, but you'll need a bigger force this time.'

Sayer nodded. The practicalities of transport, protection and supplies could safely be left to Nazeri and his men. Such mundane matters did not concern him. His thoughts were already far away as he stood up.

'I'll go and begin the preparations.'

'Not so fast,' Halion said, smiling.

'Of course, my lord,' Sayer replied, sitting down and cursing his impetuosity.

'There is still another matter I wish to discuss with you.'

The seeker could not imagine that anything would be of interest after what he had just heard – but he was proved wrong.

Halion turned to the back of the room and raised his voice.

'Come in now, my dear.'

Curtains parted and the hooded figure of a woman entered. At Halion's request she threw back her hood, revealing the most beautiful face Sayer had ever seen.

'Sayer, I'd like you to meet Kailas,' the archivect said. 'Your future wife.'

CHAPTER SIX

'Statistical records show that the combination of a seeker father and a silk mother gives the best opportunity for offspring with appreciable talent.'

From the annual report of the Chief Scribe to the Council, in the 27th year of the great task

'The way to a man's heart is through his stomach – especially if you have a sharp knife.'

Old saying of the Kavir nomad women

Sayer's first reaction after he had recovered from the shock and was capable of rational thought again was to wonder how Aphra had known. Had it just been common sense, or some intuition that he lacked? Or was there something more? His sister had shown no talent for prophecy; if she had, she would have been trained as a daydreamer. Perhaps someone had told her. But if so, who? Halion would almost certainly not have revealed his plans to anyone – other than perhaps his senior scribe – before he had informed the two people involved in the proposed match.

'Have you lost your tongue?' the archivect asked, sounding amused.

'I don't know what to say,' Sayer replied, then added

hastily, 'I'm . . . I'm honoured by your choice.' He found that he was standing again, although he had no recollection of having got to his feet.

'So you should be,' Halion remarked, smiling. 'Few people earn the right to marry one so beautiful and so talented.'

'Talent?' Sayer asked stupidly.

'Kailas's training as a silk is almost complete, and her tutors tell me she is very promising. One day you may well be able to work together. And who knows what abilities your children will possess.'

Sayer stared at the woman's face. He felt awkward discussing her as if she were not there, although she showed no sign of embarrassment. Her pale-green eyes regarded him placidly, without any obvious curiosity. Whatever her inner thoughts, Kailas had clearly accepted the betrothal. And she *was* incredibly beautiful. Her hair was golden brown, much lighter than Sayer's, and it was cut in a short, practical style, but if anything this only served to emphasize her femininity. She reminded him of the elfin creatures of light that were sometimes depicted paying court to the Snake of the Sun. Her complexion was pale and flawless, her features arranged with perfect symmetry in a heart-shaped face. Her hands – the only other part of her that was visible – were also fair skinned and soft. Even though she had come to her magical training later than most – Sayer guessed that she was roughly his own age – Kailas had clearly led a sheltered and privileged life. Those hands had neither toiled in the fields nor become coarse through the mundane tasks of washing or cooking. Although her body was hidden by her robe, she held herself well, and Sayer could not help wondering whether the rest of her was as alluring as her face. However, that line of thought made him more uncomfortable than ever and he rushed to say the first thing that came into his head.

'When will the marriage take place?'

Halion laughed.

'As soon as you return from Mazandaran,' he said. 'I imagine such a prospect will make you even more determined to succeed in your mission.'

Sayer was about to reply that he needed no extra incentive for such a task, but the thought of his impending journey – and of its goal – made him hesitate, his mind reeling at the enormity of all he had learned that day.

'As you two will have little time to get to know each other,' Halion went on, 'I suggest that you make the most of this evening. Your travel arrangements can wait until the morning, Sayer. In the meantime, I have arranged for a carriage to take you both to your apartment. In due course we may need to look for somewhere bigger, but I thought it best for Kailas to see you on home ground – and to meet Aphra.'

Halion's reference to his twin disturbed Sayer. What did her future hold now? Looking again at Kailas, seeing once again just how beautiful she was, only served to confirm that he had no genuine feelings for her. How could he have? They had only just met, after all. Aphra, on the other hand, was a large and precious part of his life. His love for her was unquestioned. Halion evidently noticed his uncertainty and, somewhat surprisingly, tried to reassure him.

'Aphra's role will change, that's inevitable, but I don't think you need worry about anything too drastic just yet.' Turning to Kailas, he added, 'The driver will wait for you and bring you back whenever you're ready, my dear.'

Kailas nodded, and Sayer realized that she had not spoken a single word since entering the room. For the first time he wondered what was going on beneath her impassive exterior and then, because he knew it was expected, he went over to her. She held out her hand and, even though he was almost certain that she had intended the gesture as a simple greeting, he acted upon a sudden impulse and raised her hand to his lips. She rewarded him with a slight smile.

Although the journey back to the city was completed quickly enough, it seemed to last an eternity. Inhibited by the driver's burly presence, Sayer was not able to ask the questions that filled his mind, but felt obliged to keep up some sort of conversation. As a result he confined himself to safe topics, asking who Kailas's tutors were, how her training was going, and whether she enjoyed the sense of purpose that magic gave her. Although he could have predicted most of her answers, he listened intently to her quiet but assured responses, wondering whether she could really be as calm as she appeared.

'We're nearly there now,' he said as the driver guided them through the lanes of the Magicians' Quarter. 'It's not much to look at, especially if you've been used to living in places like Halion's mansion.'

'I'm sure it'll be fine.'

'I expect the accommodation is the least of your worries,' he remarked, trying to sound light-hearted.

Kailas glanced at him and smiled, and for the first time he saw the glimmer of real emotion in her eyes.

'Should I be worried?'

'I . . . I hope not.'

'Halion and his advisers seem to think this is an ideal arrangement,' she told him. 'Who are we to argue?'

Who indeed? Sayer thought, but kept the question to himself.

'Talent brings its own obligations, after all,' she added, unconsciously echoing Sayer's earlier words to his sister.

'And you don't mind this . . . arrangement?' he asked quietly.

'I'll only be able to answer that when I've got to know you

better,' she replied coolly. 'But you're doing all right so far.' Her smile became a little mischievous.

The driver brought the shaft-horse to a halt with a flick of the reins, and Sayer jumped down to help Kailas from the carriage. Once his passengers had disembarked, the driver immediately set off again.

'I thought he was supposed to wait for you.'

'I told him to come back in two hours,' she said. 'We should be able to amuse ourselves for that long, don't you think?'

'Of course,' Sayer exclaimed, although he was surprised by her initiative.

'And it never hurts to have the servants like you,' Kailas added. 'He'll make better use of the time than he could just sitting here.'

Sayer would never have thought of countermanding any of Halion's orders, but he saw the sense of what she said.

'The apartment's up here,' he said, indicating the stairs.

'Will your sister be at home?'

'I expect so.'

'You're very close, aren't you?'

Now that they were alone her tongue had evidently been freed from earlier constraints and, for the first time, Sayer heard a note of doubt in her voice.

'Yes,' he replied truthfully. 'We're twins.'

'I know.'

Sayer wondered what else she knew about him. For some reason he now felt reluctant to climb the stairs and stood still, paralysed by indecision.

'Shall we go in?' she prompted.

'I'm sorry. It's just that . . . it's been quite an eventful day.' Thoughts of his forthcoming mission intruded again, and he shook his head as if to clear it.

'I did wonder whether it was a good idea for Halion to tell you about both things at once,' Kailas said. 'I can't really compete with the Eye of Clouds, can I? And you must have thought you were due a rest after retrieving the cornerstone.'

The scene at the rededication flashed into Sayer's mind.

'You were there!' he exclaimed, recalling one of the hooded figures at the back of the crowd. 'At the Ancestors' Shrine.'

'I was curious,' she admitted, nodding.

Once again Sayer found himself tongue-tied.

'It'll be dark if we don't go inside soon,' she hinted.

He started to apologize again, then thought better of it and instead led the way up the stairs. Once inside, he was instantly conscious of just how small and bare the apartment seemed. The only personal touches had been put there by Aphra. It was she who had decorated the white walls with a colourful woven rug, several painted masks and small pictures – and she was undoubtedly also responsible for the appetizing smell emanating from the kitchen.

'Dinner's almost ready. I thought you might need fortifying after today so I made your favourite spicy stew, and – oh.' Aphra's welcome died away as she came out of the kitchen and saw that her brother was not alone.

'Will there be enough for an extra guest?' Kailas asked. 'It smells delicious.'

'I think so,' Aphra replied.

The two women eyed each other warily, assessing what they could from each other's appearance, until Sayer hurried to break the silence.

'Aphra, this is Kailas. She is to be my wife.'

'I see.' His twin showed no great signs of surprise – or any other emotion for that matter. 'Welcome to our home, Kailas.'

'Thank you. I hope we can be friends. I've heard so much about you.' She slipped off her cape and handed it to Sayer, who hung it carefully on a peg. The simple dove-grey dress beneath revealed enough of her shape for him to know that seeing more would indeed be pleasurable.

'I wouldn't have thought there was that much to hear about me,' Aphra remarked, sounding defensive now.

'So you know our history?' Sayer asked quickly.

'Yes, and your progress since.'

'Then you're aware of my ignominious failure to become a mage?' Aphra said tartly.

'I would not call it that,' Kailas answered, 'but I am aware that destiny has taken you in a different direction, just as it has brought Sayer and me together.'

'That was destiny, was it?'

'Come and sit down,' Sayer cut in, wanting to avoid any unpleasantness. 'I'll get some wine.'

They followed Aphra back into the kitchen, where she set another place at the table and completed her preparations for the meal. When they were all seated and the wine poured, Aphra raised her glass.

'To the happy couple. May your union be blessed.'

Grateful for the gesture, Sayer drank some wine and then began to help serving the food.

'And what is your history, Kailas?' Aphra enquired. 'Forgive me if I'm asking you to repeat yourself, but my brother hasn't told me anything about you.'

'I—' Sayer began.

'He hasn't had the chance,' Kailas answered. 'Sayer only met me for the first time within the last hour, and we've had little chance to talk.'

'I know no more than you,' the seeker confirmed.

'Tell us, then,' Aphra said. 'I suspect you don't come from the mountains as we do.'

'No. I grew up in Kohlu. My father is a merchant there.'

'Dealing in what?'

'Spices and timber mostly,' Kailas replied as they began

to eat. 'But because he is a cousin to Archivect Halion, he has many advantages that other traders do not.'

This unexpected information, together with the honest manner in which it had been revealed, brought Sayer back into the conversation.

'I think I may have met him. Is his name Simriani?'

Kailas nodded.

'I didn't know he had a daughter.'

'I was of little consequence compared to my three brothers, until I began to show signs of late developing talent. I'm in the last stages of training to become a silk,' she added for Aphra's benefit.

'When did you come to Qara?'

'A little over a year ago.'

'Have you lived on Halion's estate all that time?' Sayer asked.

'Yes. He's been very generous.'

'He can afford to be,' Aphra commented, and merely shrugged when her brother glanced at her disapprovingly.

'That's true enough,' Kailas agreed mildly. 'I still get lost in that house sometimes.'

'You won't have that problem here,' Sayer remarked.

'Speaking of which,' Aphra said, 'why don't you show Kailas around while I clear up in here?'

Sayer did as his sister suggested. Although he felt embarrassed at showing Kailas his bedroom, she seemed to like what she saw – or at least did a good job of pretending to. They returned to the sitting room while Aphra was still occupied in the kitchen.

'Would you like some more wine?' he asked.

'No, thank you.'

'Tea?'

'You haven't told me how *you* feel about this arrangement,' she said, ignoring his question.

'I . . .'

'I know you haven't been given any choice in the matter, but I'd prefer to believe you're agreeing to something that might please you rather than merely obeying orders.'

Sayer felt himself blushing.

'You're very . . . very attractive . . .' he mumbled.

'But?'

'But it's all happened so fast!' he explained helplessly. 'It's as you said. Time will tell.'

'Fair enough.' She paused, then added, 'I like you, Sayer. That's a start, isn't it?'

'I like you too.'

'That's nice. I just wish Aphra did too.'

Sayer was about to ask how she knew how his sister felt when Aphra came into the room, forestalling his question with one of her own.

'Did I hear someone mention my name?'

'I was just saying what a wonderful cook you are,' Kailas lied easily.

'No doubt the spices from your father's warehouse should get most of the praise,' Aphra responded. 'I just threw it all together.'

'You're too modest,' the other woman said, then turned back to Sayer. 'And I should be going. You've much to do if you still intend to leave tomorrow.'

The seeker frowned, wondering whether such a schedule was unrealistic now. Although Aphra glanced at him quizzically, he said nothing but rose and followed Kailas out to the door. Farewells were exchanged and she wished him good hunting before walking lightly down the steps to the waiting carriage. Aphra stood beside him as they watched her being driven away.

'Will she be going with you to look for the Eye?'

'No. I—' He stopped abruptly. 'How do you know about that?'

'There've been rumours for days,' his sister replied. 'You can't keep something like that a secret for very long. And it was obvious that you'd be the best seeker for the job. I just put two and two together.'

'Thank you for the vote of confidence – though I'm not sure I agree with you.' The responsibility of the task had begun to weigh heavily on his shoulders.

'I wonder why Halion chose to land you with *her* at the same time,' Aphra said as they went back inside. 'A reward for past services, or an incentive for the future?'

'Do you have to be so cynical?'

'It's hard not to be. And then there's the children, of course.'

Sayer said nothing. Events were moving too fast for his liking – and his sister's attitude was not helping.

'She's beautiful,' Aphra conceded. 'It shouldn't be too much of a hardship to bed her.'

Sayer swore under his breath. He couldn't deny that he found Kailas attractive, or that he had tried to imagine what it would be like to make love to her, but he was annoyed by his twin's blunt words.

'Give her a chance, won't you?' he muttered.

'I already have,' Aphra replied. 'Rich family, political connections, easy life, *talent*. She couldn't be more perfect. When is this marriage due to take place?'

'When I get back,' he told her. He could hardly believe it himself.

'Not wasting any time, eh? When do you think you'll want me to move out?'

'Who said anything about that?' he shouted. 'There's no question of your moving out!'

'I didn't realize my cooking skills were so good,' Aphra remarked sarcastically.

'Don't be like this,' he pleaded. 'It's not an easy situation for me either. And I will not be parted from you.'

'Don't make promises you can't keep,' she warned him. 'I can't see myself fitting in as a member of Halion's family.' She went into her bedroom and shut the door.

Sayer knew better than to try and persuade her to continue the conversation and, in any case, he no longer had the energy to make the attempt. His mind was brimming over with the day's astonishing developments and, in spite of his tiredness, it took him a long time to get to sleep. It was late in the night before he remembered that he had meant to ask Aphra why she had not been at the rededication as promised. Such a small mystery seemed almost irrelevant now – but it still preyed on his mind.

CHAPTER SEVEN

'Each sentinel (shrieker) must be accompanied by two
(2) soldiers from the Port Garrison AT ALL TIMES.
Fees are payable on embarkation.'
    Standing order to the captains of all vessels sailing
        to Jazireh (also known as the Isle of the Dead)

When his ship pulled away from the harbour two days later,
Sayer's principal feeling was one of relief. On a mission such
as this he knew who and what he was. He was a seeker, and
his job defined his purpose, his actions, his thoughts, his
very existence. All his familiar colleagues were with him,
and they were embarking on the greatest adventure of their
lives. Finding the Eye of Clouds might be a long, difficult
and even dangerous undertaking, but to Sayer it appeared
simple – at least compared to the situation he was leaving
behind in Qara.

    The sight of the two women standing on the docks, each
studiously ignoring the other, only emphasized how ineffective he had been in trying to set his private life in order.
Aphra and Kailas had both come to see him off and, even
though there was no doubt as to which of them he would
miss the most, he could not help hoping that there might be
some sort of reconciliation between the two while he was

54

away. As things stood they seemed determined not to like each other. Sayer gave one last wave from the stern of the vessel – to which they both responded – then turned away and set his mind firmly on the task ahead.

It had been decided that he and his team would begin the journey to Mazandaran aboard ship. At this time of year the prevailing southwesterly winds were favourable, and it would be quicker than taking the long detour round the western shore of the Lake of Souls. At the town of Jandaq, on the far side, the party would be supplied with horses and provisions before heading north along the western bank of the Daran River. After that, their course would be guided by Sayer's instincts.

For the time being, however, he was in the hands of the ship's crew. The course the helmsman set, once they had cleared the last of the harbour watchtowers, was not directed towards their eventual destination. Before sailing towards Jandaq it was necessary to make a wide detour to the west, in order to stay outside the prohibited zone around the Isle of the Dead, the perimeter of which was mapped out by a ring of red marker buoys. The reason for this exclusion was not simply fear of contamination from the plague victims on the island, but also because of a very real need to avoid the hideous creatures that lived in the island's coastal waters. No one knew exactly what these monsters were; very few people had caught a glimpse of one and lived to tell the tale. The vague and often contradictory reports that did exist seemed to indicate some sort of obscene cross between a giant shark and an octopus. Whatever their actual shape, the strength and vicious nature of these creatures was not in doubt. Even quite large boats had been capsized by broadside attacks or entangling tentacles, while others had simply been smashed by brute force, their wooden hulls splintering at the impact of a giant tail or snout. There were even some instances of smaller craft having been literally *bitten* in two. No one ever survived such an attack, the same horrifying rows of teeth crunching through flesh and bone in a frenzy of merciless slaughter.

Many theories had been advanced to explain why the creatures lived only in the waters around the Isle of the Dead – and none of them was wholly convincing. Some said it was because of certain minerals that seeped into the lake, which had a narcotic effect and to which the monsters had become addicted. It was well known that strange plants also grew in the shallows, where luminous patches were often seen at night – and these phenomena were attributed to the same source. Others, ignoring the inconvenient fact that the creatures had been there before the island was put to its present use, speculated that the beasts were mutations caused by seepage of the plague infection. Yet another idea was that the island was the centre of some evil magic that polluted the surrounding area. Whatever the truth of the matter, the fact that the monsters could be avoided was reason for thankfulness. All sailors lived in dread of the prospect of them moving further afield, and most captains steered a course that kept their vessels well clear of the buoys.

Of course the existence of these savage guardians did have one advantage. It meant that there was no danger whatsoever of anyone escaping from the Isle of the Dead once they had been placed there. Anyone foolish enough to try was killed and eaten almost instantly, especially as their home-made craft were unlikely to be either fast or manoeuvrable. The plague colony was thus entirely secure.

In fact, the only vessels that were able to travel within the infested waters were the official plague boats. Each of these carried a specially trained talent, usually a former daydreamer, whose sole task was to repel the creatures. They did this telepathically, by entering into the nightmare world of the monstrous minds and diverting their attention for long enough for the boats to draw sufficiently close to the shore to deposit their plague-ridden human cargo and then retreat as quickly as possible. These talents were commonly known as 'shriekers' because of the noise they often made as they writhed in mental torment on the deck, and they rarely lasted more than a year in the job. Those sailors who were desperate enough to take work on the plague boats soon learned to watch their magical protectors carefully, coming to recognize the signs that might mean they were close to breaking point. Failure within the ring of buoys could mean death for all the crew, and more than one suddenly ineffective shrieker had been hurled overboard in the usually vain hope that his sacrifice would be enough to save the boat itself. Usually, however, the system worked well, providing safe passage for permitted craft but preventing any other movement. The military authorities organized the allocation of shriekers, and ensured that none of the talents ever fell into the hands of the exiles.

About two hours out of port, Sayer was standing in the starboard bow. In the distance he could just make out the nearest of the marker buoys, and he shuddered to think about what lay beyond it. His eyes were drawn unwillingly to the island. Ordinarily he would have tried to avoid looking at it, but he had never been this close to its rugged coastline before and some masochistic impulse made him study the place. It was bigger than he had imagined, rising up out of the deceptively placid water in the shape of an irregular flat-topped cone. Sayer knew that it was supposed to have been formed by the eruption of an underwater volcano aeons ago, but it was hard to believe that now. The island's upper slopes consisted of bare rock, almost black, although lower down there was plenty of vegetation – including some areas of dense forest. From this distance the place appeared peaceful, and even possessed a harsh beauty that was at odds with the sinister reality.

He felt the ship shudder a little as it turned, and knew that the helmsman was setting a new course. They would now be heading directly for the mouth of the Daran River and the town of Jandaq. The seeker had been there on several occasions, but never at the start of such an ambitious journey. Deliberately turning away from the Isle of the Dead, Sayer turned his gaze to the north, and began to dream.

The seeker had studied all the known facts about the Eye of Clouds; he had read the reports and talked to the scribes and tutors who had been present at the fateful daydreaming. He had even climbed to the top of the narrow spire inside the Tower of Clouds, to see for himself the empty space that was waiting for the return of the Eye. In that cramped eyrie, prey to both vertigo and claustrophobia, he had felt its shape with his hands and learnt what resonance was missing from the patterns of the surrounding stones. Every useful piece of information had been stored away in his brain, so that now he could almost *see* the famous relic. He could feel its weight as it would lie in his palm, trace its grooves and carved symbols with imaginary fingers and, above all, he had a firm sense of the invisible signals it would be sending out. He would recognize it – and find it – wherever it was hidden. His only doubts concerned the practical matters of transport and security, but he was not entirely responsible for such things. Nazeri and his men could be relied upon to take care of these concerns. Sayer would tell them where they needed to go; it would be up to them to work out how.

The rest of his team were equally dependable. Kebir and Damaris were almost as enthusiastic as the seeker, and were both acutely aware of the honour of being chosen for such a mission. They would not fail in their duties, no matter what hardships were encountered. The artisans who were travelling with them included not only the usual masons and structural experts, but also men familiar with mining and working underground. Thus, as far as possible, every eventuality had been covered. They were an experienced and hardy group, and Sayer was sure that between them they would be able to solve any problems arising from the physical location of the stone.

That left only Obra, the second seeker, who was to act as Sayer's assistant. At twenty-two he was four years older than Sayer, but his talent was less acute. His reputation was as a solid if unspectacular performer, and as such he had been one of many talents who had been considered for the job. What had tipped the scales in his favour was the fact that he had originally come from the mining region just to the south of the Rivash Canyon and, as a native of that bleak area, he was used to hard travelling. Although his local knowledge might be helpful, his main duties would be to confirm Sayer's intuitions if he could, and to assist in pinpointing the exact location of the Eye. Sayer had never cooperated with another seeker before and was not sure how it would work out, but the rapport that was developing between himself and Obra was encouraging. For his own part, the older seeker had been both overjoyed and overawed to be chosen. He had resigned himself to a lifelong succession of minor achievements, and to be involved in the retrieval of the Eye of Clouds – even in a subordinate role – was beyond his most fanciful imaginings. Sayer had been left in no doubt that Obra would sacrifice anything, even his life if necessary, to ensure the success of the mission. Naturally, they all hoped that nothing like that would be required, but Mazandaran was reputed to be a godless, barbarous land, its mountainous terrain populated by outlaws and cannibals, so they had to be prepared for anything.

* * *

The two seekers were together that evening when the lights of Jandaq came into view and the crew began to prepare for docking.

'It'll be good to have solid ground beneath our feet again,' Obra remarked. He and several other members of the party had turned pale when the wind had risen that afternoon, exaggerating the movements of the ship. Sayer had barely noticed, his mind firmly fixed on other things.

'Tell me about the Rivash Canyon,' he said now. 'I've never seen it before.'

'I can try,' Obra replied obediently, 'but it's so big it's almost impossible to describe. From the rim you can look *down* on the summits of mountains so tall and steep that they'll never be climbed. There are cliffs so high that it's said if the husband of a newly pregnant woman falls from the top, he'll be a father before he hits the bottom.'

Sayer laughed.

'I thought it was only mountain folk who told such tall tales,' he commented.

'You should hear some of the diamond miners after they've had a few drinks,' Obra told him. 'The canyon really is extraordinary, though, especially at sunrise or sunset when the colours change. It's a different world in there.'

'Can it be crossed?' Sayer asked, impressed by his companion's obvious reverence.

'There are trails, but they're tortuous and full of peril. Unless it's essential, I'd suggest we go round to the east instead.'

'So we should stick close to the Daran?'

'Yes. Even at the end of the canyon proper the terrain is treacherous, but it's far worse lower down.'

'All right. Let's hope—' Sayer broke off suddenly and gazed out at the dark waters of the estuary. 'Do you feel it?'

he breathed. 'Gods! This is incredible.'

'What is it?'

'The Eye,' Sayer replied. 'It passed this way. On a barge.' He was overjoyed at his discovery, having not dared to hope for anything so soon.

'You can sense that?' Obra asked in awe. 'After all this time?' He could detect nothing.

'It's very faint and fleeting,' Sayer answered, his eyes still staring at the surface of the water. 'But it *was* here. We're on the right track!'

CHAPTER EIGHT

'Not all omens are what they seem, and the paths they
lead us down may end in the pit of fire and scorpions.
So tread softly on the ghost road, and remember that
the gods use strange messengers.'

From *The Oracles of Zavanaiu*

At sunset five days later Sayer stood on the rim of the canyon
that effectively defined the northern border of Tirok.
Together with the other members of the party who had not
seen it before, he stared at the panoramic grandeur before
him in utter astonishment. Even the mountains where he
had grown up had never presented such a spectacular view
and, as Obra had said, the subtly changing colours of dusk
made the scene all the more fantastic. Sayer knew that the
Rivash Canyon was much wider further to the west, but
even here, where it was only two or three leagues across, the
array of ravines and gorges, pinnacles and ridges that lay
inside the canyon were breathtaking in their immensity as
well as their variety. Towers of rock glowed red, brown,
orange and yellow, each strata seeming to have a character all
of its own, and where shadows fell the darkness was impen-
etrable, promising further hidden wonders.

For some time no one spoke. Obra had been right when

he said that the landscape before them defied description, and Sayer was not surprised that the canyon had inspired its own extravagant mythology.

It was Nazeri who eventually broke the silence.

'How far is the trail from here?' His question was addressed to the local guide, who had been hired from a nearby village. Although Pena was dressed in little more than rags, he was a proud man who had undertaken the task gladly when Sayer explained that they were hunting for a valuable relic from the Temple of Qara.

'Less than half a league,' he replied, 'but that is a place of broken stone. You would do better to camp here for the night and begin the descent in the morning.'

'It's hard to believe there's any way to get down there,' Kebir said, peering over the cliff edge.

'It can be done,' Pena assured him. 'With knowledge and patience.'

As the camp was set up, Sayer had time to reflect on their progress. They had followed the Daran River for the first two days out of Jandaq, but in the middle of the third the seeker had felt the invisible trail shift. Until then he had received fleeting glimpses of the Eye's history as it had been taken upstream, but at this point the residual trace diverged from the water and so they followed it along a badly maintained road heading northwest. As they journeyed on at a steady pace, the path rose gently until they came to a vast plateau that stretched all the way to the border. The further they went from the river, the poorer the quality of the land became. Even though more rain fell on this part of the country than in the eastern half of Tirok, there was little agriculture here. This was mining country, and the rough terrain was made more perilous by many old shafts and pits, abandoned when the gold or gemstones ran out. Some deposits remained, and a few villagers scraped a living from these and from what crops they could coax from the stony soil, but great stretches of the plain were unpopulated.

Eventually, the sight of distant mountains to the north told the travellers that they were nearing the border, and by then Sayer knew that their route would take them not around but towards the Rivash Canyon. After consulting some of the local people, they learnt of a possible trail which the seeker hoped might even be the one along which the Eye had been taken centuries before. Either way, he was certain that was where they must go. Now, as he watched the tents being pitched and food being prepared, he could only hope that his instincts were right.

Pena took them to the beginning of the trail the next morning, but once there made it clear that he would be going no further. Nazeri glanced at Sayer to see whether he should force the issue, but the seeker shook his head. That night he had dreamt of being lost within a high-walled maze, until a green-eyed kyar had appeared and led him to safety. He had woken feeling optimistic, taking the omen to mean that the gods were guiding his path.

'We'll be able to follow the trail ourselves from here,' he stated confidently.

Pena nodded, smiling gratefully.

'It is clear enough,' he said. 'There are only two forks where you might go wrong, and in each case you must take the left turn.'

'Where do the others lead?' Nazeri asked.

'To the ghost caves,' Pena replied. 'You would do well not to disturb them.'

The captain was about to respond when Sayer interrupted quickly, knowing it would be unwise to offend local beliefs.

'We'll leave them well alone,' he said. 'How long should it take to reach the far rim?'

'Two days, unless you have to stop to clear any rock falls. There's water at the bottom, but no food until the other side.'

'We're well supplied,' Sayer assured him. 'Thank you for your help.'

Pena nodded in acknowledgement.

'May the gods grant you good hunting.'

At first the trail zigzagged down the cliff face, and was so narrow that the horses had to be led. Although the animals were well-trained and sure-footed, any slip could prove fatal. After a while the track levelled out for a time, winding around several rock pinnacles. From close to, their colours were less dramatic than they had appeared from the rim, but it was still an extraordinary landscape. Although the path made use of whatever open areas were available, it sometimes ran along the edge of terrifying vertical drops or plunged into narrow crevasses so that the rock closed in on either side and the sky shrank to a thin band of blue.

As Sayer and his group descended, the air grew warmer and more humid. Inexplicable patches of mist seemed to rise up from the baking ground. Lizards and snakes scuttled for cover at the travellers' approach and a few birds of prey circled lazily above, but the canyon was otherwise uninhabited and the few plants that clung to the steep slopes were quite different from anything Sayer had ever seen before. Inside Rivash it truly was another world.

They passed the first fork soon after midday. No one was even tempted to turn right, because that branch of the trail looked even more treacherous than the one they were on. By dusk – which came early to these depths – they had reached the river at the heart of the canyon. The slow-moving water was surprisingly cold. It was quite opaque, because of all the silt it carried, which meant that it had to be strained through cloth before it could be used for cooking. Relieved that the first half of the journey had been uneventful, the group set up camp where they were, intending to ford the river and begin their climb at first light.

However, the next day did not begin well. One of the leading horses stumbled into a pothole in midstream, unseating its rider and breaking its right foreleg. The soldier was unharmed, but there was nothing that could be done for his mount and it was put out of its misery. Great caution was exercised by the rest of the travellers, and as a result the crossing took much longer than they had hoped.

As he reached the far bank, Sayer felt a distinct sensation of cold that had nothing to do with the tendrils of fog rising from the river and, for the first time, he began to question their route. He had sensed nothing of the Eye on the trail, and that worried him. Everything had been going well so far and he did not want the mission to end in abject failure – or worse – because he had insisted on their descent into this strange and inhospitable region. However, they had little choice now but to go on, and for a time the trail was good. As they rose back towards the real world the party's spirits began to revive.

All that changed after about two hours' travelling, when the track crossed a razor-backed crag that fell away steeply on either side. Although the path itself was rough it seemed solid enough, but the horses were nervous at being so exposed and when one of them stamped down, the ground beneath its hooves gave way. Both horse and rider were swept away, tumbling over the scree in the midst of a whirling avalanche that set off several other minor landslides. Man and beast were both dead long before they came to rest a few hundred paces below the horrified onlookers. Even if they had been alive, there was nothing anyone could have done to help them. The rest of the party had more than enough to cope with in navigating the now broken and unstable path. The horses were even more skittish after that, and had to be led as they gingerly picked their way along the ridge. And then, just as they had all regained more solid ground, Sayer felt a sudden surge of confidence. The Eye had been there! It was by far the strongest resonance yet and he was about to announce this to his companions when he realized, with a sinking feeling in his stomach, that it had come from just ahead of where they were gathered. There the trail divided into two – and the signal had come from the *right-hand* fork.

Sayer glanced quickly at Obra and saw from his furrowed expression that he had sensed something too.

'Do you know where it came from?' he asked.

'From the right,' the other seeker answered quietly.

'What's this?' Nazeri demanded.

Although the discussion that followed involved all the leaders of the group, Sayer knew that it would ultimately be his own decision – and he was already certain of what it must be.

'Ghosts or not,' he said, 'that's the way we have to go.'

'I'm not worried by old wives' tales,' Nazeri said. 'What concerns me is whether we can get out of this hole that way. Should we leave some men here in case we need to retrace our steps?'

'Even if we do, we've no idea how far we might need to go along the other trail,' Kebir pointed out.

'What about sending some scouts ahead, then?' the captain suggested.

'No,' Sayer decided. 'We should stick together.'

As they set off again, he became aware of the under-current of unease among the men. The earlier accidents and now this detour were making even the most phlegmatic of his followers nervous, and they glanced around constantly, as though every boulder might conceal new dangers. An hour later the seeker was almost at his wits' end. The trail had led them through a narrow defile to a wide flat space, surrounded on three sides by sheer cliffs rising up to the clouds and on the fourth by a vertical precipice that plunged to the river below. There was nothing there except rock and dust, no ghosts, no caves – and no way out except back the way they had come. The detour had been a complete waste of time – and yet he had been sure that the Eye had led him to this place.

Nazeri recognized the seeker's confusion, and took charge. Even though it was obvious that he thought there was nothing to be found, he ordered his men to search the entire area, each crevice in the rock, in case they had over-looked anything. Sayer was grateful, but still puzzled.

'Do you sense anything?' he asked Obra.

The other seeker shook his head. He was clearly as per-plexed as Sayer.

'This won't do much for the men's confidence in you,' Kebir said quietly. 'We know the Eye's on the other side of the canyon, so the sooner we get out of here the better.'

'It was here once,' Sayer persisted. 'Maybe it wasn't a dead end then.'

The scribe gave him a sceptical look, but was prevented from making any further comment by a cry from one of the soldiers.

'Captain. Over here!'

By the time Sayer had dismounted and gone to see what had been discovered, almost the entire party had gathered and he had to push his way through. When he succeeded, he could hardly believe his eyes. Concealed between two angu-lar protuberances, a small niche had been carved into the russet-coloured cliff face, and within it lay a milky-white stone the size of his fist. Its locating grooves and the incised symbols of a star and an eye were the only marks on its otherwise smooth surfaces.

'Is it the Eye?' someone asked breathlessly.

'No,' Sayer replied, to general dismay. 'This is a faithful copy, but it's a fake.'

'Then is this what we've been following?' Nazeri asked.

'No,' Sayer answered, hoping it was the truth. 'The genuine relic must have passed here once. This is just a decoy to fool the unwary. It's worthless.' To demonstrate his point he reached out and took it from its hiding place, then held it at arm's length and dropped it to the ground. The white stone shattered on impact, and several of the onlookers gasped.

A moment later the air was rent by an ear-splitting howl and the sudden thunder of drums. As Sayer and the others swung round, they saw that they were surrounded by a band of barbarian warriors.

CHAPTER NINE

'The lives of all who are born and dwell in Tirok are blessed by the gods. Kill them not, lest their spirits return to torment you and all your works. Foreigners have no souls, and may thus be slain with impunity if the cause is just.'

From *The Oracles of Zavanaiu*

To their credit, Nazeri's company reacted instantly, moving into defensive positions at speed but without panic. Swords appeared in their hands as if by magic, and Sayer and his colleagues found themselves protected by a human shield. Most of the artisans also prepared to defend themselves, while others tried to calm the horses. The barbarian clamour went on, although no one could see the drums whose beat was echoing around the cliff faces, but the warriors made no move to attack. Nazeri shouted his orders over the din, cursing the lookouts he had posted for not giving him any warning, and wondering how the enemy horde had managed to arrive so swiftly and silently. Even so, he was confident that they would be no match for his well-drilled and experienced troops. The barbarians wore an assortment of outlandish clothes and talismanic jewellery, and their weapons looked old-fashioned. The captain was almost eager for the battle to begin, so that his men could prove their worth in godless blood.

Sayer knew better. This was magic, primitive and violent in its nature, but undeniably powerful. Ignoring the warnings of the others, he pushed himself to the front of his protectors and stared across at the warriors. They did not react to his presence.

'They're not real!' Sayer shouted. 'This is an illusion.' He stepped forward again, while around him his companions reacted with concern and disbelief. 'There is no danger here,' he added, as the noise from the attackers began to die away. 'They're not real.'

They were Pena's ghosts, he thought. It was no wonder the local people believed such places were haunted.

As the shouting and the noise of the drums became even more muted, the warriors began to melt into thin air. They lingered for a few moments, transparent phantoms, and then there was nothing. The only sound left was a soft mocking laughter that came from nowhere, before that too faded into silence. From the stillness around him, Sayer knew that his allies were in a state of shock. The warriors had seemed quite real, and for a few moments no one could quite believe that they had simply vanished. Turning around, Sayer saw that Obra was shaking and many others were still pale with fear.

'What was that all about?' Nazeri asked, making a determined effort to keep his voice steady.

'A joke,' Sayer replied. 'A joke from a diseased mind. Whoever stole the Eye was very talented, but the gods must have driven him mad as punishment for his crime.' It was a convenient rationalization.

'How?' Nazeri waved a hand at the empty space where the warriors had been.

'He knew someone would come here eventually,' the

seeker explained, 'so he set up a magical illusion to be acti-
vated when anyone touched the fake stone.'

'A booby trap?' Nazeri said incredulously.

Sayer nodded and silence fell again as the witnesses to
this strange event all struggled to come to terms with what
they had seen. It was only then that they heard the sound of
falling boulders.

Although the ground beneath their feet shook, they soon
realized that they were in no immediate danger. However,
the avalanche was in the defile through which they had
entered the ghost arena, and it was clear that they might
become completely trapped. When the horror of their situation sank in, all they could do was wait until the clouds of
dust cleared and they could inspect the damage. They had
supplies for several days, but if they were trapped and could
not find a way out, a slow death by starvation was inevitable.

'Some joke,' Damaris said quietly.

'Do you think the magic set off the fall as well?' Obra
asked. His voice was still shaky.

'More likely it was the noise of the drums,' Kebir replied.
'Either way, it's too much of a coincidence to be accidental.'

'Will we get out?'

'We're in the best possible company for a situation like
this,' Sayer answered, indicating the artisans. 'If anyone can
clear the way they can.' He was still berating himself for
having led the party into this predicament. Why hadn't he
known it was a trap? And what other surprises awaited them
on the trail of the Eye of Clouds?

When the rock fall finally stopped, the masons went to
investigate and soon reported that it should be possible to
clear some of the debris and build a new path over the rest.
However, this would take at least two days, and by then their
water supplies would be running low. The greatest difficulty

they faced, however, was to make the path fit for their mounts; men could clamber over terrain that was impossible for horses and, for a time, it seemed that they would have to leave them behind.

In the end, by dint of back-breaking work from the entire group – only the mages were not put at risk – a new track was constructed. It took three days, and the thirsty builders were in constant danger from new but fortunately minor rock falls. Finally, all was as ready as it would ever be and the first horses were led out. It was a tribute to the skill of all concerned that not a single mount was lost in their escape, and Sayer knew that if it had not been for the artisans it was possible that no one – either human or animal – would have survived the ordeal.

That night – their fifth in the canyon – they camped at the fork, and a series of smaller groups were dispatched to the river below to replenish their water supplies. The next morning they all set out to follow the route to the northern rim. They reached this at dusk, after a long, tiring but thankfully uneventful day. Most of the party slept well, having earnt their rest, in spite of the fact that they were now in a foreign land. They were just glad to be back in a world they understood after the giant haunted maze of the Rivash Canyon. Their supplies had been depleted more than Nazeri would have liked, but there was no immediate concern as long as they could find enough water.

Sayer had other things on his mind. Ever since the signal at the fork – which had deluded both him and Obra – he had felt nothing of the Eye, and so he spent most of the night in contemplation, trying to empty his mind and thus allow the resonance to make itself felt. Such was his concentration that he almost fell into a trance, but he received only vague intimations rather than any clear guidance. At sunrise he consulted with Obra, who admitted shamefacedly that he had slept all night and had sensed nothing of their target, then told Nazeri that he believed they had to go west, along the rim. The captain accepted this without question, and Sayer wished he shared the other's trust in his judgement.

That afternoon, they passed close to the edge of a forest and made camp early by a stream, while some of the men hunted and foraged, replenishing their provisions. Although there had been no sign of human habitation on the trail, it was clear that others rode this way from time to time. It was therefore no great surprise when, as the day came to an end, they were approached by another group of travellers.

Nazeri was understandably wary, deploying his men to ward off any possible attack, but the Mazandarans' party was smaller than their own, apparently carried few weapons and showed no hostile intent. In the event, with every sign of friendliness, the newcomers asked to share the campsite and set up their bivouac a few paces away. Although Nazeri remained suspicious and posted sentries to keep watch, Sayer soon felt a measure of trust and was eager to gain what information he could from the foreigners. He could see that, far from looking like barbarians, the Mazandarans were dressed in good clothes and carried with them many accoutrements of civilized society. He was equally surprised when their leader, a man who introduced himself as Mehran-Dar, asked whether they might speak together.

'I am a healer by profession, but my curiosity is still that of a child,' he remarked, smiling as they walked a little way from the others. 'I like to learn what I can from everyone I meet, and it is a rare opportunity to talk to someone from the other side of the canyon.'

'That's hardly surprising,' Sayer replied, 'given the difficulties in crossing it.'

'Ah, so you met the ghosts. Magic can be used for many purposes, but that seems to me to be the most frivolous.'

'That frivolity almost got us all killed.'

Mehran-Dar's expression grew serious.

'I did not intend to make light of your misfortunes,' he said earnestly. 'Please, tell me what happened.'

Sayer did so, but made no mention of the fake stone. He did not wish to reveal the exact reason for their journey.

'Others would not have been so resourceful in such a situation,' the healer commented, obviously impressed. 'You must be a well-respected leader for such men to follow you.'

The remark took Sayer by surprise. He had always taken his own authority for granted. It was the natural order of things, ordained by the needs of the great task.

'They respect my talent, I suppose,' he said doubtfully.

'So you *are* a fellow mage,' Mehran-Dar said. 'I thought so.'

'And I thought you said you were a physician,' Sayer replied.

'A healer,' his companion corrected him. 'That is my talent. What is yours?'

'I'm a seeker.'

'And what do you seek?'

Sayer hesitated before answering, then allowed his instincts to rule his judgement – up to a point.

'An ancient relic. It was stolen a long time ago and brought to Mazandaran.'

'I see.' The other man was obviously intrigued. 'This relic has some significance, I presume?'

'Yes. It's very important.' Sayer expected Mehran-Dar to ask why this was so, but the healer surprised him again with his next words.

'Your talent must be very strong if you can trace this relic after such a long time.'

'I've been well trained,' Sayer replied modestly. 'As you must have been if you use magic to heal.'

'Oh, I just seem to pick things up as I go along. I found that I could tell what was wrong with someone by just holding their hand or looking into their eyes, and from there it was only a small and natural step to wanting to put it right. And I have help.'

'From whom?'

'From those who have gone before me, the healers who now exist in this world in spirit only.'

'The dead?' Sayer exclaimed.

'They lend me their knowledge and a little strength to do what good I can. Mazandaran is a poor country, and illness is common. Tell me, are you familiar with the city of Qara?'

'I live there.'

'Then you are indeed far from home. Is there still plague there?'

'A little,' Sayer admitted defensively. 'Our physicians have it under control.'

'Will this relic help your people?' Mehran-Dar asked.

'Yes.'

'So it contains power to defeat the plague?'

'No. It's not as simple as that.'

'Yet it must be something important for you to travel with such a large party and to come so far.'

The two men were now standing close to the rim of the canyon, and the healer waved an arm to indicate the shadowed gulf.

'Especially over such uninviting terrain,' he continued.

'The relic will be offered to the gods.'

'Ah, the gods. It is said that religion is the last refuge of the desperate man.'

Sayer did not know how to respond to this. It sounded like blasphemy to him, but perhaps he should not expect a foreigner to understand.

'So you search for a lost piece of the Temple,' Mehran-Dar observed thoughtfully, and Sayer revised his opinions once again.

'You seem very well informed about my country,' he observed suspiciously.

'We are neighbours, even if we are separated by more than the Rivash Canyon,' the healer replied mysteriously. 'Some news inevitably travels between our lands. Tell me, do you think rebuilding the Temple will benefit your people?'

'Of course.'

'You have no doubts?'

'None. Unless we do the gods' will and fulfil the prophecy, disaster will befall us.'

Although Mehran-Dar looked sceptical, he said nothing, and Sayer began to feel a spark of annoyance. He had taken an instant liking to the man, but the healer's questions were becoming less welcome.

'I wouldn't expect someone from Mazandaran to understand,' he added.

'Because we are all barbarians?' Mehran-Dar asked with a smile.

'If you do not honour the gods, yes!' Sayer replied angrily.

'I honour all life,' the other man stated simply.

They stood in silence for a while, Sayer fretting, the healer apparently at ease.

'Where are you heading?' Mehran-Dar asked eventually. 'Do you know where the relic is located?'

'We are going west,' Sayer replied, seeing no point in denying the obvious. 'But I won't know exactly where it is until I get closer.'

'Have you heard of the ruined city of Bandan Kuh?'

'No.' Sayer wondered where this latest turn in the conversation was leading.

'It lies about twenty leagues to the west of here. It was once a great city, but is abandoned now. They say its residents were once the richest men in the world, but they ruined it all with their greed for silver and jewels.'

'How?'

'The mining was so extensive that the entire area became unstable. But even then they wouldn't stop. Eventually, many buildings simply disappeared as underground caverns collapsed, and part of the city fell into the canyon in an enormous landslide. What was left was soon wrecked by subsidence, and by the violence and lawlessness that followed. Then the silver ran out and even the brigands deserted the place.'

'And you think the relic might be there?' Sayer asked, becoming excited by the idea. 'In amongst the ruins?'

'It's possible.'

Sayer's instincts told him that this was more than a possibility. It fitted all the known facts. Whoever had taken the Eye had been a man of power and wealth – like the one-time residents of Bandan Kuh. The relic was now underground, which fitted with the story of the collapse of the houses there. And the location fitted perfectly with what had been foreseen by the daydreamer.

'It's an easy enough journey from here,' Mehran-Dar went on, 'though the road is not used much nowadays – for obvious reasons. The land in that area can still be unstable at times.'

Sayer had become confused again, in spite of his excitement.

'If you don't believe in what I'm doing, then why are you helping me?' he asked uneasily.

'I'm prepared to believe that I may be wrong,' the healer replied, then laughed. 'About this and a great many other things. Each man must decide for himself what his magic is for. I wish you luck.'

'Thank you,' Sayer responded, feeling humbled by the other man's tolerance.

'May I show you something?' Mehran-Dar enquired.

'Of course.'

'Come with me.' The healer led the seeker to the Mazandaran camp, where his followers were preparing a meal. They were mainly young, both men and women, and although they looked at Sayer with frank curiosity, they did not speak until Mehran-Dar introduced his guest. 'Sayer, these are my students.'

'Will you join us for some food, Sayer?' one of the women asked.

'No, thank you. My own companions will supply my needs.'

Meanwhile, the healer had been rummaging in a knapsack and now found what he had been looking for. He held a book out to Sayer, who took it gently. It was bound in embossed leather, with thick pages of vellum.

'Open it.'

Sayer did as he was told and was amazed by the exquisite calligraphy inside, by the resplendent decorations in blue, red and gold. Entranced, he read a few lines, part of a fable about a group of young wizards. After a few moments he tore his eyes away and glanced at his host. The healer was smiling.

'It's beautiful,' Sayer whispered. He had never seen anything quite so lovely.

'It's yours,' Mehran-Dar said. 'As a gift.'

'I can't take this . . . It must be . . .'

'It's old and valuable, but it's not unique and I know every page by heart. You will gain more from it than me.'

'But . . .' Words failed Sayer. Such extraordinary generosity to a stranger was hard to understand, and was something he had never experienced before.

'Read it as a reminder that Mazandaran may be a poorer country than Tirok,' the healer said, 'but perhaps we are not all barbarians.'

CHAPTER TEN

'The breath of clouds touches us all. The silver water
of life falls as Ailor's tears.'
> Inscription above the entrance to the
> Tower of Clouds

The next morning the two parties went their separate ways,
and Sayer and Mehran-Dar waved to each other in parting.
The book was carefully packed away in the seeker's saddle-
bag, and he was looking forward to having the time and
leisure to study it. He had reported little of his conversation
with the healer to his companions and, apart from the suggestion about Bandan Kuh, they had shown little interest. It
had been tempting to show the book to Kebir – as a scribe he
would have appreciated its beauty and value – but Sayer had
not done so, wanting to keep the gift a secret for the time
being. Mehran-Dar had given him a great deal to think about,
and he was silent for most of the morning as they rode west.
However, as they neared the outskirts of what had once been
Bandan Kuh, his mind became preoccupied again by the
search for the Eye of Clouds. Twice that afternoon he felt
short but unmistakable reverberations, and was now convinced
that the ruined city was indeed their goal. The signs were
stronger than ever, and Obra's own feelings confirmed this.

80

To everyone's immense frustration, the last part of the day's journey was very slow because of the deteriorating condition of the road. When darkness fell it became impossible to continue, even though they had been within sight of the first ruins. Sayer was so full of anticipation that he did not think he would be able to sleep, but he did, and woke to unexpectedly grey skies. Until then their travelling had been under the clear dome of summer, but now clouds had piled up and rain threatened, even though it remained hot. Far to the north the highest mountains were invisible, and within the canyon there were odd flashes of light and booming echoes that no one could explain. It was as though an impossible thunderstorm was raging within its depths.

None of this deterred the group from their purpose, however, and they moved on into the city that had been destroyed by greed. Almost at once Sayer was practically overwhelmed by a resonance so strong that he cried out, and saw that Obra had felt it too.

'We're close. It's over there,' he said, pointing. He glanced at Obra for confirmation and the other seeker nodded, his eyes bright with excitement.

Their progress was still slow, because huge craters pocked the earth and there was tumbled masonry everywhere. It was as though the place had been attacked by some unimaginable rain of giant boulders, hurled from the sky. Sayer was amazed by the fact that such devastation could have been caused by the puny efforts of mankind. Some areas were scorched black where fires had raged, while others were covered with windblown silt that softened the harsh outlines of the ruins. The remnants of some buildings were still distinguishable, and Sayer thought of the Temple of Qara, which had suffered a similar fate. Had Bandan Kuh been punished by jealous gods? he wondered, then pushed the thought aside. One thing was certain; no one would ever make the effort to rebuild this place. Its glory was gone for ever.

Thankfully, the signals he was receiving almost continuously now led them away from the collapsed edge of the cliff. If the Eye had been in a part of the city swallowed by the Rivash Canyon, finding it would have been next to impossible. As it was, with Obra's help, Sayer was able to lead the party to the relic's location within an hour. He was not surprised to find that this was within one of the steep-sided craters. As far as he could tell, the relic was buried beneath the centre of the circular depression. However, until he and Obra, working in tandem, were able to work out their bearings and angles, Sayer could not be sure just how far below the surface it was. While they were doing this, the first of the miners and masons climbed down into the pit, and found that the rubble that lined it was treacherous and unsteady. Their preliminary inspection convinced them that there was a long job ahead of them, and when Sayer announced that the Eye was more than fifteen paces below ground level, their agitation increased. Nevertheless they got to work, shoring up some rocks and removing others in order to facilitate their excavation. The process was complicated by several air pockets beneath the surface, into which both materials and men could fall if they were not careful. Their progress was also hampered by intermittent but heavy rain showers that turned dust to mud and made the stones slippery. Although this was a nuisance, some of the artisans heard Kebir's prayers and took the rain as a blessing from Ailor.

Judging by the quality of the masonry that now lay haphazardly in the crater, the building in which the Eye had originally been housed had been palatial, grander even than Halion's mansion. Its fall into the earth must have been spectacular, and the remains had obviously been smashed beyond repair. Even so, anything small and light enough to be carried away had been looted long since – unless, like the relic, it had been buried too deep.

The artisans continually revised their plans, surveying the problem from all angles. They dug tunnels, built ramps and bridges, used pulleys and levers – and all the time Sayer paced the edge of the hole, watching the swarming activity within and hearing the Eye call out to him, its voice growing ever stronger. He wished he could do more, but knew better than to interfere with the work of his team. Kebir recorded all the details of their progress and Damaris rested, waiting for the moment when his skills would be needed. That time came after three long and agonizing days.

'We're close to the Eye now,' the overseer reported. 'It's undamaged, as far as we can tell, but it's wedged between two large pieces of masonry. We'll need the silk before we lever them apart and try to get it out.'

'Ready, Damaris?' the seeker asked.

'Of course.'

Sayer insisted on going down into the crater with the silk and the artisans, but kept his distance when he was told, in no uncertain terms, to make sure that he didn't get in the way. He had already imparted everything he knew about the Eye to the silk's mind, and all he could do now was wait.

Violet light glowed through cracks in the debris, the overseer shouted orders and men strained at their tasks. Rock grated upon rock, boulders shifted, dust rose up in small eddies and stones clattered down into widening cracks. Then there was a shout of triumph, and moments later one of the artisans emerged from the mouth of a tunnel with something white in his hand, its violet halo already fading. A cheer went up as the man scrambled over to Sayer, and others watched, relaxing now, as the seeker accepted the prize.

Sayer gazed at the stone, feeling its resonance pulse

through his entire body. He was afire, breathless and triumphant. He held the Eye of Clouds in his hand!

The journey back to Qara was not without its hardships, but none of the travellers was in a mood to complain. They had only to think of the priceless stone – now carefully wrapped and carried in one of the seeker's saddlebags – to know that all their efforts had been worthwhile. They were assured of a magnificent welcome on their return home, and they would each tell the story of this adventure for all the remaining years of their lives.

Their route took them far to the east, into the foothills of the mountains, so that they avoided any possibility of having to recross the Rivash Canyon. They finally reached the Daran River and turned south, following the water's course back into Tirok. At the archivects' most northern outpost, situated at the limit of navigation, they exchanged their weary horses for passage on river barges, and the flotilla took them all the way to Jandaq in relative comfort. There they boarded a ship and sailed back across the Lake of Souls until, at long last, they returned to the docks of Qara. After almost a month's travelling, they were home.

Knowing that news of their triumphant return would spread quickly, Sayer and Kebir hurried to the Treasury to deposit the Eye there for safekeeping. The seeker was now so used to its resonances that leaving it behind was a wrench. Although part of him felt suddenly empty, he was anxious to get back to his apartment and be reunited with Aphra.

He ran all the way, his heart almost bursting with joy, and leapt up the stairs two at a time – but as soon as he went inside he knew that something was wrong. The entrance walls were bare and, on further inspection, he found that all of their furniture was gone. Each of the rooms was spotless but empty, and he stood in the middle of the sitting room in utter bewilderment.

Then he heard a sound behind him and swung round, expecting to see his sister, but the worried eyes that met his own belonged to Kailas. He had not given her a thought for many days, and seeing her there now seemed incongruous.

'Oh, Sayer,' she said. 'I'm sorry. I came as soon as I could.'

'What's happened?' he asked. 'Where's Aphra? Where are all my things?'

'They had to clear everything out.'

'Where's my sister?' he demanded, as his triumph drained away and an icy fist closed over his heart.

Kailas's expression betrayed her misery.

'Aphra has the plague,' she said. 'She was taken away five days ago.'

CHAPTER ELEVEN

'Tabrielle can make a poet out of any man.'

Tirokian proverb

Sayer woke cramped and aching after another night spent huddled on the bare floor of his empty apartment. His first conscious thought was one of despair, as it had been for each of the last five days. *Aphra's gone.* But this time, unlike the earlier mornings, it was not followed by an automatic denial. Aphra *was* gone, and nothing he could do or say would change that. Grief and rage fought for dominance in his mind until he wanted to hammer his fists into the wall in sheer frustration. Instead, he threw back his head and howled.

By comparison, his second thought provoked no emotion at all, beyond a certain weary resignation. *This is my wedding day.*

Five days had passed since Sayer's return to Qara, five days which for many people had been spent in making preparations for the rededication of the Eye of Clouds. Most ceremonies of this kind were held as soon as possible after the relic had been returned to the Temple and the rites amended according to the proper procedure for the day in question. However, Sayer's find was deemed important enough for a slight delay. This was in part because the ritual accompanying the restoration of the Tower of Clouds would be enormously elaborate and complex, involving a huge number of people, and so time was needed to make sure that everything was ready and everyone was well versed in the roles that they would play. In his misery Sayer had taken little part – and no pleasure – in the build-up to the ceremony, but he knew he would nonetheless be expected to participate.

Another reason for the delay was so that the organizers could take advantage of a fortuitous coincidence in the Temple calendar. The day chosen for the rededication was the annual feast day of Tabrielle, daughter of Ailor, and the goddess of love and fertility. Halion had decided that Sayer and Kailas should be married on this day, in the tower that had been sacred to Tabrielle's father – the tower that was finally to be restored because of Sayer's efforts. This had two advantages; it honoured the archivect's now famous seeker, and it also meant that his marriage began under the most favourable portents for the arrival of children. Sayer had taken even less interest in this aspect of the proceedings, even though Kailas had been consistently at his side, trying to comfort him.

His fiancée had been very patient, seeming to share his grief and indulging his outbursts of rancour and occasional cruelties without complaint.

Sayer's initial reaction on being told the news of Aphra's fate had been one of outright disbelief. His sister had been in perfect health when he had left, so how could she have become infected and been condemned so quickly? He simply could not understand why anyone should think to tell him something so patently absurd. But when the incredulity had gone, the anger remained. And that anger had sustained him for a while. He lashed out at anyone and anything – the physicians, the plague itself, the sailors who took its victims to the Isle of the Dead, all his friends, and even Aphra herself. How could she have done this to him? He went down to the docks and raved wildly, trying to persuade one of the captains to take him to the island so he could bring his twin back. When he accepted that this was impossible – a process that took some time – he then demanded that he too be abandoned on the island so he could join her. No one was willing to do that either. The fact that his request was insane would have been reason enough – others had made similar pleas in the past, to no avail – but everybody knew who Sayer was, and knew just how valuable he was to his master. Anyone who allowed the seeker to commit suicide in this way would have to answer to Halion.

Eventually, Sayer's rage was tempered by absolute dejection. He was frustrated beyond endurance by his inability to do anything. He had lost any semblance of control over his own destiny. In his more rational moments he was aware that he had *never* really had much influence over the course of his own life, as almost all of it had been determined by Halion and others. Tormented by his own helplessness, and more lonely than ever before, he began to see that in time he would inevitably become resigned to what had happened. But he could not – and would not – accept it. He missed Aphra more than he could have believed possible, realizing that he had depended on her steadfast presence and constant companionship to balance the bizarre nature of the rest of his existence. Without her the idea of work seemed pointless; the idea of doing *anything* seemed pointless. They had been together their whole lives – even before they were born – and to have that bond severed so completely and so unexpectedly was unbelievably painful.

Throughout his periods of monumental anger, his irrational outbursts, and then his spiralling descent into the darkest gloom, it was Kailas who had borne the brunt of his madness. At times Sayer hated her for being the bearer of bad news, for remaining healthy, for trying to persuade him that life would go on and that there was nothing anyone could do for Aphra now. On other occasions he took a fleeting comfort in her presence and, although he was now indifferent to her charms, he began to believe that she must have some genuine feelings for him. Why else would she have put up with all the abuse, all the helpless bitterness, that he had heaped upon her? On several occasions she had fled from him in tears and he had thought she would never return, but she had always come back to try again. In the end, Sayer was grateful for her persistence. Without her he might even have turned some of his more poisonous ideas into reality. He had considered trying to steal a boat and braving the monsters around the Isle of the Dead; he had thought of killing himself; and he had even devised a plan to seek out plague victims so that he too might become infected. And in each instance, Kailas had been the one to dissuade him.

It had also been Kailas who told him that all his and Aphra's belongings had been burnt, because of the danger of contamination, and the apartment purged.

'But they don't do that to other people,' Sayer objected.

'Other people aren't as important as you,' she replied. 'Halion couldn't afford to take any chances.'

'So there's nothing left at all?' he asked, meaning that there was nothing left to remind him of Aphra.

'Only these.' Kailas took two wall masks out of a muslin bag and handed them to Sayer. 'They wouldn't burn, but they've been scoured and are quite safe.'

Although the backs of the masks had been scraped and gouged, they were otherwise intact. Tears came into Sayer's eyes as he looked at them, remembering Aphra buying them years earlier, remembering her mimicking the faces – one happy, one sad.

Some days later, the masks remained his only possessions, other than the pack he had carried back from Mazandaran and some fresh clothes supplied by Kailas. He had refused to leave the empty apartment, in spite of the fact that a new home had been acquired and furnished in preparation for his married life. Ignoring his fiancée's pleas and the advice of his friends, he had not even been to see his new living quarters. He had returned to the only place where his memories of Aphra were still vivid, even though the apartment was now an empty shell. He was drawn there by feelings he could not fully explain, and the uncomfortable existence he had chosen was a kind of penance – although he could not have said what crime he had committed to deserve his self-imposed punishment.

Sitting cross-legged on the floor of what had once been his bedroom, Sayer reflected now that by evening he would be a married man and everyone, not least Kailas herself, would expect him to move into their joint accommodation that night. Halion had been understanding so far, respecting his seeker's mourning, but he would not tolerate it for much longer – especially when this day would see not only the marriage but also the rededication of the most important relic ever returned to Qara. It should have been Sayer's greatest moment, the day of his double triumph, but instead he felt only intense sadness and a great emptiness of spirit.

On impulse, he reached inside his bag and pulled out the book that had been Mehran-Dar's gift. In the throes of his torment he had forgotten its existence for a while, but now, as he glanced at each delightful page, he thought not of the words written there but of those spoken by the man who had given it to him. *I am a healer by profession.* Would Mehran-Dar have been able to save Aphra? The very idea was intolerable. *Will this relic help your people?* Sayer had been so sure of his reply at the time. Now he was not certain. What was the point of helping to rebuild the Temple if he could do nothing to help his own twin? *Each man must decide for himself what his magic is for.*

His mood of contemplation was broken by a knock at the door. At first he thought it must be Kailas, but rejected that idea when he realized it was her wedding day too. Even in the present situation some traditions must be upheld. Judging by the angle of the sunlight slanting through the unshuttered window, the day had only just begun, so it was not likely to be anyone on official business. On the other hand, there was going to be a great deal of fuss made of him today, one way or another – that was unavoidable – so anything was possible.

'Come in!' he called. 'The door's open.'

There was no response, and a moment later the knocking was repeated. Sayer swore, got to his feet and stretched aching muscles.

'Come in!' he shouted loudly. 'Or stop knocking.'

Again nothing happened. His friends had given him a wide berth recently, understandably wary of his temper, but this was ridiculous. He walked slowly into the hallway, grabbed the door handle and yanked it open. A dishevelled figure virtually fell into the apartment, clutching at Sayer's arm to stop himself from tumbling to the floor.

'Tump! What are you doing here?' The ragged ex-daydreamer was the last person Sayer had expected to see.

Recovering his balance, Tump backed away, flattening himself against the wall as though he were afraid. His eyes were wide in his pallid face, and although his mouth opened and closed, no sound came out. Sayer felt a spurt of violent anger and had to restrain himself from throwing the punch that his visitor seemed to expect. Instead, he turned away abruptly and walked back to the empty sitting room. After a short hesitation Tump followed quietly.

'What do you want?' Sayer demanded.

'I . . . I . . . I . . .'

'Durak's teeth! Spit it out, man.'

'I have a m-m-message . . . from Aphra.'

Sayer swung round and grabbed Tump's shirt front, and pulled his face to within a finger's length of his own.

'Are you mad?' he yelled, glaring into the terrified eyes. 'You can't have.'

'I . . . I . . . I . . .'

'Aphra's got the plague,' Sayer hissed venomously. 'She's on the Isle of the Dead.'

'I know. This is . . . from before.'

'What?' the seeker exclaimed, calming down a little. 'Before what?'

'Before they put her on the b-boat.'

'You heard her?'

'Not m-me.'

Sayer let go of Tump's shirt and pushed him away, realizing that he might get more sense out of the other man if he were not so frightened. And if by some miracle he was telling the truth . . .

'What did she say?'

'Tell-Sayer-that-he-has-the-power-to-change-the-world-within-and-without,' Tump recited, repeating each word with equal emphasis. This had the disconcerting effect of robbing the complete sentence of any meaning, and Sayer had to repeat the message to himself in order to make it clear. Even then it made little sense.

'What's that supposed to mean?' he demanded. He was angry because he had wanted something to lessen his pain, and had instead been presented with a riddle.

'I don't know.'

'But you're sure that's what she said?'

'Yes, yes, a kyar told me.'

As soon as the words were out both men grew very still, Tump because he sensed his mistake and Sayer because he was afraid that if he moved he might murder his visitor.

'A kyar?' he breathed eventually through clenched teeth. 'Kyars don't talk, you halfwit. They're animals.'

'No, no, no!' Tump cried, his hands fluttering like pale moths.

'Get out!' Sayer yelled. 'Get out before I kill you.'

'No, no. I didn't m-mean to say—'

'I'll bet you didn't,' the seeker replied savagely. 'Get out and take your lunatic delusions with you.' He advanced menacingly and Tump fled, scrambling out of the door and almost falling headlong from the platform before leaping down the stairs in ungainly haste.

Sayer stood where he was, willing himself to become calm. It took a long time. Kyars only talked in children's tales, although some of the madder ex-daydreamers sometimes claimed to have conversations with the sacred felines. Obviously Tump was now hopelessly insane, but Sayer could not imagine why his demented imagination should have concocted such a tale. He must surely have realized how hurtful it would be. Anger began to get the better of Sayer again until he wondered whether, in his own deluded way, Tump had actually been trying to comfort him. Nonetheless, the volcanic emotions he had raised – the hope and the longing – had been terrifyingly strong, and Sayer found that he was trembling.

'Seeker?'

The uncertain voice came from the open doorway and for a moment Sayer thought that Tump had been stupid enough to return, but then he saw two officials from the School of Rituals, each carrying some carefully folded clothes.

'We've brought your robes for the day's ceremonies,' one of them said timidly. 'May we . . . ?'

'Come in,' Sayer answered resignedly, and submitted himself to their ministrations.

CHAPTER TWELVE

'Who can predict where augury will lead?'
                    Attributed to the philosopher Nimruz,
            sometimes known as the Father of Daydreaming

'We must see beyond the horizon, hear the secrets of
silence, and touch the far side of the sky. Only then
can we hope to gather together the remnants of our
shield. Do not be afraid to search the forbidden
corners. Nothing surprises the gods.'
                                    From *The Oracles of Zavanaiu*

The long day was drawing to a close, and Sayer was glad of
that at least. The Eye was back in the Tower of Clouds, looking inward but seeing all. The rituals had been performed;
the libations had been poured, the offerings burnt, and all
the necessary words intoned. Each step had gone according
to the lore-masters' meticulous plans, with Halion at the
centre of everything, basking in the glory and leading the
ceremonies that had since turned to celebration. The city's
bells were still ringing, and a carnival atmosphere existed in
the streets. Even those who had not been directly involved
in the rededication knew of the significant events in the
Temple, and rejoiced in the certainty that only good could
come from such an auspicious occasion.

At dusk everyone left the Temple site, as the law decreed, and the celebrants, in their finest costumes, moved on to other venues. The biggest and most extravagant banquet was at Halion's mansion, and Sayer and Kailas were naturally among the guests of honour. The couple had been married as a prologue to the rededication ceremony, and everything had gone perfectly. Kailas looked ravishing in her blood-red bridal gown, and Halion had smiled benignly as he led them through their vows. But Sayer had recited his lines by rote, and the words had meant nothing to him. His senses were numb, and he had only wished for it all to be over. The rededication had left him similarly unmoved.

The seeker had taken no part in the subsequent feasting and had left his master's estate as soon as he could, in spite of the disappointment this caused the other guests. Halion, however, had silenced any protests by pointing out that this was Sayer's wedding night and that he and his bride had concerns of their own. A carriage took them away, amid much laughter, well-wishing and good-natured ribaldry – all of which was just so much unintelligible noise to Sayer. All he cared about was that he was escaping; it did not even matter where they went.

Naturally enough they had been taken to the new two-storey dwelling in the Magicians' Quarter which had been made ready for them. Kailas led her new husband inside, and he slumped into a chair while she set about tasks of her own. Sayer was just glad to rest in peace and quiet. He was not even really aware of where he was, and it was only when Kailas reappeared – dressed now in a simple, loose-fitting white robe – that he took any notice of the unfamiliar surroundings.

'Where is this?'

'Our home.'

'I don't have a home.'

'You do now. A home and a wife. Can I bring you any-thing, husband?'

Sayer stared at her without comprehension.

'A drink perhaps?' she suggested. 'Some wine? There's food too, if you're hungry. Or shall I arrange for water so you can bathe?'

He shook his head, wanting only to be left alone.

'Then the only thing I have left to offer is myself.' As she spoke, Kailas unfastened the robe and pulled it wide. Underneath she was naked.

For a few heartbeats Sayer was mesmerized by her beauty, and felt a wave of desire course through his blood. This was followed, moments later, by a surge of self-loathing which quickly turned to anger.

'Cover yourself,' he snapped, averting his eyes.

Kailas hesitated, then pulled the robe about her once more. Sayer did not look at her, but sensed her hurt and confusion.

'Do I disgust you?' she asked quietly.

'No.'

'Then why . . . ? We are married.'

'At someone else's behest,' he pointed out.

'Does that matter?'

'Of course—' he began, then shook his head helplessly, at a loss for words.

'Most men would be glad to sleep with me.'

Sayer did not reply, could not meet her gaze.

'If you . . . lack experience,' Kailas added, her voice gentle, thinking that she might have discovered the reason for his reticence, ' I can—'

'It's not that,' he told her, even though he was indeed inexperienced.

'Then what is it?'

'I don't love you.' It was not a lie, but neither was it the whole truth. In his mind, Sayer had come to associate Kailas's arrival with Aphra's departure. He knew this was illogical, but looking at her only made him see all he had lost for ever. And yet he could not tell her that.

'But you like me well enough?' she queried hopefully. 'Love will come in time. If you give me a chance.'

'I'm not sure I am capable of love.'

'That's nonsense. And even if it were true, we can still comfort each other as man and woman. How else can we produce the children that Halion is expecting?' She added the words in a light-hearted tone, smiling hopefully, but Sayer was in no mood for humour.

'I don't want children,' he replied. 'And I don't want comfort.'

'Then what *do* you want?'

Sayer hesitated, and his eyes filled with tears. Seeing this, Kailas's exasperation turned to compassion and she came to sit beside him.

'I want my sister back,' he said quietly.

Kailas held him while he wept.

Over the next month, Sayer's life fell into a new and joyless routine. At his master's insistence he continued to work, but he did so blindly, without feeling anything. Although his missions were successful, they brought him no satisfaction and he began to doubt the value of his efforts. The relatively unimportant relics he retrieved during this time disappeared into the vast expanse of the Great Temple without making any noticeable difference. More significantly, however, Sayer felt no sense of achievement or progress, no kinship with his stones. He brooded, neglected his prayers and was often surly or offhand to his colleagues. Even his faith wavered; temporarily at least, the gods had deserted him.

His change in attitude did not go unnoticed, and he

acquired a reputation for being difficult and unreliable, even though his talent was never in doubt. Kailas and his friends tried to warn him that he was taking a dangerous path, but to no avail. With Aphra's banishment and, by now, her presumed death, a part of Sayer had died as well. Even as preoccupied as he was, he became aware that he was being watched by the archivects' security forces – but he did not care. Life had lost all meaning, so what could they do to him?

His domestic situation granted him some respite but little comfort. His ambivalence towards Kailas remained so that, for all her promptings and patient attentiveness, their marriage had not yet been consummated. Whenever Sayer returned to their house – which he still could not think of as his home – she was waiting for him, always solicitous, always hopeful. He was aware that she was continuing her studies and would soon be ready to take up the duties of a silk, but her training was confined to the times when he was absent, and they never talked of the possibility of them working together in the future.

Her dogged devotion was sometimes irritating, and he jabbed at her with cruel words, rejecting her kindness and mocking her subservience. For her part, Kailas had evidently decided that the only way she could cope with the situation was to wait, to persevere in the hope that Sayer would eventually grow to appreciate her. He knew he was treating her badly and on occasion the hurt in her eyes made him uncomfortable, but he could not bring himself to behave with more consideration. Kailas gradually retreated more and more into silence, and he was grateful for that. The house became a quiet sanctuary, a refuge from the pointless noise and activity of the outside world. But the outside world was always waiting for him again the next morning.

*   *   *

'I thought it might be instructive for you to see this.' Halion was smiling as he spoke, but his black eyes held a hint of malice.

When the summons had come, Sayer had thought it was just another routine visit to the Hariolatorium – known locally as 'the dream-house' – where the daydreamers experienced their visionary hallucinations. Although it was not necessary for a seeker to be present when the approximate location of his next target was being sought through prophecy, it was occasionally thought useful, and Sayer had often been to these halls. However, the presence of his master was unusual and, for once, some sense of danger penetrated his shell of indifference.

The two men were standing in one of the many small viewing galleries that surrounded the circular hall. On the floor below were the invigilators and their scribes, waiting for their subject to make his pronouncements. Akar had been a daydreamer for longer than most, and there had been rumours that his powers were on the wane. Nevertheless, he had still made some important discoveries in recent months and was now evidently close to another. Dressed only in a pair of knee breeches, he was pacing the centre of the chamber, his bare feet making no sound on the smooth marble, while his left hand clutched a small object that Sayer took to be a fragment of The Plan. The daydreamer's eyes were unnaturally bright, but his face was haggard, his upper torso was sheened with sweat, and he was moaning softly to himself as his limbs twitched continuously.

Then, for a moment, he became still and his eyelids drooped. One of the invigilators immediately raised two metal rods and beat them together, producing a hideous clashing that was enough to rouse Akar once more.

'Horses,' he mumbled. 'Horses, horses, horses.'

The scribes went to work immediately, recording every

utterance, no matter how trivial, for later study and possible interpretation.

'In the saddle!' Akar screamed suddenly. 'Between the two loaves of rock. Between. Between!'

'Tell us about these loaves,' one of the invigilators prompted.

The daydreamer turned glittering eyes upon his inquisitor.

'Rock,' he said. 'Up and down, up and down.' His voice was softer now and had taken on a sing-song tone. At the same time he was making cradling motions with his hands.

'Are the loaves made of rock?' another onlooker asked. 'Or do they move like that?'

Akar's reply was a wordless snort of derision, and he began pacing again.

'How long has he been awake?' Sayer asked quietly. He was used to the apparently tortured actions of daydreamers when they were working, but Akar seemed unusually agitated.

'Six days now,' Halion replied indifferently. 'Time for another tincture, don't you think?'

Sayer did not reply, wondering how many potions Akar had already swallowed.

'Administer another dose,' the archivect ordered, raising his voice.

The chief invigilator turned to look up at his master, indecision etched into his face.

'But, my lord, he has already—'

'Just do it,' Halion said, in a tone that brooked no argument.

As the official went to the cabinet where the vials were kept, Halion folded his arms and nodded.

'Akar is losing his effectiveness,' he remarked to Sayer. 'But perhaps he can make one last contribution. What do you think?'

The question was obviously rhetorical and Sayer remained

silent, even though he had now realized what was going on. Although Akar had never been his friend exactly, the seeker felt pity for him in this situation.

Akar took the proffered cup gladly, swallowing its contents in one gulp. The draught was made from wine mixed with a variety of potent herbs and berries. To most people it would have been a lethal poison but for a daydreamer, inured to its toxins by innumerable smaller doses, it acted as a powerful stimulant to both brain and body. The dual effect of staving off sleep and enhancing mental powers made the chances of effective augury much greater – but at the cost of severe damage to the talent's future health. This eventual addiction was the main reason for most of them lasting only a short time in the job.

For a few moments Akar became quite still, then he flung the cup away in a convulsive movement and, opening his other hand, stared at the fragment. His pale eyes were full of visions.

'Two hills, outcrops of bare rock on top of each, the curve of land between them forms a saddle. In line with the setting sun . . .' He hesitated and the scribes looked up from their pens, waiting for him to complete the directions. But Akar was never to do so. He simply crumpled to the floor, as if every bone in his body had turned to water, and lay still. The invigilator beckoned a physician forward urgently. After a brief examination, he glanced up.

'He's dead.'

The invigilator turned to look up at Halion once more, the expression on his face one of regret but not surprise. The archivect did not react to the talent's demise, and Sayer knew that his callousness had been deliberate. Halion was demonstrating that all his servants owed him allegiance – even to the point of death.

'You're lucky your duties are not so rigorous, Sayer,' the

archivect commented pointedly, and turned to leave.

The seeker needed no special powers to recognize the threat implicit in his master's words.

When Sayer returned home later that day, he knew at once that it would not be the quiet haven he had longed for. Kailas was waiting for him, the habitual caution in her eyes replaced by something close to desperation. He saw that there was no way he could avoid a confrontation, and so he beckoned her to follow him into the kitchen where he poured himself a large glass of wine. He offered some to his wife but she shook her head.

'You never used to drink so much,' Kailas said.

Sayer ignored the comment, knowing it to be true. Drinking solved nothing, but it dulled the pain. He took another mouthful and waited.

'What did Halion want?'

'He wanted me to witness a daydreaming.'

'Akar?'

'Yes.'

'And now he's dead.'

'Yes,' Sayer confirmed, surprised that the news had travelled so fast. 'How did you know?'

'I was there too,' Kailas answered quietly. 'In one of the upper galleries.'

'Why?'

'Because my tutor got a message from Halion.'

So, Sayer thought, I was not the only one he wanted to threaten.

'These things happen,' he said, without conviction.

'It was deliberate!' Kailas exclaimed. 'Almost murder,' she added in a whisper, as though she were afraid of being overheard in her own house.

'Don't be absurd. Halion is not above the law, and killing

a Tirokian would be the worst of all crimes. You know that. It was just an unfortunate accident.'

'You're right,' she said, accepting his lie with relief. 'I just thought . . . Perhaps I will have a little wine.'

Sayer poured, and she took the glass and sipped.

'You must be careful, Sayer,' Kailas said abruptly, as though she had been steeling herself to speak. When he did not respond, she went on. 'You're being watched. You know that, don't you? I don't want anything to happen to you.'

'I'm not a daydreamer,' he replied, picking up her obvious implication.

'Even so, there are ways a seeker can be put in danger.'

'My work is what I am. I'm not going to run away from it.'

'Of course not, but you could . . .'

'Could what?'

'Be a little more cooperative,' Kailas suggested tentatively. 'Your reputation—'

'I'm as cooperative as I need to be,' he cut in. 'Does anyone question my talent?'

'No,' she admitted. 'Only your attitude.'

'That's irrelevant,' he snapped.

'Not if we suffer because of it. The great task—'

'I play my part in the great task,' he said, interrupting her again. 'Whether I think it's worth doing is another matter.'

'How can you say such a thing?' Kailas exclaimed, obviously shocked. 'You'd better not let anyone else hear you talking that way. They'll think you're as mad as Hurghad.'

'Who?' Sayer had never heard the name before.

'The hermit,' Kailas replied. 'Halion's tame hermit.'

'What are you talking about?'

'You know those so-called ruins Halion had built at the eastern end of his estate? He called it his "romantic folly".'

Sayer nodded. He had only ever glimpsed the artfully

constructed ruins from a distance, and had wondered at the pretentious nature of such a project.

'Well, just to complete the picture, Halion has hired an old lunatic to live there,' Kailas went on. 'He shows him off to visitors like some wild animal in a cage. Except that Hurghad can talk – and he says the most stupid things.'

'Like I do?'

'Sometimes. It doesn't matter when you're talking to me, but you might give other people the wrong idea. Promise me you'll be careful.'

'I'll try,' he said, recognizing the sense of what she said, although he still wondered why it was so important to her.

There was a long silence, each of them occupied by their own thoughts.

'You have to live your *own* life,' Kailas said eventually. 'You know that, don't you, Sayer?'

'And forget Aphra?' he asked, following her train of thought.

'Not forget,' she replied. 'But forgiving her would be a start. It wasn't her fault she caught the plague.'

'I don't—' He shrugged helplessly. 'You don't understand.'

'I can't if you won't let me.'

'She was a part of me,' Sayer replied with a touch of anger. 'Without her I'm incomplete. There's a hole inside me.' He thumped a fist into his chest for emphasis.

'Is it too much to hope that someone else might fill the void?'

'You?'

'I'd like to try. If you'll let me.'

Sayer shook his head.

'You can't. Nobody can. We were *twins*.' He paused, then added gently, 'But I appreciate your concern.' For almost the first time he wondered what it must be like for her, locked in a barren union with a man obsessed by a dead woman. Kailas could not flee, any more than he could, and so had to continue living a lie.

She saved him from this uncomfortable line of thought by changing the subject.

'Halion wants us to work together on your next mission.'

'Together? But—'

'I passed my final examinations today. I've been awarded my silk.' She took a violet headband from her pocket and held it up for his inspection. 'All I lack now is practical experience.'

'Congratulations.' Sayer smiled. In spite of his confused feelings, he found that he was proud of her.

'Thank you.'

'But Damaris is my silk.'

'He will step aside gladly if you tell him why,' Kailas said confidently.

In that moment, Sayer knew that she had already spoken to Damaris and gained his approval. He also realized that he was no match for his wife's persistence.

'Let me show you I'm worthy of your trust,' she begged, seeing the obvious uncertainty on his face.

'You must be tired already after the tests.' He picked up his wine glass again. 'Save your strength.'

'What for?' she asked. 'Besides, it'll only be a demonstration. Please, Sayer. I don't want you to have any doubts. What about that glass? Can you give me its shape and location?'

'Now?'

'Of course, now!'

Sayer looked at the glass, which he had replaced on the table. It had its own resonance, its own history, and he instinctively registered it all. It was a thin and pale echo of the ancient stones of the Temple, but was unique nonetheless.

'All right,' he said, knowing that this was the least he could do for her.

He stood up, leaving the glass where it was, crossed round to where Kailas sat and gently placed a hand on her head. He had always avoided physical contact with her, but now her hair felt warm and soft. Thoughts flowed, describing the object, and almost at once there was a fleeting violet glimmer that perfectly matched the outline of the glass. However, as fast as it had appeared, it was gone – but the link between seeker and silk remained. Before Sayer had even grasped what was happening, the link expanded and shook off its original shackles of purpose and simplicity. Then Kailas was standing before him, even though he had not realized that she had moved, and their arms were around each other. Warmth flooded through him, and this time desire was not followed by revulsion. He felt her body pressed against his and accepted his defeat. *Love will come in time.* Not yet, perhaps, but in the meantime their minds had decided jointly that this was right.

'Is this how you try to replace Aphra?' It was the first time he had been able to mention his sister's name with a smile on his face.

Kailas grinned back, her whole face glowing with triumphant happiness.

'I can never be Aphra,' she said. 'Nor do I want to be, but I do want to bring some joy back into your life. Will you let me? Will you let me be your wife?'

For answer he stooped to kiss her, then allowed himself to be led into the larger of the two bedrooms in which, until then, she had slept alone. He knew he had been tricked into the intimacy of telepathic contact, and that she had deliberately allowed forbidden emotions to intrude upon the exchange, but as they undressed each other, he did not care.

The barriers that he had erected between them had all

been destroyed by that simple touch of minds, and trust came – literally – overnight. Each time they made love Sayer's sense of wonder grew, until his head was reeling and he hardly knew where – or even who – he was. All he knew for certain was that a little laughter had crept back into his soul.

Much later, in the dead of night, Kailas lay deep in exhausted slumber but Sayer was awake, tired but too intoxicated to sleep. He realized that Kailas's renewed efforts to seduce him might well have been prompted by fear, perhaps even by a direct order from Halion, but that too did not concern him. If children came of their passion, then so be it. If not, it had been its own reward. For this night at least, he put cynicism aside.

Later still, just before he sank into his own oblivion, the seeker remembered part of their earlier conversation, and came to a decision. He was determined to speak to Hurghad as soon as possible. After all, he thought, we madmen must stick together.

Sayer fell asleep with a smile on his face.

CHAPTER THIRTEEN

'Broken bones can be set, fevers cooled and wounds
bound up, but there is nothing that can cure the midnight illness of the mind. It is too fleeting, too elusive,
and no two men may agree on its cause or its treatment.
Madness, like beauty, lies in the eye of the beholder.'

From the collected texts of Jowzuan,
the founder of the Qarian College of Physicians

The first thing Sayer noticed about Hurghad was that his
hair was green. The old man, who had apparently emerged
from a hole in the ground in answer to the seeker's call,
looked like a giant, deranged rodent, with crazed eyes and
long tufts of hair that seemed to be covered in moss or
lichen. He also had strange marks painted on his face.

'Shells break at midnight,' the old man hissed. 'Are you a
demon or a sprite?' He rolled his eyes and waved his thin
arms, making the ragged sleeves of his tunic flap wildly.

'Neither,' Sayer replied. 'I'm a man.'

'That's what they all say,' Hurghad responded, an expression of imbecilic cunning on his pointed face. 'But what *kind*
of man?'

'Just a man,' the seeker answered, torn between laughter
and pity.

'A demon then,' the hermit said, now sounding completely matter-of-fact. 'Shall I cast you back into the abyss?'

'No, thank you. I just wanted to talk to you.'

'Talk is seven marks a bushel. Cheap at half the price. But then most things would be, wouldn't they? Figs, for example.' He laughed at his own joke.

Sayer was about to turn away, having decided that he was wasting his time, when the hermit's eyes narrowed and he stopped capering about.

'You have talent.' It was a statement rather than a question.

'I'm a seeker,' Sayer admitted.

'You can't be very good,' Hurghad remarked. 'You missed the gatehouse by a long way.'

'I was looking for you, not the gate.'

'Why?'

'Because I was curious.'

The two men watched each other over the broken stones of the fake ruin, and Sayer got the impression that he was somehow being measured.

'You're the one who won't sleep with his wife,' Hurghad said suddenly. 'Very suspicious, that.'

Taken aback, Sayer did not respond.

'And after they went to such trouble to arrange the match,' the hermit added. Sayer thought he could hear a hint of mockery in the other man's voice.

'How do you know such things?'

'Of course, being so attached to your sister was a bit suspicious too,' Hurghad went on, ignoring the question. 'But there's no problem with that now, is there?'

'You watch your tongue, old man,' Sayer exclaimed with an angry gesture.

'The plague. How sad.'

Although the seeker was now close to losing his temper completely, he was also intrigued.

'How do you know about all this?' he demanded again.

'Oh, I know all about you, Sayer. Who doesn't know about the seeker who found the Eye of Clouds?'

The use of his name rendered Sayer temporarily speechless once more. This was not at all what he had expected from Kailas's description of the hermit.

'They all talk in front of me,' Hurghad explained. 'They assume that because I'm mad, I'm deaf as well.'

'You're no more mad than I am.'

'Kind of you to notice.' This time the hermit's sarcasm was unmistakable.

'Then why do you live here?'

'Every man needs a job, and a roof over his head.'

'In a false ruin?'

The old man's gaze carefully checked the nearby gardens, making sure they were alone, then beckoned to Sayer. The seeker followed him between two tumble-down walls, down some broken steps and through an archway into darkness. He heard a key grate in a lock, then a door opened onto a small, lamp-lit room. This was comfortably furnished with a narrow bed, a padded chair, a desk and stool, a small stove and two shelves full of books. There was even a faded rug on the stone floor and several paintings on the walls.

'A modest residence, but my own,' Hurghad commented, as Sayer looked around in amazement and a little envy. This was just the sort of the private refuge he would once have coveted. Now that his relationship with Kailas had changed, that time was past, but he was still enchanted by the idea of this secret, underground bolt-hole.

The hermit grabbed one of the longer locks of his dishevelled mane and pulled hard. The hair came off in his hand and he tossed the stained wig onto the floor. His own hair was grey, and cut so short that it stuck out like bristles on a brush. Sayer laughed, no longer surprised by anything this eccentric old man revealed. His madness was an act, at least in part, but the seeker realized that there were varying degrees of sanity.

Hurghad fell into the chair and waved Sayer over to the bed.

'Have some mead,' he said, indicating a stone flagon on the nearby desk. 'And while you're at it, pour me one too.'

Sayer did as he was told, taking a drink over to his host then returning to sit on the pallet. His own cup was made of metal, finely etched around the outside rim. The hermit saw him looking at it.

'Beautiful work, isn't it?' he commented. 'It's old too. Can you hear its resonances? I used to be able to once, but now . . .' He shrugged.

Sayer let his mind wander into the past, saw the original craftsman at work, heard the toasts of earlier owners and smelt the bouquets of a thousand wines.

'It's remarkable,' he said.

'Too good for the likes of me?' the old man said, smiling.

'No, I . . .'

'It was a gift, long ago.'

Sayer nodded, wondering who the giver had been, and what the hermit had done to earn it.

'Your wife came here a few days ago,' Hurghad said, disconcerting the seeker again.

'In here?'

'Oh, no! Outside. I only let the ones I can trust in here.'

'How do you know you can trust me?' Sayer asked, bewildered again.

'You're on your own,' Hurghad replied simply, as if this explained everything.

'And Kailas – my wife – was with others?'

'Oh, yes. I put on the usual show, but they weren't really interested. So I just listened.'

'Who was she with?'

'Halion's personal chamberlain and one of the other servants. They were talking about you.'

Sayer began to feel chilled, even though the room was quite warm. Had the plot been even more devious than he'd thought? Had Kailas been party to the decision to push Akar beyond the limits of his endurance? If so she was a remarkable actress, because she had seemed genuinely distressed when talking about it. Nevertheless, Sayer was assailed by doubts. He had taken great pleasure in Kailas's company during the four days since their new understanding, but now even that seemed tainted, almost certainly the result of intrigue.

'Have I said too much?' Hurghad asked, noting the expression on his guest's face.

'I don't know,' Sayer replied truthfully. He was not sure whether he really wanted to learn so much about his world, just when it had seemed to be becoming a little happier.

'Don't blame her for seeking help,' the hermit advised. 'She's in love – and that's always confusing.'

Sayer said nothing, wondering how much else of what he had fondly imagined to be his private life had been discussed with Halion or his aides.

'What made you want to come and see me?' Hurghad asked.

'Ironically enough, it was something Kailas said. She thinks you're mad – and dangerous.'

'Half right,' the old man said, laughing.

'Which half?'

'I'll let you be the judge of that.'

Sayer realized they had both been assuming that his visit had been made without Halion's knowledge.

'It took me a while to come up with an excuse to visit the estate,' he said, 'but once I was finished at the house I simply came here on my way out.'

'So you've not lost all your self-destructive urges then?'

'What do you mean?'

'Visiting someone who is dangerous – or mad – might not be very good for your career.'

'I'm not sure I care about that any more,' Sayer replied, aware that he might be revealing more than was prudent.

'Really? Has the Temple lost its lure?'

'I'm just not sure there's any point in going on. If the gods aren't satisfied with all the efforts we've made so far, they're never going to be satisfied.'

'Sacrilege!' Hurghad exclaimed, pretending to be shocked. 'And in one so young. But, as it happens, I agree with you.' He laughed at the response his words provoked. 'Don't look so surprised. I can say what I like. Who's going to take any notice of a lunatic?'

'Surely Halion knows you're not—'

'He's as blind as all the rest. I'm safe enough. However, you might not be if you stay too long. They keep records at the gatehouse, so you'd better go now. Tell one of the guards you went for a walk in the grounds. That'll explain the time gap.'

'Is that really necessary?' Sayer asked.

'They watch everybody,' the hermit replied, 'but especially the valuable ones like you.'

The seeker stood up reluctantly.

'If you want to come here again,' Hurghad added, reading Sayer's mind, 'go to the old tax collector's hut by the Gold Road.'

'But that hasn't been used in years. It's just a ruin.'

'So is this,' the old man replied, waving a hand at his chamber.

'What do I do? Leave a message?'

'You'll see. Now, go.'

Sayer went, feeling his way back up the stairs in the semi-darkness. Behind him he heard the key turn in its lock.

*   *   *

'You're late,' Kailas said, putting her arms around his neck as he came in.

'I went for a walk in the gardens to clear my head,' he replied, repeating the lie he had told Halion's sentry.

'From the mead?' she asked, grinning.

'No. I only had a little.' The question had taken him off guard, and he realized he was not very good at keeping secrets.

'Do we have an assignment yet?' Kailas asked.

'No. They're trying to get one of the other daydreamers to finish Akar's prophecy.' He watched her carefully for any sign of guilt, but all he saw was the pain of an unpleasant memory. If she had collaborated in that vile act, then she was disguising it well.

'Is it so important?' she asked quietly.

'It's a relic from the Raven Dome. Or that's the theory, at least. It might be one of the missing roof carvings.'

'Gods!' Kailas breathed. 'I was hoping they'd give me something less valuable as a first mission.'

'They wouldn't send you unless they were certain you were ready,' he assured her.

'I won't let you down,' she said bravely. 'I just wish we could get started.'

They went into the kitchen for their evening meal, and talked about the inconsequential events of the day. Sayer said nothing about his visit to Hurghad, knowing that Kailas would disapprove, but he could not resist using a little of what he had learnt from the hermit.

'Halion must be happier now that we're sleeping in the same bed,' he remarked.

'I should think he assumed we always were,' she responded.

'So you didn't discuss our little problem with him or his chamberlain?'

Kailas had the grace to look embarrassed, and took her time replying.

'I didn't know what I was doing wrong,' she said eventually. 'I needed advice.'

'And it worked, didn't it?'

'No. Using the link was my own idea. But being able to talk to someone did help me clear my thoughts. I . . . I won't do it again.' She paused. 'I didn't seduce you for Halion's sake. I did it for me, for us. And I'm not sorry. Are you?'

'No.'

'I think I came to you at the time I did for a reason,' Kailas said earnestly. 'The gods knew you'd need someone else beside you, and they brought us together.'

'I thought that was Halion's decision.'

Kailas smiled.

'The gods use strange messengers,' she said.

The next day, when it became clear that the daydreamers were making no real progress, Sayer took advantage of his free time to leave the city once more. Following the Gold Road, he came to the hut where merchants and prospectors had once declared their goods and paid the city's tolls. That system had long since been abandoned, and the building had fallen into disrepair. Although the roof had collapsed and the door had vanished, most of the stone built walls were still standing, making a genuine but decidedly unpicturesque ruin.

Without really knowing why he did it, Sayer glanced around. There was no one in sight – the midday heat had driven most people to seek shade – and he felt confident that his movements were unobserved. Even so, he was nervous as he edged his way through the open doorway and surveyed the hut's interior. There was not much to see; bare walls, a few pieces of broken masonry, windblown piles of dust and sand. Sayer walked slowly round the edge of the floor, stepping over the rubble, and it was only then that he heard a faint sound. It rose and fell softly in a vaguely musical whispering, but he could not locate its source. Was this the clue to his search? You'll see, Hurghad had said, but Sayer didn't think there was anything *to* see.

He was about to give up and leave when the resonance came to him. It amounted to little more than a ghostly echo, and if it had not been for his particularly refined sensitivities he would not have heard it at all. That he did – and that he recognized it as coming from Hurghad's cup – made him certain that there was more to the hut than met the eye. The resonance had come from below his feet, and a little to one side. Listening now, he tracked it down to one dusty corner and when he cleared away the accumulated silt, he found a trapdoor.

It took him some time to shift it, because the door was heavy and grit had filled the cracks around it, but he eventually succeeded and looked down what seemed to be a well shaft. The musical sound of running water came from the invisible depths, and the signal from the old cup was much clearer now. Iron pegs had been driven into one side of the well and, after a moment's reflection, Sayer lowered himself down gingerly, testing each support as he went. When his head was below ground level, he reached up and closed the door above him. As he did so he was plunged into total darkness, and had to rely on his senses of touch and hearing to guide him. He had no idea how deep the shaft was, and was terrified of falling, but gradually the rippling of the underground stream drew closer. Eventually, one of his feet slipped into water and then, almost immediately, onto the rock bed beneath. The water was icy cold and the shock almost made him lose his balance on the slippery surface, but he steadied himself, then lowered the other foot.

Turning around, he sensed the stream running past from right to left and the resonance from the cup on the far side. Cautiously, his arms stretched out in front of him, he felt his way towards it and soon found himself on dry ground. There was a clatter as his foot knocked something over and he stooped to retrieve the cup – then realized that the echoes had revealed that he was in a new tunnel. Further investigation told him that both the floor and walls were unnaturally smooth, and he went on blindly but with more confidence now, sure that Hurghad was guiding him onwards. After what seemed like an age, the tunnel simply came to a dead end. For a moment Sayer panicked, thinking that he must have taken a wrong turning and that he might be lost in this dark labyrinth for ever. Then he told himself firmly that there had been no other turnings and therefore this *must* be his destination.

'Hurghad?' he called, his voice echoing hollowly behind him. 'Hurghad!'

The absolute darkness was grating on his nerves and he hammered on the blank wall in front of him, hurting his knuckles in the process.

A sudden creak was followed by a grinding noise, and then by the appearance of a blessed crack of light. Moments later the stone-clad door opened wide enough for Sayer to slip through, and he found himself in the welcome lamplight of the hermit's sanctum.

Hurghad was glaring at him, his face pink from his exertions in opening the concealed entrance.

'Next time you could at least try and push,' he remarked crossly.

CHAPTER FOURTEEN

'Accepted historical truth is a distillation of rumour
and wishful thinking, revealing more about the author
than about his subject.'

From the preface to *A True History of Tirok*

'It can only be opened from this side,' Hurghad explained
breathlessly. 'And then only if you know it's there.'

They had closed the door again together, having to push
quite hard against the stiff hinges, and now it was all but
invisible. If Sayer had not already been aware of its existence, he would never have noticed the paper thin cracks in
the stone that marked the door's outline, nor the inden-
tation that allowed the hidden catch to be released.

'So it's supposed to be a way out, not a way in?' he guessed.

'Very astute,' the hermit commented. 'The underground
stream's been there as long as anyone can remember, but Halion
had this tunnel built a few years ago, as a means of escape.'

'Escape from his own estate? Why?'

'Because the richer and more powerful a man gets, the
more suspicious he becomes of everyone else. Our revered
master sees conspiracies everywhere, and his walls can keep
people *in* as well as out. This gives him another option, should
leaving discreetly become advisable.'

'That's absurd.'

'I didn't say it was logical.'

'Who would dream of threatening Halion anywhere, let alone in his own home?'

'No one, but I should think there are some who would like to.'

'But he's the leader of the Council!' The very idea of such disloyalty ran contrary to everything Sayer believed. He had always taken Halion's superiority for granted.

'Does that make him infallible?' Hurghad asked. 'Or invulnerable?'

Although the seeker's thoughts had been running on unaccustomed paths recently, to hear such ideas expressed openly was still shocking. He began to wonder whether Kailas might be right in believing Hurghad to be both mad and dangerous. But if that's the case, he asked himself, then why am I here?

'Why did you come here, Sayer?' the hermit enquired, uncannily echoing the seeker's thoughts.

'I don't really know,' he confessed.

'Then think about it. I can't help you unless I know what you want.'

Do I want help? Sayer wondered silently.

'While you're thinking,' Hurghad went on, 'pour us some mead. It might speed up the process.'

Sayer obediently fetched some of the honey-scented wine for his host but, remembering Kailas's reaction, took only water for himself. The hermit raised his eyebrows at this abstention, but made no comment. When the young man still did not speak, Hurghad prompted him again.

'You're disillusioned, that much I can see. But why? The loss of your sister must have been a shock, but was that enough on its own?'

'Everything changed then,' Sayer admitted, then hesitated.

'But there's more. Your arranged marriage?'

'Perhaps. Although that seems to be working out now.'

'I'm glad.' The hermit smiled. 'What else, then?'

'Do you believe that foreigners have no soul?'

Hurghad looked surprised for a moment, then laughed.

'I see,' he said. 'You want to start with the easy questions.'

'I'm serious,' Sayer protested.

'So am I, but in order to answer you I'd have to know whether Tirokians themselves have souls.'

'Of course we do!'

'I envy your faith,' the hermit said, serious again. 'If I shared it, I would say that all foreigners are likely to be so blessed. It doesn't seem possible that such matters could be decided by a mere accident of geography.'

'But the gods . . .' Sayer began, then fell silent.

'If you're on speaking terms with the pantheon, young man, then you have the advantage over me.'

'Don't mock me!' the seeker cried angrily. 'The oracles came from the gods.'

'But they still had to be written down by a man,' Hurghad pointed out calmly. 'It would not be the first time men have used religion for their own ends. It's a powerful tool, after all.'

Sayer was surprised to find himself reassessing the very foundations of his beliefs, amazed that such heretical ideas did not shock him more.

'Why the interest in foreigners?' the old man asked curiously.

'Because I met a remarkable man in Mazandaran.' Sayer went on to tell Hurghad of his conversation with Mehran-Dar, and of the disconcerting effect the healer's words had had on him. 'I always believed that the people there were barbarians,' he concluded, 'and yet he seemed the most civilized of men.'

'He certainly sounds as if he is just that,' Hurghad agreed.

'He even gave me a b— a beautiful gift.' For some reason he could not understand, Sayer was reluctant to share the secret of the book's existence with anyone.

'Civilized *and* generous,' the hermit commented.

'The frightening thing was that I could have told Nazeri to kill Mehran-Dar and all his party – and he would have butchered them without a second thought.'

'Animals to the slaughter,' Hurghad said, nodding.

'With no souls. That can't be right.'

'No.'

'So is *everything* I believe wrong?'

'Of course not, but you are a little innocent in the ways of the world.'

'Then teach me,' Sayer pleaded. 'I need to know the truth.'

'Truth is an elusive thing,' the hermit remarked. 'It can change from person to person, or from year to year. How do you know that what *I* believe is not simply another set of delusions? I'm just a madman, after all.'

'I trust you,' the seeker replied, realizing that was true at least.

'You've demonstrated that already. In turn, I'll share some of my secret thoughts with you. Is that a fair bargain?'

Sayer nodded.

'So where do we begin?' he asked.

'With economics.'

'What?'

'Have you ever wondered how the archivects and their friends live in such luxury and yet still manage to finance a massive project like the rebuilding of the Temple?'

'I . . . Not really.'

'Because that's just the way things are? Think about it,

Sayer. Tirok has many valuable resources, after all – the rare herbs, the minerals and gemstones, the agricultural land to the south – but none of that would mean anything if we weren't able to trade with the countries beyond our borders. Those same despised foreigners – the ones with no souls – are the ones who enable Halion and his cronies to perpetuate their supremacy. It's hypocrisy gone mad! Why do you think so few people are ever allowed to travel outside Tirok? They might glimpse the lives of those barbarians and start making odious comparisons with the slums outside Qara. And no foreigner ever comes here. What do you think a healer like Mehran-Dar would think of the living conditions?'

'He'd be appalled.'

'So to him, perhaps *we* are the barbarians.' Hurghad paused to allow that idea to sink in, then added, 'Life may never be fair, and the inequality of wealth may only be one of the injustices in Tirok, but many of the others stem from it.'

'The way things are,' Sayer quoted softly.

'And the way they'll remain,' the hermit said. 'Too many people have a vested interest in keeping things just as they are.'

'People like me.'

Hurghad shrugged.

'You and many more,' he concurred. 'But the thousands who would benefit from change are either powerless or too frightened.'

'But what can *I* do?' Sayer asked helplessly.

'By yourself, nothing.'

The answer was both frustrating and a relief. It was all very well to talk, but Sayer was not sure he had the courage to *act*. He took a gulp of water, aware of Hurghad's cool appraisal, and in an attempt to steer the conversation back to less uncomfortable areas, he returned to one of the old man's earlier comments.

'You said there were some who would like to threaten Halion. Did you mean the other archivects?'

The hermit nodded.

'Some of them, yes. Although the Council members are all supposed to be equal, that's obviously nonsense and it leads to resentment. Even though everyone knows Halion is the leader, that doesn't stop the intrigue or the competition among them. The ruins around us – which, by the way, were an after-thought, intended to disguise the tunnel entrance – are evidence of just how absurd the whole thing has become. As soon as Halion built his own ruin, several of the others had new antiquities built. No doubt my fellow hermits are also being sought. We're the latest status symbol – though I never thought lunatics would become a collectors' item.' The old man laughed. 'Some of them may really be mad, but they'll soon become boring. Being an *interesting* loon is a lot of hard work.'

'Doesn't it ever bother you?' Sayer asked. 'That people think you're mad, I mean.'

'I take it as a compliment. And I have other ways of amusing myself.'

'What?'

'We'll have to keep that for another visit. Having the tunnel makes it easier for you to stay as long as you want, but it would not be wise to vanish from sight for too long.'

Recognizing his dismissal, Sayer rose to his feet. In the windowless room he had no way of telling how late in the day it was, and he saw the sense in Hurghad's advice. In any case, he already had more than enough to think about. The fact that both men were assuming that their meetings would continue to be of a clandestine nature was not lost on the seeker, and he was glad the hermit had made it plain that he was welcome to come again.

Together they opened the door, and Sayer prepared to slide back into the tunnel.

'I shan't offer you a candle,' Hurghad said. 'You obviously managed perfectly well on the way in, and you'll hear the stream before you get to it.'

Sayer glanced down at his shoes, which were still damp, and was glad he had not drunk any mead. The prospect of climbing up the well in the pitch dark was unappealing enough already.

'Why didn't you just tell me about the tunnel?' he asked. 'It would've saved me a lot of time and trouble.'

'I wanted to see if you really were as talented as they say,' the old man replied, his eyes glinting with mischief. 'Besides, knowledge is more valuable when it is earned. Get on now.'

Sayer went through the doorway, listened to Hurghad straining to close it, and was immersed into total darkness again. He began to walk slowly back towards the stream.

CHAPTER FIFTEEN

'Lucky is the man who can scent wildhorn.'
                                   Tirokian proverb

It was several days before Sayer was able to make another visit to Hurghad. This was because he was sent on another mission, this time with Kailas acting as his silk. His over-seers had decided not to wait for usable results from the fragment that had caused Akar's downfall – although the daydreamers continued to work on it – and had settled eventually on a relatively simple task, involving only a short journey, to retrieve part of an ornamental pillar. To their joint relief, Sayer and Kailas worked well as a team, and the extraction was a complete success. Kailas did not allow the telepathic link to stray beyond the boundaries of pro-fessional need, and afterwards – despite her exhaustion – she was so elated that Sayer could not help but share in her happiness.

However, he was now looking at the world through dif-ferent, jaundiced eyes, seeing things he had never noticed before. For the first time he was aware of being under obser-vation. This was not continuous and so he retained some privacy, but for much of the time he was watched unob-trusively, especially when he was in public. He was careful now, doing his best to act normally, treating his colleagues in a friendly and respectful manner and, above all, trying to work to the best of his ability. Having Kailas beside him actually helped in this endeavour and, for her part, she was obviously delighted by his reformed behaviour.

It was only in the silence of his own thoughts that Sayer was troubled. Although he was not yet ready to throw out all his beliefs, or to accept everything that Hurghad had said, his mind kept filling with questions. He became more aware of the people who had previously only been incidental to his life – the lowly servants, the bystanders, the beggars and ragged children of the city streets. The same soldiers who watched him were regarded by these people not with reverence for authority and the law but with fear and ill-concealed malice. And, by inference, they must regard him in the same way – to some extent at least. He was one of the privileged few, one of those for whom the system worked, converting his talent into material benefits.

In the past he would have turned a blind eye to examples of corruption and petty tyranny, but he now saw them clearly for the unjustifiable cruelties that they were. And yet everyone, even the victims, seemed to accept such things as normal. Sayer's newly acute senses picked up other things too; conversations he would once have ignored, sidelong glances, half-heard murmurings and other signs of discontent. He overheard men cursing their overseers, the soldiers, the archivects and even the gods. He saw how many workers regarded the great task as merely the source of income – the one certain way to earn a decent living – instead of a divinely ordained duty. And worst of all, given his new and rewarding relationship with Kailas, he had to keep this all to himself. She was so happy, in the belief that both her marriage and her work were now going according to plan, that he did not want to disillusion her.

Sayer took pleasure in his wife's company, and especially in their nights together, but he could not have said with any degree of certainty that he loved her. Although their arrangement was enjoyable and convenient, it was not a true meeting of hearts and minds. This was partly because of Sayer's self-imposed secrecy, partly because of his growing sense of guilt at his own fortunate position, and partly because Aphra's absence still left a gaping hole in his life. In truth, Sayer was also not quite sure that he could trust Kailas. Although she appeared open and honest on the surface, he could not forget the way she had gone to see Halion's chamberlain behind his back, nor the fact that their betrothal had been ordered by the archivect. Could it be that she was not as innocent as she seemed, that she was one of those assigned to watch him and report on his progress? Sayer hoped not – and he had no evidence to back up his suspicion – but he could not be certain. His wife's role in Akar's death and the fact that her arrival had coincided with Aphra's illness and exile still bothered him. As a result, Sayer was now leading two lives – one of them confined to the inside of his own head.

Sayer's second meeting with Hurghad was the first of several over the next month. The seeker fitted these meetings in between missions, and became adept at slipping away alone in his free time and reaching the old tax collectors' hut without anyone seeing him – or so he hoped. Each time he climbed down into darkness and knocked on the stone door his heart raced but – even when there was some delay – the hermit always let him in eventually, greeting his guest with gruff words and a smile that spoke of their growing friendship.

Even so, a couple of incidents served to remind Sayer that he was playing with fire. In the first, one of Halion's servants rapped on the outer door of Hurghad's lair to tell the hermit that visitors were approaching and that his presence was required. Although Sayer was close to panic, the old man merely motioned for quiet, donned his absurd wig, left to put on another eccentric performance – locking the door behind him – and returned some time later wearing a grin that dispelled his visitor's fears. In the second, they both heard footsteps approaching and realized to their horror that the outer door had been left wide open, to allow fresh air to enter the sometimes stuffy room. Sayer had to hide beneath the bed and spent a short but very uncomfortable time there, while Hurghad talked amusing gibberish to another curious visitor and one of Halion's senior stewards. After that they resolved always to lock the door, no matter how hot the day was.

The only other difficulties encountered by the seeker were at the other end of the tunnel. He was soon able to make the journey in the subterranean dark with ease, but he was always afraid of being discovered when he emerged from the trapdoor. Although it was unlikely that anyone would see him inside the dilapidated hut, it was possible that passers-by would hear him and come to investigate. He was always very cautious, and on a few occasions had to retreat and wait for travellers to move on. Once he was already above ground, and was sweeping dust back over the trapdoor when he heard the approach of a large number of soldiers. He had to stay where he was, flattened into the most obscure corner of the ruined hut, until they had all marched past and were out of sight.

These alarms were rare, however, and the two men were usually able to talk for as long as they liked – although Sayer never stayed for much more than an hour at a time, respecting Hurghad's earlier advice. They discussed many things and, although Sayer asked most of the questions, the hermit often avoided direct answers and wanted instead to hear his visitor's opinions and impressions. Sayer got the feeling that he was being tested. He had no idea why this might be so, beyond mere intellectual curiosity, but he endeavoured to be as honest as he was able, knowing he had already gone too far to turn back now. The ideas expressed by both men would certainly have got them into trouble had they been uttered within range of the wrong ears, and they were left with little option but to trust one another.

Their discussions ranged over a wide selection of topics, including the use and abuse of power by the military, corruption within officialdom and various social injustices. They speculated on the reasons for the apparently relentless progress of the plague and for the taboo on killing Tirokians, without reaching any firm conclusions. They talked about the continual intrigue within the Council, including the rumour that Halion's arrogance at the rededication of the Eye of Clouds had been too much for at least two other archivects – Becerra and Seigui – who had apparently made scathing comments after the ceremony. They argued about the nature and purpose of magic and about the plight of daydreamers in particular, trying to define a justifiable balance between suffering and achievement. This led on one occasion to some claims by Hurghad that, at the time, Sayer thought outrageous.

'So you think talent is a gift from the gods?' the hermit said. 'And as such should be dedicated to their service?'

'Yes, I do. Don't you?'

'In most cases.'

'What do you mean?'

'Have you heard of wildhorn?'

'What?' Sayer was bemused by this apparent irrelevance.

'Have you ever eaten them?'

'No.'

'Neither have I,' Hurghad went on, 'but they're reputed to be the most delicious food in the world, although how a rotting fungus can taste that good is beyond me. They're also supposed to be good for the health and, as no one has ever found a way to cultivate them, hunting for the plants can be a profitable business.'

'There are dogs trained for that, aren't there?' Sayer added, wondering where this was leading.

'Indeed there are, but do you know what make the best wildhorn hunters?'

'Oh, no,' the younger man exclaimed, realizing now where the hermit was headed. 'I don't believe it.'

'Seekers,' Hurghad confirmed. 'Not the good ones like you, of course. Some of your less gifted brethren use magic like a dog uses its nose. And all so that Halion and his friends can eat like gourmets.'

'That can't be true. It can't.'

'Go to the kitchens,' the hermit suggested. 'Ask around. And while we're on the subject, you should be aware that talent has other, distinctly impious uses.'

'Such as?' Sayer demanded.

'It's possible to enhance the pleasure of lovemaking through telepathic suggestion. For the older archivects especially, this has a certain attraction.'

Hurghad's wry smile made Sayer want to scream.

'I don't believe it,' he repeated. 'You're lying.'

'Why don't you ask Kailas?' the hermit suggested quietly, serious again now.

The colour rose in Sayer's cheeks then as he was caught between doubt and fury. It couldn't be true – and yet he could not deny the way in which he had first been seduced.

'That's horrible,' he breathed. 'No one who respects the gods would even consider such a thing.'

Hurghad said nothing, letting the silence force his guest to keep thinking.

'It's sacrilege,' Sayer went on. 'The Council promised to use all the talent available for the good of the great task, and for the gods.'

'I think you'll find much hypocrisy concerning the gods,' the hermit remarked. 'When a man is so powerful that he can effectively do what he likes, the pantheon seems a little less omniscient.'

From there the discussion turned, as it nearly always did, to the Temple and the reasons for rebuilding it. Sayer argued, with decreasing conviction, that it had provided all Tirok with a purpose, and that society would collapse if this were taken away.

'Would that be so bad?'

'Of course!' the seeker replied, responding to the older man's deliberate provocation. 'It would lead to chaos.'

'Perhaps,' Hurghad conceded. 'It always comes back to the Temple, doesn't it?'

'Yes,' Sayer agreed cautiously.

'Have you ever considered that the great task may be a device that not only gives the people of Tirok a purpose, but also keeps them in their place? As long as there is hope of salvation at the end of the reconstruction, few will complain about the present. So those in power *stay* in power, and enjoy all the benefits.'

'Are you saying that the whole thing is just an elaborate trick?' the seeker asked, disbelieving.

'Maybe not,' the hermit replied evenly. 'But my theory certainly fits the facts. The rebuilding might have begun as a genuine project, undertaken in all humility, but it's gone far beyond that now. It's become fanatical, and that's always dangerous. Even you've had some doubts, haven't you? And do you really see any great spiritual conviction in Halion's attitude, for example?'

'If that's true, then I've wasted my whole life!' Sayer cried. 'Is that what you're asking me to believe?'

'I'm only asking you to consider it,' Hurghad replied. 'I don't expect you to change your mind overnight.'

On that occasion, Sayer left the hut in a state of considerable agitation and did not return for several days. He was not sure he wanted to go back at all, but the evidence of his own eyes and ears supported much of what the hermit had said, and so he eventually returned to knock again on the secret door. For a long time there was no response and Sayer waited in the blackness, hoping nothing was wrong. He had often wondered what would happen if he knocked when another – legitimate – visitor was in the room with Hurghad. The hermit had laughed at his anxiety when the matter was raised, saying that visitors came inside so rarely that it was not worth worrying about.

When he could stand it no longer, Sayer rapped his knuckles on the stone again and, to his great relief, the door creaked open. He began to push.

'Don't be so impatient,' Hurghad chided. 'I can manage.'

'Are you all right?'

'Of course I'm all right. Why?'

'You were a long time.'

'I was busy – and you've not been here for so long I'd almost given up on you. Did I say something to offend you?' Although the hermit was frowning, the glint was in his eyes once more.

'Many things,' Sayer answered. 'But I forgive you. What were you doing?'

'What?'

'You said you were busy.'

'Oh, nothing important,' Hurghad replied airily.

'Has it anything to do with that?' the seeker asked, pointing at a sheet of paper sticking out from under the straw-filled mattress.

'No,' the hermit said, but Sayer knew he was lying.

He stooped to retrieve it, but Hurghad, moving with surprising agility for a man of his age, grabbed it first and held it protectively against his chest. Sayer did not move, but he was thoroughly intrigued now.

'I thought you were going to share all your secrets with me.'

'Not all of them.'

'What is it? Why try to hide it from me?'

Some of the belligerence went out of the old man's expression.

'If I show this to you, you must promise never to mention it to anyone.'

'I promise.'

Hurghad handed him the sheet. It contained only four lines at the top of the page, in a tiny, insect-like scrawl.

'A poem?' Sayer asked, wondering why this had been worth so much fuss. He read:

'Forbidden landscapes, shadows deep,
The moonlight whispers, kyars creep.
Others lie blind within the keep,
But the night people cannot sleep.'

'I'm still working on it,' Hurghad said defensively.

'It rhymes,' Sayer commented, not knowing what else to say. He was no connoisseur of poetry. 'What's it called?'

'The whole thing?'

'There's more?'

Hurghad snorted.

'Of course.' He pulled back the mattress and there, between the palliasse and the boards, were reams of paper in neat stacks. 'Six hundred and forty-two pages so far.'

Sayer whistled, looking at the multitude of sheets, all of

them covered by Hurghad's minute writing.

'So this is how you occupy your time.'

The hermit replaced the mattress carefully.

'It's my only passion now,' he said. 'And no one must find it until it's finished.'

'What's it called?'

'*A True History of Tirok*.'

'The whole history?' Sayer asked, looking again at the single page he held.

'Without the layers of conceit,' the hermit replied.

'Can I read it?'

'No. Not yet.'

The seeker took one look at the old man's face and decided not to argue, then returned his gaze to the one brief excerpt he had been permitted to see.

'The "forbidden landscape" is the Temple, right?' he guessed. 'So who are the "night people"?'

Chapter Sixteen

'Inter the ancient bones within a tomb of silent curves, so that their spirits may return to light our pathway to the gods. When I am done, and if my words prove worthy, I would lie there too and add my candle to the beacon's flare.'

From *The Oracles of Zavanaiu*

'Where are you going?' Kailas murmured.

'For a walk,' Sayer replied.

'But it's the middle of the night!'

'I can't sleep. I won't be long. Go back to sleep. You need your rest.'

He had not expected her to wake at all. Kailas was still recovering from her latest endeavours as a silk and, as usual during such a time, she slept very soundly. His wife had proved herself to be resilient, and regained her strength as quickly as any of the best of her talent, but their recent heavy workload had had a cumulative effect that was now taking its toll.

'You've been so restless lately,' Kailas mumbled, sounding concerned, but then she closed her eyes again and returned to her dreams.

Sayer would have preferred to be able to slip away

without her knowledge, but there was nothing he could do about it now. It had taken him a long time to persuade Hurghad to talk about the night people, and longer still to learn how to make contact with them. In fact, he still did not know how tonight's meeting had been arranged, and when he had been told what to do he'd almost wished he had not been so persistent. With hindsight he knew he should have foreseen this, but that didn't make it any less daunting.

Now, as he finished dressing in black clothes, he was glad that the night chosen was one with only a new moon. The darkness would increase his chances of being able to move unobserved. With one last glance at his wife, who was now fast asleep again, he slipped from the room and out onto the quiet street. He spent a few moments just listening as his eyes adjusted to the faint silvery light provided by the stars. All colour was bleached to varying shades of grey and everything looked unfamiliar, almost alien, as he left the doorway and moved silently along the alleyways.

Knowing that the Magicians' Quarter was often watched, even at night, he went north first, leaving the district as quickly as possible. Even though he was almost sure he could have avoided the sentries, he saw no point in taking unnecessary risks. Then he turned west and strode towards the Gold Road Gate. As always, the massive gates stood open and the sleepy guards took little notice of an anonymous cloaked man who left the city and set off towards the archivects' estates. Sayer had his story planned if he were to be stopped, but no one paid him any attention.

Once he was far enough away from the city walls to be invisible to the sentries, he doubled back and cut across the open scrubland to the west of the Causeway, then walked down beside the long northwest wall of the Temple. He had never been this close to the hallowed site during the hours of darkness, and he was extremely nervous, even though all

about him was very still and quiet. Hurghad had told him to
enter by the second set of steps over the wall, and when he
reached them, Sayer hesitated. To go on now was to commit
himself to breaking one of the most sacred of all the laws of
Tirok. Entering the realm of the gods was not something
to be undertaken lightly, and all he had to balance against
his fear was curiosity. He had no idea what would happen
or who he would meet when − if − he went on, and
Hurghad had given him no clue, but he knew that the consequences were likely to be far-reaching. Even though Sayer
was no coward, there were some things he would rather not
face.

You'll never know unless you try, he told himself firmly
and, after one last look around to confirm that he had not
been followed, he began to climb.

As he crossed the invisible threshold at the top of the
wall, the seeker expected to feel something − some frisson of
power or a sudden chill − but there was nothing. His heart
was already racing in anticipation, and the darkness that
greeted him was almost disappointing. He went on a few
paces, trying to get his bearings in this unfamiliar part of the
Temple. It would be quite possible to become lost in the
maze of lanes and alleys, especially in the dark. That thought
brought home to him again the enormity of what he was
doing, and he swallowed hard. What was he supposed to do
now? Just wander on blindly?

Then it occurred to Sayer that there must be some of his
stones nearby; all he had to do was locate them and then set
his course by them. That way he would at least avoid the
possibility of wandering around in circles for hours. He
opened his mind carefully, summoning up the resonances
he remembered so well − and then lost concentration
instantly. As if in response to his efforts, a light had appeared.
It seemed to float in midair, perhaps thirty paces away along

the alleyway in front of him, but whoever was carrying it remained paradoxically invisible. The light itself glowed like a candle flame but was more diffuse, as though it were surrounded by some semi-transparent material.

'Hello?' Sayer ventured, not daring to raise his voice much above a whisper.

Although there was no audible response, the light bobbed slightly. Sayer took a pace forward and then another and, as he did so, the light moved too. The seeker soon realized that it was keeping its distance ahead of him, showing him a way through the labyrinth. Although it then led him round many twists and turns, disappearing from sight at frequent intervals, it was always there again when he turned the corner. He made another attempt to speak to his guide, but received no answer. The ever-changing shadows cast by the strange light made the Temple seem alive, and Sayer often glanced around nervously, thinking he saw movement where there was none. Before long he was completely lost – and then, just as he was wondering how long this tortuous journey was going to last, he and his guide came to a much wider street that he recognized. It was the part of the Penitents' Way that ran around the Oracle's Tomb. He automatically went to turn right so that he could circle the building in the correct direction, but the light, which until then had been hovering directly ahead of him, now went left.

Sayer hesitated, then told himself that he was already breaking so many taboos that one more would hardly matter, and followed. A few paces further on, the light abruptly blinked out of existence. Deprived of his guide, the seeker felt the night close in upon him and his fear returned. He knew this place well enough by day, but now everything seemed mysterious. The circular road was surrounded by broken shapes that all looked vaguely threatening, as if they might conceal any number of unexpected terrors, while inside the ring the bulk of the Oracle's Tomb rose up in convoluted waves of darkness.

Sayer knew that the tomb was a remarkable construction, defying almost all the normal rules of architecture; it seemed to grow from the earth like a gigantic snake that had twisted and tied itself into a complex mass of knots, curves and loops. Inside, it was like an insane rabbit warren, with its stone tunnels, chambers and galleries all built in the same serpentine manner. There were sudden chasms and slides, corridors that ended in open skylights, crescent halls and coiled shafts that resembled the insides of a vast seashell – but there was not a single straight line in the entire place. Even the sepulchres, which housed the long-dead bones of earlier mystics, were rounded. Privately, Sayer had always thought that the building must have been conceived during a nightmare but, as one of the holiest shrines in the Temple, it had been faithfully reconstructed. Now, in part because its components had been so easy to identify, it was almost complete. Sayer himself had contributed several stones and he sensed them now, like old friends.

'Hello?' he tried again. He was sure he had been led there for a purpose, and wondered why he seemed to have been abandoned now.

He was answered not with words but with light. All over the surface of the Tomb, in every niche and hollow, tiny flames sprang up. They were like candles, but burned in every colour imaginable – green, blue, purple, white, red and orange. It was an awe-inspiring sight, beautiful and terrifying at the same time. In the flickering of the overlapping shadows, the Oracle's Tomb seemed to writhe, as if the giant snake were waking – and Sayer's thoughts inevitably turned to the gods. Surely only they could have created such a spectacle. Could it be that the Snake of the Sun was rousing from its usual slumber?

All at once Sayer was petrified, appalled by his own

recklessness, his presumption. This must surely be a warning sign; the gods' anger would soon crush him to nothing.
His legs felt weak, and he could hardly breathe. What had
possessed him to embark on this doomed misadventure? He
considered falling to his knees to pray for forgiveness, but
knew that he could not find the necessary words, nor even
make himself heard. Even in silence the gods' vengeance was
deafening. He could only stare at the many coloured lights
and wait for his punishment.

'Pretty, isn't it?' said a voice from behind him.

Sayer jumped violently and swung round, his heart hammering even more wildly. Even though the voice had been
very human, he had not sensed or heard the other man's
approach, and faced now with this apparition, he could only
think he must be one of the gods' chosen messengers. His
face was the colour of gold and his eyes were like black holes.

'We like to put on a good show every so often,' the messenger added. Even when he spoke his lips did not move.

'It's a mask,' Sayer blurted out, finding his tongue at last.

'Yes. I'm sorry about that,' the man replied. 'But until we
know you're one of us, a little caution is necessary.'

'One of us?'

'Our society of like-minded souls.'

'Then you're not a god?' Sayer said, thinking that maybe
– just maybe – he was not going to be struck down.

'Sadly, no.' The other man laughed. 'If I were, things
would be very different around here. I am merely the one
chosen to speak to you. The others watch.' He raised a hand
and from all around there came a variety of soft calls, each
human voice mimicking the cry of an owl, a kyar or a dove.

Sayer looked about him and saw movement, darker shadows within the night, in the outer ring of half-rebuilt shrines
or upon the surface of the Oracle's Tomb itself.

'You're the night people.'

'We prefer to call ourselves kyars, because we are not afraid to walk at night in the forbidden places.'

A glimmer of something stirred in Sayer's memory, then was lost again.

'Why here?' he asked.

'Because it gives us a measure of safety and strength, as well as a sense of camaraderie.'

The seeker considered this as his mind began to adjust to the new situation.

'So what are you trying to achieve?' he asked eventually. Hurghad had only told him that he might find the night people interesting, that they would help him see Tirok from another perspective.

'Why are *you* here?' the kyar spokesman asked.

'Because I see much that is wrong in our society, and no one seems to have the power to do anything about it. I hoped you'd help me see what I could do.' His argument sounded feeble, even to himself, but there was nothing Sayer could do about that now.

'So you came here at night,' the masked man commented, 'when the gods walk among us. That showed courage. We will all need such bravery if we are to change anything.'

'Do the gods really . . . ?' Sayer whispered.

'The gods are with us all the time. They don't need the cover of night. The lights you see are ours.'

'Isn't that risky? Surely it draws attention to your presence.'

'On the contrary. Our little displays reinforce the belief that the gods are present here in the darkness, and thus ensure our privacy.'

'So all the stories, all the sightings . . . that was you?'

'I wouldn't presume to lay claim to every legend, but a great many of them, yes. It was us. Does that shock you?'

Sayer shook his head. He had learnt too many shocking things recently to be taken aback by this latest revelation.

'What is it you want for Tirok?' he asked.

'Justice, a degree of equality, an end to persecution and tyranny. At least that will do for a start,' the kyar added dryly.

'And how will you achieve that? Do you want to overthrow the Council?'

'If there is no other way of making the archivects see sense, then we have little choice. We don't want bloodshed, but sometimes it's the only way. The prejudices and inequities are too deeply entrenched.'

A chill sank into the seeker's bones. To hear this man talk in such a matter-of-fact way about what amounted to revolution – civil war! – was horrifying, and his reaction must have shown on his face.

'Do not despair yet,' the kyar said. 'There is much we can do before it comes to violence. And for that we need friends like you. Will you join us?'

'Do I have a choice?'

'Of course. You cannot betray us without betraying yourself, admitting to having broken the law by entering the Temple at night. That would do you little good. You haven't seen any of our faces, you've heard only my voice, and you wouldn't be able to find us again unless we want you to. If you choose not to become one of us, we have nothing to fear from one another. That's not to say we wouldn't be disappointed. If you remain part of the existing system, sooner or later we will inevitably become enemies by default – and that would be a shame. We've followed your career closely, and always hoped you'd become a kyar one day.'

Sayer felt a renewed sense of disorientation. Evidently it was not just the archivects and their soldiers who had been observing him. Had any part of his life ever been truly private?

'Why me?' he asked. 'What made you think that I . . . ?'

'I'm surprised you haven't already guessed,' the kyar replied. 'Your sister Aphra was one of us.'

CHAPTER SEVENTEEN

'"You know the law," the lackeys say,
To justify the tyrant's claim,
Yet then they look the other way.
The law depends upon your name.'
From *A True History of Tirok*

Sayer was stunned. He stared into the blank eyes of the mask, quite unable to speak or even to think rationally.

'We felt Aphra's loss deeply,' the man went on. 'She was committed to our cause, and anyone with talent is especially valuable.'

'Talent?' Sayer queried, clutching at a single recognizable straw in the maelstrom of his thoughts. 'But her talent failed.'

'Only in the sense that she chose not to put it to use for the archivects. She failed them deliberately.'

'No!' Sayer cried. 'She could not have hidden that from me!'

'Your sister was most resourceful,' the other man said, calm in the face of the seeker's frantic disbelief, 'which is another reason for her loss being so tragic. You were away from home when it happened, weren't you?'

'Are you seriously telling me,' Sayer exclaimed, ignoring the question, 'that Aphra was a kyar? That she came here?'

'Yes, but not often. Her role—'

'But that's impossible!' He had known everything about his twin. They had shared *everything*. Although Sayer had been forced to reassess a great deal of his life recently, this was just too much. How could Aphra have led a secret life? The very thought was preposterous.

'She did not like deceiving you,' the other man added. 'That was the one thing that gave her second thoughts. In time she would have—'

'Tump!' the seeker cut in. The nagging memory had suddenly crystallized within his disordered mind. 'He said "a kyar told me", but I thought . . . There really *was* a message!'

'"Tell Sayer that he has the power to change the world within and without",' his informant quoted.

Sayer could only stare once more.

'It's good advice,' the man added.

'But Tump . . . ?'

'We sometimes use him as a messenger – in spite of the obvious disadvantages of his less than perfect mental state. His innocence allows him to wander where others cannot.'

'Gods,' Sayer breathed wretchedly. 'And I nearly tried to kill him.'

Somewhere in the darkness a wolf howled.

'Who else knew you were coming here tonight?' the kyar asked quickly.

'Only Hurghad.'

'Not your wife?'

'No. Why? What's the matter?' Sayer was still reeling from all he had been told, and was not sure he could cope with anything else.

'Come with me.' His companion grabbed Sayer's arm. 'Quickly.'

'Where are we going?' the seeker asked in alarm. 'What's happening?'

'There's a patrol coming,' the kyar replied as he led the way into the deeper shadows.

Sayer wanted to protest that it couldn't be so, that the soldiers were forbidden to be there at night, but he kept his mouth shut. What was one more official lie? One more flouting of Tirok's laws?

They had now reached one of the half-built structures on the outer edge of the circle, and his guide led him inside, through a sequence of open-roofed chambers and into a small courtyard. Away from the candles the night seemed very dark, but as his eyes readjusted Sayer recognized the place. It was the Cloister of Skulls, so-called because of the many skeleton shapes carved into the walls and pillars surrounding the quadrangle. At the centre of this macabre space stood the Primal Chair, at the top of its own small pyramid of stone. Directly beneath the chair itself was an open compartment inside the tower with a 'chimney' leading up from it; when potent relics were placed inside, their power rose up like smoke to imbue whoever sat in the chair with new strength and insight. However, such things were far from Sayer's thoughts now. The idea that he was actually in danger of being caught was appalling.

'Wait here,' the kyar whispered urgently.

Sayer made a half-hearted attempt to stop his guide from abandoning him, but his hand was brushed aside impatiently. He shrank back into the shadows at the edge of the courtyard and watched his companion run swiftly to the pyramid and climb the outer steps. Reaching the top, he clambered up to the Primal Chair, took off his mask and looked around. At another time the seeker would have been shocked by such irreverent behaviour, but he was beyond that now. All he cared about was that his guide risked being seen by the soldiers. He did not even try to recognize the kyar. It was too dark, and he was too far away for Sayer to see his real features clearly. In fact he was not even sure he wanted to. He had enough sense left to realize that some knowledge was just too dangerous.

More calls echoed in the night, making the Temple sound as though it were inhabited by a bizarre menagerie, and Sayer wished he could interpret them so that he would know what was going on. When one of the muted howls came from just behind his left ear, he jumped violently and turned to see two bright green eyes regarding him curiously. For a few moments he wondered if his heart was ever going to start beating again, then realized that the eyes belonged to a real kyar. The cat-like creature leapt silently from his perch, gave Sayer one last disdainful glance, and padded away across the quadrangle.

Before Sayer had a chance to recover either his breath or his wits, his guide was back at his side. The mask was in place once more.

'We should be safe here. The guards are milling around the Oracle's Tomb, and they don't like this place. Too many skeletons watching them.'

Sayer heard the amusement in his companion's voice, and wondered who he was.

'Will your people be all right?' he asked softly.

'Oh, yes,' the other replied confidently. 'They'll evade the patrol easily enough. We have better night skills. Most soldiers are usually afraid of what they might find, so they carry *torches*.' He sounded contemptuous. 'They can't see anything beyond their own circles of light, but we get to see them clearly.'

'Do they often patrol the Temple at night?'

'They inspect the perimeter regularly, but they rarely come inside.'

'So what do we do now?'

'Wait until it's all clear. Unless you want to see for yourself.'

'No!' Sayer responded quickly.

'I just thought you might like to confirm it with your own eyes,' the kyar explained. 'You only have my word that the soldiers are actually here.'

'I trust you,' the seeker said, thinking that there was no reason for the kyars to lie to him. And besides, he was already at their mercy here.

'Good. You've been faced with many new things tonight, and there are many more that you can't be expected to know yet, but at least we've made a start.'

They stood in silence for a while. Before them the court-yard was still and silent, and Sayer realized that the faint radiance of colour was gone. The candles on the Oracle's Tomb had evidently been doused and everything had returned to the silver grey of night.

'Were the candles real?' he asked quietly. 'Or an illusion?'

'Real.'

'How is it done?'

'Magic can be used for many purposes,' the kyar replied, echoing the words of Mehran-Dar. 'This was a demon-stration of that fact.'

'For my benefit?'

'Yes. Frivolous, I know, but it served another purpose too.'

'Perpetuating legends.'

'Exactly. Except tonight—' He broke off abruptly as an owl hooted mournfully. 'Be still,' he whispered.

Sayer froze as two soldiers entered the cloisters on the far side of the quadrangle. One of them carried a burning torch, but they were clearly reluctant to explore much further.

'You sure it was in here?' one of them asked, his voice carrying easily on the still night air.

'I thought so,' the other replied doubtfully. 'Gods, this place gives me the creeps.'

'It's meant to. I can't see anything.'

At that moment the real kyar emerged from the shadows, and took a few paces out into the open before stopping and turned its emerald-green gaze upon the soldiers and the flames of their torch. It sniffed the air delicately and waved its tail before continuing its progress.

'It was just a cat!' one of the guards said, laughing with relief.

'Let's go,' the senior man decided.

As the soldiers disappeared, Sayer let out a long sigh. When they had arrived, his immediate instinct had been to run, and he was very glad that his guide had been there to prevent him from doing so. Movement would have been the one sure way of getting himself noticed in the gloom. And discovery then would have been doubly catastrophic. The glow of the torch had been enough for him to recognize one of the guards. Unless his eyes had been playing tricks on him, it had been Captain Nazeri.

Some time later, while he was still trying to come to terms with this latest revelation and its ramifications, another call sounded softly in the air.

'They've retreated. We can go now.'

'That's it?' Release from immediate danger had left Sayer feeling almost intoxicated, and there were innumerable questions clamouring in his brain.

'We can't achieve anything more tonight,' the kyar told him. 'Most of the others will already be on their way.'

'How many of you are there?'

'More than Halion would ever guess, but less than we need. For obvious reasons only a few of us gather together at any one time, even here. If we are ever to act, then a great deal of planning will be necessary first, but we just have to hope that others will join us when they realize what's happening. Until then we must be careful. We watch, listen and learn – and try to persuade others to join our cause.'

'Like me?'

'Like you,' the kyar confirmed. 'I won't lie to you, Sayer. If someone like you were to join us it would be a huge step forward, but it would put you in a great deal of danger. Halion couldn't afford to have one of his most important talents defy him openly.'

The same thought had already occurred to Sayer.

'For the same reason,' his guide went on, 'we would welcome you with open arms, and do all in our power to protect you. But our resources are limited. Whatever you decide, you must be cautious, and aware of the risks involved.'

'That's not a very enticing recruitment speech.'

'The truth rarely is.'

Truth is an elusive thing, Sayer thought, remembering Hurghad's comment.

'How do I contact you again,' he asked, 'if I want to?'

'You don't. We contact you. Don't worry, you'll be given the opportunity to refuse – if you want to. Can you find your own way from here? Or do you need me to guide you further?'

'I'll make my own way.'

His companion nodded.

'I wouldn't recommend leaving by the Kyar Gate,' he said dryly. 'There are times when a theatrical exit is appropriate, but this is not one of them.'

To his amazement, Sayer found himself laughing.

'Farewell, Sayer. Can I hope to see you again?'

'I don't know,' the seeker replied honestly. He was frightened, and his thoughts were still in turmoil.

'Here's one last thing you should know,' the kyar said. 'It might help you decide. We think Aphra was betrayed somehow, and that her exile was punishment for her involvement with us. There's a good chance she never contracted the plague at all.'

CHAPTER EIGHTEEN

'Next to the sun a candle's flame is nothing, but at
night it defines the world. It illuminates as it burns,
measures time by growing less, and kills the moth that
ventures too close.'

　　　　From the writings of the philosopher Nimruz

The first light of dawn was already showing in the eastern
sky when Sayer eventually got home. He had been away
much longer than he had intended but, to his relief, Kailas
was still fast asleep. He undressed and slipped into bed
beside her but was far too agitated to sleep. He lay, staring at
the ceiling, trying to get his thoughts in order. He simply
did not know what to believe.

If only half of what he had been told that night was true,
then his entire world had been stood on its head. Sayer was
astute enough to know that he had been played like a musical
instrument by the kyar spokesman. He had danced to the
other man's tune, and the fact that his guide had saved the
most incredible and horrifying revelation until last was
proof of his expert manipulation. That Aphra might have
been one of the night people was extraordinary enough, but
the idea that she had been sent to the Isle of the Dead as a
punishment for this treason, and not because she was a

plague victim, was almost too dreadful to contemplate.

At the time Sayer had been too paralysed with horror to respond, and the kyar had turned to go.

'Wait,' the seeker had gasped. 'How do you know this?'

'Scabs can be painted on. It's been known before. The soldiers are in the archivects' pockets, and some of the boat captains are none too scrupulous if the money's good enough. And Aphra was in perfect health the day before she was taken away. Work it out for yourself.' The kyar had paused briefly. 'I have to go.'

'You can't just leave me like—' Sayer had begun, but was left clutching at thin air. His companion had vanished into the night.

Could it possibly be true? Was Aphra still alive? From one point of view, the possibility contained a kind of sick logic. If Aphra was indeed one of the kyars, if their organization represented a genuine threat to Tirok's rulers, and if the Isle of the Dead really was a prison colony and not just somewhere to isolate plague victims, then his sister's fate made sense. Killing Tirokians was the ultimate taboo, the law that superseded all others, so the disposing of allegedly dangerous criminals in this way would salve the consciences of those involved.

Sayer was distraught. He needed proof of what the kyar had told him, but had no idea about how to go about getting it.

And perhaps the kyar had been lying. Sayer had already learnt that the rule of Tirok was based in part upon lies and distortions – and Nazeri's presence in the Temple that night had been further proof that the laws were not sacrosanct – so why bother to exile traitors, rather than silence them permanently by killing them? Sending them to join the genuine plague victims on the island was effectively a death sentence, albeit a passive one. Could the people who mocked the other laws possibly take account of such a fine distinction? Was keeping up appearances so important? Sayer thought briefly about Akar's death and the fact that his 'accident' had been premeditated, and began to feel sick.

He knew now that for a long time he had been wilfully blind to many of the wrongs of Tirokian society, but he still found it hard to believe that he had been equally blind to the realities of his sister's life. Everything came back to that – and the only person who could tell him the whole truth was now marooned on the Isle of the Dead, out of reach. 'You can't hide anything from me.' Sayer had once spoken those exact words to his twin, and cringed at the memory now. He was being forced to reassess the whole of their lives together. What other secrets had she kept from him? Had she – as the kyar had implied – spied upon him, biding her time until she judged him ready to be approached? When would that have been? Had her frequent headaches been a result of the stress of her dual life? And was that why she had never let him even try to ease her pain with his talent? Was she afraid of what the telepathy might have revealed? Such speculation seemed far-fetched, but it did fit a kind of pattern. It was also possible that the real reason their old apartment had been scoured was in case Aphra had left any clues to the identity of her fellow malcontents, or any dangerous messages for her brother. The idea that his twin's closeness to him might have contributed to her supposed fate filled Sayer with stomach-churning dread. Had she been disposed of so that her rebellious attitudes could not contaminate Halion's best seeker?

The crucial question was, had Aphra really been a kyar? If she had, then everything else flowed from that. Only a short time ago Sayer would have thought the idea laughable, but instinct now made him inclined to believe that she had. The apparent anomalies surrounding her disappearance, together with the fact that his guide had known the exact wording of Tump's message, were the most convincing evidence. Tump's embarrassment when he had mentioned 'a kyar' had been genuine, but not for the reason Sayer had assumed. Somewhere in the young man's addled brain, he had known he was not supposed to mention the secret organization. Of course, it was also possible that the night people were merely using a convenient set of circumstances to try and attract the sympathies of an important talent. The kyar spokesman had certainly been telling the truth when he said that the seeker's recruitment would be something of a coup. So was it not possible that in trying to bring this about he could have been as devious as any archivect?

Sayer also realized that if the kyar *had* been telling the truth, then this raised another unsettling question. Had Halion timed his introduction of Kailas to Sayer because he knew that Aphra was soon going to be arrested? Had he wanted someone more responsible – pliable – as a companion for his best seeker? That seemed all too plausible. Sayer glanced at the sleeping face of his wife, and was filled with new doubts. Had she known? Had she been part of this intrigue from the beginning? Or was she, like Sayer himself, another puppet whose strings were being pulled by their master? Lying there, completely relaxed, she looked so gentle and so guileless that it was hard to believe she might be that deceitful – and yet the kyar's instant reaction to the alarm had been to ask whether Kailas was aware of Sayer's visit to the Temple. By implication, he suspected her of duplicity. Then again, given her family background, that would hardly be surprising. And Kailas had *not* known of Sayer's plans. The most she could have done was tell someone that he had gone out unexpectedly in the night; as he had apparently not been followed, even that was unlikely.

Sayer felt so confused and so alone that he was close to

tears. The worst thing about all this uncertainty was that he now suspected *everyone*, with the possible exception of Hurghad. Captain Nazeri had never been a close friend, but the two men had worked closely together on many occasions, respecting each other's abilities. Sayer now knew that the captain had secrets too. Although he paid lip service to the laws, he was clearly quite prepared to break them if the situation demanded it. So who else among his colleagues and friends had been hiding things from him? Who was left for him to trust?

The idea that Aphra might be living still, stranded upon that abominable island, was literally nauseating. Sayer knew that one thing was clear. He had to rescue her – but how? It was obvious he could not do it on his own; the odds were too heavily stacked against him. He needed help, and the kyars represented his only real hope of this – but his guide had not even raised the possibility of saving Aphra. His attitude had been one of anger and sadness at her loss, assuming her fate to be irreversible.

As the light outside their window grew bright and Kailas began to stir, Sayer was at a loss. For all his attempted reasoning, he was no further forward.

What now? he wondered. What am I supposed to do?

The sound of his knocking echoed through the tunnel. It was a measure of Sayer's desperation that he had now tried four times to attract Hurghad's attention, knocking and then waiting as long as he could stand in between attempts. But there was still no response. The hermit was either unable or unwilling to answer his summons and, try as he might, Sayer could not hear anything from the room on the far side of the stone door.

At last he yielded to the inevitable and turned to leave, stumbling wearily through the stream as he retraced his footsteps. Where could Hurghad be? Sayer had waited more than long enough to ensure that the hermit had not simply been above ground giving one of his 'performances', so there had to be another reason for his absence. A variety of explanations, all of them unpleasant, flashed into the seeker's mind, but none of them helped reconcile him to the fact that his mentor was not there to speak to him. The one person he could have asked for advice was suddenly and inexplicably unavailable.

Sayer's preoccupation did not stop him from being cautious as he emerged from the trapdoor and, after disguising its existence once more, he walked slowly back to the city. His lack of sleep was beginning to take its toll, but rest was still the last thing on his mind. At the gates he was startled to be hailed from on high by one of the sentries and waited, trying to remain calm, while the guardhouse door opened. The man who came to join him was one of Halion's stewards.

'Ah, there you are, Seeker. We've been looking for you most of the afternoon.'

'I've been walking.'

'Archivect Halion wants to see you.'

'Now?'

The steward nodded.

'Bring us some horses,' he called to a nearby stable lad, then turned back to Sayer. 'It'll make the journey that much quicker. You look as if you've done enough walking for one day.'

The two men did not talk on the way, but Sayer could not help speculating about the reasons for and the timing of this summons. When they reached Halion's mansion and servants had relieved them of their mounts, the steward led him to a part of the vast building Sayer had never visited before. An octagonal room had been added to the top of one of the wings – yet another enhancement to the archivect's grandiose home. Although it was constructed mainly of wood, two adjacent sides included several large panes of clear glass – a rare and very expensive adornment. However, the most interesting feature was the fact that the entire room revolved upon a giant turntable, and the windows could therefore be made to face in any direction. This was done by servants inserting long poles into special metal rings – which had been fitted to the outside of the chamber – and pushing it round to the desired position. Sayer had heard of its design, and considered the new addition to be a vain waste of both materials and manpower, but Halion had evidently not shared his concerns.

As Sayer arrived, using the door that was currently at the top of the external staircase, Halion was lounging on a large seat, surrounded by plump cushions, his colourful garb made brilliant by the late afternoon sun.

'Sayer. Come in.' He waved a hand towards another chair. 'One more rotation, please,' he added to the steward, who bowed and then withdrew.

Moments later, with a slight rumbling vibration, the complete structure moved round an eighth of a turn.

'Now we'll have the benefit of the last of the sun,' Halion explained affably.

The movement had made Sayer feel a little queasy, and his master's apparent bonhomie did nothing to improve his mood.

'You are well, I trust, Sayer?'

'Yes, my lord. Thank you.'

'And Kailas? I am told she has proved to be a very gifted silk.'

'She is all I could have asked for.'

'Good. No doubt your children will be equally talented. Let's hope so, anyway.'

Sayer said nothing, knowing that he had not been brought here to make small talk, but having no wish to learn the real purpose of the visit.

'Where did you go before dawn last night?' the archivect asked. Although he spoke lightly, and his smile was still in place, his eyes were now fixed upon Sayer with an unnerving intensity.

'I . . . I went for a walk,' the seeker replied, hoping that his awkwardness would not betray him. 'I couldn't sleep and decided to go out rather than disturb my wife. Kailas is still recovering from her last mission, and she needs—'

'Where did you go?' Halion repeated.

'Along the Gold Road. I like to climb the hill at Esauru and look down upon both the archivects' estates and the Temple.'

'You can't have seen much in the dark,' his master commented.

'I find it a soothing place, nonetheless. Starlight can be—'

'So you didn't see anything unusual?' Halion asked, interrupting Sayer again.

'There were some coloured lights in the Temple, but it's not unusual for the gods to show us such a display,' the seeker replied, hoping he sounded suitably reverent. 'It is their province, after all.'

'I only heard of it. You were lucky to be able to see the spectacle for yourself.'

'The gods granted me that favour.'

Halion paused, apparently considering this statement.

'Are you happy in your work, Sayer?' he asked eventually.

'Yes, my lord. It's most fulfilling.'

The archivect nodded.

'There are a few godless heathens who do not believe in the great task,' he remarked casually. 'Such heresy is immensely dangerous.'

'Surely no one takes these madmen seriously?' Sayer heard the words as if they were coming from someone else's tongue. His newfound fluency in lying still took him by surprise.

'A few misguided fools, no more,' Halion said. 'But such creatures sometimes try to prey upon others when they are at their most vulnerable. I know it's been a difficult time for you since your sister's illness, but I would hate to think that you might begin to doubt your vocation.'

'Never.'

'I'm pleased to hear it. It would be a tragedy for you to throw away all you have earned, let all your talent go to waste, simply because of the irresponsible actions of others.'

The archivect's words were still couched in polite terms, but Sayer knew a threat when he heard one. His recent exploits had obviously not gone unnoticed and, even if their extent was not yet known, he realized that he would have to watch his step even more carefully from now on.

'I am fully aware of my responsibilities,' he said, 'to my-self as well as to others.'

'I'm glad we understand each other. Tell me, how are you enjoying married life?'

His purpose achieved, Halion was now content to talk of unimportant matters. He was pleasant and charming, but all Sayer wanted to do was escape, to put as much distance as he could between himself and his lies. He even began to won-der whether Hurghad's disappearance might have been because Halion had somehow found out about his own visits to the hermit.

Servants came in, one bringing wine, the second a new set of candles. Now that the sun had set, the room was grow-ing dark. Having poured the drinks, the first woman departed, while the other lingered, setting up the candles and lighting them.

'I prefer candles to lamps, don't you?' Halion commented. 'They give a softer, more welcoming glow.'

'Aren't they a danger, with all this wood around?' Sayer asked, for the sake of something to say.

'Oh, I don't think we need worry about that. Galieva knows her business, don't you, my dear?'

The servant bowed her head and smiled in response, but did not speak. She had just lit the last of the candles and was carrying it across the room, one hand cupped to the side of the wick. Turning now so that she had her back to her master, she glanced straight at Sayer – and something in her eyes made him take note of her. At that moment the flame of the candle she held flickered, turning blue, red and green in quick succession before returning to normal. Sayer looked away quickly, not wanting to betray his astonishment to Halion, who had not been able to see this display. Fortunately, the archivect did not seem to be aware of anything unusual.

'Fine vintage this, don't you think?'

'It's delicious,' Sayer agreed, taking another sip.

Galieva had set the final candle in its holder now and turned to leave, giving no indication that anything out of the ordinary had happened. The seeker knew better. And he knew what the signal had meant. It seemed that the kyars had eyes everywhere – even in the heart of their enemy's stronghold.

CHAPTER NINETEEN

'No mask like open truth to cover lies,
As to go naked is the best disguise.'
From *Duplicity*, by the poet Evergnoc

Sayer had accepted the offer of a horse to ride back to the
city. Although he would have liked to go and see whether
Hurghad was all right, he had not dared to do so, especially
after Halion's warning. So the only thing left for him to do
was to go home, and his own weariness, compounded by the
effects of wine, made him want to get there as soon as
possible. He wanted to rest, to sleep and, above all, to be able
to stop thinking.

However, when he reached the city and left his mount at
the stables near the Gold Road Gate, his feet led him not to
his new home but to his old one. He did not even try to resist
the impulse, even though he told himself it was a pointless
exercise. The forces that drew him back to the apartment
were beyond his understanding, but he could not ignore
them. Perhaps, he thought hopefully, there is something
there after all, some hidden message from Aphra that I've
missed, something that will tell me what to do.

However, as soon as he stepped inside he knew it had
been no more than a foolish whim. There was nothing in

those bare, empty rooms. Even the memories were fading. He wandered aimlessly for a while, then told himself he was being stupid and left.

'Have you been to see Halion?' Kailas asked as he came in.

'Yes.'

'Good. One of his stewards was here earlier but I wasn't sure where you were. What did he want?'

'Just a chat. About work.'

'Do we have a new assignment yet?' she asked eagerly. 'I'm ready.'

'Not yet,' he told her, and sighed.

'You look tired.' Her voice was full of concern. 'Are you hungry? Safi prepared a meal for us before she left for the night.'

Since Kailas had taken up her duties as a silk, Halion had arranged for a servant to help her around the house. Safi cooked, cleaned and did their laundry, but Sayer had seen little of her and could hardly remember what she looked like. Now he wondered idly whether she was another spy, sent to keep an eye on him.

Although he was not really hungry, he followed his wife into the kitchen and sat down obediently at the table.

'Safi's a good cook, isn't she?' Kailas remarked after they had been eating for a while.

Sayer nodded.

'Where did you find her?' he asked.

'She used to work in Halion's kitchens. This gives her a chance to spread her wings a little. She jumped at the chance when he suggested it.'

'I expect she gives him reports on us,' Sayer commented, half joking.

'Why would she want to do that?' Kailas asked, obviously confused.

162   Julia Gray

'Just to make sure we're behaving ourselves.' He smiled, but she did not share his dark amusement.

'I don't like it when you talk like this.'

'Sorry.' Her distress seemed genuine, and Sayer felt a pang of guilt.

'Halion's done a lot for us, for both of us,' Kailas went on. 'Do you think we'd have all this, or be able to live as well as we do, without his help?'

'There are a lot of people who aren't as lucky as us,' the seeker pointed out.

'Exactly my point!' she exclaimed. 'You should be grateful.'

'I am, but haven't you ever thought that perhaps we ought to try and help all those people? If we used even half the resources that are going towards rebuilding the Temple, who knows what we could achieve.'

'That's crazy talk!' she said, angry now. 'Unless we rebuild the Temple we'll all be destroyed, all of us.'

'But—'

'Stop it!' Kailas got to her feet. 'I'm not listening to this.' She almost ran from the room, leaving the rest of her food on the table.

Sayer stayed where he was. Although he knew that Kailas did not share his opinions, he was nonetheless surprised to have provoked such a violent reaction. Eventually he stood up and followed her upstairs. He found her sitting on their bed, her eyes brimming with tears. As he sat down beside her, she took out a handkerchief and blew her nose.

'I thought you'd got over all that nonsense,' she told him quietly.

'I can't help thinking.'

'Why can't you just accept the way things are? We have a good life, don't we? Why jeopardize that? It's not just yourself you have to think of now. There's me . . . and our

children.' There was a catch in her voice as she spoke the
final words, and Sayer jumped to the obvious conclusion.

'Are you pregnant?' he whispered.

'No. I thought I was, but I'm not.' She was crying now. 'I
wanted to be. I wanted . . .'

Sayer put an arm round her shoulders and she moved
closer. He did not know whether to be disappointed or
relieved. He had not really got used to the idea of being a
husband yet, and the possibility that he might become a
father soon was unnerving.

Some time later Sayer tiptoed out of the bedroom again.
He had held Kailas in his arms until she fell asleep, feeling
immensely protective, but had then been unable to get to
sleep himself. Aphra haunted his thoughts and would not let
him rest. There had to be some way to be sure, to find out
the truth.

He went to the bedroom he had first used, and took the
two masks out of the chest there. For Sayer these masks were
now symbolic of his twin's personality and of the hidden life
she had led. Handling them now, feeling their weight, the
coldness of the metal and the jagged edges at the back, he
could not help thinking that they were not very practical to
wear. Of course, they had never been intended as anything
other than wall decorations. Aphra's real masks, unlike these
and the one worn by the kyar in the Temple, had been
invisible – but just as effective.

He realized that, in all his thoughts that evening, he had
been assuming that Aphra *had* been one of the night people.
In his heart he knew that he wanted to believe the kyar's
version of the truth, especially after Galieva's earlier demonstration. She had shown faith in him by risking herself. He
could have denounced her and, even without proof, he
would have been taken seriously enough to get her into a lot
of trouble. Of course he would then have risked exposing his

own illegal contact with the secret organization, so her message had been a calculated gamble. But what was it supposed to prove? That the night people were serious, courageous, well-organized? Galieva was the only kyar whose face he had seen, so perhaps that meant she was to be his contact. But did he even want to have any further contact? Apart from the dangers involved, if he accepted what the kyar spokesman had told him, then he would have to admit that he had *never* known Aphra – and that was hard.

His reflections were interrupted by a sudden loud banging. Someone was hammering on the front door, and he hurried down to see who it was. Two grim-faced soldiers, whom Sayer did not recognize, were waiting on the doorstep. One of them had raised his fist to knock again, but had been forestalled when the seeker opened the door. Although he lowered his hand, the impatience remained in his eyes.

'I am Captain Akander,' he announced shortly. 'This is Lieutenant Maier.'

'Good evening, Captain. Can I help you?'

'May we come in?'

'Of course.' Sayer ushered them into the living room and offered refreshments, which were refused. All the time he was wondering what part of his story to Halion had been found wanting, and devising ways to explain any discrepancies. However, when Akander next spoke it was about another matter entirely.

'I understand you visited Archivect Halion this afternoon?'

'That's correct.'

'Where did you go after you left his estate?'

'I came home. Here.'

'On foot?'

'Yes. I left my horse at the stables by the city gate.'

'And from there you came straight here?'

'Not exactly. I went to my old lodgings first.'

'Why?'

'It's hard to explain, Captain. That's where I last saw my sister, and . . .' He hesitated.

'And?' the captain prompted.

'I miss her. I just wanted to remember our times together.'

'I understand the apartment was cleared after your sister caught the plague.'

'That's correct.'

'So there would hardly be much to remind you of her, would there?'

'Not really, no. I didn't stay long. It was a foolish idea.'

'And you didn't meet anyone there?'

'No. What's all this about, Captain?'

'Do you know a daydreamer called Tump?' Akander asked, ignoring the question.

'Yes,' Sayer replied. 'But he no longer works. Why?'

'He was found dead early this evening, below the entrance to your old apartment. It seems likely that he fell from the landing at the top of the steps. His neck was broken.'

'Gods,' Sayer breathed, taken aback.

'You know nothing about this?' the soldier asked.

'Of course not! Surely you don't think—'

'You were heard threatening him on an earlier occasion,' Akander said mildly.

'Yes, but—' The truth suddenly dawned on Sayer. This was another warning. Whether Tump had fallen by chance or had been pushed, it was clear that Sayer was under suspicion. And if it *was* murder and Halion was responsible – albeit indirectly – then this was proof that the last barrier of law had been cast aside. The archivect was capable of doing anything to ensure he got what he wanted.

'I swear that I never even saw Tump today,' he said.

'No doubt it was an accident,' the captain replied evenly, 'but you understand that we have to investigate such matters.

The violent death of any Tirokian citizen is a serious matter.'

'Of course. I assure you I had nothing to do with it.'

Although Akander's face betrayed no emotion, his lieutenant looked decidedly sceptical.

'Did anyone else see you leave the apartment?' the captain went on.

'Not that I can recall,' Sayer answered. He wanted to ask why the military's own lookouts had not seen him, but knew better than to do so.

'And presumably your wife can confirm the time you arrived home?'

'Of course.'

'Is she here now?'

'Yes, but she's asleep. She's a silk, and needs her rest. I'd rather not wake her.'

'That won't be necessary.' Maier looked surprised by Akander's words, but said nothing. 'We'll be going now. Thank you for your cooperation.' All three men got to their feet.

As the two soldiers headed towards the door, Maier turned back and fixed Sayer with a vengeful glare. In that moment the seeker knew that, even if Akander was aware of what had really happened, his colleague actually believed him guilty of murder.

'Just because you're a seeker,' Maier snarled, 'it doesn't mean we won't be watching you.'

'That's *enough*, Lieutenant,' Akander snapped.

When they'd gone, Sayer leant against the door and took a deep breath. He was shaking badly. He was overpowered by fear and knew that he had neither the courage nor the resolve to risk everything by aligning himself with the kyars. Even if Aphra was alive, there was nothing he or they could do about it. With a wrench that almost broke his heart, he decided to turn his back on the past. Life had to go on.

* * *

Two days later, Sayer found a note in the pocket of his tunic. He had no idea how it had got there – a fact that made him even more nervous – but the contents were more worrying still. The unsigned message suggested he go to the Cloister of Skulls at midnight on any of the next seven nights, whichever was most convenient.

Three days after that Sayer left Qara on a new mission, but knew that he would not have gone to the Temple anyway. The night people would have to do without him.

CHAPTER TWENTY

'Within the black dome the wings must gather, to look down through the eyes of the gods. Each carries a gift in beak or claw, and we must accept them all before we are blessed. The magpie is a thief of hearts, and the jay hides secret treasures. The raven carries the sword of vengeance, while the rook is the emblem of war. The keeyaa wakes the dead; the crow guards the gate of heaven. The jackdaw . . .'

From *The Oracles of Zavanaiu*

When he reached the crest of the mountain pass, Sayer gave a slight tug on the reins and his mount came to a stop. They had been climbing steadily for the last three days, and the horse was glad of the chance to rest. The wind was cold, carrying with it a foretaste of winter, when the ice and snow would invade from the north; although summer lingered on the central plains, it was already autumn here.

This was the first time Sayer had travelled so far west since he had been taken to Qara as a child. During his early years as a seeker, the overseers had chosen not to give him any missions to the mountains that had once been his home-land, presumably because they had not wanted to subject him to the strain of divided loyalties, should he see his old village – or his parents – again. Later there had been no call for an experienced seeker in that area. Few major pieces had been transported so far, and fewer still had been taken to the high borderlands which supported only a small and generally poor population. The relic Sayer was currently tracking down was an exception.

The fragment that had caused Akar's downfall had finally been interpreted. The lore-masters were almost certain that their earlier guess had been correct and it was indeed one of the missing bosses from the Raven Dome. However, the apparent location of the roof carving had caused some consternation. According to the daydreamers it lay high in the mountain range between the two major tributaries of the Kul River, each of which flowed from the even greater peaks beyond Tirok's border in the vast and mysterious country known as Helmand. That alone would have made any seeker's task almost impossible, because the area between the two branches of the river was immense, but, using Akar's description of the actual site, the invigilators had been able to make several educated guesses as to the most likely places to start looking. Sayer had then steeped himself in all the available information, and hoped to be able to pick up the relic's trail when he got closer. He had achieved that with an ease that surprised even him, and now he knew that they were near.

Their next move would be to follow the trail down into the shelter of the rugged glen that lay before them. After camping for the night, they would climb once more, reaching a pass that was higher still – and which would be their destination. However, Sayer felt a strange reluctance to let anyone know just how soon they would reach their goal. Part of him wanted the journey to go on for ever, amid the wild beauty of stone and tough mountain grass. On several occasions he had been tempted to lead the party by a roundabout route, and had even considered diverting them to the valley that had once been his home. No one would have been any the wiser, but in the end he decided against it. What would have been the point?

'Can you feel the resonance?' Kailas asked as she drew up beside him.

'Yes,' he answered truthfully.

'Are we close?'

'I'm not sure,' Sayer replied with his by now habitual evasiveness.

Kailas shivered.

'Gods, this is grim country.'

In contrast to Sayer's almost complete lack of emotion, his wife had been very excited when they had first learned of their new mission. Confident now of her own abilities, she was looking forward to greater responsibilities, and thought of helping to find one of the few remaining pieces of the Raven Dome as an excellent opportunity. It was not on the same scale as the Eye of Clouds, but if they succeeded it would be far and away the most significant relic that she had helped retrieve.

Although her enthusiasm had not waned, Kailas had grown more subdued as the practical realities of travelling in such bleak terrain had become apparent. She had only ever known the comparatively gentle landscapes of Kohlu and Qara, and Sayer could tell that camping out in empty valleys in the shadow of forbidding peaks had made her nervous. She had not said anything, but it was obvious that she would be glad to be able to turn back towards the familiar comforts of home. The trip had already lasted several days, and she needed the reassurance that they were near their target in order to rekindle her earlier exhilaration. The fact that Sayer chose not to give her that reassurance made him feel guilty.

The whole party had come to a halt now, and Nazeri

came to join the seeker and his wife in looking at the valley ahead.

'Down?' he queried.

'Yes.'

'We'll camp at the bottom. The wind will be less trouble-some there.' The soldier glanced at Kailas. It was the closest he would ever come to criticizing the decision to bring a woman into such savage territory. Although Nazeri respected her abilities as a silk, it was clear that he regarded her as a liability when they were forced to travel rough. Sayer was aware of his attitude but Kailas seemed oblivious to it, mere-ly accepting the special provisions that were made for her as her due.

'At least the skies are clear,' she commented. Two nights earlier, heavy rain had reduced their camp to a quagmire.

'We're all grateful for that, ma'am,' the captain replied, then wheeled his horse away and began shouting orders.

At first Sayer had felt a little better, glad to be leaving Qara behind. For a start, there was no chance of catching an acci-dental glimpse of the Isle of the Dead – and that was one place he did not even want to think about. However, as they travelled, his thoughts kept betraying him, and he was forced to defend his position to himself.

Aphra's message – even if it was genuine – was wrong. He had no power to change anything. He had once believed that he might make a difference, but he realized now that that had been a delusion. And yet when he thought of Aphra, all logic was thrown aside. He was continually reminded of the hypocrisy and lies that surrounded his life. Each time he spoke to Nazeri he remembered seeing him in the Temple, and came close to confronting the soldier about it. He did not, however, because he knew that it would be a futile and possibly self-destructive act. At other times Sayer was tormented by the fact that Akar had *died* for the sake of the relic he was now pursuing. But the most damning evidence of all was the reaction of the few villagers they had encountered in the mountains. Some of them had simply run away, abandoning their homes as the armed and obviously official party drew near. Those that remained had been suspicious and afraid, parting with information only grudgingly. It was clear that they saw no benefit to themselves in the rebuilding of a distant temple, and Sayer had been glad when his group moved on to the higher regions, an area that was virtually unpopulated.

Now, as the soldiers and artisans pitched camp, he found himself recalling the words of Mehran-Dar. *Each man must decide for himself what his magic is for.* And that, the seeker thought, is my problem. Although he was using his magic, he no longer knew what it was *for*.

As the sun sank, he watched the shadows creep up the sides of the valley, deepening the pool of darkness in which he sat. The sky was still clear, and several peaks glittered in the last of the sunlight, apparently floating on the air, above the mundane world he occupied. The strange beauty of this landscape was lost on most of the party, who regarded the region as hostile and barren, but as the unseen sun set beyond the distant horizon, there came a sight that even the most dour of his companions could not fail to appreciate. Sayer heard their expressions of astonishment and turned to look for himself. In the curving space between two peaks, the sky was filled with a shimmering fan of light, composed of all the colours of the rainbow. It was as fleeting as it was beautiful, and faded within moments, leaving them wondering if they had really seen it at all.

'What was that?' someone asked.

'It looked as though the whole pass was full of dragonflies,' one of the soldiers added, with uncharacteristic poetry.

Sayer turned away and made no comment. He *knew* what it had been, and the knowledge made him feel sick.

The next day, Sayer's premonition proved correct. They spent most of the morning climbing up the rough and twisting trail that led them from the valley to the pass, and once there the scene was immediately recognizable. *Two hills, outcrops of bare rock on top of each, the curve of the land between them forms a saddle. In line with the setting sun . . .* Akar's last words echoed in Sayer's brain, adding another layer of bitterness to his sour mood. Between the two tors – which did indeed look like the loaves that had been prophesied – stood a small building. It was circular, with a domed roof made of some dark grey stone, and as they drew closer, Sayer could see that set atop the graceful curve was a spike of translucent crystal. It winked and flashed in the sunlight, and he was sure that this was what had produced the miraculous display the previous evening. As darkness fell, the last rays from the final arc of the sun had been caught by the crystal, and divided into the radiant colours they had seen. *In line with the setting sun . . .*

The chief mason confirmed Sayer's worst fears as soon as they had verified that the relic was indeed part of the structure.

'It's an awkward job,' he reported. 'The boss is directly under the crystal, at the crown of the dome. It's like a central pin, holding the whole thing up. Take it away and the entire roof will cave in.'

'Can't we bolster it to prevent that?' Sayer asked.

'We could try, but it would take several days just to gather the materials we'd need. The nearest wood is two days away, and—'

'We've no time for that,' Nazeri cut in. 'There's no chance of replenishing our supplies up here. We could all starve to death before you're ready.'

The captain obviously did not see what was causing the difficulty. He had seen larger and more important buildings demolished for lesser rewards. On the other hand, Sayer felt a kind of sick dread at the thought of destroying this lovely wayside chapel. It was not only a place of prayer, but also served a practical function, sheltering travellers from bad weather. The fact that it was well maintained, sound and clean, in spite of being in the middle of nowhere, was proof of its usefulness in this regard. And above all, the craftsmen who had built the chapel had put their hearts into their work, creating the rainbow beacon Sayer's group had seen the night before. What right did he have to destroy all that?

Seeing his hesitation, the chief mason spoke again.

'Seeker?'

'Give me a moment.'

Sayer went back inside the dome and looked up. Although it was dark, he could just make out the relic. The carving depicted a bird – probably a crow – in flight, with a strange object clutched in its talons. Sayer did not recognize the symbol, but in gazing at it he experienced a feeling of peace and knew that this was a place of tranquillity, a true haven. Instinctively, he knelt as if in prayer.

'Are you all right?' Kailas asked softly. She had followed him inside but he had not heard her approach.

'No.'

'I can do it,' she said, mistaking the reason for his unease. 'I'm ready. You needn't worry about—'

'Come on,' he rasped, rising abruptly and taking her arm. 'Let's get this over with.'

Kailas glanced at him anxiously as he almost dragged her outside, but Sayer did not notice. Rage had engulfed him, though he did not let it show.

'Knock it down,' he instructed the overseer. 'Let us know when you're ready to begin.'

The chief mason nodded.

'This is going to be a messy one,' he said gravely, looking at Kailas. 'It'll mean you'll have to protect the relic for longer than usual, ma'am. Until we can dig it out.'

'That's fine,' she replied confidently. 'I'm ready.'

He turned away and began issuing instructions to his men. For more than an hour they swarmed around the chapel, both inside and out, preparing for the demolition. Sayer forced himself to watch as they weakened certain areas, identified key points of attack and arranged their positions, so that on a given signal they would be able to complete their work without any of them being trapped or injured by falling rubble. Meanwhile, Kailas sat on a rug that had been laid out on the ground, composing herself and gathering her strength for the task ahead. She clearly shared none of Sayer's qualms, and by the time the masons announced that they were ready she was practically in a trance.

'Give me its shape,' she intoned, her voice hollow and unnaturally deep.

Sayer came up behind her and placed his hand on her head in the now familiar ritual. Moments later a violet glow, brighter than any Sayer had ever seen before, filled the inside of the dome with an eerie radiance.

'Go!' the overseer called.

As one, half a dozen sledgehammers crashed into stone. The dome shivered and cracked, but did not fall.

'Again.'

Once more the air rang with the clash of metal on stone, and this time it was followed by a dreadful creaking.

'Back!' the chief mason yelled, and his men leapt clear as the dome seemed to give one last sigh and then collapsed in on itself with a deathly slithering roar. With a final spark, the crystal spike shattered into a million pieces. As dust filled the air, other artisans were already running forward with their tools, ready to dig towards the partly buried violet aura. They worked quickly and with the efficiency of a well-established team, but it was still some time before they were able to uncover their prize – and when they did there was a sudden dismayed silence.

'It's clear,' the chief mason called eventually, and Kailas slumped to the ground, unconscious. Sayer knelt beside her as Kebir hurried forward to inspect the find. When he returned his face was grave, but Sayer already knew what he was going to say.

'Part of the relic's been crushed,' the scribe reported. 'The shield must have failed.'

'Is it reparable?'

'The masons aren't sure yet. It'll be a long and delicate job just to retrieve all the pieces. What happened?'

'I must have given her the wrong shape.'

'Are you sure it wasn't Kailas's error?'

'She's too good for that.'

'So are you. And she's a lot less experienced. I know she's your wife, but I'm going to have to report on this in detail and I need the truth.'

'Truth is malleable,' Sayer told him and waved the scribe away. 'Leave us alone.'

For the rest of that afternoon and well into the evening, the artisans toiled patiently, collecting even the tiniest fragments of the relic. There was a large crack down the centre of the crow's body, but that could be repaired easily enough. Much worse was the fact that the carving of the bird's feet and the symbol they grasped had been shattered into many pieces, with some of it reduced to little more than dust. Even the most pain-staking restoration would probably never recreate the original properly. Kebir watched the work intently, noting as many details as he could, but no one approached Sayer and Kailas, who sat apart, paying no attention to what was going on.

When Kailas did eventually regain consciousness, she knew from the look in her husband's eyes that something was wrong. Glancing round at the continuing excavation, she realized instantly that she had failed. Having held the aura for longer than normal, she was exhausted, and although her wordless distress kept her awake for a few moments, she was unable to stop herself from falling asleep again. She shivered, her dreams obviously troubled, while Sayer held her, regretting his actions now. He had been driven by fury, but in his madness he had not considered the effect they would have on his wife, and now all he could do was curse his own stupidity.

He had indeed given her the wrong shape, but it had been a deliberate act of sabotage. Kailas was blameless, but she would assume otherwise unless he could convince her that it had been his fault. However, he could not tell her the whole truth. Sayer had been hoping to anger the gods, to provoke them into giving him some sign that what he had done was wrong. He had destroyed one of their most sacred relics, made a mockery of his commitment to the great task – and that should have prompted some response. Sayer had been ready to accept whatever punishment was his due – because the gods would know whose fault it was. But he had been waiting for hours now. And there had been nothing. Nothing at all.

CHAPTER TWENTY-ONE

'Ceaseless labour sent to build
What now should be but dust,
Senseless faith allowed to gild
An obsession born of lust.'
                    From *A True History of Tirok*

Sayer had been back in Qara only a few hours when he
realized that he had no friends left. He knew now that he
had only ever had a very small number; those he would
previously have included in the list were no more than
acquaintances. Of the few he had been sure of, Aphra was
gone – and now it seemed that he had never really known
her at all – he had not seen Damaris since Kailas had
become his silk, Tump and Akar were dead and, since the
latest mission, both Kailas and Kebir could hardly hide
their disappointment in him. The journey back from the
mountains had been torture. When she had been awake,
Kailas had been alternately silent and tearful, and no matter
how hard Sayer had tried to convince her that she was
blameless, she simply refused to believe him, assuming that
he was just trying to comfort and protect him. The scribe, on
the other hand, had eventually come to accept that Sayer
had been at fault, but he had had difficulty coming to terms

with the seeker's claim that it had been a simple mistake. Finally, when Sayer had refused to discuss the matter any further, Kebir had given him a piece of his mind and then maintained an indignant and disapproving silence. Yet, even with all that weighing on Sayer's mind, the worst blow was still to come.

His visit to the Treasury on their return to Qara had been utterly humiliating, and he had wanted to run away and hide. The damaged relic had caused much horrified consternation, and specialists were called in immediately. Other stones had been recovered in similarly poor condition, and the profession of 'stone-binder' had thus come into being. However, it was rare for a relic to be in need of their expert attention when it had been located intact – and it had never happened with such an important piece. The atmosphere of shock had been palpable and Kebir's explanation, which had been brief to the point of curtness, did little to improve matters. In due course there would be an inquest into exactly what had happened but, for now, the priority was to see whether the boss could be restored.

Sayer fled as soon as he was able, and spent the next hour walking aimlessly around unfamiliar streets in the northern part of the city. He did not want to go home. Kailas was already there, asleep once more, and he had no wish to disturb her and face those sad green eyes again. Even after six days she was still very tired, but Sayer feared that she suffered from more than exhaustion. Her spirit was broken – and that was his fault.

Instead of returning to the Magicians' Quarter, he slipped out of Souls' Gate and wandered on through the ragged shantytown that lay between the city and the docks. He was still dressed in his stained and crumpled travelling clothes, and no one paid him much attention. For once he did not feel nervous walking among the people who lived in such squalid conditions, and this was not just because he did not really care what happened to him. He saw in their faces the signs of poverty and resignation, but also a resilience, a perverse strength born of misfortune. They have friends, Sayer thought, and families – and even a sense of community. I have none of these things.

He eventually found himself at the harbour, striding along one of the many jetties, staring disconsolately down at his feet. When he reached the end, he looked up and stared across the lake at the Isle of the Dead.

'Tell me what to do, Aphra. Why aren't you here?'

There was no answer, of course, and it was only when he turned away and noticed some dockers regarding him curiously that he realized he had spoken aloud. Head down once more, he hurried away, knowing that there was only one person who might be able to help him now.

Sayer breathed a massive sigh of relief when Hurghad opened the underground door almost immediately. Then he grew slightly uneasy when he saw that the hermit was wearing his wig and there was a look of drunken incoherence in his eyes.

'Come in, come in,' Hurghad said loudly, then turned away. 'Seetrecka, this is Sayer.'

For a moment Sayer was filled with panic. Was someone there? Was that the reason for Hurghad's performance? But, if so, why had he let him in? He walked slowly into the room, but could see no one else there – and the outer door was firmly shut.

'There's no reason to be coy, Seetrecka. Come and meet our guest.'

Sayer was about to speak when movement under the bed caught his eye. Two green eyes stared up at him, framed by long whiskers and pointed ears. The kyar emerged slowly, still regarding the newcomer with suspicion. It was a small animal, with the soft fur of an adolescent male. Once out in the open it seemed to relax, and sat on its haunches, curled its long tail around its paws and mewed once.

'That's right,' Hurghad responded. 'He's a friend. A seeker, a very important person.'

'Hurghad, I need to talk to you. Are you all right?'

'Perfectly. Tell him, Seetrecka.'

'Stop it,' Sayer exclaimed, as his unease turned to genuine alarm.

'Stop what?' The hermit looked puzzled.

'There's no need to put on an act with me. Kyars can't talk.'

'This one can,' Hurghad replied, with a sly glance. 'Of course, it's not the cat speaking, but the soul of the man he used to be. He was a prophet, and he's told me so many—'

'You're not serious?' Sayer cut in.

'Ah, but I am. He's told me secrets. How else would I know who you are?'

'What are you talking about? Of course you know me. I've been here many times before.'

'No,' the hermit said, shaking his head. 'I don't think so.'

'But you said I was a friend.'

Hurghad looked confused for a few moments, then smiled brightly.

'Would you like to see something I wrote?' He had evidently dismissed the problem of the seeker's identity.

'Yes,' Sayer replied doubtfully.

The old man picked up a sheet of paper from his desk and held it up in front of his visitor's face. Although it was covered in writing, none of the words made any sense. It was complete gibberish.

'Seetrecka told me that story,' the hermit stated proudly. 'Good, isn't it?' He snatched the paper away again, as if he were afraid that Sayer would steal it.

'But what about your epic poem? *A True History of Tirok?*'

'Burnt. All gone. Up in smoke.' Hurghad laughed and the kyar yowled softly.

Sayer leant down and lifted the corner of the mattress. Underneath, still in neat stacks, were the reams of paper that contained the hermit's poem, but he knew there was no point saying anything to Hurghad now. Something had happened since he had last seen the old man – something terrible.

The kyar mewed again, and Hurghad chuckled.

'Where are my manners? It's taken a cat to remind me of the laws of hospitality. Seetrecka asks if you would like a drink.'

'No, thank you.'

'This mead is really very good.'

Sayer shook his head. The liquid he had been offered was clear, and was almost certainly water. Even if the evidence of Hurghad's words had not been enough, the seeker had now seen other clues to his host's fate. There was a faint bluish tinge to his lips, and there were black rings around his irises. Sayer had observed the same symptoms in those day-dreamers who had received too many doses of the poisonous tincture. Hurghad had been a daydreamer once so the toxin had not killed him, but whether he had taken it voluntarily or under duress, the end result was not in doubt. This was no act.

Had it been some kind of punishment? Had Halion learned of the hermit's involvement with Sayer and decided to arrange another 'warning'? Perhaps the archivect had simply been ensuring that Hurghad's performances were authentic. Whatever the reason, Sayer had lost his last friend, his last hope of someone to talk to. After years of pre-tending, Hurghad was now quite insane.

* * *

The next day, Sayer was feeling enormously depressed. The repercussions of his latest mission were rumbling on and promised to do so for some time to come, even though the stone-binders had reported unexpectedly good progress. He was worried by the fact that he had received no summons from Halion. Was the archivect simply biding his time? Kailas was still very upset, in spite of the fact that — given the lack of any evidence to the contrary – she had been officially absolved of any responsibility for the mishap. After days of silence, she now wanted to examine what had gone wrong in minute detail, while Sayer was equally determined not to talk about it any more than necessary. It was only Kailas's continuing tiredness that prevented their conversations escalating into full-blown rows. And none of Sayer's other colleagues even spoke to him, as if they were trying to disassociate themselves from the whole sorry affair.

Late in the afternoon he was sitting alone in his kitchen, half-way through his second bottle of wine, when there was a knock at the front door. His spirits were at such a low ebb that he considered just ignoring the visitor and hoping they would go away, but the businesslike rapping was repeated. Moving a little unsteadily, Sayer went to answer it. He had expected some soldiers or officials with more pointless questions, but he was wrong. The sight of the face that greeted him jolted him back to some level of alertness.

'Safi wasn't able to come today,' Galieva said. 'I'm her replacement.'

When he did not react, she raised her eyebrows in query. 'May I come in?'

Sayer stood aside and she entered, walking without hesitation towards the kitchen. He followed more slowly and arrived to find her glancing round at the wine bottles and the general mess. In that moment he realized that the kyars were not going to let him go; they could be just as ruthless and persistent as any archivect. They might claim to be his friends, but they just wanted to use him, like everyone else.

'I'll make you something to eat as soon as I've tidied up a bit,' she informed him.

'I'm not hungry,' he said with a trace of drunken petulance.

'You need to eat,' she replied, 'especially if you're going to drink so much.'

'Mind your own business,' he snapped rudely.

'It *is* my business. Can we talk while I work? Where's Kailas?'

'Asleep.'

'Are you sure?'

'Yes. Do you want to go and check? And anyway, why should I want to talk to you?'

'Because we can help each other.'

'How?'

'You already know that a person of your standing could be very useful to us.'

Sayer laughed.

'My standing's getting lower by the day.'

'I heard about that. Was it your doing?'

'Yes.'

'I guessed as much. It was a sign of your frustration, your pent-up anger. We could help you direct that anger to a more worthwhile purpose.'

'Really?' he said sarcastically. 'How?'

'I can't give you specific details now, but if you'll agree to another meeting—'

'And what do I get out of this?' he demanded. The wine was blurring his thoughts, making him prey to any number of conflicting emotions.

'Two things,' Galieva replied. 'Revenge, and—'

'Revenge for what?' he asked, interrupting again.

'For the harm done to your sister – and you – by our revered master.'

'I only have your word for it that Aphra's exile was Halion's doing.'

'The Isle of the Dead is a prison as well as a plague colony. That's common knowledge, and you'd be aware of it if you hadn't buried your head in the sand.' She sounded angry now. 'Usually the threat of sending someone there – or some of their loved ones – is enough to keep them in line, but occasionally it's more than a threat. Halion exiled Aphra because he found out she was one of us, and *you* were too valuable to risk. But that's not the worst of his crimes and you know it.'

'What could be worse than that?'

Galieva stopped what she was doing and regarded him steadily.

'You really don't know? Aphra never told you?'

'Told me what?'

'Halion raped her when she was twelve.'

The words were spoken evenly, in a matter-of-fact tone, but for a few moments Sayer could make no sense of them. When he did, his first reaction was one of disbelief. How could this possibly have happened while he remained oblivious? Then he remembered that at that age the twins had often been apart for days at a time while their training was in full swing. Aphra had often been miserable, and reluctant to talk about what she had been doing – and he had looked no further than the obvious.

'How do you know this?' he asked fiercely.

'Aphra was my friend. She kept few secrets from me.'

'Secrets that she kept from her own brother?'

'What could you have done? You were both helpless. The whole affair was swept under the carpet, of course, but it was not the first time such a thing had happened. Halion still has quite a reputation among us serving girls.'

Sayer found that he believed her, and the implications made his head reel. Had he ever known *anything* about his sister?

'Did he . . . touch you?'

'I was already a bit too old for his tastes when I went to the estate,' Galieva replied grimly. 'If he tried it with me, I hope I'd have the courage to slit his filthy throat.'

'You'd kill a Tirokian?' Sayer exclaimed, shocked in spite of all he had heard.

'Some people deserve to die,' she answered calmly. 'Maybe some *will* die before we're finished – and Halion would be at the top of my list.'

Rage was replacing horrified astonishment in Sayer's mind.

'Is this true?' he whispered.

'I swear it.'

'If you're lying to me I'll kill *you*.'

'I'm not lying. I can tell you a great deal about Aphra. Do you want to test me?'

Sayer shook his head, thinking that Galieva probably did know more than he did. Testing her would prove nothing.

'Why did she tell you and not me?'

'Because I'm a woman. And a kyar. Most of those who join us have good reasons to dislike the present regime. Your sister's reasons were better than most.'

'But why not tell *me*?'

'Probably because she was too afraid at first, then she knew there'd be no point. Later, when she joined us, we would have told her not to.'

'Why?'

'We knew you had great talent and would rise high. Someone like that would be very valuable at the right time.'

'And that time's come?'

'Yes. Or it will do soon, if you join us.'

They were silent for a while, and Galieva went back to stacking dishes. Sayer watched her, wondering how she could remain so calm and controlled while his own thoughts raced and his hands shook.

'I . . . would like . . . revenge,' he said eventually.

Galieva turned to look at him again. The smile on her face held a hint of triumph, but there was also some genuine pleasure.

'There's another good reason for you to join us,' she said.

'What?'

'We've found a way to communicate with the people on the Isle of the Dead.'

Sayer stared at her in astonishment.

'How?'

'I can't tell you yet. You'll have to come to a meeting to find out. All I can say is that it's slow and limited, but if it works we might soon be able to get word of Aphra. There might even be a message *from* her.'

Just when he had thought that nothing could surprise him any more, Sayer found himself taken aback again. It was almost four months since Aphra had been taken, and he realized that he had begun to think of her in the past tense.

'If she's still alive,' he said quietly.

'I'd bet on it. Aphra's a fighter. And she's not the only kyar on the island, so she'll have had help. Being able to talk to the prisoners is just the first step.'

'To what?'

'We plan to rescue everyone on the Isle of the Dead and bring them home,' Galieva said.

CHAPTER TWENTY-TWO

'May you live in interesting times.'

Ancient Khorasian curse

'. . . the crow guards the gates of heaven. The jackdaw is the court jester, the skylark brings the music, and the serin leads the dance.'

From *The Oracles of Zavanaiu*

As Sayer arrived home he was tempted to turn and wave to the soldiers who had been following him. They did not even bother to disguise their purpose now, not caring that he must notice them. The seeker's recent failure was common knowledge and, coming on top of his possible involvement in Tump's death, it meant that the military authorities regarded him with suspicion. Sayer knew that it was only Halion's influence that kept him from being harassed even more. The archivect himself had made that very plain during their meeting that afternoon, a meeting that Sayer had found almost unbearable. Coming face to face with his sister's rapist was never going to be easy, but because the confrontation was inevitable he had steeled himself to be suitably contrite, and waited for it to end. He could still hear Halion's parting words.

'Only I can protect you, Sayer. Remember that. But you must be careful. If you do anything too stupid, even your talent will not be worth the trouble that protecting you entails.'

Under the circumstances, Sayer decided not to do anything that might provoke the wrath of the guards, and walked straight up to his front door. To his surprise it was locked, and he had to fumble in his belt pouch for his key.

'Kailas? Safi?' he called once he was inside, but there was no response.

He was about to go up to his bedroom to change when a stranger appeared in the kitchen doorway. Sayer froze in alarm, wondering how best to defend himself, but the man appeared to be unarmed and came no closer.

'Be calm,' he said, spreading his hands wide.

'Who are you? What are you doing here?'

'Would you prefer it if I wore a mask?'

The voice was suddenly familiar. Galieva had said that one of the kyars would contact him about a meeting, but that had been three days ago. Nothing had happened since then, and Sayer had begun to wonder if anything ever would. Trying to act normally while he waited had been difficult, especially because he knew he was being watched more closely than ever. Now, it seemed, the waiting was over.

'How did you get in here? The door was locked.'

'There are more ways of getting into a house than through the front door,' the man replied. 'It's important we keep our contact a secret for as long as possible. With the scouts constantly on your tail, a midnight jaunt to the Temple would be most unwise, so your home seemed the safest place.'

'What about my wife? She'd normally be back by now.'

'Kailas has been delayed – her overseers want to go over some matter of technique with her again. She won't be free for at least an hour.'

'How do you know—' Sayer began, then stopped. Either he trusted the kyars' spokesman or he did not. 'And Safi?' he asked.

'She is more concerned with a budding love affair at the moment,' his visitor replied with a smile. 'Galieva volunteered to come in her place, but she's been and gone. You'll have to make your own supper tonight.'

Sayer did not feel like eating.

'So we have time to talk,' the kyar concluded.

Belatedly, Sayer glanced around, checking that the shutters that faced the street were closed, then waved his unexpected guest to a chair.

'You've trusted me with your face,' he said. 'Will you tell me your name as well?'

'Call me Serin. My trust is necessary, Sayer. Galieva believes you're ready to lend your weight to our cause, and I respect her judgement. Some risk is unavoidable in such matters. If you betray me, others will carry on – and the kyars can make unpleasant enemies. We *all* know who you are.'

Sayer found to his surprise that he was not angered by the threat. There had been so many astonishing twists in his life recently that he had no idea when the turning point had come, but he was committed now. The kyars offered him his only chance for some sort of personal redemption, a way of making up for all the time and talent he had wasted until now. They offered him the opportunity of playing a part in Tirok's new future – and the chance of seeing Aphra again. With them it was possible that he would be able to do something after all. Therefore he had to believe everything they told him, as a matter of faith, and push his doubts to one side. If he were to be of any use, he had to be as strong as they were. Until now the kyars' resolution – and that of their enemies – had far outstripped Sayer's own, but that was about to change.

'I won't betray you,' he stated firmly.

'I wouldn't be here if I thought you would.'

'Galieva said you've found a way of communicating with the Isle of the Dead.'

Serin nodded.

'One of our number has a remarkable gift, almost amounting to talent. He has an affinity with all living creatures, but especially with birds. Some months ago he found three orphaned fledglings, hooded crows, and reared them himself. Now they're grown they remain loyal to him, and the understanding between them is almost telepathic.'

'These crows carry messages?' Sayer guessed. It made sense. If you could not travel *on* the water, then you had to go over it. 'But how did he get them to go to the Isle of the Dead?'

'Graovac had to take them there,' Serin answered simply.

'But—' Sayer was aghast. 'You can't mean . . . He *volunteered* for exile?'

'Yes.'

The seeker was speechless, and for a moment his determination faltered. How could he possibly match such extraordinary self-sacrifice? It was the most convincing proof yet of the kyars' deadly serious attitude to their self-appointed task.

'Faking the symptoms of the plague is easy,' Serin went on. 'If someone is more or less willing to go, no one's going to argue. It happens more often than you'd think. The crows simply flew alongside the boat.'

'But won't they just stay on the island if Graovac is stranded there?'

'No. Even though he's always given them their freedom, he trained them to return to his home every so often. His son fed them too, so the theory was that they'd go back again if Graovac told them to.'

'And they have?'

'Only one so far, but that's just what was planned. The others are being held in reserve for when more important information has been gathered.'

'Is there any word from Aphra?' Sayer asked eagerly.

'No, not yet. We asked for news of her, so we should hear something soon.'

'When?' Sayer asked, not even trying to hide his bitter disappointment.

'There's no way of telling. I know it's hard to wait, but if we are ever to effect a rescue of any sort, there's much vital information we need that's more crucial than news of any one person.'

'So what *did* you learn?'

'The most important thing was to confirm that Graovac and the birds had arrived safely, and that the system works. The rest of his message was a brief report on the conditions on the island, and most of the news is good. Many of the people who were not stricken before they went remain healthy, and the community there has become quite organized. But the most exciting news is that they've found the plague is not always fatal.'

'You're sure?' Sayer exclaimed in disbelief.

'Absolutely. They've obviously been trying to help the victims as best they could, looking for ways to ease the pain and stop the infection spreading, and they saw that in a few cases they simply got better.'

'That's incredible!'

'I know. No one on the mainland had ever recovered, so it must be something special to the island. Talent is part of it, they think, but—'

'Talent? You mean healing by magic?' Sayer asked, thinking of Mehran-Dar.

'Yes, but that's not all of it. They're working in the dark, picking up techniques as they go along, so it's hit and miss so far. According to the report there may be some herbs involved, an antidote to whatever causes the illness.'

'Then if we could cultivate it here . . .'

'Don't get too carried away,' Serin warned. 'They don't know which herbs are effective yet, and complete recovery is still very rare. The vast majority of the victims are dying eventually, but this *is* a start. You see now why we need to know more? Apart from anything else, this would be a tremendously powerful weapon if it ever comes to outright confrontation with the Council. They've never even tried to find a cure. If we can provide one, or even the hope of one . . .' He let the implication hang in the air.

That hint of cold political reasoning was convincing. It had occurred to a small faithless part of Sayer's mind that this could just be another lie, to help recruit him to the kyars' cause through a – false – hope for Aphra's safety. But he was in no doubt now that they really would be searching for a cure.

'If we can prove the plague can be cured, it would also show that we don't have to rely on the gods,' he said. 'We can solve our own problems.'

'Exactly,' Serin agreed, smiling. 'The resources of manpower and talent that are currently being wasted on the rebuilding of the Temple could be used for something else – something that would actually change the lives of thousands for the better.'

'I could be a healer,' Sayer whispered to himself.

'We've a long road to travel yet,' the kyar said, 'but I believe you could.'

The two men regarded each other steadily, each seeing the passion reflected in the other's eyes.

'We live in interesting times,' Serin remarked eventually.

After another pause, Sayer realized that the room had grown dark and went to light a lamp.

'It's a long way from getting messages from a few crows to being able to get everyone off the island,' he observed soberly.

'It is,' his visitor agreed, 'but the first step has always been the need to establish communications. We've tried other methods – lights, smoke, and so on – but it was too far away, too unreliable, and the codes were too restrictive for any sensible dialogue. We've always known we could get a message *to* the island, but there was no point until now because there was no way of getting a reply. Besides, no one was keen to be a messenger when they knew they'd never return. That's why the birds are so important. We already know the other two will return to Qara and bring back a great deal, but if we're lucky we may be able to get them to go to the island again without having to sacrifice anyone else. Graovac was sure that's what would happen, otherwise we wouldn't have let him go.'

'He can call them telepathically from such a distance?'

'That's the idea. We don't yet know if it works in practice.'

'What do they carry?'

'Graovac took a small supply of paper with him. They'll use that first. After that they'll have to improvise.'

'You will let me know if . . . if . . .'

'If there's any word of Aphra? Of course. Your situation is not unique. We all know how you feel.'

Sayer rather doubted that, but was not inclined to argue the point.

'I know why *I'm* so keen to see them rescued,' he said. 'Why is it so important to you?'

'Aphra is far from being the only kyar on the island,' Serin replied. 'Some of them are no doubt dead by now, but we owe it to them all to try, to help those we can, and to make the sacrifice of the others worthwhile. We need all the good men and women we can get. But beyond that, it would be symbolic of our whole struggle. What represents the archivects' tyranny more clearly? Their laws set up the plague colony, they turned it into a prison for their political enemies, and their soldiers guard it. So if we can demonstrate that even the Isle of the Dead is not invincible, then the people will start to believe that anything is possible. We must have popular support, or we've no chance at all. The only thing that can beat the Council and their military forces is weight of numbers – and a just cause. We could have both on our side. The people who return from the island will help us, but the effect on the morale of everyone else would be even more important.'

'I can see the sense of that,' Sayer conceded, 'but surely it's impossible. Getting a few people off, maybe. But everybody? There must be hundreds there now.'

'It has to be all or nothing,' the kyar replied. 'Who are we to choose who lives and dies? If we did that, we'd be no better than Halion and his cronies.'

'But what about the monsters? How can you possibly get past them?'

Serin shrugged.

'Either we have to train our own shriekers – and to date there haven't been too many volunteers – or we have to obtain some of theirs. We're already working on that, even though they're heavily guarded. Alternatively, we need to devise a new method altogether. Magic, in one form or another, seems the best bet, which is why people with talent – any talent – are so important now.'

'So what do you want me to do?'

'We obviously have to be patient about the Isle of the Dead, so in the meantime there's something else I'd like you to try.'

Serin went on to outline a proposal that sounded stupid at first, but the longer he talked the more sense it seemed to make.

'You think you can do that?' he asked.

'I don't see why not.'

'It's risky,' Serin admitted, 'but it's plausible, and could be very interesting. And the knock-on effects in the military might work to our advantage.'

'I'll do what I can.'

'Be careful.'

'But not too careful?'

'Exactly. Your wife'll be back soon. I should go.'

They stood up.

'Which way will you go?' Sayer asked curiously.

'From upstairs.'

'There's no way . . .' the seeker began, then fell silent.

'Perhaps I can fly,' Serin remarked, smiling. 'You stay down here to greet Kailas.'

As the kyar reached the bottom of the stairs he paused and turned back.

'It's obvious that Halion knew of Aphra's arrest in advance,' he said. 'Do you think *Kailas* knew what was going to happen?'

'I don't know, but I don't think so.' Sayer had often wondered the same thing himself.

'Yours is not an easy situation, Sayer. Only you can decide who you can trust.'

'I'll remember that.'

'Discretion is a valuable characteristic.'

'You've made your point,' Sayer replied irritably.

'Forgive me. Let's think of the positive aspects of what we've discussed.'

Sayer nodded.

'The carving that I partially destroyed was a crow,' he said. 'I know now what it was carrying in its claws.'

'What?'

'Hope.'

'I trust ours will not be crushed so easily,' Serin replied, then ran up the stairs.

CHAPTER TWENTY-THREE

'Each member of the Council agrees to promote harmony and cooperation between all their families and households, both now and in the future, until the great task is completed.'

From The Decree

As Sayer joined the good-humoured throng converging on the mansion of Archivect Seigui, he felt a mixture of fear and excitement. This would be his first rebellious act to have any meaning. After today there could be no turning back.

His plan had taken several days to set up and, ironically, it had been at the long-delayed rededication of the crow stone that he had finally got his opportunity. That had been a comparatively quiet affair – because of the rumours that had surrounded the damaged relic's retrieval – with none of the pomp that had accompanied the Eye of Clouds. The stone-binders had done a remarkable job, and the repairs to the boss were only noticeable at close quarters. Once it was back in place in the roof of the Raven Dome, no one but a seeker would be able to tell that part of it was not the original carving. Despite the lack of ostentation, however, the necessary rituals were all still observed, and several archivects had been present.

At the same ceremony a second, less important relic had also been rededicated. This had been found by Mayumi, a seeker whose master was Seigui. Afterwards, the two seekers walked together in the procession from the dome, and fell into conversation.

'The stone-binders did fine work,' Mayumi remarked. 'Even the resonance was not too distorted.'

'I can't complain about that,' Sayer replied. He thought he detected an undercurrent of spite in his fellow talent's words. They were colleagues in one sense, but rivals in another.

'A little bird tells me you have other things to complain about, though,' Mayumi said.

'Well, you know what they say about bird-brains,' Sayer replied. 'I'm surprised you listen to them.'

'Your discontent is well known.'

'That's rubbish.' He tried to appear angry, but was secretly delighted that his hints had been interpreted as he had intended.

'Have you ever wondered whether employment might be more congenial elsewhere?'

'Keep your voice down,' Sayer hissed, glancing ahead to the archivects.

'They're too wrapped up in themselves to listen to us,' Mayumi responded casually. 'Seigui is having a celebration in my honour this evening. Why don't you come?'

'What for?'

'Don't play dumb with me!' Mayumi snapped. 'You may be an arrogant son of a bitch, but you're not stupid.'

The procession had ended by then and, now that the ritual was over, the participants were all milling around in the section of the Penitents' Way between the dome and the Oracle's Tomb. Sayer could see Halion and Seigui chatting together, laughing as if they were the best of friends.

Moments later, before he had had a chance to respond to Mayumi's invitation, Seigui left his fellow archivects and strode over to the two seekers.

'Congratulations, Sayer. Everything turned out well in the end.'

'Thank you, my lord. Each of us tries to serve the gods to the best of his abilities.'

'Quite so. I trust Mayumi here has told you of my little gathering tonight.'

'He has, my lord.'

'Good. I would consider it an honour if you – and your wife, of course – could join us. Or do you have plans of your own?'

Sayer shook his head.

'A celebration in my honour would hardly be appropriate on this occasion,' he said dourly.

'You are too harsh, I'm sure,' the archivect replied. 'In any case, why not come to my estate? That is, if you're not too proud to honour another seeker who may one day equal your accomplishments.'

'Mayumi has already done so,' Sayer claimed. 'Each relic is of equal importance to the gods.'

Seigui laughed, but his seeker's expression was unreadable.

'Your pious sensibilities do you credit,' the archivect commented. 'Will you come?'

'Of course,' Sayer replied, bowing. 'Thank you.'

Later that afternoon he had told Kailas of the invitation.

'Are you sure we should go?' she asked. 'Does Halion know?'

'I expect he'll be there too. Why shouldn't we go? We deserve to enjoy ourselves after the last few days.'

They had been out on one further mission, an almost menial task that would not normally have been assigned to such a high-powered team. They had all known that they were being tested, but although everything had gone smoothly, their general mood had remained uncertain. This had been made worse for Sayer by the fact that he had heard nothing more from either Serin or Galieva. It had been six days since the last meeting, and the second crow must surely have returned by now. It had occurred to him that the kyars might be waiting for him to show his good faith by acting on Serin's suggestion, and this had made him all the more determined to attend the party.

'All right. We'll go,' Kailas said, though she still sounded doubtful.

Now, as she walked beside him, there was a little more enthusiasm in her face, and when they were swept up by the festivities – the food, wine, music and general gaiety – Sayer could not help thinking that this was the world his wife had been born to. In the four months since their marriage her life had been quite different, confined for the most part to the company of one man, and with no social life to speak of. He felt a pang of regret that she had given up a good deal for him – and he had not reciprocated. Kailas deserved to enjoy herself on occasions like this at least.

However, such thoughts were driven from his mind later, when Mayumi appeared at his shoulder, an empty goblet in his hand. Most of the guests were watching a fireworks display, and took little notice of the two seekers.

'Come with me for a drink.' Mayumi's eyes were slightly glazed, and it was obvious that he had already had several.

As the true reason for his presence there returned to Sayer with renewed force, he followed the other seeker to one of the serving tables and accepted some wine. From there, the two men slipped into the shadows of the house and went inside, climbing a spiral staircase to a small circular terrace where Seigui was waiting. The archivect was looking out at the gathering below, and the whole scene was intermittently illuminated by brightly coloured explosions.

'Welcome, Sayer. Thank you, Mayumi. I'm sure the guest of honour should not leave his guests for too long, so I won't detain you.'

Mayumi went with as much grace as he could muster.

'I'm not a man to mince words,' Seigui stated when he and Sayer were alone, 'so I'll come right to the point. I know you're unhappy with the way Halion's treating you, and I can't say I blame you. He's an arrogant bastard at the best of times, and he deserves to be brought down a peg or two. I want you to transfer your allegiance to me. I'll make it worth your while.'

Sayer waited a long time before replying, to give the impression that Seigui's outburst had come as a total surprise.

'How?' he enquired at last.

'Money, possessions, a new home, servants. Anything you want, really, but most of all, respect. Halion doesn't appreciate your worth. I do.'

'Halion is still a powerful man. Could you guarantee my peace of mind if I made an enemy of him?'

'I'm not without power of my own. In any case, if your decision is made of your own free will and announced publicly in front of the Council, he would not dare move against you.'

Although Sayer found this argument less than convincing, he pretended to consider it carefully.

'And Kailas?' he asked eventually.

'Naturally she would also come under my protection. I know she's related to Halion, but that shouldn't be allowed to stand in the way of what's right.'

'I'm not sure I know what that is any more,' Sayer confessed.

'You're confused. That's natural. Let me help you.'

The last of the fireworks had died away now, and most of the party had moved inside. It was dark on the terrace, but Sayer knew that some of the flashes of light would have illuminated them both. He wondered if anyone had been watching.

'Archivect Becerra has already made me a similar offer,' he said. This was a lie, but even if he were caught out, Seigui would assume it was just a bargaining tactic. If he wasn't, it might divide the Council in more ways than one.

'Becerra knows as well as I do that Halion's domination of the Council must be ended. His family is almost as wealthy as mine, but my troops are more numerous, better equipped and better trained. That's something you would be foolish to ignore.'

Once more, Sayer waited for as long as he dared before speaking again.

'May I have a little time to consider your offer?'

'Of course. But don't take too long. I'm a patient man, but events sometimes move quickly whether we like it or not.'

That, Sayer thought as he descended the steps again, is certainly true. On the other hand, some things did not move fast enough. He had found it frustrating not being able to get in touch with the kyars, and having to wait for them to contact him. Perhaps now that he had begun his own machinations he would be rewarded with the news he longed for.

'Where have you been?' Kailas asked when he rejoined the party. 'I've been looking for you.'

'Here and there. Mayumi wanted me to have a drink with him.'

'He's very drunk,' she told him. 'And he's been talking about you. I think he's jealous.'

'I have you,' Sayer replied, smiling. 'Any man would be jealous.'

'That's not what I meant,' Kailas said, although he could

tell she was pleased by the compliment. 'He envies your talent.'

'We're all working towards the same goal.'

'You wouldn't think so sometimes,' she remarked. 'The archivects are always trying to outdo each other.'

Sayer was tempted to tell her everything then, drawn by the hope that her good sense would overcome her inbuilt prejudices, but he held his tongue. There would be time enough for that before too long. He had no doubt that word of his meeting with Seigui would soon reach Halion's ears. Mayumi's efforts would see to that. He was gambling on the belief that Halion would not want to lose his seeker, in spite of his recent failings.

'Have you had enough of this?' he asked.

'Yes.'

'Then let's go home.'

They made love that night with an intensity that left both of them almost delirious, and then fell asleep in each other's arms. However, they were not permitted to rest undisturbed. A sudden violent hammering on the door below woke them both with a start and left Kailas trembling. As Sayer hurried down the stairs, pulling a robe about him, he heard the lock splinter and the door crash inwards. By the time he reached ground level Halion was waiting for him, legs planted, arms folded, with thunder in his black eyes. The archivect's reaction had come even sooner than expected.

'Rumour has it that you're thinking of betraying me.' His voice was deceptively quiet and calm.

'My lord?'

'Please don't insult me by lying, Sayer. I know you met with Seigui this evening.'

'That's true. He invited me—'

'And what did he invite you to do? Switch your allegiance to his house?'

'Yes, my lord, but—'

'You admit it?' Halion's voice rose dangerously.

'Yes, but I had no thought of accepting his offer. I swear.'

'You refused him?'

'Not at the time. I am no match for any archivect in a battle of words. I gave him no answer. All I wanted was to escape.'

'Why didn't you come straight to me and tell me of this outrage?'

'Because I had no wish to promote ill feeling among members of the Council.'

'Oh, there is ill feeling already,' Halion growled. 'I can deal with that easily enough. What I can't stomach is your treachery.'

'There was no treachery,' Sayer insisted. 'The meeting was at Seigui's instigation, not mine. I had no idea what he wanted. How could I refuse the summons of so eminent a host?'

Halion paused, apparently considering this argument.

'You're stepping very close to the line, Seeker,' he said, although he seemed to be calming down a little. 'Be sure you don't step over it. If I find you've been lying to me, you'll be envying your sister her fate.'

The reference to Aphra almost broke Sayer's hard won composure, and he felt bitter hatred well up inside him. But he held himself in check.

'I meant no offence,' he said meekly. 'I am your loyal servant.'

Halion fixed him with a long, intimidating stare, until Sayer began to wonder if his master could somehow read his thoughts. When the archivect finally spoke again, his voice was controlled once more, carrying with it a chill of menace, but Sayer knew that the first crisis was over.

'Remember what I am, Sayer. Whatever you were offered,

I can take away again. I gave you all this.' He waved his hands at the house around them. 'I can take it all away too – and that includes your wife. Don't give me any more reasons to doubt you.'

With that he turned on his heel and strode out of the open door. Sayer heard him yelling orders to the soldiers who had been waiting outside, and took a deep breath, trying to ease the tension that had filled him since Halion's noisy arrival. A small sound behind him made him turn and look up. Kailas was sitting on one of the upper steps, huddled up with her arms around her knees. Her face was deathly pale and she was shivering. When he climbed up to sit beside her and put his arm around her shoulders, she did not exactly flinch, but sat rigid and did not respond. Her skin was very cold.

'What have you been doing?' she whispered.

'Nothing. It's all been a mistake.'

'We should never have gone to the celebration.'

'It was Seigui's idea, not mine. I didn't know what he wanted.'

'Didn't you guess?' she asked. 'Mayumi was dropping enough hints.'

'It did cross my mind,' he admitted, 'but I had no intention of working for Seigui. It was flattering in a way, though.'

'Flattering? You're mad! Don't you see how dangerous it was?'

'How was I supposed to know? Should I have refused to even talk to him?'

'You could have made some excuse,' she replied stubbornly. 'Are you sure you didn't encourage him somehow?'

'Of course not. Forget it. It's over now.'

'I hope so,' she said tearfully. 'Why do you keep doing this to us, Sayer? We have a good life. And I . . . I don't want to lose you. I love you too much.'

Once again he was tempted to tell her everything, hoping that her love would be enough to allow her to join him on the path he had chosen, but he could not. There was too much at stake. Instead, he simply held her closer.

'I love you too,' he said and, for the first time, he felt as if he actually meant it.

CHAPTER TWENTY-FOUR

'History is written into the fabric of all things. We need only learn to read.'

From the writings of the philosopher Nimruz

The following day, neither Sayer or Kailas had any need – or desire – to go anywhere. They wanted only to remain quietly at home, in each other's company, but their peace was to be disturbed by a succession of visitors. First to arrive were some artisans who set about repairing the shattered lock. A pair of guards had been on duty outside overnight and Sayer noted, without any great surprise, that they stayed where they were even after the door had been refitted.

Next came Kebir. The scribe had clearly been troubled by recent events, and had overcome his natural reticence to talk to his young protégé. Sayer had no way of telling whether the visit had been Kebir's own idea or prompted by Halion, but he endured the fatherly lecture on the responsibilities of talent as best he could. He knew that Kebir would always remain dedicated to the rebuilding of the Temple. It had been his whole life. There was no point even trying to convert him to another way of thinking, so Sayer just agreed with everything the other man said, saddened by the realization that there was little hope that they would remain friends.

Less than an hour after the scribe left, muttering about having to complete some research, another even more unexpected caller knocked at the door. Although he seemed vaguely familiar to Sayer, he could not put a name to the face. The mystery was solved when Kailas, coming to see who it was, exclaimed aloud.

'Zanu! What are you doing here?'

'Father sent me to see whether my little sister was ready to produce his first grandchild yet,' the man replied, laughing. 'But you look much too thin. I trust you *have* been trying?'

'That,' Kailas replied tartly, 'is none of your business.' She hugged the newcomer. 'Sayer, you remember my brother, don't you? He has no manners, but he's not a bad sort really.'

'That's not what you used to say,' Zanu remarked. Turning to Sayer, he added, 'She used to call us all sorts of unpleasant names.'

'That's hardly surprising,' she protested happily. 'What chance did I have against you three hulking brutes?'

'Ah, but you had talent. The first in our family. Father's very proud of that.'

'He'd never have noticed me otherwise.'

'Now don't be bitter,' her brother chided. 'Do you have anything to drink? I'm parched.'

'I'll get you something,' Sayer volunteered.

He went to the kitchen, leaving the two of them to talk. He remembered meeting Zanu at the wedding, but he had had little chance to get to know him. On first impressions he seemed very much a junior version of his father, with the same self-confidence and faintly condescending air. Sayer knew that – whatever his own achievements or celebrity as a seeker – such men would always regard him as one of the servants. What was more, Zanu was a reminder of the privileged life Kailas had once enjoyed. In his presence she became more like one of them and less like the woman he had begun to love. He couldn't imagine Zanu having any sympathy with the kyars' point of view, and so they seemed destined to be enemies. As a result, Sayer played little part in the ensuing conversation, which centred on family news and the real reason for Zanu's being in Qara – which was to oversee the delivery of a shipment of rare herbs to another trader. This turned Sayer's thoughts to the possible healing properties of plants on the Isle of the Dead, and he hardly noticed when Kailas asked him a question.

'I'm sorry. What did you say?'

'Typical magician,' Zanu commented, grinning. 'Always leagues away.'

'I said, is it all right for Zanu to stay with us?' Kailas repeated.

'I . . . Of course.' Sayer had been caught off guard and seeing this, Zanu laughed again.

'It's all right, Sayer,' he said. 'I've no intention of impos-ing upon you. I've lodgings arranged which will allow me more comfort than your spare room. Besides, Father would want you to have your privacy.'

'You're a beast,' Kailas complained. 'At least come and have dinner with us one night.'

'Agreed. I'll be here for quite a while. Qara has a lot more to offer than Kohlu, I can tell you. I'll let you know.'

He took his leave soon after that, and Kailas was unable to hide her disappointment.

'My brothers made my life miserable when I was at home. Now I miss them. Silly, isn't it?'

'No,' Sayer replied heavily. 'I know how you feel.'

'Oh! I'm sorry, my love. I didn't think. I'm sorry.' She put her arms around him.

'It's all right,' he said. 'It doesn't matter.'

* * *

Their next visitors were the security officers who had interviewed Sayer after Tump's death. Captain Akander explained that it was just a courtesy call, to tell him that the cause of death had been officially recorded as accidental.

'So you're off the hook,' Lieutenant Maier added, his disapproval obvious.

'No witnesses came forward and the physical examination revealed nothing,' Akander went on, ignoring his colleague's remark. 'So there was no other choice. There was some concern over the circumstances of his fall, but there was nothing anyone could do about that. The case is closed.'

Sayer said nothing. It had been almost a month since Tump had died, and he doubted that the investigation had gone on that long, no matter how thorough it had been.

As the soldiers were leaving, a rather flustered official from the Treasury arrived, with the news that Sayer and Kailas were to leave the next morning to retrieve a large stone that had been located somewhere to the south.

'That's all the detail you have?' Sayer asked.

'For the moment, yes. It's all rather a rush, I'm afraid, but Archivect Halion is insisting you go immediately. We'll do what we can overnight – there are two daydreamers at work now – so we may have better information tomorrow.'

After he had gone, Sayer and Kailas exchanged glances.

'This is ridiculous,' she said disgustedly.

'Halion is obviously making sure I'm removed from all temptation,' Sayer replied. He was annoyed not only by the archivect's transparent motive, but also by the fact that this wild-goose chase would delay even further the chance of him receiving any news from Serin. Kailas had her own reasons for being disappointed.

'I'd better go and leave a message for Zanu at his lodgings,' she said. 'He'll probably have to go home before we get back.'

Sayer knew that he ought to go to the Hariolatorium to follow the daydreamers' progress but, once he was alone, could not summon up the necessary energy to leave the house. Instead, he took out the book Mehran-Dar had given him and began to read one of the stories. It concerned a great sea of salt and the city buried in its dry, crystalline depths, and Sayer became so engrossed that he jumped when there was yet another knock at the door. When he opened it he found Galieva outside, carrying a basket piled high with fresh fruit and vegetables, and engaged in a relaxed and jovial conversation with the two sentries.

'I'll bet they're not as fresh as you are,' one of the guards said.

'Mind your tongue,' Galieva told him, 'and I might see if there are any leftovers.'

'Scraps are all we ever get,' the soldier grumbled, but his grin made it clear that he was not serious.

'Liar. Soldiers eat better than most.' She turned towards the door. 'Hello, Sayer. See you later, boys.'

She came inside, and Sayer closed the door and followed her into the kitchen.

'Is there any news?'

'Yes,' she replied with a smile. 'Aphra's alive.'

'Thank the gods!' Sayer burst out.

'And as far as we know, she doesn't have the plague.'

'As far as you know?' he queried, sudden fear making his voice shrill.

'I'll explain,' Galieva said, motioning for quiet. 'The second crow has returned with much of the information we wanted. You don't need to know most of it yet, but the most important news is the confirmation that it is possible to cure the plague. Aphra is among those working on the problem, and the general opinion from their experiments so far is that they're getting closer. They're making progress all the time, but there's obviously still a long way to go.'

'If Aphra's working on the cure, then she must be in danger.'

'Everyone on the island is in danger,' Galieva rebuked him.

'I know that. I'm sorry.'

'The crow brought something else back,' she went on. 'We don't exactly understand what it is, and hoped you might have better luck.' She took a small strip of paper out of her pocket and handed it to Sayer. 'Do you recognize the writing?'

He glanced down at the words.

'It's Aphra's,' he said, feeling a strange mixture of emotions. ' "Give this to my brother",' he read aloud. ' "Tell him I put everything I could into it." Into what?'

Galieva removed some of the produce from her basket and took out a small muslin bag.

'It's in there,' she said, placing it on the table. 'But you'd better be careful. Everyone else who's touched it either blacked out or became nauseous. Serin thinks magic has been used somehow to guarantee that only the right person can make use of it.'

'Me?'

She nodded.

'We weren't sure it was meant for you at first, but if that's Aphra's writing . . .'

Sayer automatically probed for any resonances emanating from the bag, but could detect nothing.

'I don't feel anything.'

'You need to touch it directly. That's when the others reacted.'

Sayer carefully picked up the bag and opened the drawstring. Peering inside, he saw a shiny cylinder of rock about the size of his thumb. The smooth surface was covered by a mottled pattern of red and black that had a mysterious depth to it. It was beautiful, in a bizarre way, but he still could not sense anything coming from it.

'If it does contain anything more about the island, then we need to know as soon as possible,' Galieva said.

'All right. Here goes.'

Sayer stretched his fingers inside, and was just about to touch the stone when he heard the outer door open and Kailas call in greeting. He swiftly closed the bag again and slipped it into a drawer, while Galieva quickly began to prepare food.

Sayer's frustration increased as the evening wore on. Before Galieva left, he had let her know that he would be setting out on another mission the next day, and they had agreed that she would return in the morning to see whether he had had any success. After that, all he could do was wait until he had a chance to be alone. He dared not touch the stone while Kailas was still around, in case he was affected as the others had been. If that happened, she would naturally want to know why. If, on the other hand, he was successful and there *was* some hidden message from Aphra, he had to be able to concentrate without fear of interruption. Either way, he knew he must wait until his wife was asleep.

Fortunately, Kailas was a sound sleeper and, after the disturbances of the previous night, she was dead to the world soon after they went to bed. Sayer cautiously slid from under the sheet, went downstairs and lit a candle. Now that winter was drawing in, the nights were cold, even in Qara, but he hardly noticed. Retrieving the bag from its hiding place, he lay on his back in the sitting room and tried to relax. After taking a few deep breaths, he opened the bag and reached in, grasping the stone firmly.

Instantly, a feeling that was half pain, half pleasure ran

up and down his arm, and then the room went black. He could not tell whether the candle had blown out or if he had gone blind, and there was a horrible squirming sensation inside his head. He fought it at first, until he realized he was being probed, tested somehow, and he surrendered, allowing the magic to do its work. Random memories surfaced in his mind's eye, memories that only he and Aphra could share. There was just enough time for him to be impressed – if Aphra was responsible for this, she did indeed have real talent – and then it was over. He had passed the test.

He woke to find himself on the Isle of the Dead.

CHAPTER TWENTY-FIVE

'Henceforth, the uninhabited island known as Jazireh is reserved for the isolation of those suffering from the plague, so that they may live out the remaining part of their natural term without danger to any other. Approaching or landing on the island for any purpose other than disembarking such persons is forbidden by law.'

Public decree issued by the Council in the 18th year of the great task

It was like the most extraordinary dream. He kept his own identity, and the ability to think, but he had no control over what he did or where he went. He saw through another's eyes; when he spoke it was with another's voice – but he was there! And he was Aphra.

Aphra took the red and black stone from the crude wooden box, finding its glassy surface cool to the touch. There were no luxuries on Jazireh – no one here called it the Isle of the Dead – but she had treasured this strange jewel ever since she'd found it on one of the upper slopes of the volcanic crater. It had become her talisman, a reminder that beauty still existed in the world – and now it would be something more.

Holding the stone tightly, she went out of the hut to join a man who was standing there, looking about him with a slightly bemused air. Behind him, three large, handsome crows strutted on the ground. A group of islanders were watching both man and birds with a mixture of curiosity and hope.

'Could one of them carry this?' Aphra asked.

Graovac took the cylinder and weighed it in his hand.

'Yes. Why?'

'I'm going to record a message for my brother, in a way he'll understand.'

'How?'

'All things absorb a certain amount of what happens around them, their own history if you like,' she explained. 'That's what seekers mean when they talk about following the resonances of a particular object. Stone is especially receptive because it's so old and strong. If I can make the impressions powerful enough, Sayer will be able to see what's going on here.'

'You can do that?' a second man asked. He was tall and bearded, and had the look of wiry strength. His deeply sun-tanned skin showed many scars and pockmarks, but he seemed healthy enough.

'I can try,' Aphra replied. 'Looking inside things is what I do best. You know that, Tyler. And if anyone will be able to read it, my brother will.'

'Can we be sure of him?'

'I know his heart. This will convince him if our friends haven't done it already.'

'What if it falls into the hands of someone else – another seeker?' Tyler persisted. 'We can't allow the archivects to find out what we're doing.'

'I'll make sure that won't happen,' Aphra replied. 'And I can get more information on here than on a dozen sheets of paper.'

Tyler smiled at her enthusiasm.

'Go ahead, then. Start recording your message.'

Aphra returned his smile.

'I already have,' she said.

Aphra and her three assistants strode out of the village with a renewed sense of purpose. About them, many of the wooden shelters were being repaired, ready for the winter ahead. Meals were being prepared over communal fires and, everywhere Aphra looked, supplies were being gathered. Water was brought from the inland springs, the last of the wild fruit was being harvested, and nuts were being stored away. Fishermen added their catches to the small bounty brought home by the hunters and trappers. Salt scraped from evaporated pools of seawater was used to preserve what meat was not to be eaten immediately. Outside the village, the small fields that had been cleared for their crude efforts at cultivation lay mostly barren now, but by spring they too would be a source of nourishment and hope.

During the months of her exile, Aphra had come to take all this for granted. Now, for the sake of her talisman, she saw it all anew. She knew that the island had once been a hideous, barbarous place, where only the strongest and most ruthless endured, but with the arrival of increasing numbers of kyars that had slowly changed. They had been determined to prove that they could only survive in the long run by cooperation, and over time their methods had gained acceptance. Now the healthy worked, the sick were cared for, and, although the hardships were still great, the law of the jungle had been supplanted by a genuine collective spirit. For a long time there had been no hope of ever leaving the island and, in some ways, that had been a good thing. Aphra doubted whether so much would have been achieved if Jazireh's inhabitants had not been certain they would spend the rest of their lives there. That was beginning to change now, especially since Graovac's arrival, but the routines of survival were well established.

'You know where we're headed?' Aphra asked.

They were walking along one of the many trails that made a network over the lower slopes of the island.

'The cemetery?' Jase guessed. Although he was the youngest of the group, he had a sharp mind and a little talent.

'That's right. I found a new herb there a few days ago and tried it on one of the new patients – the old woman who came on the same boat as Graovac.'

'She's doing well,' Cainas said. 'When she arrived I thought she'd be dead within two days.'

Aphra smiled to herself. Cainas had a gift for repeating the obvious, but she had a good heart and was willing, and her talent was strong, if unfocused.

'I've got a feeling about this one,' Aphra went on. 'I'd never seen it before, and I've no idea what it's called, but it only seems to grow around the graves. There's not much of it, so we're going to have to be very careful.'

'Perhaps it's effective *because* it grows there,' Skehan suggested with typical insight. He was the oldest of the group, and although his magical talent was minimal he made up for it in other ways. 'Most of the people buried there died of the plague, so maybe the plants are creating their own antidote so they can grow in soil that's been tainted.'

'Perhaps,' Aphra said cautiously.

'We should call it aphran,' Cainas suggested, 'because you discovered it.'

'Let's find out if it really works first,' Aphra replied.

The cemetery was situated in a rare area of relatively flat but mostly infertile land. The graves were laid out in rows, hundreds of them, each marked with a small boulder with a name scratched upon it. The dead deserved that at least, and now they were repaying the respect shown to them with a gift of their own.

Aphra led the party to a small clump of greenery amid the predominantly black stones.

'This is it,' she said, kneeling and separating some of the leaves so the others could study their shape. 'I want you to spread out and look for more. Don't pick any or uproot it, but mark the location. We may be able to transplant or take cuttings later, but it's not a good idea at this time of year. We just have to hope they'll seed themselves naturally.'

'Aren't we going to take *any*?' Jase asked. 'For more tests?'

'Meet me back here in an hour,' Aphra replied. 'We'll compare notes and decide how much to take then.'

As the others went off, Aphra raised the fingers that had bruised the leaves to her nose and sniffed gently.

'Make this the one,' she whispered to herself.

Walking into one of the houses that made up the infirmary, Aphra was struck, as always, by the contrasting emotions generated by such places. There was so much fear and suffering here, so many sights that would once have moved her to both pity and revulsion, and yet there was also a tangible sense of purpose and even laughter. Anyone with talent was encouraged to develop the skill of 'looking inside' the patients, not just to locate and combat the sickness in the blood but also to help them fight the pain. Although more often than not the progress of the disease was irreversible, it was always possible to ease the last days of its victims. By the time most people reached the island the plague had usually done too much damage for any hope of a full recovery, but no one was ever abandoned to die alone. As always, seeing the self-taught healers at work made Aphra proud to be among them.

She went to one of the pallets at the far end of the dormitory and knelt beside an old woman. Her face and neck were disfigured by purple swellings but her eyes were bright and she smiled weakly in greeting.

'Hello, Kelara. How are you feeling?'

'Better.' Her voice was little more than a hoarse croak, but it was remarkable that she was able to talk at all. When she had arrived on Jazireh she had been practically comatose. 'I'll be up and dancing soon.'

'I'll look forward to that,' Aphra said.

'Is there any more of that drink you gave me?' the old woman asked hopefully.

'A little. I'll fetch it in a moment. May I look first?'

'Be my guest.'

Aphra placed her fingertips on either side of Kelara's head and closed her eyes. She concentrated first on shutting out all external influences – the noises and smells of the infirmary – then let her mind expand. Tendrils of awareness crept out from her fingers, through the old woman's temples and into the fabric of her being. It was an inward journey that could not be measured in terms of distance or time, but it was full of both wonders and horrors. At Kelara's age, the onset of the disease and the shock of her exile had been devastating and her body had almost succeeded in shutting itself down, choosing oblivion over unbearable pain. Now, however, her internal systems were coming back to life. Aphra saw this not in visual terms, but in senses that were outside the normal world of experience – flashes of intuition that illuminated the dark patterns within. The resilience and sheer bloody-mindedness of the human body in combating illness continued to amaze her, and for Kelara the war against the contagion was slowly being won, against all the odds. There were still signs of the plague everywhere, which Aphra felt as unnatural knots of evil that made her cringe, but they were less tangled now, smaller and less virulent.

Aphra withdrew, feeling breathless as she always did, and smiled encouragingly.

'I'll get you that drink.'

'Thank you, dear.'

The small kitchen was at the end of the building, and it was here that the various mixtures were produced that were used to ease the lives of the patients. With any prospective remedy various forms were tried; whether they were to be ingested raw, infused in boiled water or as a dried powder, or placed upon the skin as a salve or poultice, all the plants and herbs were brought here first. The properties of most were well known and the results they achieved monitored, but with any new tuber or leaf it was especially important to make the preparations exact and to record all of the effects.

Aphra set about her task methodically, using the few precious leaves she had allowed herself to gather. As well as tending to Kelara, there was one more experiment she need-ed to try.

The plague boat had been spotted well before it reached the island, and several of the villagers had gathered on the shore to watch the approach and help the newcomers gain dry land. A few sometimes drowned in the last, often desperate part of the voyage, but these were usually the passengers who were the most sick and for whom death could be seen as a welcome relief.

Aphra stood back a little and, for once, did not join those who waded into the shallows. She had listened to the thin screaming of the shrieker, seen the thrashing under the surface of the water where the monsters lurked, and could not help recalling her own terrifying journey. Her reception on the island had astonished her. Each boat brought with it more work for the healers, but it might also bring other able-bodied exiles who would be able to help the islanders. And, most precious of all, the newcomers carried with them news of what was happening in Qara.

For a few moments Aphra felt a sudden dread, watching all the faces as they came ashore, but there was no one she knew among them, no one whose eyes matched her own.

Aphra looked around the meeting, trying to gauge its mood. Tyler was there, his worried expression telling its own story, and the others were all equally grave. The men and women gathered there were the leaders of the island community. They gained no privileges from their generally acknowledged status, but had earned it through their own toil and ingenuity.

'This is *good* news,' Aphra insisted. 'As I told you, a small dose, when given to a healthy person, creates mild symptoms that mimic the contagion. But in someone who already has the disease, it lessens them.'

'I don't understand,' Tyler said. 'Why doesn't it make them worse?'

'I'm not sure, but I can guess,' she replied. 'Perhaps by making the body fight what the herb does to it, it also makes it fight harder against the plague itself.'

'You mean the patients themselves might be producing their own antidote?' someone else asked.

'Yes, if their systems are stimulated in the right way. Anyway, it works. At least half the patients we've treated have responded favourably, and the rest have got no worse. Aphran is our best hope yet. The problem is, there's not enough to go around.'

'Then we need to find more, to cultivate it,' Tyler said.

'We should search the whole island,' another man added. 'So that we're sure to conserve what supplies we do have.

Give the scouts a description of the herb,' he told Aphra, 'and let them know what to do if they find any.'

'Of course. In the meantime, there are decisions to be made that I'm not comfortable with.'

'Who gets the medicine we do have?' Tyler said gravely.

'No one feels comfortable with such decisions,' one of the women said. 'You're the best authority we have, Aphra. You're the only one who can decide who would benefit most.'

Aphra nodded reluctantly, and felt the burden of responsibility settle upon her shoulders.

She stared across the black water, wondering. The new moon was a pale crescent in the night sky and there were a few luminous patches in the sea, but she was looking at the distant glow to the south. The lights of Qara.

Footsteps sounded behind her, but she did not turn around, knowing who was coming to join her silent vigil.

The message ended there, and the stone released him. Sayer gradually came to terms with the fact that he was back in his own home, beneath the distant glow he had seen through Aphra's eyes. The candle burned serenely still; it did not seem to have melted down at all.

It had been an incredible experience, and had left him with memories as real as his own. After her initial decision had been approved, Aphra had obviously chosen specific parts from several days of her life – presumably from what she considered important. The abrupt jumps between scenes had been disconcerting, and Sayer could not help wondering about the times she had left out. For instance, how had she known about the effect of the herb on a healthy person? Had she tested it on herself?

As it was, Sayer had been given an astonishing picture of the society that had developed on the island. He was not sure what he'd expected, but he had been surprised by what he had witnessed. He had even seen children in the village who were too young to have been exiled from the mainland. The idea that some of the islanders might have been born there, and grown up knowing nothing of any other world, was staggering. And the island itself had come as a surprise, with far more trees and vegetation than he would have believed.

However, it was Aphra herself – his eyes and ears – who concerned him most. It was only when he had returned to his own body and was able to consider all he had seen that he realized that the entire message had been selfless. Even though his twin had been his guide, there had been nothing about her own arrest or exile, about her present state of health . . . nor anything of a personal nature. She had let the island and the work of its people do her explaining. There had been no pleas for rescue or for help, just facts.

The closest Aphra had come to revealing anything about herself was to record the way the man Tyler looked at her. He had featured in several of the scenes, and their relationship was obviously close. During her earlier life in Qara, Aphra had never seemed to have any time for men, and that was easy to understand. Being raped by Halion when she was little more than a child would probably have ruined any chance of a normal relationship with anyone of the opposite sex, but now Sayer wondered if there had been more to it than that. Had she avoided any entanglements simply because she had known her first duty was to the kyars, because a time like this was bound to come? That she had considerable talent was now obvious, but she also shared the incredible dedication that seemed so common among the night people. Even though Sayer could only admire her for it, he was saddened by the thought that this same devotion to the cause might have robbed her of a chance of pleasure or happiness.

He hoped that on the Isle of the Dead – where she no longer had to hide anything – she might find someone to console her.

Now that the impossibly vivid dream was over, Sayer had a yearning to go back, to be with her again, but knew there would be no point. The stone could not give him what he wanted. What he needed was reassurance, some direct contact, an expression of love or longing, some acknowledgement of his presence.

And then he realized that Aphra had given him all this and more. By addressing her message to him alone, she had given him the greatest gift of all. Her faith.

CHAPTER TWENTY-SIX

'Revenge was piled upon revenge until no one knew what the original offence had been. Eventually, all that was left to be done was to appeal to the gods – and their justice was harsh.'

From *The Chronicles of a Barbarous Time*

Sayer was understandably exhausted when Kailas woke him early the next day. For the second night in a row he had hardly slept, and when it dawned on him that they were due to leave for the south in a few hours, he groaned aloud. He remained distracted all morning, his thoughts far away, until Kailas finally grew angry with him. Unable to explain his preoccupation, Sayer could only accept her irritated comments and apologize. Even though he knew he should be preparing for the mission, all he could think about was the stone's message, and he waited impatiently for Galieva to arrive so that he could pass on what he had learnt. Knowing he would not have time to tell her everything, he kept trying to put together a concise summary that contained all the important facts, but each time he did so, he realized he'd forgotten something and had to start again.

At the same time, he went over what he had learned for his own benefit. The most important fact, the one thing that dominated everything else, was that Aphra was alive. Beside that joyous news everything else was almost incidental, even though he still had some lingering worries over the state of her health. Although she was clearly not a victim of the plague, Sayer had not seen her face nor experienced any of her internal feelings, so there was no way of knowing if she was in pain. That she had been able to work at the time she recorded the message was an indication that she was well enough, but either the illness itself – or her experiments in trying to cure it – might still take their toll. Sayer was filled with a sense of urgency. If he was to be sure of seeing his twin again, then there was no time to waste.

The second thing that he reflected upon at length was Aphra's amazing talent. Anyone who could work as a healer as well as creating a secure message in the stone was a magician to be reckoned with. Keeping her gift secret for so long must have been very difficult, and Sayer believed that she would never have been exiled if the archivects – and Halion in particular – had known about it. Given sufficient time and determination, it was possible that someone as talented as Aphra might be able to duplicate the effect of a shrieker, even though their training was surrounded in mystery and strictly monitored by the military authorities. She would thus be able to help a boat escape from the island. However, this possibility had not even been mentioned in the message, and it was clear that Aphra wanted to concentrate on healing, the task she felt best equipped for. Given the results she had already produced, Sayer could not blame her.

Beyond that, Aphra had achieved her object of securing her brother's allegiance to the cause. *This will convince him if our friends haven't done it already.* He now had proof that the kyars were right. It was true that he could not use the proof to convert anyone else, but it was more than enough for him.

When Galieva finally arrived, she nearly did not get past

the front door. In spite of Sayer's vigilance, Kailas got there first and was about to turn her away, explaining that they were leaving and wouldn't need anything doing, when Sayer intervened.

'There's still some fruit in the kitchen,' he said quickly. 'It'll only rot if we leave it there. Why don't you take it for the soldiers?'

Ignoring his wife's exasperated glance, Sayer led the maid into the kitchen.

'Well?' Galieva asked quietly, as soon as they were out of earshot.

'It was from Aphra, a picture of her work on the island. It—'

'Will you come to a meeting?' she interrupted. 'There are people who need to hear this.'

'I can't. I have to leave this morning. Just listen.' As quickly as he was able, he gave her an account of the main points of the message. 'There's more,' he finished, 'but there's no time now. I'll do what I can when we get back.'

'Do what?' Kailas asked, coming into the room.

'Galieva would like to work for us all the time,' Sayer improvised. 'Now that Safi's so preoccupied, it seems like a good idea. I was going to see if I could arrange it.'

'We've more important things to worry about at the moment,' Kailas replied tartly. 'The horses are here and you're not even packed yet.' She turned on her heel and strode out again.

'You'd better go,' Galieva said. 'We don't want to give Halion any more excuses for being annoyed with you.'

'I don't want . . . If I could . . .' He shrugged helplessly.

'It can't be helped,' she told him. 'You've already stirred up a hornet's nest with Seigui. Should be interesting. I'll pass on what you've told me, and we'll talk when you get back.'

Her smile told him that he had been accepted. For better or worse, he was one of the kyars now.

'This is hopeless!' Sayer threw the notes he had been given back on the bed. For the first time ever, he had no real feeling for a mission. 'How am I supposed to do anything when this is all I have to go on?'

Kailas glanced up at him sympathetically, but she had no answers. They had been travelling south for three days, moving slowly and more in hope than expectation. Because Sayer's uncertainty had communicated itself to the rest of the party, it had not been the happiest of journeys. Everyone knew that the seeker was under a cloud, and there seemed little hope of that changing unless he succeeded in this task. However, that prospect seemed increasingly unlikely, and Nazeri had decided to end that day's riding early in order to give Sayer the chance to gather his thoughts. The captain had been surly, and was clearly ill at ease. Sayer was not even sure whether the soldier actually wanted the mission to succeed.

The seeker and his wife were now installed in a room at a travellers' inn, and Sayer was no closer to knowing what to do next.

'Hasn't the resonance become any clearer?' Kailas asked.

'Not really. I keep getting faint echoes of something, but it could come from any number of stones. It was vague enough to start with. It could be anywhere between here and the Restless.'

'You'll find it eventually,' she said loyally.

'We should never have been sent out,' he said. 'It's like looking for a particular grain of sand in the Kavir Desert.'

'I know. This is such a stupid waste of time and talent. Halion's a fool.'

The antagonism in her words gave Sayer pause for

thought. He wondered, for perhaps the thousandth time, whether he could trust Kailas with what was really happening in his life. His appreciation of his wife had deepened, from a superficial enjoyment of her beauty to an understanding of her apparently single-minded devotion to their marriage and their life together. Although her history and family background dictated many of her attitudes, she was far from being stupid, and Sayer could not believe that she would approve of the way Tirok was being run if she knew the truth. He realized that he had grown to love Kailas, and believed that she genuinely returned his affection. Surely he owed it to her – and to himself – to tell her the truth.

'Do you really think Halion's a fool?' he asked tentatively.

'In this, yes.'

'I mean generally.'

Kailas looked at him apprehensively.

'No. Do you?'

'No.' He hesitated.

'But?' she prompted.

'I've come to despise and hate him,' Sayer admitted. As he waited for her response, he was aware of a sense of relief at having said the words aloud.

Kailas sat very still for a time, her face a perfect mask.

'Are you going to leave him for Seigui, or one of the others?' she asked eventually.

'No.'

'Don't lie to me, Sayer. I couldn't stand it if you lied to me.'

'The archivects are all as bad as each other,' he said. 'There'd be no point changing. I despise them all.'

'But you *hate* Halion. Why?'

'He's my master. He's the one who shaped my whole life.'

'And has that been so bad?'

'Not all of it, no.'

'Then there must be something else.'

Sayer felt himself teetering on the brink of confessing everything, but his doubts made him hesitate again.

'I'm Halion's second cousin, not his spy,' Kailas said, discerning the reason for his caution. 'You can tell me. If you want to.'

Sayer found that he believed her. Even if he had not, he needed to unburden himself.

'Halion raped Aphra when she was twelve.'

Kailas did not respond for so long that he began to wonder if he had made a huge mistake. Had his confidence in his wife simply been wishful thinking?

'How long have you known?' she asked at last, her voice no more than a whisper.

Sayer was not certain what reaction he had expected, but this was not it. Shock had registered in her soft green eyes, but there had been no outrage, no disbelief. She seemed perfectly calm.

'Not long,' he replied. 'Aphra never told me about it, but a friend of hers did, a few days ago.'

Kailas nodded. Her eyes were haunted now and, with a sickening rush of insight, Sayer realized why she did not seem surprised.

'You too?' he breathed.

Kailas shook her head.

'No. But he tried.' Her voice shook, and Sayer went to comfort her.

'You don't have to tell me if you don't want to.'

'I want to,' she replied, but it was a long time before she spoke again, and she could not look at Sayer as the words spilled out. 'It was more than five years ago, in Kohlu. I was only thirteen, and very innocent. I didn't know what was happening at the time, but I didn't like it . . . and then Meydan, Halion's father, found us and there was a lot of shouting. I ran away and hid.'

Sayer swore angrily under his breath.

'And your father still let you come to Qara and stay at Halion's mansion?'

'My father didn't know. I knew I must've done something wrong, something terrible, and I didn't want to get into trouble, so I just kept quiet and tried to forget about it. I didn't want to come to Qara, but I had no choice. My father thought it was a great honour to live in an archivect's house, and . . . Halion never treated me badly when I was there. I began to think there must have been some sort of misunderstanding, but then I heard some gossip and wondered . . .' She paused, then added, 'Poor Aphra. How horrible. Now I know why she didn't think much of you marrying into Halion's family.'

Sayer heard his sister's words again. *I can't see myself fitting in as a member of Halion's family.* It was no wonder she had been so antagonistic.

'So now we both know what Halion's really like,' he said gently. 'Is that the sort of man you want to work for?'

'Do we have any choice? I thought you said—'

'Can I tell you something else about Aphra?' Sayer cut in. 'Did you actually see her before she was sent to the Isle of the Dead?'

'No. After you left, she and I weren't exactly on the best of terms. I saw her once or twice, but not to talk to. I regret that now. When she caught the plague—'

'Aphra never caught the plague,' he said, interrupting her again.

'Of course she did.' Kailas was obviously bewildered. 'That's why she was sent to the island.'

If she was acting, then it was a bravura performance, and Sayer went on with renewed confidence in her innocence.

'She was never ill,' he reaffirmed. 'Aphra was arrested and exiled. The Isle of the Dead is a prison as well as a plague colony.'

'That can't be true!'

'I didn't want to believe it at first either, but I've seen Aphra recently and—'

'*Seen* her?' Kailas exclaimed incredulously. 'Where?'

'It's complicated,' he replied, wishing his wife could see what he had seen. 'But it involves magic.' He tried to explain, but he could see that Kailas barely understood what he was saying. When he reached the part about a cure for the plague, she latched onto that as if something made sense at last.

'You mean Aphra cured herself?'

'No. She was never ill. You remember we thought it was odd that Halion introduced me to you just when I was about to go in search of the Eye? Well, he timed it like that because he knew Aphra was going to be arrested before I got back.'

'And I'd be there to look after you?'

'And keep an eye on me,' he confirmed.

'But why was Aphra arrested? What had she done?'

With a jolt, Sayer realized he had already told Kailas far more than he had originally intended. However, the flood-gates were open now and there was no way he could hold back the tide.

'There's a secret organization made up of people who want to change the way Tirok is governed. Although I never knew it, Aphra was one of them.' Without giving her any specific details, he went on to tell Kailas about the kyars, their methods and their aims. Although she listened in silence, her changing expressions betrayed a mixture of emotions, predominantly amazement and fear.

'How do you know all this?' she asked when he had finished. 'Have you met any of these people? Are you one of them?'

'I've met them,' he admitted. 'I'd like to join them.'

'This is madness!' she burst out. 'Don't you see what this

means? It's treason. And how can you even *hope* to succeed against someone like Halion?'

'Something has to change,' Sayer replied. 'The injustices have to stop, and we finally have a chance to rid ourselves of the plague. That must be worth any risk.'

'But why you?' she cried. 'Why us? You'll ruin everything.'

'It's already ruined. I can't unlearn all the things I know now. I can't go back to being blind. You're the only good thing left in my life, Kailas.'

'And this is how you repay me?'

'I'm doing this for me,' he stated firmly. 'For the first time in my life, I'm not being used by others. This is my decision. It might turn out to be a huge mistake – but at least it'll be *my* mistake.'

He watched her face closely, realizing suddenly just how young she was. Before that moment she had always seemed so mature, but now his wife looked vulnerable and tiny, like a child. Even though he had asked her to absorb a great deal, she had not cried once – and he was grateful for that, knowing that her tears would have unmanned him completely.

'I'm truly sorry to burden you like this,' he went on, 'but I love you and I'd rather have you at my side, whatever happens. I don't want to keep any more secrets from you.'

'How do I know you're telling me the truth?' she asked softly.

'You don't. There might be some things I can prove to you, but in the end it just comes down to trust. What reason could I have for lying to you?'

Kailas regarded him gravely for a few moments and then, incredibly, she smiled.

'I don't suppose you've got the imagination to make up a story like that,' she said.

'No,' Sayer agreed, returning her smile.

'How do you know I won't go to Halion and tell him everything?' Kailas asked, serious again now.

'That's your decision, but I don't think you will.' He had no need to spell out the consequences of such an action for their marriage. If he meant anything to her at all – and he believed that he did – then she would already know the price of betrayal. He felt strangely liberated by the fact that his wife effectively held his life in her hands. Aphra had never been able to confide in him fully, in the way he was doing now with Kailas, and that was something he regretted a great deal.

'I'm sorry, my love,' he said. 'This is not a situation of my choosing, nor did I mean to involve you so suddenly—'

'When *were* you going to tell me?' she demanded. 'When you were arrested too?'

'I . . . I don't know.'

'You didn't know if you could trust me, did you?' she said quietly. 'What made you change your mind?'

'I wasn't even sure of myself until now,' he replied. 'I want to be a healer, if I can.'

'You're a seeker. Doesn't that mean anything to you?'

'Not any more. The kyars are right. Rebuilding the Temple is pointless.'

'This is so hard!' Kailas groaned. 'On top of everything else, you're asking me to give up the only thing I've ever believed in. I've just found what I thought was my vocation, and now you tell me it's pointless.'

'You can put your talent to use in other, better ways,' he assured her.

'Become a healer too?'

'Why not?'

'I don't know. The gods—' She broke off suddenly and looked at him with a new fire in her eyes. 'It wasn't an accident, was it? You broke the crow stone deliberately!'

Sayer nodded, shamefaced.

'You gave me the wrong shape on purpose, and I thought . . . How could you do that to me?'

'I'm sorry. I tried to tell you that it was my fault. I was angry and confused.'

'Why did you do it?'

'To see whether it really was important to the gods.'

'And they were supposed to strike you down with a thunderbolt?'

'Something like that,' he mumbled.

'You're an idiot,' she told him disgustedly. 'Don't you think the gods would be capable of a little more subtlety when it comes to exacting revenge?'

CHAPTER TWENTY-SEVEN

'I will stand any test of faith, any trial of piety. My meditations have led me to the light of truth, and nothing – no temptation, no threat, no torture – can make me turn aside now. Although I am but a portal, I speak with the voices of the pantheon and my words will shake the earth itself. I have been blessed.'

From *The Oracles of Zavanaiu*

They eventually found the elusive stone three days later. Following intermittent flashes of insight, rather than any consistent trail, Sayer had led them to another small town further to the southwest. Once there he could find no trace of the resonance he was seeking, but Kailas had the good sense to describe the stone to the landlord of their tavern.

'The calf-stone, you mean?' he had replied. 'Bloor will be glad if you get rid of that for him. It's in the middle of one of his best fields.'

'Is that it?' Kailas asked later, when they had found the farm the innkeeper had described.

'Yes,' Sayer replied, staring in disgust at the slab of white rock. It lay in the open, surrounded by a herd of cattle who regarded the human newcomers with a gentle curiosity. 'Who, in their right mind, would carry anything that big all the way down here, and then just dump it in the mud?' He went over to the stone, placed a hand on the grimy surface and muttered to himself.

'What's the matter?'

'There's hardly any resonance, even here. Either this has had the dullest history in the entire Temple or I'm losing my touch.'

'Don't even think that,' Kailas whispered.

Sayer looked at her anxious face and tried to smile. He could not help remembering the last stone he had touched. It had been so vibrant, so alive. Aphra had created a miracle in just a few days, whereas this insensate lump had endured centuries and yet absorbed almost nothing.

'At least it saves you some work,' he remarked, waving the artisans forward. 'The only thing this needs protecting from is cow dung.'

In spite of the delay – while Nazeri commandeered a cart sturdy enough to transport the bulky relic – the journey back to Qara was accomplished in good time. All but one of the party were glad to be returning from such an undistinguished mission, hoping for better things next time. The exception was Kailas. Although she too had found the earlier days frustrating, she knew that a return to the city would bring with it the need to answer several uncomfortable questions. Sayer's revelations had shattered her cosy little world and forced her to look at wider issues. Whenever they had had a private moment, they had discussed it further, although she had not come to any firm conclusions. She could not remain blind to the evils that Halion and his cronies had imposed upon her country, and wanted desperately to support the man she loved, but the stumbling block was the kyars' belief that rebuilding the Temple was a pointless – and potentially even harmful – exercise. As she told Sayer, the pantheon was real for her; the gods had spoken to the people of Tirok through the oracles, so how could she cast all that aside?

'Oracles are notoriously ambiguous,' Sayer had argued on one occasion. 'Perhaps they've been misinterpreted.'

'That's ridiculous. Zavanaiu was the greatest mystic of all time. Everyone knows that.'

'It doesn't alter the fact that the Council has used his revelations to oppress and control the entire country.'

'But that doesn't invalidate the prophecy itself,' she had countered.

Sayer had simply shrugged. His mind was made up. Although he did not fear betrayal by Kailas, he knew now that it was terribly important to him that his wife both understood and supported what he had to do. Whatever happened now, their lives could not remain the same for much longer. If they were to be ruined, he did not want to feel that the responsibility was his alone.

The walls of Qara finally came into view in the late evening. Darkness had fallen some time ago, but because they were now on a good road – and most of the party were keen to complete the journey – they had continued on their way. To their left, the outlines of the Temple could just be made out against the night sky but, as they drew closer to the city, Sayer became aware of torches to the other side of the trail. Such activity was unusual, to say the least, and, to his horror, he soon realized what was going on. The rush lights were held by a group of soldiers, while labourers were digging a large pit in the waste ground. Laid out next to it were several jumbled rows of dead bodies.

As they rode nearer, the travellers could see that both the guards and the workmen were wearing cloths over their mouths and noses, and instinctively they all spurred their mounts forward, wanting to pass by the macabre scene as

quickly as possible. They were encouraged in this by one of
the sentries, who yelled at them to stay clear as he waved his
torch angrily.

The chill of that experience lasted until they reached the
gates of Qara, where another unpleasant surprise awaited
them. Ordinarily, an official party such as theirs would simply
have been able to ride on into the city, even at such a late
hour, but on this occasion the great gates were closed and
the guards would not open them until formal identifications
had been made. Even then the travellers were forced to
enter one by one, to give their names and other details to the
attendant scribe.

'What's this all about?' Sayer asked. He was used to his
status granting him many privileges, and was irritated by
this seemingly endless delay.

'I'm only following orders, Seeker,' the captain of the
gate detail replied. 'There's been some trouble in the city
recently, and security's been tightened.'

'What sort of trouble?'

'General unrest. Sedition. A few troublemakers spoiling
it for the rest of us. But we've got everything under control
now.'

After that Sayer was waved on and was unable to learn
any more. When he and Kailas were inside their own home
and able to talk freely at last, they fell into each other's arms.

'I'm frightened,' she whispered.

'Me too.'

'Do you think it's the kyars?'

'I expect they've got something to do with it,' he replied,
wondering what had been happening while they had been
away.

'What are you going to do?'

'I don't know,' he replied truthfully. 'Until we find out
what's going on, there's no way to decide anything.'

They were silent for a while.

'And on top of all this, the plague is obviously getting worse,' Kailas said, referring to the mass burial outside the city walls.

Sayer decided not to tell his wife what he had seen in the flickering torchlight. Unless he was very much mistaken, some of the bodies piled next to the grave had displayed no signs of the contagion whatsoever.

They were roused early the next morning, and although Sayer hoped the visitor would be Galieva, it was not. Instead it was one of Halion's stewards, who had come to summon both Sayer and Kailas to the archivect's estate. As they rode out of the city, the seeker's mind was full of misgivings. He looked around for signs of unrest, but apart from the unusually thorough checks at the gate, everything seemed normal enough. Beside him, Kailas was pale and silent, and he began to wish he had not told her so much. Facing Halion would have been less of an ordeal for her that way. As it was, he could not imagine what their master wanted to see them about.

To their joint surprise and relief, the archivect turned out to be in buoyant mood. As soon as they were ushered into his presence, he offered them refreshments, thanked them for their prompt arrival and complimented them on their latest success.

'It was hardly the most prestigious find,' Sayer replied.

'All relics are equally precious in the eyes of the gods,' Halion remarked. 'And this one told me a great deal.'

'Really?'

'I owe you an apology, Sayer. I was overhasty in my judgement of you. The faults, such as they were, lay elsewhere, and I gave you what amounted to an impossible mission. And yet you succeeded. Such loyalty should be rewarded.'

'Assisting in the great task is its own reward,' Sayer answered.

'Quite so. However, there are some, such as yourself, who have done more than anyone could have expected, and such service should be publicly acknowledged. And that is what I intend to do.' Halion went on to explain that in two days' time there would be a public feast in Dominion Square, the largest open space within the city walls, with himself and the other archivects as hosts and Sayer and a few others as the guests of honour. 'There'll be few ceremonies, but it should be a pleasant occasion and, after the recent troubles, a display of fellowship between us can do nothing but good.'

'Forgive me,' Sayer began, 'but we've had no time since we returned to learn the nature of the unrest. Has it been serious?'

'No,' Halion replied confidently. 'More irritating than dangerous. A few deluded fools have been spreading absurd rumours, that's all.'

'What rumours?' Kailas asked.

'Irresponsible nonsense about magicians being abused by the Council, and similarly misguided rubbish.'

So that's what this is all about, Sayer thought. It explained why Halion wanted a public display of cooperation between the archivects and their talents.

'There's even been one ridiculous claim that it's possible to cure the plague,' Halion went on. 'Can you imagine anyone believing that?'

'Do you know who's been spreading these rumours?' Sayer asked.

'They call themselves the kyars.' The archivect's contempt was clear in his tone. 'I won't dignify the rabble by calling them an organization, but they're making a nuisance of themselves.'

'Have you caught any of them?'

'A few. And we'll get the rest soon enough.'

Halion's words sent a chill down Sayer's spine, but he did his best not to show it.

'How can anyone give credence to such fools?' Kailas asked.

'I have no idea,' Halion replied. 'I sometimes think that madmen like Hurghad talk more sense than some people.'

'The hermit?'

'Yes. He lives in the ruins. You should visit him some time. He's really quite entertaining.' Halion smiled. 'In the meantime, I want you both to relax. For the rest of today I insist that you stay here and enjoy all the facilities my home can offer.'

Sayer was about to indicate that they would rather return to their own home when he caught Kailas's warning glance and held his tongue.

'That would be delightful,' Kailas said. 'Even though I wasn't needed as a silk, the travelling *was* tiring.'

'You know your way around, don't you, my dear? Tell the servants if there's anything you need. Alas, I have work to attend to, but we can talk again at the midday meal.'

'What's he up to?' Sayer wondered aloud.

They had achieved some degree of privacy at last by making use of the vast marble bathhouse in the basement of the mansion. Here, immersed in hot water and wreathed in steam, they were more or less alone. The servants who had followed them around all day had withdrawn once the couple had discarded their clothes, but they still spoke quietly.

'I don't know,' Kailas said, 'but we have to play along for the time being. There's no point in antagonizing him now. And if you stay in his good books, there'll be all the more chance of helping the kyars later.'

Sayer stared at her.

'Does that mean you're with us?' he asked hopefully.

'I'll do what my conscience allows,' she replied. 'If it comes to a choice between Halion and you, who do you think I'd choose?'

A feeling of immense relief flooded through Sayer. He reached under the water, took his wife's hand and squeezed it.

'Is that all the reward I get?' she enquired.

He moved closer, grabbed her round the waist and pulled her, laughing, under the water. They emerged a few moments later, spluttering but still in each other's arms.

'I thought water was supposed to have a certain effect on men's bodies,' Kailas remarked, her eyes wide in innocent surprise.

'That's *cold* water,' Sayer replied.

'So I see.'

Some time later, their brief mood of euphoria had evaporated. There were still too many unanswered questions.

'We should go,' he said.

Kailas nodded, but when the attendants brought in their clothes, they were informed that Halion expected them to join him for the evening meal. They had no choice but to obey. Over dinner, several of the other guests were joking about Hurghad in a way that made Sayer's blood boil, but it gave him the excuse to suggest that he and Kailas take a stroll in the last of the evening light to go and see the hermit. As they set off, they were both aware of being followed at a discreet distance.

'Why are we doing this?' Kailas asked.

'Hurghad was the one who first put me in touch with the kyars.'

'The madman?' she exclaimed. 'Then this is too dangerous.'

'I have to see what's happened to him,' Sayer replied, and did not explain further.

They reached the ruins just before sunset and went down the steps while their chaperone sat on a nearby boulder, looking very bored. The door to the hermit's cellar stood open, but there was no response when Sayer called out. The underground room was dark but, as their eyes adjusted to the light, two things became clear. The first was that Hurghad was not there. The second was that the secret door to the tunnel was wedged open.

CHAPTER TWENTY-EIGHT

'The moon is not composed of white cheese, but if
enough people can be made to believe that it is, then
you can dine on it very handsomely.'

Attributed to the philosopher Nimruz

'What's in there?' Kailas asked, as Sayer peered into the
tunnel.

'It's a secret way out of the estate.'

'Has Hurghad gone, then?'

'Looks like it.' He stepped inside and listened, but there
was not a sound to be heard. At this distance not even the
burbling of the stream was audible.

'So now what do we do?' Kailas asked.

Sayer knew that she was hoping they would abandon
their search for the hermit, but he was intrigued as well as
worried now and not inclined to give up just yet. It was clear
that Hurghad meant to return – or he would not have
wedged the door open – and because he had been seen by
other guests earlier that day, the chances were that he had
not gone far.

'I'm going to look for him.'

'Down there?'

'Yes. It's quite safe. I've done it before.'

Kailas took a moment to absorb this information, then indicated the servant waiting for them above ground.

'What about our friend up there?'

'You can stay here and—'

'Oh no!' she cut in. 'You're not leaving me here alone.'

'Then let's lock the outer door,' Sayer suggested. 'With luck we'll be back before he notices we've gone, and even if he does, we'll just tell the truth. Hurghad wasn't here, but we saw the tunnel and were curious. We can say we went so far, lost our nerve in the dark and came back none the wiser.'

'Why would we lock the other door if we were doing that?'

'To stop anyone closing *this* door and trapping us in the tunnel,' he replied promptly. 'Come on. The sooner we—'

'All right.' Kailas gave in, shut the door at the bottom of the steps, locked it, then joined her husband. He took her hand and together they crept along the silent corridor. The dim light faded to complete darkness, and only the sound of running water warned them that they were approaching the far end. There was still no sign of the hermit.

Sayer guided his wife across the stream, told her to stay where she was, and climbed up to the trapdoor. It was closed, but opened easily enough when he pushed it. He waited, listening, but there was no reaction from above and he pulled himself into the ruined hut. Hurghad was nowhere to be seen. When Sayer turned round to call down to Kailas, he found that she was already reaching the top of the shaft.

'I couldn't stand it down there on my own,' she explained. 'When I saw the light . . . Is he here?'

'No.' Sayer helped his wife up, then went to the crumbling doorway and peered out into the gloom. 'I wonder where he's gone?'

'Is there anyone around?' Kailas asked.

'Not as far as I can see.' He was about to step out into the open, to get a better view, when the sound of distant hoof-beats made him hesitate. 'Riders are coming,' he whispered. 'Keep still.'

Kailas had joined him now, and they crouched down in the shadows as five horsemen approached. The Gold Road ran close by, and they were able to see the travellers clearly enough to tell that the central figure was Seigui, flanked by four soldiers dressed in white uniforms. They looked like ghosts in the half-light. They were coming from the city, heading towards the archivect's estate, which lay further to the southwest.

Just after they passed by, a ragged figure suddenly emerged, apparently from nowhere, and ran in front of the horses, waving his arms wildly. The two leading horses shied, causing the others to swerve with a thudding of hooves and a jingle of harness. Shouts filled the night air, but Sayer could not make out what was being said.

'What's going on?' Kailas whispered, staring at the bizarre scene.

'I've no idea,' Sayer replied, 'but that was Hurghad.'

'He really must be mad,' she commented. 'It's a wonder they didn't run him down.'

One of the soldiers was now flailing at the hermit with his whip, angrily yelling at him to get out of the way, and then more actors entered the stage and the scene took on a more sinister aspect. The newcomers were on foot, dressed in black, and they moved from their hiding places silently and with purpose. Within moments all four soldiers had been dragged from their mounts and, after one vain attempt to spur his terrified horse into action again, Seigui was surrounded and the reins torn from his grasp. Hurghad vanished as quickly as he had come, but such was the confusion that Sayer could not tell whether he had run away or whether, like the unseated guards, he had been hauled off into the darkness.

The fading light of dusk glinted on drawn swords.

'What's the meaning of this?' Seigui demanded, though his voice shook with fear.

'Get down,' one of his assailants ordered. 'Now!'

The archivect did as he was told, and as he dismounted the man in black struck him a vicious blow across the back of his neck with the flat of his blade. Sayer could hear the bones snap from where he was and, beside him, Kailas gave a whimper of shock and revulsion as the archivect crumpled to the ground. The raiders disappeared into the night, taking the soldiers' horses with them, but leaving Seigui's to stamp nervously beside his fallen master.

'I think I'm going to be sick,' Kailas gasped.

Although Sayer was feeling as appalled as his wife, his own reactions were dominated by a sudden fear.

'Come on,' he urged her, taking her shoulders and guiding her into the hut. 'We have to get back as soon as we can.'

Kailas did not argue, and simply followed him down into the darkness. It was only when she reached the bottom and stood beside the stream that she caught her husband and held him close. Sayer could feel her trembling.

'That was Nazeri, wasn't it?' she whispered. 'The one who killed Seigui?'

'Yes.' Sayer had been hoping she had not recognized the captain, but his face had been clearly visible for a few moments and the harsh voice was unmistakable.

'I can't believe what he did,' Kailas breathed.

'We haven't got time for this now,' he told her, and pulled her across the water. 'We've got to get back before we're missed. If anyone thinks there's even a possibility of us seeing what we did, we'll be in danger ourselves.'

She recognized the urgency in his tone, and hurried along behind him, taking comfort from the clasp of his hand.

When they reached the underground room, Sayer drew the stone door to, so that it was almost shut. Although it would still be possible to open it from the other side, the tunnel was now less noticeable. Then he quietly unlocked the outer door and led Kailas up the steps.

'That's a remarkable collection of books, for a madman,' he said loudly. 'Pity he wasn't there to tell us more himself.'

'We can come back another time,' Kailas replied gamely, realizing that the conversation was for the benefit of their shadow. He was still sitting where they had left him, looking even more bored than before.

As they set off for the gatehouse, Sayer began to believe that they might get away with it. After all, they had been gone for a relatively short time, and it did not look as though their unwanted companion had bothered to investigate their progress underground. At the entrance to the estate, Sayer asked for transport back to the city and they were given horses from the stables there. Two guards accompanied them home, and Sayer was very glad that their route would not take them past the spot of the ambush. He had no wish to be there when the archivect's body was discovered. As it was, he and Kailas could not speak freely until they were at their own home and alone again.

'How could they do that?' Kailas burst out. 'They murdered him!'

'I know,' Sayer replied. 'And I think I may have been the cause.'

'You?' Then she saw what he meant. 'You mean the idea that you might change your allegiance? That surely wouldn't be enough to make Halion commit such a vile crime against the gods.'

'Maybe not in itself,' he agreed, 'but the feud between those two was already bad – and Nazeri is Halion's man.'

'I can't believe this is happening.' Kailas was on the verge of tears. 'If Halion is responsible for this, then nothing is sacred to him. Nothing!'

'We can't let a man like that rule Tirok,' Sayer vowed. 'After this, the Council will do anything he says. The price of opposing Halion has been made horribly clear.'

'But surely he can't admit what he's done?'

'No,' Sayer agreed. 'It'll be interesting to hear what the official explanation is.'

They found out early the next morning, and the messenger was Halion himself.

'I can't stay long,' he said after Sayer had let him in. 'I'm on my way to an emergency meeting of the Council.'

'More trouble?' Sayer asked.

'Something quite different, but grave news all the same,' the archivect replied. 'There was a terrible accident on the Gold Road last night. Seigui fell from his horse and broke his neck. He's dead.'

'How awful,' Kailas whispered.

'We had our differences, as you know, but this is an unfortunate business, to say the least.'

It was a credible performance and, just for a moment, Sayer wondered whether Nazeri could possibly have been acting on his own initiative, and Halion was genuinely unaware that his rival had been murdered. Then he remembered how many other lies Halion had told so convincingly.

'Do you know how it happened?' Sayer asked.

'Not yet. The investigation will clear it all up, no doubt, but it seems that his horse was spooked by Hurghad, of all people.'

'Hurghad?' Sayer exclaimed, trying to sound utterly bemused.

'Yes,' Halion replied. 'He was found dead too. His skull was crushed, probably by a blow from the horse's hoof. The gods know what he was doing out there.'

'Oh!' Kailas looked distraught.

Sayer went to her side and put an arm around her shoulders.

'We went to see the hermit last night,' he said quickly, 'but he wasn't there. Kailas and I spent a little time looking at some of his books, then gave up and went home.'

'I don't suppose you saw anything on the way?' Halion enquired.

Once again, Sayer answered for them both. Kailas was pale now, but he hoped that this would be interpreted as a shocked reaction to the news.

'No. Two guards went with us, and none of us saw anything unusual. Didn't Seigui have an escort?'

'He set out with one,' Halion replied, 'but he must have dismissed them for some reason. No one knows where the men are now. It's all very distressing. However, I wanted you to know that our celebration is still going ahead. It can also serve as a wake for Seigui, if necessary, but it's more important than ever that the Council shows its solidarity now. None of Seigui's children are old enough to take his place, so we've some urgent decisions to make.' He went to the door, then paused and turned back. 'I trust you both had a pleasant day yesterday.'

'It was wonderful,' Sayer replied. 'Thank you.'

'I'll let you know the arrangements for the feast as soon as they're finalized,' the archivect said as he left.

After Sayer had shut the door again, he turned to look at Kailas.

'Are you all right?'

'Just about.' Her voice quavered a little. 'But I'm not sure how much more of this I can stand.'

'You're doing fine,' he assured her, taking her in his arms again. Then another knock at the door made them both jump.

'Go upstairs, and try to get some more rest,' he said quietly. Neither of them had slept well that night. 'I'll deal with this.'

'Come and join me when you can,' Kailas responded gratefully.

'All right.' He kissed his wife and, as he watched her climb the stairs, wished that he could somehow distance her from all danger while still keeping her in his life.

To Sayer's utter disappointment, it was Safi and not Galieva who stood on the doorstep. The maid came bustling in but, rather than simply getting down to work as usual, she seemed intent on talking.

'Good morning, Seeker. I suppose Archivect Halion's told you the news.'

Sayer nodded.

'Dreadful, isn't it?' she went on. 'They say it was an accident, but I wouldn't be surprised if these so-called kyars've got something to do with it.'

'Why would you think that?' Sayer asked in some alarm.

'Well, they've been putting up all these posters full of blasphemy and lies. Haven't you seen them?'

'No,' he admitted. 'What do they say?'

'I can scarcely bring myself to tell you, it's such nonsense. They're all about how the Council's supposed to be ruining Tirok and we need a new government or something – can you *believe* that? Maybe they've decided to get rid of the Council one by one – and Seigui was their first victim.' She paused for breath. 'Then, to top it all, there was one notice that claimed they could cure the plague with magic! Well, I ask you, if that was possible, the archivects would've got all the people with talent – like you – to do it, wouldn't they? It's just getting people's hopes up for nothing.'

Sayer knew there was no point trying to argue with her. The kyars had obviously struck the first blows in the propaganda war, but if Safi's reaction was anything to go by, they had not yet been very successful.

'These kyars are making life difficult for all of us honest, law-abiding citizens,' the maid continued. 'The sooner the guards arrest them all, the better. Pack them all off to the Isle of the Dead, that's what I say. Let them use their magic to cure the plague there. If they can!'

CHAPTER TWENTY-NINE

'Accretions or erosion (such as is due to the action of
the elements) may be treated according to the needs of
each individual case. In repairing such damage, care
must be taken to retain the unique properties of any
part of the Temple's structures. The reconstruction
must be sound, but as close to the original as possible.'

From Herat's appendix to the 'yellow' ledgers of
The Plan (Archive reference ZL246)

Later that day, Sayer found himself at a loose end. Kailas
was asleep and he went to ask Safi, who was still at work in
the kitchen, if she would stay a while to look after his wife.

'Of course, Seeker.'

'Don't you have a young man waiting for you?'

'Oh, him!' she exclaimed dismissively. 'I've finished with
him. I've no time for anyone who tries to defend the kyars.'

'I'll be going out, then. Will you stay until I get back?'

'Certainly. Where are you going? In case your wife asks,'
she added, trying to hide her curiosity.

'To the Treasury.'

In fact, Sayer really only needed to get out of the house.
His destination was irrelevant. The fact that he was unable
to contact the kyars, and had to wait for them to get in touch

with him was becoming terribly frustrating. He recognized that this was the most sensible arrangement, but that did not make it any easier; if he went out, he might at least learn a little more about what had happened during his absence.

For want of something better to do, he actually did go to the Treasury, on the pretext of enquiring about their plans for the stone he had brought back from the south. Two of the guards, who were now stationed permanently outside his home, accompanied him on the way, and Sayer began to wonder how the kyars would ever be able to reach him. The soldiers waited outside after the seeker had been greeted by the official doorman.

'Good to see you've got your own escort,' the doorman commented. 'We all need protection these days, more's the pity.'

Sayer merely nodded as he went inside. When he reached the records office he discovered, to his surprise, that the relic had been sent to the stone-binders.

'But it wasn't damaged,' he protested.

The Treasury scribe consulted his ledger.

'That's true, as far as we can tell,' he said, 'but there was extensive cleaning to be done, so we decided to send it to the experts. We don't have the staff here for such tasks – and, to be frank, the thing *smelled*,' he added, wrinkling his nose in distaste.

'I see,' Sayer replied, suppressing a grin.

'In fact, there's a note here asking you to go and give them some advice,' the scribe went on. 'Do you know where their premises are?'

'Yes. I'll go there now.'

'There's no great urgency,' the official added, making his opinion of the find clear.

Pompous little bureaucrat, Sayer thought, then wondered whether he should try sneaking out of a side door, to avoid his guards. He was given no chance to do so, however, and as he came out onto the street again, the two soldiers got to their feet. On impulse, Sayer decided to confront them.

'Is this really necessary?' he asked. 'I'm only going to the stone-binders' workshop, and I doubt anyone's likely to attack me in broad daylight.'

'We have our orders, Seeker,' the senior man replied. 'If anything happened to you while you were out in the open, it'd be our responsibility, and you know what Captain Nazeri's like.'

'I do indeed.' The assumption that the soldiers' presence was purely for the seeker's own safety was a pretence, and all three men were aware of this, but Sayer also knew that if he tried to elude them he would only bring renewed suspicion upon himself.

'Come on, then,' he said resignedly. 'You must find this all very boring.'

'We've had worse assignments,' the second man replied as they set off.

'Really? What?'

'Better you don't know,' the senior partner cut in, giving his colleague a warning glance.

'Anything to do with the kyars?' Sayer asked.

'Don't worry about them. We'll soon take care of that problem.'

'They're scum. Preying on people's fears.'

They trudged on in silence for a while, and Sayer wished he had not begun the conversation.

'Are you looking forward to the feast tomorrow?' he asked eventually, unable to bear the awkward silence any longer.

'Should be a grand occasion,' the senior guard said, his tone carefully noncommittal.

'Just more work for us, though,' his companion complained. 'I don't suppose we'll even get the chance of a drink.'

'Bad luck,' Sayer said. 'Will you be on duty all the time, then?'

'Almost all the units will be. Halion's got everyone in a spin. Daft, if you ask me.'

'That's enough, soldier,' the other man said sharply.

At the entrance to the stone-binders' building, the guards once again left Sayer to go in alone. One of the senior overseers greeted him immediately.

'I'm sorry to inconvenience you like this, Seeker, but it does seem necessary. According to Bylar – he's one of our artisans, and especially good at this sort of thing – there are some accretions on the stone beneath the dirt, and he's not sure whether to remove them or not. We don't know if they're part of the original block or later additions, so you see our problem. I hope you don't mind coming here for such a menial task.'

'It's no trouble,' Sayer replied. 'I've no other official duties today. You helped me out recently,' he went on, 'so it's the least I can do.'

As he followed the overseer through a series of interconnected workrooms, most of which were in use, his senses were assaulted. An assortment of strange smells filled his nostrils, the heat from furnaces and braziers was intense in places, and the noise from various rasps and chisels was intermittently very loud.

'How do you work in a place like this?'

'You get used to it,' the overseer replied with an indulgent smile.

By comparison, Bylar's yard – at the rear of the complex – was light and airy. The relic lay on solid wooden trestles in the middle of the yard, surrounded by various utensils and pots of liquid. The artisan himself had his back to them as he washed his hands in a stone trough, but he turned around as the visitors came in – and Sayer had to struggle to remain impassive. The artisan might be known as Bylar here at his workplace, but when Sayer had met him before he had called himself Serin.

'Bylar, here's the seeker you've been asking for. His time is valuable, so try not to detain him for too long.'

The artisan shrugged.

'The job in hand dictates how long it'll take,' he said bluntly. 'If you want it done right.'

'Yes, well, do your best.' The overseer glanced apologetically at Sayer. 'I'll leave you to it.'

'I'm worried about these nodules,' Bylar stated, beckoning Sayer over to join him. 'Come and take a look.'

The seeker knelt down beside him and looked to where Bylar was fingering some small, dark protrusions on the surface of the block.

'Don't worry about this,' the kyar said in a quieter voice. 'It's simple enough, but I can make it last an hour or two if necessary. And if it looks as though we're talking about the relic, no one will know if we also discuss a few other matters.'

'Is it safe?'

'As safe here as anywhere. We're not likely to be overheard. Life's become a great deal more complicated since we last met.'

'So I gather.'

'Are you still with us?'

'If I'm not, then you're in a lot of trouble,' Sayer pointed out. 'I know your real name now.'

'I'm aware of that,' Bylar replied coldly.

'I'm still with you,' the seeker confirmed hurriedly. 'More than ever now.'

'Good.' The artisan took a cloth, dipped it in one of the pots and dabbed at the pitted surface of the relic. 'I'm risking my own life by trusting you, Sayer, but with the soldiers following you around like lost sheep, this seemed the only way I could get to talk to you.'

'You needn't worry about me.'

'That message from your sister must have been quite something, to have made you so sure of yourself,' Bylar commented.

'It was,' Sayer admitted, 'but even if it hadn't been, I'd still want to join you.'

'Has something else happened?'

'I saw Seigui murdered last night.'

For the first time since their initial meeting, Sayer saw the kyar look shocked.

'You *saw* it happen? Do you know who did it?'

'One of Halion's men. A captain called Nazeri.'

Bylar whistled softly.

'You're sure?'

'Yes. I work with him.'

'We didn't believe it was an accident. There are a lot of rumours flying about, but most of them seem to think *we're* to blame. Did anyone else see it happen?'

Sayer hesitated, then decided to tell the truth.

'Yes. Kailas was there with me. And Hurghad was involved, but he's dead too. I don't really know what he was doing. He might have been trying to warn Seigui, or he might just have been caught up in the ambush by chance.'

Bylar took a few moments to absorb this information.

'Did anyone see you?' he asked eventually.

Sayer shook his head.

'I don't think so.'

'They'd have let you know if they had,' Bylar said dryly. 'What does Kailas think of this? It must've been quite a shock for her.'

'It was,' the seeker agreed, 'but not as much as you might think.'

'Why?'

'I'd already told her about the kyars – and that I'm trying to help you.'

'That was a mistake,' Bylar said gravely.

'It was a risk,' Sayer conceded, 'but I can't do this without her. I haven't told her anything that could compromise you or Galieva. I'm the only one she can betray – and I don't think she will.'

'I hope you're right,' the kyar said. 'At least she knows now that Halion is the real enemy. Our scheme to provoke a little enmity between archivects worked all too well, didn't it? Halion will have the entire Council in his pocket soon, if he hasn't already.' He paused, deep in thought, still working absently on the stone. 'Do you honestly believe Kailas can be one of us?'

'Yes. I'm sure of it. I'd bet my life on it.'

'You already have,' Bylar said heavily.

'It's done now,' Sayer added with a touch of anger.

'You realize there's still a chance that your wife is Halion's spy?'

'I don't believe that, but I won't tell her any more than I have to, until you're satisfied.'

'Fair enough. I was actually going to ask you a favour involving Kailas, so this might make it easier.'

'What favour?'

'The third crow returned yesterday. It—'

'Is there any news of Aphra?'

'Nothing specific, no. We know her work is continuing, though, and that's what the favour is about.' Bylar reached into a pocket, took out a tiny bag and handed it to Sayer. It was so light he assumed it was empty.

'What's this?'

'There's a leaf inside, from the herb they've called aphran. The crow brought it, and we were wondering if you could show it to your wife and see if she recognized it. Her father's an expert on herbs and spices, so we thought she might be able to help.'

'Aphra thought it only grew at the island graveyard.'

'I know, but there's no harm in looking over here. If it does exist on the mainland—' Bylar broke off as the overseer came out into the yard again. Both he and Sayer stood up, stretching cramped muscles.

'How are you progressing?'

'One step at a time,' the artisan replied gruffly.

The overseer turned to Sayer.

'If Bylar can spare you for a few moments, I'd be delighted to show you our other work in progress.'

'Later, perhaps,' the seeker replied. 'I'm happy to help here.'

'I need him to confirm each layer as I clean,' Bylar explained.

'Very well.' The overseer went back into the building, and the two men squatted down again to resume their conversation.

'I'll do what I can,' Sayer said. The bag was already secreted inside his own tunic.

'Good. We could do with a bit of luck at the moment. To be honest, things haven't been going as well as we'd have liked. We can shout about a cure for the plague until we're blue in the face, but without some proof . . . ' He shrugged. 'What I wouldn't give to be able to get just one boat off the island.'

'No progress with the shriekers, I presume.'

'It's worse than that,' Bylar replied ominously. 'We found out a little about their training. It seems that unless a shrieker is given a particular drug before they go to work, they die on contact with the monsters. That's one of the reasons they're always accompanied by soldiers. Simply capturing one of the sentinels would be useless by itself, and even if we managed to steal some of the drug too, I couldn't ask any of my people to administer it.'

'Why not?' Sayer asked, although he had already guessed the answer.

'Because it slowly destroys the brain of the user. That's what kills them, not the creatures' thoughts.'

'So we have to find another way.'

Bylar nodded.

'If we can. Any ideas?' He sounded despondent.

'Not at the moment, no.'

'It's one of the reasons we *have* to find a cure here. We must face the fact that we may never get direct help from the island.'

'I won't accept that,' Sayer declared.

'None of us will until we've tried everything,' the kyar vowed. 'But we still have to stop Halion.'

'Can you tell me what else you're doing?'

'It's better you don't know,' Bylar replied, ironically echoing the soldier's words. 'At the moment, we're concentrating on getting as many people as possible to question what they see around them. It's working to an extent, but too many of them have a vested interest in the existing system, and most of the rest don't care about anything beyond their own misfortunes. I can't really blame them for that. We need to offer them something better, something real.'

'Is there anything I can do?' Sayer asked. 'At the feast tomorrow, maybe?'

'No,' the kyar answered firmly. 'I don't know what Halion is planning, but he's probably hoping to draw us out into the open – and that's the last thing we can afford right now.'

'I've been told that almost all the army units will be on duty,' Sayer added, realizing how foolish his offer had been.

'We guessed as much. What you have to do is go and play

your part like a good servant of the Council. The more you're identified with Halion, the better it'll be when you reveal your true allegiance.'

'And when will that be?' the seeker asked apprehensively.

'Not until we're ready – and there's no telling *when* that'll be.'

'Halion told me that some kyars had been captured. Is that true?'

'Unfortunately, yes. Three of us were caught putting up posters. Fortunately, it wasn't anyone who can do our organization any real damage,' Bylar said grimly. 'The chances are that they'll be on the Isle of the Dead before long. At least I hope so.'

'You *hope* so?' Sayer exclaimed.

'After what you've told me about Seigui, exile seems the best they could hope for,' the kyar said.

CHAPTER THIRTY

'Who is to say how secrets are revealed? A true prophet does not need a clear day to see into the distances of time. Within the swirling clouds of capnomancy, the air is bright.'

From *Rituals of Fire and Air*,
by Kudrak of Namakzar

Dominion Square was bright with flags and banners, and filled with people. The early morning clouds had dispersed so that, at the appointed hour of noon, the sky was clear and the sun was warm, even though midwinter's day was little more than a month away. It was as though not even the weather dared spoil Halion's plans.

For the last few days the preparations had involved large numbers of carpenters and other artisans, as well as all kinds of merchants, cooks, scribes and soldiers. A huge wooden platform had been erected along the western side of the square. This was where the archivects and their guests now congregated, looking down on the long lines of trestle tables set up across the rest of the large open space. These tables groaned under the weight of huge joints of roast meat, piles of fruit, pyramids of bread, barrels of wine and ale, and a great deal more besides. No expense had been spared, and the lure of free food and drink meant that the entire area – and several of the nearby streets – was thronged with eager citizens, all anxious to claim their portion of the spoils. It could have been a recipe for chaos, but it was not, thanks to the huge number of soldiers who were keeping order. They marshalled the flow of humanity and ensured, as far as was possible, that everyone would have a chance to share in the feast.

On the raised wooden dais there was less of a crush, but it was still crowded. The dignitaries were all in their best clothes, with everyone who was entitled to do so wearing the coloured headband that denoted their status. All nine remaining members of the Council were there, together with their families and most of their prominent servants – especially those with talent. Seekers, silks and scribes were well represented, and there were even a few daydreamers present, as well as some high-ranking military officers, senior representatives of the artisans, and guests from the world of commerce.

Sayer, with Kailas by his side, was feeling more than a little apprehensive, but did his best not to show it, and entered into the generally affable conversation with as good a grace as he could muster. He had already been greeted warmly by many people, including Damaris – whom he had not seen for some time – and Kebir, who seemed, for once, to be in good humour. Mayumi, the seeker who had tried to recruit Sayer for his recently deceased master, had been less cordial, and several of the archivects, careful of their dignity, had been polite but formal.

Overall, the mood was a strange mixture of merriment and a slightly uneasy sense of anticipation. Although Halion had announced earlier that the feast was intended to be a joyful affair, the death of Seigui – and the general supposition that the archivects would not have been so extravagant without good reason – meant that Halion's promised speech of welcome was awaited with considerable curiosity and a little trepidation. This was especially true for Sayer, and all the music and other entertainments failed to distract his ominous thoughts.

The noise level in the square had risen to a clamorous roar of several thousand separate conversations, but when Halion stepped up onto the small pulpit that had been constructed at the edge of the platform, silence spread out around him. He waited, his face impassive, as a slight wind ruffled his yellow robes, until even the furthest corners of his audience were quiet and all eyes were upon him. Even from his position behind and to one side, Sayer could tell that his master was in his element, revelling in what the archivect saw as his rightful position as the centre of all things. He was filled with confidence and power, and the sunlight made him look both strong and impossibly bright, as though he were lit by some inner fire. When he spoke, his voice was strong and resonant, carrying easily across the crowd.

'My friends, this feast is meant to be a joyous occasion, and so it will be.'

There was a smattering of applause and a few cheers at this, but these faded quickly when Halion held up his hands, his expression still solemn.

'However, as you all know, there is one matter of concern to us all, a matter that cannot wait, and which I intend to address now. The death of Archivect Seigui came as a great shock to everyone, especially those of us fortunate enough to have known him well. He served Tirok admirably, and his untimely passing is a tragedy that will be mourned for some time to come. There are members of his family and household here today, and our thoughts and prayers are with them in their time of grief.

'Sadly, none of his children are old enough to assume his place on the Council. In our discussions, the remaining members have in any case reached the conclusion that Seigui was irreplaceable. It has therefore been decided that, until his eldest son comes of age, I will become guardian to all the children and assume responsibility for his household and army units.'

At this a ripple of comment ran through the crowd, a murmuring of surprise that died away slowly. As Halion waited to continue, Sayer recalled Bylar's words, which had now taken on the chilly significance of prophecy. *Halion will have the entire Council in his pocket soon.* The process had already begun.

'I do not take these new duties lightly,' the archivect went on. 'All my resources will be made available, to ensure that the change is as painless as it can be in these unhappy circumstances.' He paused, gazing round the assembled throng with mesmeric eyes. 'Which brings me to the exact nature of Archivect Seigui's death. At first it was believed that it had come about by an inexplicable but fateful accident. However,' he added, raising his voice over the buzz of speculation in the audience, 'I have now been informed that there were more sinister forces at work. Seigui was murdered.'

During the uproar that greeted this declaration, Sayer groaned inwardly. He knew what was coming. In retrospect, it had always been inevitable. He glanced at Kailas, sensing the tension in her and wondering if she knew it too. The hubbub eventually subsided, at the urging of a large number of soldiers, and Halion was able to speak again.

'This most heinous crime, which all the gods abhor, was committed by those people who call themselves the kyars, the same blasphemous fools who have spread so many vile rumours of late. Until now I had thought this small group of insurgents to be worthy of only our mockery and contempt, but with this act they proved me wrong. They are truly dangerous, a pernicious blight on our whole society, a blight which we must eradicate.'

As the crowd muttered its many-throated approval, Sayer could only bite his tongue. He longed to shout out the truth, to expose the appalling hypocrisy of Halion's words, but he knew he had to play his part 'like a good servant of the Council'.

'Therefore,' Halion continued, sensing the general mood and knowing that the time was ripe for his next revelation, 'the Council has unanimously decided to deal with these kyars in the most severe manner possible. As of this moment, every single member of the kyar organization – and anyone who aids or protects these criminals – is no longer one of us. We are revoking their Tirokian citizenship.'

Sayer found that he could not breathe. His mouth and throat were dry, and his lungs seemed incapable of action. This was worse than he had feared. In themselves, Halion's words seemed innocuous, but their implication was clear to all, as the volume of gasps from the onlookers testified. Anyone who was no longer a Tirokian citizen was, by definition, of the same status as a godless foreigner – and their lives would no longer be sacrosanct. The terror could come out into the open now; no more midnight burials, no more secret ambushes . . .

'We do this in sorrow as well as righteous anger,' Halion stated. 'It was not an easy decision, nor did we take it lightly, but by flaunting their disregard for the most sacred of our laws, the kyars have proved themselves to be beyond the reach of common decency. This punishment is just.'

The murmur of speculation from the crowd swelled once more. However, when three soldiers climbed up onto the stage, each of them guiding a dejected prisoner whose wrists and ankles were encased in iron manacles, the sudden silence became profound. A new and selfish dread entered Sayer's mind as he wondered if any of the three captured kyars knew of his own involvement. Had any of them been in the

Temple that night? Although he immediately felt ashamed of his thoughts, he avoided looking at the pitiful trio as much as he could. For their part, the three – two young men and a woman who was little more than a girl – hung their heads in misery and perhaps pain, and did not look at anyone around them.

'These three were arrested as they tried to put up more of the illegal posters you have all seen or heard about,' Halion went on. 'Like the rest of the kyars' notices, they were full of sedition, unforgivable lies designed to undermine the authority of the Council and all those who serve Tirok loyally. Some of their claims are laughable, while others are more plausible on the surface but false nonetheless. All the kyars are deluded, but not all of them are lunatics. Some are fanatics, and they are the most dangerous of all. Because of the menace that they pose, the Council has agreed on new laws, giving the military authorities greater powers than usual. This is a temporary measure, which will be repealed as soon as this crisis is over. It is a small price to pay to rid ourselves of this canker in our midst.'

Sayer quailed at the thought of the oppression that was bound to follow this announcement. Judging by the subdued reaction of the audience, he was not alone in his doubts. Halion sensed it too, and went on swiftly.

'In the meantime, we must decide what to do with these self-confessed traitors. Take them away,' he ordered, waving a dismissive hand at the kyars. 'We will leave it to the gods to decide their fate later,' he announced as the prisoners were led from the platform. 'And that is what we must all do. Submit ourselves to the will of the gods. The oracles have told us what the future of this great country can be. It is our duty to fulfil the promises of our forebears. Completing the great task is the only way we can meet our destiny with pride. I am here now to rededicate myself and all of my fellow archivects – and all of you – to that task. Together we can succeed. And that is why we have all come here today, to celebrate the achievements of the last three decades, to toast the men and women whose skill and talent have made it possible, and to pledge even greater efforts in the future. So eat, drink and enjoy yourselves!'

On that positive note of largesse, Halion touched head and heart, then stepped down to a roar of approval. He had given his audience much to think and talk about, and the noise level rose again as the feasting began in earnest.

'What will happen to those three?' Kailas whispered anxiously.

Sayer shook his head.

'I don't know,' he said, and once again heard Bylar's words. *Exile seems the best they can hope for.*

'What did Halion mean about letting the gods decide later?'

'I don't know,' he repeated. Sayer had sensed the crowd's disappointment when the prisoners had been taken away without their fate being determined, and could not help thinking that Halion had missed an opportunity then. 'I'm sure we'll find out soon enough.'

Then there was no more time for private speculation because, as one of the guests of honour, Sayer was expected to meet many people. Although he did his best to appear good-humoured, he found the whole process agonizing and longed for the ordeal to be over.

Several hours later, when the platform was in shade and the air was growing cold, there was still no sign of the gathering dispersing. Although the feasting had lost its urgency now, the square was still packed with revellers, and the musicians, jugglers, acrobats and clowns were still performing. Sayer and Kailas had become separated when Zanu had taken his sister off to meet some of his business associates, and Sayer had been trapped in conversation with one of the older archivects. Izod's headband was yellow with flecks of red and purple and, after several cups of wine, it was now slightly askew. The old man had been bemoaning recent events and praising Halion lavishly, without allowing Sayer to do much more than nod in agreement, but now he tugged at the seeker's sleeve and pointed to the pulpit.

'This should be interesting,' he remarked eagerly.

Sayer turned to look, and saw that a ceremonial brazier had been set up on the upper level of the stand, where everyone could see it. A thin column of hot air wavered above the coals within, distorting the scene beyond. All the music ceased, and a sudden roll of drums announced the next scene in the afternoon's performance. Flanked by two of his fellow archivects, Halion climbed the steps to stand before the brazier, and waited once more until he had everyone's undivided attention. Then, without a word, he placed a variety of sacrificial offerings into the fire. Sayer noted some herbs, bark and twigs, a few drops of oil and several other items he could not identify. As the flames leapt up, those closest to the stage were able to smell the diverse scents within the smoke.

At last Halion broke the silence.

'I promised you that the gods would decide the fate of the prisoners. In the name of Zavanaiu, pray that the oracles may guide us. Let it be done now.' He was handed a goblet of wine by each of his companions and poured the libations onto the fire, adding a few quiet words in the old tongue. Although the fierce hissing lasted only a few moments, the column of smoke and steam that rose up was thick and carried within it fleeting glimpses of colour, like lightning inside a thundercloud.

Everybody there watched intently as the column shifted and expanded, waiting for a sign. As it rose higher, the smoke left the shadows and emerged into the slanting rays of sunlight and, as it did so, Sayer felt the air around him grow thick and slippery. There were sparks before his eyes and, without needing to look for her, he knew that Kailas was similarly affected. He had known such a sensation only once before – in the Rivash Canyon when the false warriors had appeared. However, others did not share his sensibilities or his experience, and took what they saw at face value.

The sunlit smoke turned red and slowly began to form into a shape. Before long, the many-fanged head was recognizable to everyone there as the most terrifying of all the pantheon. Yet it took one young man, whose pale-blue headband marked him as a daydreamer, to put the awe of the crowd into words.

'Durak!' he cried. 'Behold the drinker of blood!'

The illusion was dispersing now, as the smoke drifted on the breeze, but it no longer mattered. The people had their answer. What had begun as a few isolated voices grew into a low rumble and then to a repeated chorus of ever-increasing volume.

'Blood!'

The chant took on a malevolent life of its own, became a torrent of sound.

'Blood. Blood. Blood!'

CHAPTER THIRTY-ONE

'Rakeharrow: Apart from its healing properties, which
are well attested, this herb is enshrined in the mythology of rainmaking. It is said that the steam released
from boiling the leaves, together with certain ancient
chants and dances, causes clouds to form in clear skies
and rain to fall if clouds are already present. Such
legends are, in the opinion of this author, quite without foundation.'

Entry in *Royle's Herbal Index*

'That was horrible,' Kailas whispered, as Sayer held her in
his arms. 'Horrible.'

It was only now that they were home again that they were
able to speak about what they had seen and heard. Although
Sayer had gone to his wife's side as soon as the smoke began
to rise, instinctively knowing where she was, they had been
forced to listen while Halion promised the crowds that the
gods' will would be honoured. Although they had desperately wanted to escape, it had been some time before they
were able to leave – and even then their journey through the
congested streets had taken longer than usual, with their
escort having to force a way through in places. Halion's manipulation of the throng had produced a degree of hysteria

that amounted to madness, and Sayer could only hope that saner counsel would prevail the next morning. What he could not understand was exactly how Halion had achieved his purpose.

'You felt it too, didn't you?' he said, knowing that Kailas would follow his train of thought.

'The magic, you mean?' she replied. 'Yes. That was one of the things that made it so terrible. How could anyone abuse their talent like that?'

'They were just doing what Halion told them, the same as us.'

'We don't create false illusions to condemn innocent people!' she protested. 'That's quite different!'

'There aren't many of us who actually know they *are* innocent,' he pointed out.

'The gods know,' Kailas stated fiercely. 'Halion won't be allowed to get away with this. It's sacrilege.'

'That doesn't seem to have bothered him recently. It's just one more way of twisting the truth.'

'Do you think we're the only ones who know it was a trick?' she asked.

'I doubt it. There were plenty of others with talent there, but they're not likely to make a fuss, are they? Most of them won't *want* to believe their instincts.'

'How can you be so calm about this?'

'If we're ever going to fight back, we *have* to stay calm,' he told her. 'Have you any idea how it was done?'

'No, but I can guess. The image looked very like one of the stone idols on Halion's estate.'

'Of course. It was a memory projected onto the smoke.'

'Probably with the help of a small piece of the statue,' Kailas added. 'I'm not sure how memories can be converted into a vision, or actually used to shape the smoke, but we're so specialized in what we do. Who knows what magic can be turned to?'

'"Magic can be used for many purposes",' Sayer quoted, remembering Mehran-Dar and his own experiences in the Rivash Canyon.

'And now we must decide what to use ours for,' Kailas said, unconsciously echoing another of the healer's statements.

'You really think we have a choice?' her husband asked uncertainly.

'Why not? It's only our training that's restricted us.'

A horrifying possibility occurred to Sayer then.

'Do you think we might have been able to disrupt what happened today?' he said. 'Could we have stopped what Halion was doing?'

'I doubt it,' Kailas replied. 'Even if we'd known how to counteract the magic, we'd had no time to prepare. We didn't know what was coming.'

'Or who was responsible,' Sayer added soberly.

'We'll never find out now,' his wife told him. 'Whoever it was isn't likely to boast about what they've done. Halion will see to that.'

Zanu arrived later that evening and, even though Sayer and Kailas would have preferred to be left alone, they could hardly refuse to entertain this visitor. As a result they were forced to endure a long discussion of the afternoon's events, which Kailas's brother had clearly found both astounding and awe-inspiring.

'One thing's for certain,' he concluded. 'The kyars won't be getting too many new recruits after that little exhibition.'

Belatedly sensing their reluctance to talk, he moved on to other topics.

'Anyway, I had a splendid time today. Made all sorts of contacts which should be good for business. I'm off to Jandaq tomorrow, so I'm afraid I won't be able to honour you with my presence for dinner this time.'

'On your next trip, then,' Kailas suggested.

'Definitely.'

'While we're talking of business,' she went on, 'I've something that might interest you.'

'Is it something Halion wants?' Zanu asked eagerly. He obviously realized where the power lay in Qara, and was eager to ingratiate himself.

'Not that I'm aware of,' Kailas replied, smiling at her brother's transparent ambition. 'And I'm sure you don't need my help to wheedle your way into his household.'

'I'll take any advantage I can,' he replied, grinning. 'So, what is it?'

Kailas stood up and opened the small box where she had placed the leaf from the Isle of the Dead. When Sayer had shown her the fragment of aphran it had seemed vaguely familiar, but she had not been able to put a name to it.

'Do you know what this is?'

Zanu took the leaf gently and peered at it closely, then raised it to his nose and sniffed.

'Hmm. Where did you get this?'

'From a travelling merchant. He knew our family were experts in the field, but I didn't recognize it. He said the locals told him it was supposed to have some beneficial properties.'

'Such as?'

'He wouldn't say. And he wouldn't tell me where it came from either, except that it was somewhere near the Lake of Souls.'

'It's still reasonably fresh,' Zanu commented. 'So it can't have come too far.'

'Have you come across it anywhere?'

'I don't think so.' He turned the leaf over in his fingers. 'But it's difficult to tell just from this. Let's see. Entire, ovate blade, ordinary petiole, interesting scent. I don't suppose the merchant told you the leaf structure?'

'I think he said they came in threes,' Kailas answered.

Sayer had been about to say the same thing, wishing he had described the herb he had seen in more detail, and Kailas's words took him by surprise. He could not remember telling her about the plant's shape.

'Trifoliate then,' Zanu said, nodding. 'Any flowers? Fruit?'

'Not that we know of,' Kailas replied, again anticipating Sayer's thoughts.

'Reminds me a little of rakeharrow,' her brother concluded thoughtfully. 'There's something different about this, though.'

'Is rakeharrow common?' Sayer asked.

'Not really. And it's useful in the treatment of fevers, so it's quite valuable. What's this merchant willing to give you in return for information?'

'He wanted Father to test it. If it's any good he'll give him an exclusive contract for the next crop.'

'Interesting. Can I keep this?'

'No,' Kailas said, to Sayer's relief. 'I need it back.'

Zanu handed it over without protest.

'Perhaps we should have let you help with the business after all,' he remarked with a grin.

'And let me spoil your fun by being better than any of you boys?' she taunted him.

'Don't push your luck, sister. I was paying you a compliment.'

'Why, thank you, kind sir,' Kailas said, curtseying extravagantly.

Zanu glanced at Sayer, his eyebrows raised.

'I hope you don't let my sister mock you like this.'

'Only when I deserve it,' the seeker replied gravely, amazed that he was able to join in with their banter after the events of the day.

* * *

'Should we tell the kyars about rakeharrow?' Kailas asked, after Zanu had gone.

'Of course.'

'How do we go about it?'

'I'll find a way.'

'Can't I talk to them myself?' she said. 'They may have questions, and I know a lot more about herbs than you do.'

Sayer hesitated, and knew from his wife's expression that she had guessed the reason.

'They don't trust me,' she said.

'It's not that. It's just better if we all know as few of the others as possible. Do you see?'

Kailas looked at him, obviously unconvinced.

'So we don't endanger anyone else if we're arrested?' she guessed.

'Exactly. It makes sense, Kailas. This isn't a game.'

'I know that,' she snapped. 'Makes planning difficult though, doesn't it? What do I have to do for them to trust me?'

'I don't know,' he admitted.

'Where did you first meet them?'

'In the Temple. At night.'

'Oh.' Kailas was taken aback.

Sayer recognized that she found it difficult to come to terms with such heretical behaviour, but after all she had learned recently, he was not sure why.

'You know—' he began.

'Just because other people have lost their respect for the oracles,' she cut in, 'it doesn't mean I have to.'

The next four days saw considerable upheaval in the city. A curfew was imposed within the walls and military patrols seemed to be everywhere, but despite this the kyars did not give up their campaign. More posters were tacked up in different sites and, as fast as the soldiers tore them down, others appeared. There was no way that all the rumour and gossip they provoked could be prevented from spreading.

One of the kyars' claims that was widely discussed – usually with a great deal of scepticism – was that the demonstration in Dominion Square had been misinterpreted, and that the treatment of the three prisoners was a travesty of justice. This was followed by the even more outrageous claim that *Halion* had been responsible for Seigui's death – with jealous rivalry between their two houses given as the motive. Although few people took this theory seriously, it provoked an angry response from the Council, with official denials posted wherever the accusations had appeared. The authorities' frustration was compounded by the fact that none of those responsible for putting up the seditious posters was caught and, in spite of public reassurances, it did not seem as if the kyar organization would soon be destroyed. Some token arrests were made, but the true identity of the rebel leaders remained a mystery. In the meantime, however, the date for the trial of the three captives was announced – even though everyone knew that their fate had already been decided.

Sayer was aware of this only through the unreliable means of hearsay. Nevertheless, between that and his own observations, a reasonably clear – if depressing – picture emerged. He had managed to pass on what he had learnt about the herb to Galieva, in a hurried conversation at his home. The maid had been able to visit him only for a short time because Safi was taking her duties very seriously now, and too many unexplained appearances would have been risky. Because of this, and because of his certainty that trying to contact Bylar would be dangerous, Sayer could learn nothing more about what was happening on Jazireh or what the kyars' plans were. The enforced inactivity grated on his nerves, and he began to appreciate his wife's misgivings about the rebels' system of communication. In earlier times Kailas would have been the one to calm him down, but now she was obviously in a state of some anxiety herself. Her researches into rakeharrow had revealed that it grew wild, mostly at the western end of the Lake of Souls, in the delta area of the Kul River, and that its properties included the reduction of fevers, the healing of sores and – improbably – the ability of those who consumed it to affect the weather, most specifically as rainmakers. She had wanted Sayer to pass this information on to the kyars, but he had no opportunity to do so until – much to the seeker's relief – Bylar appeared on the stairs of his house as if by magic, and beckoned Sayer to join him on the upper floor.

'I was beginning to think you'd forgotten me.'

'It's difficult,' Bylar replied. 'Now that there are so many more guards about, I have to pick my times carefully. How long will Kailas be gone?'

'About an hour.' She had been called away to assist another silk with a stone that had been found – against all the odds – embedded in the walls of Qara itself. 'Maybe longer if she has to use her talent. What's happening?'

Bylar gave him a quick rundown of recent events, without telling Sayer anything much he didn't already know, then ended by admitting that they were not really achieving very much.

'It's all we can do to keep our spirits up at the moment. And after the trial it'll be even worse.'

'Isn't there anything you can do about that?'

'A daring rescue, you mean?' Bylar said bitterly. 'We may try, but there's not much hope. Security's very tight.'

'So what *do* we do?'

'Our best hope is that people will be so revolted by the

prospect of more bloodshed that Halion will have to back down.' His tone made it clear that he did not feel very optimistic. 'In the meantime, we're still working on a way of getting a boat off the island. We need proof that what we've been saying is true. If we can do that with just one thing, then it'll be much more likely that people will accept the rest.'

'I'm proof that you're right about Seigui's murder,' Sayer put in. 'Kailas and I were there. We saw what happened. Surely we can use that in some way?'

'Who'd believe you?' the kyar replied. 'You may be our trump card, Sayer. Once you declare yourself, it'll be all or nothing – and we can't risk that yet. We need something that can't be denied – like the return of some healthy plague victims.'

Sayer could see his point. At the back of his mind an idea began to form.

'We've finally persuaded the crows to return to the island,' Bylar said. 'At least, they flew off in that direction.'

'That's good news,' Sayer responded, setting his own thoughts aside.

'Let's hope the messages they bring back are good too,' the kyar added.

Sayer told him what Kailas had discovered about rake-harrow.

'We already know that much,' Bylar said. 'We've got people investigating in the delta now. We're pretty sure it's already been tried on the plague, though, to no effect.'

'Perhaps aphran is a hybrid, rakeharrow mixed with something else.'

'If it is, then it's possible that it only exists on the island,' the kyar said gloomily. 'We'll keep trying, though.'

'Have you thought any more about Kailas?'

'What about her?'

'She wants to help, to prove herself worthy of your trust.'

'As it happens, I would like to meet her.' Bylar seemed mildly amused by the seeker's obvious surprise. 'Provided certain precautions are taken. Will she come to the Temple?'

'At night?'

'Yes.'

'I'm not sure. Her faith's been stretched recently, but not broken.'

'Let me know if she decides to stretch it a little further.'

'How?'

'Leave something you want cleaning at the stone-binders. Don't ask for me. I'll find out. We'll wait for her that same night.'

'He was here, wasn't he?' Kailas asked, almost as soon as she had come through the door.

'What do you mean?'

'The kyar. I can see him in your eyes.'

'Don't look too closely,' Sayer advised her, wondering how she suddenly seemed to be able to read his thoughts. 'He wants to meet you.'

'At the Temple?'

'Yes. At night.'

'I'm not ready for that yet,' she said, not bothering to hide her annoyance. 'It's stupid and dangerous, especially now there's a curfew. There must be another way to gain their trust.'

Sayer did not reply and, as she turned away, he felt part of her anger and disappointment.

'I take it you didn't have to work tonight,' he said, wanting to break the silence.

'Do you think I'd still be standing up if I had?' she enquired caustically. 'Darte was quite capable of handling it on his own. He just wanted some advice.'

For a moment Sayer caught a glimpse of the scene, with the artisans crowded round as the violet-enclosed stone was carefully removed.

'Well, we can't have the city walls falling down, can we?' he said.

'I'm tired,' Kailas said, without responding to his smile. 'I'm going to bed.'

The trial was a formality. Although the defendants denied the charge of murder – all they admitted to was membership of the kyars and putting up posters – and no proof was offered of any direct involvement in Seigui's death, their actions were being treated as treason. This was a very serious matter in itself, and all doubts about the outcome of the deliberations had already been swept aside by the demonstration of the gods' will in Dominion Square.

When Halion, as chairman of the panel of judges, announced the verdict and sentences, there were a few half-hearted pleas for mercy from the appointed lawyers, but these were summarily denied. As Halion pointed out in his summation, their fate was necessary as an example to others.

Sayer was not in Qara when the executions were due to be carried out, and a cowardly part of him was glad of that. It absolved him from the responsibility of trying to do anything about the barbaric injustice being inflicted on three young people whose only fault was to believe in the wrong cause. He had been sickened and horrified by the general blood lust that Halion had stirred up, and did not know whether the kyars would risk any attempt to save their comrades – or how he could help if they did. Nevertheless, his absence helped to salve his conscience.

When he and Kailas returned from their latest mission, they discovered that there had been no rescue attempt. Whether this had been due to callous calculation or merely to help-lessness was something they had no way of knowing. How-ever, once the mob hysteria of Dominion Square had worn off, the deaths of the young people – even if they were no longer citizens – had disgusted many, and Sayer could only hope that public opinion would now begin to work in the kyars' favour. Even if it did, he reflected dismally, it would do little good for those who had already paid with their lives.

CHAPTER THIRTY-TWO

'Telepathy is the mind's way of telling the tongue to
shut up.'
           Graffiti in the basement of the Hariolatorium

Sayer had been back in Qara for several days before he
realized what was making his life unbearable. There were
many things wrong with his world, and there was no sign of
any of them getting better, but in recent days the one thing
that had kept him sane and given him a little hope had been
his relationship with Kailas. During the mission they had
naturally talked about the situation they found themselves
in, and although they had not reached any firm conclusions
about what they should do, they were in almost total agreement about how they felt. Very often words were unnecessary.
They both acknowledged this occasional sharing of their
thoughts and were glad of it. Something had blossomed
between them, something inexplicable and probably unique
but oddly comforting. They felt closer than they had ever
done before, and the strength of their newly discovered
bond had been demonstrated clearly when they located the
relic. There had been no need for the usual physical contact
between seeker and silk to facilitate the telepathic exchange.
As soon as the precise thought formed in Sayer's head,

Kailas knew the necessary location and shape of the stone perfectly. Sayer had been aware of the fleeting touch of minds then, and had been warmed by the sensations of love and trust that surrounded it. It was not a complete sharing by any means – they retained their individual privacy – but it was more than they had any right to expect.

However, something had changed during the last few days. Kailas had begun to seem remote, almost as though she were trying to hide something from him. It was not that she acted differently, but simply that the almost supernatural link had faded, the special warmth was gone. This added another layer of distress to the way Sayer was feeling, but he was unable to confront his wife about it; he knew that she would simply deny that anything was wrong, and he would be unable to offer any tangible proof to the contrary. He was left to contemplate the world around him – a world that was becoming more hateful by the day.

Halion's grip on the city, on the machinery of government and control of the army, grew tighter all the time. New laws, new restrictions and edicts, were issued almost continuously, so that even those loyal to the Council glimpsed the fear and saw the tyrant for what he was. Although many still defended his actions as necessary, others were secretly less enthusiastic. Even so, no one was in a position to oppose him. That task was left to the kyars, and even their efforts dwindled to almost nothing in the face of continual surveillance of the city streets.

Although there had been no more executions, there had been a number of arrests, and many people had been exiled to the Isle of the Dead. There was no longer even a token pretence that the island was purely a plague colony, and prisoners and victims shared the boats on their fateful one-way journeys. Sayer had no way of knowing whether those exiled had really been kyars or not – and neither did the authorities. One of the reasons for there being no further executions was because there had been no proof that any of those arrested were members of the outlawed organization. Confessions were in short supply, even under duress. However, Halion's new powers meant that mere suspicion was enough to justify their exile, and Sayer suspected that some of the archivect's political enemies had been caught in the same net.

For his own part, the seeker had had no further contact with the rebels. He assumed that they were biding their time until the worst of the present crisis was over. The fate of the three original prisoners was acting as a deterrent and, heeding Bylar's earlier warning, Sayer tried to content himself with the thought that his time would come. However, he found it very hard to remain patient, and the waiting was awful. He longed for news – of Aphra, of the kyars' progress, anything! – but it never came, and he could not go anywhere without an escort, making it impossible for him to seek it out for himself. He was stuck in limbo, and now it seemed that the one person he could rely on, the person who had become central to his existence, was drifting away from him too.

Late one afternoon, when Sayer was alone, he realized that he could stand it no longer. He suddenly had an overwhelming need for physical exertion – and an escape to memories of an earlier, simpler time. He thought fondly of the long solitary walks he used to take and, on impulse, set off to retrace his footsteps.

Although there were usually five guards on duty outside the house, two of them were currently accompanying Kailas, so only three men stood to attention as Sayer came out of the front door. He knew that two of the guards would follow him and, even though the house would then be empty, one would remain on sentry duty. He had never worked out why it was done that way, but he had got used to the system by now.

'Come on,' he said shortly, and strode away.

Two of the soldiers hurried after him.

'Where are we going, Seeker?'

'For a walk. To Esauru.'

The two guards exchanged long-suffering glances, but did nothing to try and dissuade him. Curfew was still some time away and they had no authority to tell Sayer where he could or could not go, unless he broke any of the new rules.

'Why are you going there?' the senior guard asked as they fell into step.

'To be alone,' Sayer replied pointedly. Then, realizing that his answer had made no sense – he had been alone at home – he added, 'To get some fresh air, to think.'

At the city gate Sayer went through the security formalities with a bad grace, repeating his reasons for going and refusing the offer of horses.

'I want to walk. That's the whole point.'

At last they were allowed to continue on their way along the Gold Road and it was then, with a sudden surge of excitement, that Sayer remembered the idea he had had when he had last talked to Bylar – which now seemed like a lifetime ago. He walked on with renewed determination, setting a fast pace and thinking all the time. Although the soldiers kept up with him easily enough, they muttered darkly under their breath. When they reached the ruined hut they were happy enough when Sayer came to a halt.

'Wasn't it somewhere around here that Archivect Seigui was killed?' the seeker asked.

'So I'm told.'

Sayer was studying the ground, moving slowly over the road as though he expected to glean some clue from the marks upon its surface.

'You won't find anything here,' the other guard told him. 'Captain Akander had his men go over the whole area with a fine-toothed comb.'

Sayer ignored him and kept looking, moving onto the verge and hoping against hope. The soldiers waited patiently, watching his efforts disdainfully and glancing every so often at the setting sun.

'What are you looking for, Seeker?' the senior guard asked eventually.

'I don't know,' Sayer answered truthfully, trying to hide his disappointment.

'Are we going on to Esauru? If we are we'd best be moving along, or we'll not be back in time for curfew.'

'All right,' Sayer agreed wearily, annoyed with himself for having raised false hopes. 'Let's go.'

They set off again at a brisk pace. When they reached the foot of the hill, Sayer turned to face his escorts.

'Will you wait for me here?'

'We're supposed to stay with you all the time.'

'All I'm going to do is climb the hill. I'll be in sight the whole time. I just want some peace and quiet to meditate. What could possibly happen to me up there?' He could see that neither soldier was keen on further exercise, and he was longing for some solitude to nurse his misery.

'All right,' the senior man conceded. 'But stick to this side of the hill.'

'Agreed.' Sayer turned to go before the guard could change his mind.

The shadows lengthened as he climbed, and his legs were aching from the unaccustomed strain when he reached the ledge of bare rock from where he could see both the archivects' estates on the far side of the Gold Road and the Temple to the east. He sat down and tried to catch his breath. Below him he could see the two guards. They were resting, but their eyes were fixed upon him. He thought of waving, then decided against it, not wanting to antagonize them any more than he had already done. Inhaling deeply, Sayer looked around at the view he had once found so tranquil, but found no peace.

'This is pointless,' he said aloud. 'What am I doing here?'

He was answered by a soft mewing from behind him, and swung round to see a pair of bright green eyes regarding him curiously.

'Seetrecka? Is that you?'

The kyar stalked forward, moving with graceful deliberation as if he was not sure whether he should grant this human the favour of his presence. In the two months since Sayer had last seen him, the cat had grown considerably and his coat had lost the softness of youth, but the seeker knew it was the same animal.

'I wish you could talk, Seetrecka. I bet you could tell me a thing or two.' He stretched out a hand, which the kyar sniffed carefully before allowing Sayer to stroke his head and neck. The action was oddly soothing and Sayer closed his eyes, wondering whether this unexpected meeting was some sort of omen. He opened them again when he heard the distant thud of a horse's hooves approaching from the city, and watched as the rider drew up next to the two soldiers. Their subsequent conversation appeared heated, with a good deal of arm waving and pointing, some of it in the seeker's direction, but Sayer could hear none of it. At length the guards ran off back the way they had come, while the horseman dismounted and began to climb towards him. Seetrecka bounded off, and Sayer stood up and walked slowly down to meet the newcomer.

'You must return to the city, Seeker!' the man called when he was near enough to be heard.

'Why?'

'Dangerous matters are afoot.'

This sounded ominous, but Sayer doubted he would get any more information from the army captain who was now approaching him. He tried anyway, when they met halfway up the hill.

'What's happening?'

'I can't tell you that now. Please, take my horse and return to Qara.'

'I couldn't—' Sayer began.

'Consider it an order, Seeker,' the soldier said firmly. 'I have to go elsewhere.'

'Very well.'

As Sayer went on down to where the horse was tethered, the captain set off around the northern side of the hill, heading towards the Temple. From where Sayer was now, the site was invisible, but when he reached the road and had ridden a little way, he could see lights flickering amid its towers and spires, and his sense of foreboding deepened. Was this the long-awaited confrontation? And if so, what was he to do? He would hardly do the kyars' cause – or his own – any good by blundering into a situation he knew nothing about, but he desperately wanted to do *something*.

Then he realized that, for the first time in ages, he was abroad alone, with no one to keep watch over what he did. With the army obviously preoccupied elsewhere, it seemed too good an opportunity to miss and, with uncharacteristic decisiveness, he knew exactly what he was going to do. Seetrecka's appearance *had* been an omen.

It took only a few moments to reach the old tax-collectors' hut. There was no way Sayer could conceal the horse, so he merely tied it up a little way from the ruin and ran inside alone. He told himself that he was unlikely to be noticed. The light was fading fast now and, in any case, he was in the grip of a kind of madness. He did not really care if anyone saw what he was doing.

The trapdoor opened easily enough, and he climbed down into the chill of the underground passage. The stream had risen since he had last been there, and he almost fell as he crossed it in the darkness, but he made it to the other end of the tunnel without further mishaps. As his hands reached out towards the stone-covered door he could see no chink of light, and he prayed that it was still possible to open it from this side. Pushing with all his might produced a tiny but encouraging movement, and renewed efforts allowed him to push the door far enough for him to edge through, even though several objects were jammed against it. The room was in almost complete darkness, and it took Sayer some time to find a tinder box and a candle. It was only when he had succeeded in lighting it that he was able to see the mess all around him. All the furniture was either overturned or broken, books were strewn about, and crumpled pages of Hurghad's epic poem littered every surface. Someone had obviously searched the place in a less than subtle manner and then just left it all in a shambles, as if they had been disgusted by what they found. The outer door was locked from the other side.

'I need your help, Hurghad,' Sayer whispered. 'I need your help.'

He had been drawn there by a hunch, but now he did not even know what he was looking for. He picked up a few sheets of paper and read the lines without really taking in their meaning. His sense of failure became desperate. Swearing under his breath, he tried to relax and think coherently.

The resonance came to him like lightning out of a clear sky, so powerful and insistent that he wondered how he could have missed it at first. It was familiar in that he had sensed it twice before, once when he had drunk mead with the hermit and once when he had first come to the hut and been lured underground. This time, however, the metal cup had had a new chapter added to its history. He found it easily, lying on its side, discarded in the corner of the room. As soon as he touched the fine etching around the rim, he heard Hurghad's voice as clearly as if he had been in the room.

Sayer? Sayer! They're coming. I don't suppose I'll be able to stop them, but . . . Find my message. Use it well.

The words faded, but the contact went on. After a few moments, Sayer set the cup down. As he did so a small, screwed up piece of paper fell out from its base, where it had evidently been hidden. He scooped it up and unfolded it, only to find another section of incomprehensible verse. Stuffing the paper into his pocket, Sayer moved quickly, returning to the tunnel and pulling the door until it was almost closed, then all but running down the corridor in his haste.

He was returning to the scene of Seigui's murder. And this time he knew what he was looking for.

CHAPTER THIRTY-THREE

'Let all your labours cease at sunset. Darkness is the
province of the gods, and night is the time of their
walking on the sacred earth.'

From *The Oracles of Zavanaiu*

It was an ordinary piece of rock, indistinguishable from a
million others beside the Gold Road, but now that Sayer had
been told what to look for he had no difficulty finding it.
When he had searched the road before, he had only been
looking with his eyes. This time he also used his mind,
employing the finely honed instincts of a seeker to home in
on the unique resonance that Hurghad had set up. As he
picked up the stone, he caught a glimpse of all it contained,
of everything the hermit had stored there, but he quickly
shut the images away, knowing that this was not the time.

The stone itself was about the size of a plum, its straw-
coloured surface rough to the touch, and covered with dust.
It looked nothing like the beautiful jewel Aphra had sent
him, and yet it had the potential to be just as important.
However, that was for the future. At this moment Sayer's
only concern was to return to Qara before his absence was
noted by anyone in authority. He ran back to the horse and
untied it, then swung himself up into the saddle and set off

at a canter towards the city. As he rode, he prayed for the soul of Hurghad, grateful that the hermit had managed to utilize his last vestiges of sanity in order to create and then pass on this final legacy. Whether the old man had been prompted by instinct or some vaguely remembered sense of duty, he had paid for his actions with his life – and Sayer was determined to ensure that his friend's sacrifice had not been in vain.

At the city gate, the seeker's arrival, alone and mounted, caused some consternation. He was questioned at some length by the duty officer and told the truth, leaving out only his visit to Hurghad's room and any mention of the stone that now lay in his pocket. While he was there, several groups of soldiers left the city and there was much commotion in the guardhouse itself, but his interrogator remained unnervingly focused, watching the seeker with hawklike intensity and apparently considering every aspect of his explanation. Eventually, however, he seemed satisfied, and called for one of the guards to escort Sayer back to his home.

'I'm sorry I can only spare one man tonight,' he said, 'but as you've no doubt gathered, our efforts are concentrated elsewhere at the moment.'

'What's going on?'

'I thought you'd have guessed,' the officer replied in a condescending tone. 'We're going to end the menace of the kyars once and for all.'

Sayer tried not to let his dismay show. He desperately wanted to know more, but the soldier did not volunteer anything further.

'At the Temple?' Sayer guessed.

'What makes you think that?' the officer asked sharply, his half-smile fading instantly.

'I saw the lights . . . and the captain who gave me his horse was headed there.'

The officer considered this answer, then evidently decided to accept it at face value.

'You should go home,' he said.

'I don't really need an escort here in the city,' Sayer offered. 'If you're short of men.'

'Best if you do, Seeker. The curfew's passed and we wouldn't want you to get into trouble, would we?'

Sayer admitted defeat and went out, followed by his guard. The streets were silent and deserted, and their footsteps echoed loudly in the darkness. Sayer tried several times to engage the soldier in conversation, but to no avail. The man did not reply, did not even respond in any way, until the seeker began to wonder if he was deaf and dumb, and gave up the attempt.

At last they reached Sayer's home, and he was a little surprised to note that there were no sentries posted outside. He had been assuming that Kailas would be back by now. Although the door was unlocked, he knew as soon as he went inside that his wife was not there. It was not just the quiet stillness of the house, but also a subtle absence in the air itself, a sense of loneliness that he felt deep inside him. He had wanted to share his success with his wife, and also tell her of his fears over what was happening that night. The fact that her overseers had seen fit to detain her after the curfew was disappointing.

Although Sayer's first impulse was to pour himself a drink, he went upstairs first and hid the stone at the back of a cupboard. Once again he experienced brief flashes of Hurghad's story, but he already knew most of what was there and did not need to relive it now. The hermit could not have known that, of course. He had gone there, into the ambush that had claimed his life as well as Seigui's, believing himself to be the only witness to the deed. That he was not did nothing to reduce the value or bravery of what he had done.

If he ever got the chance, Sayer fully intended to use Hurghad's posthumous gift to serve the cause that the old man had believed in.

After the stone had been hidden away, Sayer remembered his other find and removed the crumpled scrap of paper from his pocket. Smoothing it out, he read the verses again, but they still made little sense to him. The telepathic message Hurghad had left within the cup itself had been done in haste, but in such a way that it was likely only Sayer would find it. Which meant that what was written on the paper was meant for him too. This torn page had been chosen out of hundreds strewn around the room, and there had to be a reason for that. Sayer frowned and studied the enigmatic lines once more.

A mirror, black and full of light,
A mirror that assigns our roles,
Reflects the yellow flame of might,
False suns illuminate the scrolls.

Blind Yma turns her face aside,
And the scryer's madness ceases.
Her fire is doused, his masters hide,
The dark mirror lies in pieces.

He still could make neither head nor tail of it – and had no idea why Hurghad might have thought it important enough to leave it where he did. It was possible, of course, that it had no meaning at all, that it had just been picked out at random – or had perhaps been prompted by a part of the hermit's mind that really was insane. But Sayer did not want to believe that. He puzzled over the words for some time, then took the paper to the ground floor so he could pour himself some wine. As he went down the stairs, his thoughts strayed back to the events outside, and his stomach knotted at the idea that the kyars' fate might be being decided at that very moment – and that there was nothing he could do about it.

Then he found the handwritten note on the kitchen table and all such thoughts vanished.

'Sayer, I left the lizard tablet at the stone-binders for cleaning this afternoon. I told them you would pick it up in the morning, so don't forget! Kailas.'

Time froze, and for a moment Sayer's heart stopped beating.

He knew what the message really meant – and the enormity of it smashed down on him like an avalanche, crushing him in its icy grip. Kailas had gone to the Temple.

Oh gods, no! Not tonight, of all nights, when half the army was converging on the Temple. Sayer's thoughts spiralled down into a yawning abyss of dread, in which the darkness swallowed everything. He struggled not to scream, his heart racing now as his numbed senses struggled to cope. And then fury took him, and he began to move.

Sayer threw open the door, startling the taciturn soldier who had stayed to guard the house, and dashed out onto the street.

'Where are you going?' the soldier demanded, proving that he did have a voice after all.

'I have to go to the Temple.'

'No,' the guard replied flatly.

'I'm going.' Sayer began to head south, only to be halted and swung round as the soldier grabbed his arm.

'I said no. The curfew—'

'Damn the curfew! This is urgent.' He shook his arm free, but his adversary still blocked his path.

'No one goes to the Temple in darkness. My orders—'

Sayer hit him. The guard was bigger and stronger than

the seeker, but Sayer's punch carried with it all the weight of his desperation, his anger and fear. It landed squarely on the other man's jaw and sent him sprawling. Sayer was running almost before the unconscious soldier hit the ground. For the moment he was not even considering the possible consequences of his own actions. All he knew was that he had to get to the Temple.

As he ran, he wondered how Kailas had managed to escape from the soldiers who were supposed to accompany her. Had she given them the slip when they were out somewhere in the city, or had she discovered a route from the house over the roofs – the same route used by Bylar? Or had she simply been left unguarded – as if she were of no importance – when the army was mobilized for the night's operation? Whatever had happened, Sayer could only hope that she had not reached the Temple before the situation had become dangerous. Unfortunately, he suspected that this was not the case. He had enough respect for his wife's resourcefulness to believe that she would not have sent the coded message to Bylar if she had not been practically certain of being able to make the rendezvous. The best way of ensuring this would have been to sneak onto the site in daylight, then hide until all the overseers and artisans went home. Once darkness fell, she could emerge and go to the Oracle's Tomb – where Sayer had first met the night people – and wait for them there. But it would not be the kyars who came for her.

When Sayer reached Temple Gate, he was greeted by an astonishing sight. A large crowd had gathered, in defiance of the curfew, and there was a good deal of shouting going on. As he drew closer, the main gates swung open and a ragged cheer went up as people poured out onto the Causeway. Utterly bemused now, Sayer joined the jostling throng and was swept out of the city and past the harassed-looking guards, who were still shouting at the crowd – and at each other.

Having been saved the trouble of negotiating his own passage, Sayer ran on, moving to the front of the ragged stream of citizens, many of whom were carrying torches. However, these were not the only lights in the darkness. There were more torches and lamps all around the giant silhouettes of the Kyar Arch, and beyond that some eerie, many-coloured flames flickered and glowed inside the Temple itself.

Sayer slowed his pace, trying to make sense of the bizarre scene. The lights below the Kyar Arch belonged to soldiers, of whom a great many were milling around in apparent confusion. Others were posted along the outer walls of the site, and a few could be seen inside the Temple. Sayer presumed that the night people were responsible for the distant, multi-coloured display. If any of the rebels *were* inside, it looked very much as if they might be trapped – and if she was there too, so was Kailas.

Sayer became aware of the mood of those around him at the same time as the soldiers noticed the mob approaching. The crowd kept advancing for a time, but less confidently now. More shouts rang out and, as far as Sayer could tell from the confusion of voices, it seemed that the citizens were expressing outrage at the desecration of the sacred site by the military. However, none of them wanted to get too close to the soldiers – for the obvious reason that they were breaking one of the new laws themselves by being out after the curfew. Their earlier bravado was dissipating, and they eventually came to a halt about thirty paces away. Their only safety was in numbers; the guards could hardly arrest them all at once.

'The gods will curse you!' someone yelled.

'Blasphemers!'

'We are not the ones to break the sacred trust,' an officer

yelled back angrily. 'There are kyars inside. They're the real blasphemers!'

'Then show them to us,' another onlooker shouted.

'Can't you see the lights?' the captain responded, pointing.

'The gods walk at night,' the heckler replied.

Sayer did not really understand what was going on, what had prompted the mass exodus from the city, but that was not his concern now. He had no time for this kind of debate. Cautiously, he moved to the side of the crowd, then left the Causeway and crept into the darkness of the wasteland beyond. He needed to get inside the Temple, and he could not do that in the midst of so many people.

Some time later, after skirting round the corner of the site and along part of the northwest perimeter, Sayer spotted a section which was dark and where there were no guards, and made a dash for it. Clambering over the massive, sloping walls was something he had never tried before, but he made it, with an agility born of absolute determination, almost falling headlong into the alleyway beyond. He ran on blindly for a time, heading in the general direction of the Oracle's Tomb. He had expected the Temple to be crawling with soldiers and kyars, the hunters and their prey, but it seemed deserted and his confusion intensified. What was going on?

At last, when he reached the section of the Penitents' Way where it circled round the Tower of Clouds, he heard voices, and crept closer to hear what was being said. Several officers were standing in the open, with large numbers of men waiting nearby. Even though he had to strain to hear them clearly, Sayer recognized two of their voices.

'No one at all?' Nazeri exclaimed.

'No one,' Akander confirmed. 'The sweeps are all complete, and we also searched the inside of the tomb.'

Nazeri swore violently.

'All we found was this,' added a man whom Sayer did not know. He held up a board on which some writing had been daubed.

'We can't show *that* to Halion,' Nazeri growled. 'He'd go mad.'

In the torchlight it was difficult for Sayer to read what had been painted on the board, but he was almost certain that one of the words was 'kyars'.

'He'll be mad enough that we didn't catch any of them,' Akander agreed.

Sayer had to stifle a gasp. If the soldiers had not captured anyone, then Kailas had escaped, or had never come there at all. And if that was the case, he had put himself in danger for nothing . . .

'One piece of wood and a few hundred candles is hardly what he had in mind,' Akander went on.

'They tricked us,' Nazeri muttered. 'Halion's intelligence is obviously not as reliable as he thought. He'll have to accept that.'

Another platoon of soldiers, headed by Lieutenant Maier, approached from the direction of the Kyar Arch.

'What's going on out there?' Akander asked.

'There's a crowd of townspeople come out to see our progress,' his deputy replied. 'Or lack of it.'

'That's all we need,' Nazeri grumbled angrily.

'Why haven't they been arrested?'

'There's too many of them. Halion forbade it. He's still waiting to show off the kyars we've captured. He said that was the only way to justify our actions now.'

'Wonderful,' Nazeri said. 'We've no chance. Even if we *have* missed any kyars, when they sneak out now all they have to do is join the crowd and we'll be none the wiser.'

'We didn't miss anyone,' Akander snapped.

'I could hide a dozen of my men in here and you'd never

find them,' Nazeri replied contemptuously.

'Would you care to place a wager on that?' Akander asked coldly.

'Another time, maybe. Right now we have to explain this debacle to Halion.'

Sayer had heard enough. His relief over Kailas was now balanced against his own precarious position. He turned around and prepared to sink back into the darkness. Everything would be all right if he could just get away . . .

'Movement!' a soldier cried, and a moment later pandemonium broke out.

Sayer ran, knowing in his heart that it was hopeless, but unable to quell his instincts. Terror lent him speed and strength, and he seemed to fly through the jagged, shadowy landscape. Shouts echoed all around as the soldiers moved to cut off his escape, but for a time he kept ahead of them. His luck ran out when his boot caught on an unexpected ledge and he fell heavily, winding himself. Soon after that, as he limped round another corner, he saw torches ahead of him and knew it was over. A quick glance around confirmed that he was trapped and he came to a halt, his heart thumping. The pain in his leg was nothing compared to the dreadful ache in his chest as he watched the guards approach.

'Well, well,' Akander remarked. 'Look what we have here.'

Sayer was marched along the Penitents' Way towards the Kyar Arch. Ahead of him one of the guards carried the board on which the message 'The only kyars here are cats' had been written in blood red paint. The soldiers' mood had improved since their capture, realizing that they finally had something to show for their efforts, something to avert the worst of Halion's wrath. The seeker remained silent, sunk in misery and self-recrimination.

As he reached the top of the steps beneath the ceremonial archway, he looked at the scene spread out before him. The citizens and soldiers still faced each other at a distance, but now there were the yellow robes of at least three archivects among the army officers. Everyone turned to look at the prisoner, and the babble of conversation melted away as he was led down the steps.

'One of the rats didn't desert the sinking ship,' Nazeri announced. 'Here's your kyar, Halion.'

The archivect stared at his seeker with a mixture of emotions showing on his face. This had not been what he had expected – or wanted.

'So, you show your true colours at last, Sayer,' Halion said. 'What do you have to say for yourself?'

Sayer did not reply. He had neither the heart nor the energy to defend himself. When Halion realized this he turned to the crowd and raised his voice again.

'You see how even the best of the pantheon's servants can be corrupted by the kyars' treason. We will rid ourselves of this menace. There will be another execution.'

'No!'

Kailas's voice rang out from where she stood at the top of the steps. She had emerged unnoticed from the Temple and now waited calmly, facing the entire crowd below.

'Sayer is no kyar!' she cried. 'He only came here to look for me.'

Sayer stared at her, a new panic constricting his chest, as the onlookers muttered and gaped in astonishment.

'Sayer would never have had the guts to join us,' Kailas went on, above the noise. 'He's too fond of his luxuries, too loyal to the gods and to the Council.' The contempt in her voice cut him like a knife, but another small voice inside his head left him even more shocked and bewildered. *Let me do this.*

'Are you saying *you* are a kyar?' Halion demanded.

'I am, and proud of it,' she declared.

'Then my statement stands,' the archivect cried. 'There *will* be another execution. Take her.'

'No! No!' Sayer screamed as the nearest guards ran up the steps towards his wife, but no one took any notice of him.

Kailas made no move to try to escape, but held up her hands.

'Wait!' she shouted, then went on quickly as the soldiers hesitated. 'I am not afraid to die for my beliefs, but my daughter is innocent. You cannot kill her.'

This announcement brought a further round of astonishment – not least for Sayer, who was struck dumb. Kailas glanced at him with a mute smile of apology.

'Are you claiming to be pregnant?' Halion asked eventually.

'I *am* pregnant,' she replied simply.

The soldiers, who had come to a halt halfway up the steps, turned to look at Halion, awaiting his orders. Everyone else was watching the archivect too, except Sayer who continued to stare at his wife in horror and disbelief. Unanswerable questions piled up in his brain. Why hadn't she told him? Why had she chosen this night to go to the Temple? Why had she confessed to being a kyar? *What was she doing?*

Again the quiet alien voice sounded calmly in his head. *Let me do this, Sayer.*

The seeker tore his gaze away from Kailas and glanced at Halion – and saw the mixture of fury and calculation on the archivect's face. He was caught in his own trap. Kailas had to be punished – her own very public admission of guilt demanded that – but not even barbarians would execute a woman who was with child. That would do Halion's public image irreparable harm. In addition, the child was likely to have a great deal of talent – talent that by rights belonged to Halion – and ending its life before it had even begun would mean all that was lost. Yet the only way to remedy the situation was to throw Kailas into gaol until the baby was born, which meant that any punishment would have to wait for several months. Halion had to make an example of her – and he had to do it now.

Sayer knew what his master had decided even before he spoke.

'Then you leave me no alternative,' Halion decreed at last. 'You, and your child, will be exiled to the Isle of the Dead. At once.'

CHAPTER THIRTY-FOUR

'It is despair and humiliation, not pain, that are the torturer's greatest weapons.'

From *The Chronicles of a Barbarous Time*

As Kailas was led away, Sayer struggled briefly in the grasp of the two guards who held his arms, then gave up the unequal contest. He stared at the retreating figure of his wife, trying to fight the blizzard that filled his head. His thoughts had been scattered to the four winds and every time he tried to gather them in again, a numbing despair left him reeling. The Isle of the Dead had already claimed the only other person he had truly loved; now he was to be effectively bereaved a second time.

For a moment he had considered adding his 'confession' to hers, so that he could join her on the island, but the small part of his brain that remained rational had stilled his tongue. Halion's earlier words, and the simple fact that this would be much too easy a solution, made it certain that Sayer would not be exiled but executed. He would gain nothing and lose everything, so he kept quiet. It occurred to him a little later that Kailas's actions might have saved him, and it was now very important that he lived, whatever the cost. To do otherwise would be to make a mockery of her sacrifice – a sacrifice that still made him feel utterly bewildered. She had risked her life – and the life of their unborn child – on a hunch. How could she have done that? The gamble – if that's what it had been – had paid off, but . . .

Sayer's thoughts were brought back to the present by Nazeri.

'What shall we do with him?' the captain asked Halion.

The archivect glared at the seeker with eyes full of rage, and it occurred to Sayer that he was by no means safe yet. Knowing that Kailas was being sent to Jazireh gave him a little hope to cling to, and the fact that she was carrying his child gave him an extra reason to fight, but his own actions were suspect now. It was up to him to ensure that he was still around if and when the kyars enabled his wife to escape.

'Is it true that you only came here to look for Kailas?' Halion asked, his voice deceptively mild.

'Yes.' Sayer was glad he was able to answer truthfully, and was surprised to find that his voice was steady.

Halion remained silent for a long time, as the crowds started to drift back the way they had come, urged on by the menacing presence of so many soldiers.

'Akander, you and Maier are to interrogate the seeker,' the archivect said eventually. 'I don't want him harmed, but I want the truth. Then I'll decide what to do with him.'

'Yes, my lord,' the captain replied. Behind him, his lieutenant smiled with relish.

'If it had been anyone else,' Halion went on, glaring at Sayer again, 'they would already have been condemned. This evening has cost me a great deal. I hope you won't make it worse.'

With that he turned on his heel, his yellow robe flaring out around him, and set off back towards the city.

* * *

'So, are you a kyar, Sayer?'

'No.'

Akander had already posed the question several times.

'And you wouldn't tell us even if you were, right?' Maier added.

Sayer remained silent. He was standing, stark naked, in the centre of an underground cell beneath the military headquarters, while Akander and Maier paced around him. The windowless room reeked of sweat and fear. It was also very cold – and Sayer had been doused in icy water, so that he was shivering violently and his teeth were chattering. The interrogation had already gone on for several hours, deep into the night, and he was close to exhaustion. The security officers had kept him on his feet and forced him to go over every event of his day time and time again, picking him up on every tiny inconsistency until he wanted to scream. It was only the thought of Kailas, and his determination to see her again, that kept him from breaking down completely. It could not be allowed to end this way.

'And did you know your wife was a kyar?' Akander asked.

'N-no.'

'It came as a complete surprise?' Maier said, obviously not believing Sayer's answer.

'Yes, I t-told you.'

'Then how did you know she'd gone to the Temple?' the captain asked.

Sayer's earlier hesitation over this question had not gone unnoticed. This was one of the few lies he had been forced to tell, and probably the least plausible. The soldiers sensed it, and returned to the same point over and over again.

'She told me. This morning,' he repeated. 'I d-didn't know she meant to stay after s-sunset, b-but when I heard about the trouble I thought she must have been c-caught up in it.'

'Because she was late home?'

'Yes.'

'You were pretty slow to react, though, weren't you?' Akander commented. 'Why did you wait so long before going after her? You already knew what was going on at the Temple.'

'I wasn't thinking straight. It only occurred to me later.'

'You're lying,' Maier stated contemptuously. 'I know Halion said he didn't want you harmed, but I know how to cause you pain in ways that'll never show.'

'Go ahead,' Sayer declared. 'Do you think I c-care? My life is already ruined. And I'm t-telling you the truth.'

The lieutenant laughed at the prisoner's false bravado. In one sense Sayer's torment was already close to unbearable, but in another he was terribly afraid of physical pain. His bruised and swollen fist throbbed cruelly, and the ache in his numbed feet – where they stood in a puddle on the stone floor – was almost unendurable. He was not sure how much more he could take. In everything he had said so far he had been careful to stick to what had actually happened, whenever possible, knowing that certain parts of his story would have been checked with the others involved. However, he was now tempted to tell them everything, whatever they wanted to hear, just so that they would stop. He would have given almost anything for warmth and rest, but a stubborn remnant of hope would not let him yield.

'Why did you strike the guard?' Akander went on remorselessly. 'If you thought Kailas was innocent, why not explain the situation and ask for his help?'

'He wouldn't listen. It was the only way.'

'Your hand doesn't look too good,' Maier remarked. 'You're not much of a fighter, are you?'

'Have you ever been in the Temple at night before?' the captain asked.

This was a rare new question and almost caught Sayer off guard.

'N-no,' he stuttered. 'N-never.'

'You seemed to know your way around quite well.'

'So did you,' Sayer replied with a tiny measure of defiance.

Akander smiled, and did not attempt to deny the accusation or defend his presence on the site.

'We've had your house searched, you know,' he remarked casually.

'What for?'

'Just to see what we might find. You've been living with a kyar, after all. It's hard to believe there'd be no telltale signs.'

'And did you find anything?' Sayer asked, thinking of the two message stones that were so precious to him.

'Oh, a few things,' the captain replied and did not elaborate, deliberately leaving Sayer dangling.

Akander was behind him now, still pacing slowly, while his lieutenant leant against the wall to one side, his gaze fixed upon the seeker's face.

'Would it surprise you to learn that your sister was also a kyar?' the captain asked eventually. 'That's why she was sent to the Isle of the Dead.'

'That's ridiculous. Aphra c-caught the p-plague.'

'That's what you were told, but it's not true.'

'Curious, isn't it?' Maier put in. 'Living with one kyar might be considered back luck. Living with two looks like carelessness.'

'Or was it you who turned them into traitorous whores?' Akander suggested.

Sayer tried to turn and flail at his tormentor, driven beyond the tattered remnants of his composure, but his legs gave way beneath him and he fell heavily. The two soldiers regarded him indifferently as he curled up into a ball and then, to his own horror, began to cry.

Akander went to the door and opened it. Maier collected the single lamp from its hook and followed the captain outside. The door clanged shut and Sayer was left alone in darkness.

When they returned, an indeterminate time later, they found that their prisoner had crawled into the corner of the cell, where the floor was dry. His skin had a bluish tinge to it and the shivering had stopped, so that in the muted lamplight he looked almost like a corpse. They forced him to get up and move around, loosening stiff muscles and reawakening a thousand agonies.

'Right,' Akander said. 'Let's start at the beginning again.'

Sayer groaned.

'Unless there's something new you'd like to tell us.'

'No,' he croaked.

The endless questioning went on, covering the same old ground, with Akander asking most of the questions and Maier making a few sarcastic asides and threats. Sayer gritted his teeth and repeated everything he had told them before, with the same crucial omissions and lies. Much as he wanted the torture to end, the respite had given him fresh courage. He only had to think of his unborn child for his resolution to remain firm, and his obstinacy eventually gained him the grudging respect of his interrogators. However, that did not stop them from trying to break his spirit one more time.

'How do you suppose Kailas knew her baby was a girl?' Akander asked unexpectedly, as they reached the end of another round of questions.

'What?'

'She said "my *daughter* is innocent",' the captain explained.

The same thought had occurred to Sayer at some point, but his recent ordeal had driven it from his mind.

'I've no idea,' he said, though he continued to wonder in silence. Did Kailas know, or was she guessing? Could there be some sort of link between a mother and her unborn child? More improbable still, could her pregnancy have been the reason for the increased strength of the telepathic link between her and Sayer? Now that there was a very real physical connection between the two of them, was a mental bond so far-fetched?

'Of course, it doesn't really matter now,' Maier commented. 'Whatever it is, it's not likely to be born alive on the Isle of the Dead, is it? If Kailas even makes it that far. Even if she doesn't catch the plague, a pretty woman like her is going to attract some attention among the scum there.'

Knowing more about conditions on Jazireh than his interrogators helped Sayer to steel himself against their barbed words. He said nothing, hoping that Kailas would survive as Aphra had done, until there was a chance to get them both back home.

'You don't seem very concerned,' Akander remarked.

'There's nothing I can do,' Sayer whispered. 'I loved her, but she deceived me.'

'She certainly didn't have a very high opinion of you,' Maier pointed out. 'She said you were gutless and soft.'

'And loyal,' Akander added. 'We should give the seeker his due, lieutenant.'

Maier snorted derisively.

'And I'm inclined to believe it,' the captain went on.

Sayer looked up at him, fresh hope in his eyes. Could this be the signal that the end was in sight? Or was it just another trap?

'I'll make you a deal,' Akander offered. 'Answer me one more question in a way that satisfies us both, and we'll be finished here. Agreed?'

'What question?' Sayer asked fearfully.

'These were found on your kitchen table.' He took two pieces of paper from his pocket and handed them over. 'I'd like to know what they mean.'

Sayer's fingers were so cramped that he could hardly hold the scraps, but he already knew what they were. Nevertheless he glanced at them dutifully.

'Well?' Akander prompted.

'The one from Kailas is just a straightforward message,' Sayer began.

'So it would seem. What significance does the lizard tablet have?'

'It's a sculptured tile we had hanging on the wall. It was a present from her father, and it's very old. We'd been meaning to get it cleaned and restored for some time.'

'That's it?'

'Yes. The stone-binders will confirm the story. What else is it supposed to mean?'

'Ugly piece of crap, if you ask me,' Maier remarked. 'A bit of dirt would improve it.'

'We collected it ourselves this morning,' Akander explained. 'What about the other message?'

'It's not a message, just part of a poem.'

'What poem?'

'I don't know.'

'Then what's it doing in your kitchen?'

'Kailas liked it. I think she found it in the archives at the Hariolatorium.'

'It's not her writing, though.'

'She must've got one of the scribes to copy it out for her.'

'Which one?'

'I don't know.'

'What a surprise,' Maier said, feigning shock.

'And you don't know what it means?' Akander went on.

'No,' Sayer replied truthfully, then added, 'It's just some

nonsense that appealed to her, I suppose.' He handed both pieces of paper back to the captain.

'Don't you want to keep them?' the lieutenant asked. 'For their sentimental value?'

Sayer shook his head, ignoring the jibe. He already knew the verses by heart, even if he did not understand them.

'They don't mean anything to me,' he replied. 'Do what you like with them.'

No one spoke for some time, and Sayer tried hard not to let his hopes rise too high.

'Can I go home now?' he asked eventually, when he could stand it no longer.

'I don't see why not,' Akander replied. 'But you have new living quarters.'

'Why?'

'You're a single man now,' Maier taunted. 'That house is too big for you.'

'Halion has arranged rooms for you above the archives at the Hariolatorium,' Akander said. 'You'll be safer there.'

'And we'll be close by, to keep an eye on you,' the lieutenant added. 'You won't be able to sneeze without us knowing about it. Doesn't that make you feel nice and secure?'

Sayer was dismayed. His present suffering might be over, but he was being taken from one cell to another.

'And who knows?' Akander concluded. 'If Halion decides you're no longer reliable enough to head off all over the place as a seeker, he might decide to turn your talents to day-dreaming.'

CHAPTER THIRTY-FIVE

'Only prayers that are unworthy are left unanswered.'
Attributed to Archivect Meydan

It took only a few days for the new routines of Sayer's life to settle into a depressing rut. His existence had never seemed so pointless. He was virtually a prisoner, and spent much of his time in his tiny bedroom, brooding about all he had lost. First Aphra, then Kailas and now his freedom – and with it any hope of getting in touch with the kyars. His sister's absence still had the power to hurt him, but the loss of his wife was an aching void, something that dominated his thoughts and emotions even when he was occupied with other matters.

His new quarters had been practically bare when he had first been taken there, and everything that had been brought in since – however insignificant – had been checked thoroughly by Akander's men, two of whom were on duty outside the apartment at all times. As this was on the second floor, and the roof of the building was inaccessible, the single front door was the only way in and out of his lodgings. Not even Bylar would be able to enter any other way. The fact that Sayer was still under suspicion was reinforced by the manner in which his requests to visit his old home had been refused. Instead, essential items had been brought to him by the guards and, as a result, Sayer had no idea what had happened to the two message stones. He would have liked to have Aphra's for personal reasons, but Hurghad's was the more important, should he ever be able to escape from his confinement. What was more, it was possible that another seeker might get his hands on the hermit's stone and realize its significance – and then Sayer would be doomed. As it was, there was nothing he could do about any of these things, so he set himself to wait, to cooperate with his master's wishes, hoping that time would provide him with the opportunity he longed for. But time weighed heavily on his shoulders.

He was hardly ever allowed outside the Hariolatorium, and then only under guard. Most of his waking hours, when not alone, were spent in completing a series of tests for the invigilators, to determine whether his talent was suitable for a second career as a daydreamer. These trials consisted mainly of his being given various fragments of The Plan and other documents or antiquities, and being asked to give his impressions of their resonance and histories, as well as anything else that occurred to him. Some of the visions he experienced were quite vivid, but he deliberately played down his ability to read the hidden clues. He did not pretend to be so insensitive that the invigilators would realize he was lying, but he toned down his responses a little, made a few trivial errors, and protested frequently that he found it impossible to think like a daydreamer rather than as a seeker. He got the impression that his mentors were not really serious about his training, that they were merely testing his reactions, but he remained on his guard. Although the questioning some-times went on for a long time after each experiment, the invigilators rarely tried to trick him into contradicting him-self. Even when they attempted to trip him up by offering him a false relic, they seemed to take it for granted that he would not be fooled. It was as though they were simply going through the motions and, like Sayer, waiting for the real purpose of the tests to become clear.

One thing the seeker wanted to avoid at all costs was being subjected to tests involving the various tinctures commonly used to supplement a daydreamer's natural instincts. He had no way of knowing how his brain would react and what secrets he might inadvertently reveal – to his own peril – if he was not fully in control of his own faculties. This possibility was never raised, however. He was also glad that he was not deprived of sleep for days on end, as the real daydreamers often were. He was sleeping badly enough as it was. When he did manage to rest, his nights were full of dreams. Kailas appeared in many of them, but there was always something wrong. She would be trying to tell him something he could not hear, or she would slip away from his outstretched hand, leaving him sad and alone, denied even the illusory comfort of her presence.

The testing process went on in a half-hearted manner for several days, and then just stopped. It was as though the invigilators had suddenly forgotten Sayer's existence and, with nothing else to do, he grew bored and angry. He was vaguely aware of a great deal of activity in the Hariolatorium, but he was not involved in any of it, and eventually he could stand his solitary confinement no longer. Devising – and rejecting – various escape plans only left him feeling even worse. He was aware that he was on the brink of risking anything just to try to break out of his isolation. He had to get out somehow and, in the end, decided simply to ask – to beg if necessary.

As luck would have it, Lieutenant Maier was talking to his regular sentries when Sayer opened the door of the apartment.

'What can we do for you, Seeker?'

'I need to get out.'

'I'm not aware of any official business that requires your presence.'

'This is personal.'

'Isn't the dream-house big enough for you?' Maier asked sarcastically.

'I'm wasted here, and you know it,' Sayer replied. 'But I need to pray. At the Temple.'

The lieutenant regarded him thoughtfully. The antagonism between the two men would have been obvious even to a casual observer, and the two guards were already aware of it. They waited, stony-faced, expecting Maier to refuse the prisoner's request.

'Well, you've been a good boy for a while,' the lieutenant said eventually. 'I don't see why we shouldn't all go for a walk together.'

Sayer was surprised. He had been all set to argue that he had the right to practise his religion, and that it would be wrong to deny him his contact with the gods, but it had proved unnecessary.

Their journey to the Temple was uneventful. The streets of the city seemed a little quieter than Sayer remembered them, but that could just have been his imagination. He glanced at everyone they passed, hoping that one of these strangers would be a kyar – and would thus be able to let Bylar know that, for a short time at least, the seeker had escaped the confines of his gaol. He was not exactly free – Maier was walking alongside him and the two guards marched close behind – but, for all Sayer knew, the kyars might have believed him to be dead by now. Having set off with no clear idea of what he wanted to do, apart from distancing himself from the stultifying atmosphere of his rooms, the seeker was content to leave the rest to chance. He was happy with a change of scenery and some fresh air. Anything else would be a bonus.

'Did you have a specific deity in mind?' Maier asked as they passed beneath the Kyar Arch. 'For your prayers, I mean.'

'They'll all hear,' Sayer replied.

'So you don't have a particular shrine in mind?'

'No.'

'Then we'll go to the Tower of Clouds. The scene of your greatest triumph seems appropriate, don't you think?'

'Fine with me.' Sayer did not care where they went, wanting only to prolong the visit as much as possible. The more people he saw – and who saw him – the better the chance of news reaching his allies.

As they walked down the Penitents' Way, he was aware of being watched by many of the artisans on the site. Their expressions varied from indifference to suspicion and scorn. No one smiled or greeted him as they would have done a month ago. Sayer tried not to let this bother him.

At the Tower of Clouds, the two guards remained outside while Sayer and the lieutenant went in. Then Maier allowed the seeker to go on alone, giving him a small amount of privacy as he touched head and heart, then knelt in the centre of the empty, cavernous space beneath the vast white roof. The idea of praying had only been an excuse for Sayer to get out for a while, but now he was at the Temple old instincts took over and he found he really did want to address himself to the gods. Silently, he asked for the safety of Aphra, Kailas and her child, for a chance to be reunited with them, and for the success of the kyars in their battles against injustice and the plague. He was not comforted, however, and felt as though his sincere pleas vanished into an uncaring void. Even though his faith had been eroded a great deal by recent events, there was still something missing, an indefinable atmosphere of failure. Feeling unaccountably disappointed – what had he expected? – he stood up and walked slowly back to Maier.

'All right?'

'Yes.'

'Notice anything different?'

'No. Why?'

'You must be losing your touch,' the lieutenant commented, ignoring the question.

Before Sayer could ask what he meant, a young man ran in through the main entrance.

'Are you the seeker?' he asked breathlessly.

'Yes.'

'Come quickly. There's been an accident, inside the Oracle's Tomb. We need your help.'

Sayer glanced at Maier who, after a moment's hesitation, nodded his agreement. They all ran outside and then circled round the tower, followed by the two guards.

'What's happened?' Sayer asked.

'One of the inner chambers was being renovated, and part of a wall collapsed. It's only big enough for two men down there, and we need someone who can match the resonances quickly if we're to get it repaired before sunset.'

It was a matter of honour among artisans that any damage or removals be replaced the same working day. The gods must not be allowed to see anything but positive progress each night.

'All right,' the seeker gasped. He was not used to such sudden physical exercise and was now out of breath.

'Time to earn your keep,' Maier said, sounding amused.

'This way.'

The young man led them up a curving ramp to one of the oval entrances into the serpentine labyrinth of stone, and they plunged inside, leaving the two guards at the door.

Candles flickered ahead of them as they followed the winding corridor until they halted at the top of a steep slope.

'It's down there,' the young man said, pointing. 'Can you slide? Or do you need a rope?'

'I can slide.' Sayer had done it before. One of his relics made up a part of the wall of the tiny cave below, and he remembered it well. Peering down, he could see more candles in the depths.

'This place gives me the creeps,' Maier remarked. 'It's like walking into a giant's intestines.'

The others ignored him.

'The seeker's here!' their guide called down, then turned back to Sayer. 'Ready?'

'Yes.'

'Shout when you want to come up again and I'll lower a rope. We'll keep a check on the time for you.'

Sayer nodded, sat on the floor and launched himself feet first into the chute. The slide took only a few moments, and threw him from side to side, but the surface of the rock was polished smooth and he came to no harm. Strong hands caught him and steadied his progress as he reached the bottom, and the seeker found himself in a tiny candlelit chamber, face to face with a man who motioned him to silence. It was Bylar.

'He's down safe!' the kyar yelled, and received an echoing acknowledgement from above. 'Are you all right?' he asked quietly.

'Better for seeing you,' Sayer replied, hardly able to believe his luck. 'What's—'

'We can talk, as long as we keep our voices down,' Bylar cut in, 'but we need to work as well. As soon as I heard you were here, I arranged this little accident, but I rather overdid it. It won't do either of our reputations any good if the repair isn't finished in time.'

The two men shuffled round in the cramped space, and Sayer surveyed the irregular hole in the wall and the jumble of curved stones that had come from it. He explored one of the recesses with his fingers, then pointed to a fragment. Bylar picked it up and slotted it into place. It was like a three-dimensional jigsaw puzzle, and would have taken hours to complete without the seeker's talent. As it was they worked smoothly as a team, each assisting the other whenever a particular manoeuvre presented the need for more than two hands. In between the exchanges necessary for the task in hand, they talked.

The first topic of conversation, naturally enough, was the fateful night at the Temple when Kailas had been captured. Bylar explained that the kyars had deliberately started the rumour that they would be meeting there that night.

'Why?'

'It was a trap. We wanted people to see that the soldiers had no qualms about entering the Temple at night. Breaking the sacred laws, in other words. The plan was for some of us to get inside, set up a few lights and so on, then slip away via our prepared escape routes, leaving the soldiers to chase shadows.'

'But what about Kailas?'

'By the time I found out about her message, it was too late to call it all off. No one could find her, so we weren't able to warn her to stay away. The only alternative was to meet her as promised and help her escape before the troops arrived.'

'So what went wrong?'

'Nothing. We met and talked briefly. Her way out was set up. She should have got away easily. I've no idea why she didn't.'

'That's crazy. Kailas would never have simply walked into a trap.'

'She did say . . .' Bylar began, then stopped uncertainly.

'What?' Sayer demanded.

'She said she had an idea, but that she needed to go to the Isle of the Dead to carry it out. I told her that was impossible, that the only way was to catch the plague. But she refused to say any more about it.'

'You're not suggesting she was trying to get caught on purpose?' Sayer exclaimed incredulously. Until now he had blithely assumed that Kailas had given herself up only to save him.

'Keep your voice down,' Bylar hissed. 'I'm not suggesting anything, just trying to work it out.'

'She was pregnant!' Sayer objected.

'We didn't know that,' the kyar pointed out.

But *she* did, Sayer thought. Had she been so confident of being exiled, and not being put to death, because of it? The idea made him feel nauseous.

'And we didn't know you'd go looking for her,' Bylar added. 'There was nothing we could do. I'm sorry.'

Sayer remained silent, lost in further speculation.

'I know it's not much,' the kyar went on, 'but at least we were able to make sure Kailas really was sent to the island. We'd organized the mass protest of the citizens to witness Halion's men breaking the law, and with so many people around he was forced to stick to his word.'

Sayer looked blank. He had not even considered any possibility other than Kailas's exile.

'I saw the boat sail myself,' Bylar continued, 'and Kailas wasn't the only one on board. Rivolier had come down with the plague, and a lot of people were there to see him off too.'

Sayer was not really listening. He knew of Rivolier by reputation, a storyteller who was called 'the people's poet' because he preferred to perform in the city slums rather than at parties of the well-to-do, but his fate was of no real concern to the seeker.

'Is there any news from the island?' he asked.

'One of the crows returned a few days ago. They're making progress with the herb. It seems as if it really does have—'

'Any news of Aphra or Kailas?' Sayer cut in impatiently.

'Nothing specific about Aphra, and the bird left before Kailas got there.'

'Are we any further forward in trying to rescue any of them?'

'Not really. We're doing our best.'

By this time their work was almost finished.

'What's been happening with you?' Bylar asked.

Sayer told him, wondering aloud when they would be able to talk again.

'We certainly can't go on meeting like this,' the kyar said. 'People will begin to talk.'

'I'm trying to persuade them that I'm trustworthy,' Sayer said, unsmiling. 'If they'll let me work as a seeker again, I may have a little more freedom.' Then he remembered Hurghad's message stone, and told his companion where it was hidden.

'That could be just the break we're looking for,' Bylar said, obviously relieved. 'I'll see what we can do. Good work, Sayer. We've no reason to give up hope yet.'

'I can't afford to,' the seeker replied, thinking once more of the people he had lost.

The last stone was fitted into place, leaving the surface smooth and rounded once more. Both men used their different abilities to check that all was well.

'Anything else?' Bylar asked.

'Not that I can think of. Unless you'd like to rescue me.'

'Don't worry. We won't forget you. We'll come for you if and when it's necessary.'

'In the meantime, I just have to be patient, right?'

'We all do,' the kyar agreed.

Sayer nodded resignedly.

'We're finished!' Bylar yelled to his colleague above.

Moments later the end of a rope slithered into view and Sayer tied it round himself and crawled out into the upper chamber and thence out of the Oracle's Tomb. He did not wait for Bylar, rejoining Maier and the other soldiers at the base of the ramp.

'It's all go for you today,' the lieutenant told him. 'I've just got word that Halion wants to see you. At once.'

'You want *me* to go?' Sayer queried, hardly able to accept this second piece of good fortune.

'You're still a seeker, aren't you?' Halion snapped. 'It's time to prove yourself again.'

'Thank you. I won't let you down.'

'You'd better not. Believe me, if I could send anyone else I would, but I don't have much choice on this occasion.' The archivect sounded distinctly unhappy about the fact.

'Why not?' Sayer enquired.

'The relic you'll be seeking is one you're uniquely quali-fied to find. It's the Eye of Clouds.'

'What!'

'It's been stolen from under our very noses.' Halion paused, glaring at the astonished seeker. 'This is something that must not become general knowledge, you understand. Such sacrilege defies belief.'

Sayer nodded. Such incredible incompetence on behalf of the Temple guardians would not enhance the Council's reputation. He almost wanted to laugh at the absurdity of the situation, but he could not. Besides, the Eye was *his* relic; such an unheard-of theft was an insult to his work, in spite of everything that had happened since. Why hadn't he sensed its lack at the Temple that afternoon? Maier's remark about losing his touch made sense now, and so did the fact that the tower had been unusually deserted. Then the seeker remembered feeling that something had been missing when he'd tried to pray. Perhaps, subconsciously, he had known after all.

'Do we have a new location?' he asked.

'Yes. The daydreamers found it yesterday.' Halion paused, seemingly reluctant to continue. 'This might just be your most difficult mission yet.'

'Why?' Sayer asked. 'Where is it?'

'On the Isle of the Dead,' Halion replied.

CHAPTER THIRTY-SIX

'Most battles are won and lost long before they are fought.'

General Orszula, First Marshal of Khorasan

'What's *he* doing here?' Maier demanded, glaring malevolently at Sayer. 'It was his wife who stole the damn thing!'

'Assuming you're right,' Nazeri replied calmly, 'it gives him all the more reason to get it back.'

'Of course I'm right,' the lieutenant exclaimed. 'Who else could it have been? Halion's going soft. He should have executed the bitch, instead of shipping her off. Then we wouldn't—'

'Enough!' Akander cut in, while Sayer had to force himself not to respond to Maier's hostility. 'The decision has been made. We're here to make plans, not deal in recriminations. You would do well to remember that, Lieutenant.'

The meeting was taking place in a sparsely furnished room within the army's headquarters. Three captains, accompanied by their respective lieutenants, sat around a large table, while Sayer stood a little apart. Like Maier, he was not really sure what he was doing there. It was already clear that this would be a mission unlike any he – or any other seeker – had ever taken part in. The seeker would ordinarily have been in overall command, at least nominally, but on this occasion Sayer was to be wholly subservient to the military.

As Maier fell silent, accepting his admonishment with ill grace, the third captain – a man Sayer did not know – spoke for the first time.

'This is a unique situation, gentlemen, and it may be that an unusual strategy is required. If the seeker can assist us in that, then I for one welcome his presence.'

'Whether you welcome him or not is of no consequence, Theisen,' Nazeri stated flatly. 'As commander of this operation, I take responsibility for Sayer. He will travel with me, and he will do his job – or pay the price of failure.'

'But how can we trust him?' Maier burst out, unable to keep quiet any longer. 'For all we know he's a *part* of this plot.'

'The seeker's loyalty has been questioned,' Nazeri conceded, 'but we need him to get the Eye back. I will make sure he does not let us down.'

Sayer listened to them talking about him as though he were not in the room, and found the whole situation utterly bizarre. The fact that he was actually going to the Isle of the Dead seemed completely unreal. That was where Aphra was, where Kailas was . . . where so many of his hopes lay. This was an opportunity that would only come once, and was so unexpected that it could not be a simple coincidence. He had made the same assumptions as Maier about the theft of the Eye, but if Kailas *was* responsible, had it been the most extraordinary impulse of the moment or a carefully planned decision? Ever since Halion had told him of the robbery, various possibilities had been occurring to him. Bylar had told him that Kailas had mentioned needing to go to the Isle of the Dead, so was this her unexplained idea? If so, what exactly was she expecting to happen next?

The soldiers seemed to be wondering the same thing.

'Whoever stole the relic,' Nazeri went on, 'we have to assume they took it to the island for a reason.'

'That may not be true, though,' Theisen said.

'I know that,' Nazeri responded impatiently. 'It's also possible that whoever took it planned something quite different – to demand a ransom, or even keep it for their own use – and the fact that they were caught and exiled may just have been an unfortunate accident. But I believe it would be dangerous for us to assume that.'

'We have to be prepared for the worst,' Akander said.

'Exactly. And I reckon the theft was designed to lure us to the island. They must have known we couldn't just ignore such a crime.'

'Why would anyone want to lure us *there*?' Theisen asked.

'To help them escape,' Akander guessed.

'So you think the kyars are responsible?' Maier said.

'I believe so,' Nazeri replied. 'Quite a few of them have been sent there, and Kailas probably thought she'd be giving them a chance by doing this.'

'Assuming it was her,' Maier muttered.

Nazeri gave the junior officer a withering look.

'Perhaps she was taken in by this nonsense about a cure,' Theisen suggested. 'Maybe she thought the kyars would be safe from the illness, and this is a way to try and help them get back to the mainland.'

'It's more likely they're all dead of the plague,' Maier said. 'The whole island's probably been riddled with the sickness for years by now.'

'And even if it isn't,' one of the other lieutenants added, 'it's likely to be in a state of anarchy, given the sort of people that've been sent there.'

'All that may be true,' Nazeri admitted, 'but we must assume that we may encounter organized opposition. The kyars have caused enough trouble on the mainland. Out there, they've had a free hand. We have to be ready for anything. This is too important for us to take any chances.'

'What exactly do you think the kyars are hoping to achieve?' Akander asked.

'In order for us to retrieve the Eye, we'll have to land, bringing a boat closer to the shore than normal. My guess is that they'll try to capture one of the vessels, together with a sentinel.'

'They're hardly likely to be able to match us in a fight,' Theisen said. 'They can only have primitive weapons.'

'But they'll know the terrain, and that gives them a considerable advantage. They can hide the Eye anywhere they like.'

'We also don't know how many people are on the island,' Akander pointed out.

'Or what lengths they're prepared to go to,' Nazeri added. 'They'll obviously be pretty desperate.' He paused. 'There's one thing we should all bear in mind. The Council have agreed that exile, for whatever reason, implies the loss of Tirokian citizenship. Make sure your men are aware of that.'

Until that moment, Sayer had been listening to all their speculation in an almost trancelike state of disbelief. He knew more than any of them about the real situation on Jazireh, and he was certain now that the kyars were using the Eye as bait. He wished that Nazeri were not so perceptive, and wondered what part he might play himself as the drama unfolded. What did Kailas expect him to do? But all such thoughts were banished by the mention of citizenship, and the reality of what was about to happen became horribly clear. The soldiers would have the freedom to kill anyone who opposed them – and the chilling half-smile on Maier's face showed that he for one would have no compunction in murdering the exiles.

'Before we get down to logistics,' Nazeri continued, 'do you have anything to add, Seeker?'

Sayer was so surprised to be included in the discussion, after having been ignored for so long, that at first he could think of nothing to say. But then he saw the opportunity to sow a little doubt in the soldiers' minds.

'Have you considered the possibility that the kyars might simply want to trade?'

'What for?'

'I don't know. Some things to make their lives more comfortable? They must know how valuable the Eye is to us.'

'They must also know that we can take it back,' Akander pointed out.

'They can't hide it from me,' Sayer admitted, 'but they could presumably make it very difficult for us to get to it. They've had nothing to bargain with before now.'

'Maybe whoever's got the Eye will try to exchange it for their own freedom,' Theisen suggested.

'That makes no sense,' Maier said. 'Whoever stole the Eye went *to* the island. Why do that if they were just going to try and get away again?'

Nazeri turned to Sayer once more.

'Do you think Kailas might have had some insane idea about rescuing your sister?'

'I doubt it,' the seeker replied. 'They didn't even like each other.' He was finding it hard to remain calm while the lives of the people he loved were being discussed in such a way.

'Well, it can't do any harm to listen if they *do* offer to trade,' Nazeri concluded, 'but I want to be ready to fight if necessary. We'll be taking three boats, and they won't be the normal ferries. I'll be on the *Dryad*, Akander you'll command the *Saltrunner*, and Theisen takes the *Dawn Flame*. Make yourselves familiar with your ships. All the normal crews will be on board but they answer to you, understood?'

He received nods of agreement.

'Each vessel will carry three shriekers. That way they can take it in turns, if necessary, because we'll probably be inside the danger zone much longer than usual.' He had no need to add that the arrangement would also be a safeguard against failure by one of the sentinels. 'As you know, each of these ships normally carries cargo, so there'll be plenty of room for troops and equipment. Any questions so far?'

No one spoke, and Nazeri went on.

'Sayer, you'll be with me. I assume you'll want a silk?'

'I don't think we'll need one, but it would be best, just in case.'

'And a scribe?'

'Yes.'

'What for?' Maier asked. 'They'll just get in the way.'

'Our job is to make sure they don't, Lieutenant. We're dealing with a sacred relic here, and the protocols must be observed.' Nazeri paused. 'Seeker, you will return to your quarters now. The rest of us will go to the docks to make our preparations. We sail at first light tomorrow.'

The three vessels set off under overcast skies that mirrored the sombre mood of those on board. No one was looking forward to the voyage, and no one knew what to expect at the other end. The sailors of the ships that had been commandeered, and the soldiers who were now their passengers, were all silent as they left the harbour, probably cursing their ill luck at having been chosen for this task. Ahead of them the lake was being churned up by a fitfully gusting wind, the iron-grey water flecked with white.

Sayer stood alone in the bows of the *Dryad*, looking ahead towards the dark smudge on the horizon that was their destination. He had had no difficulty in picking up the relic's trail. Having become accustomed to detecting the faintest echoes of an ancient passage, he found that the Eye's recent journey had left behind a resonance so strong that, to him, it was like a path of fire leading across the water to the north. It was so powerful that he could not help wondering whether his presence had really been necessary. Surely any seeker would have been able to follow such a trail, even if they had never dealt with the Eye before. Did that mean that this was yet another test of his loyalty?

Some time later, just before they reached the ring of red buoys, Sayer spotted a black dot in the sky ahead. As it grew larger, he recognized the heavy wingbeats. The crow passed quite close to the ship, but did not alter its flight towards Qara, and only the seeker paid it any attention. He did not watch it for too long, in case someone else noticed his interest, but he could not help wondering what messages it carried.

Such thoughts soon vanished as the lookout aloft cried out in warning, pointing past the starboard bow to where a patch of unnaturally disturbed water marked the approach of the first of the monsters. Everyone tensed as the first of the sentinels went into action, his piercing voice shattering the morning air with a wordless howl. In the distance to either side of the *Dryad*, the shrieking was echoed faintly as the talents on the other ships joined in. The noise was horrible, but everyone put up with it because there was no alternative. Even so, Sayer felt physically ill after a time, and could not bear to look at the writhing figure on the foredeck. He had to shut down his own magical gift for a while, because something of the agonized telepathy was leaking into his thoughts. It was close to madness, with touches of great sadness as well as evil and violence, and he could not stomach it. This meant he could no longer see the relic's trail, but that did not really matter at this stage. They knew it was on the island, and it was only when they reached Jazireh that a more accurate location would be needed.

The Isle of the Dead gradually loomed up ahead of them, first its shape and then finer details becoming clear. When they were close enough to observe the coastline, Nazeri ordered the ships to sail around to the east rather than attempting to land immediately. They spotted the huts of the village almost at once, and the size of the settlement caused some astonishment. Even though the place appeared deserted, Sayer was not the only one to sense the atmosphere of watching and waiting. A little further on, all was still quiet, but a few corpses bobbed in the surf at the water's edge, a sight that filled the observers with revulsion.

'Perhaps the plague's got them all,' someone suggested.

'That might be just what they want us to think,' Nazeri said.

Further reconnaissance revealed a few more signs of the island community, but not a single glimpse of any people.

'Where was the Eye taken ashore?' Nazeri asked.

Sayer had been able to use his talent again for a while now. Although the shrieking went on, there had been no sign of any of the creatures for some time.

'On the other side of that headland,' he said, pointing back to the west beyond the village. 'Where we first came close to the shore.'

'That's where they expect us to land, then,' the captain said. 'We'd better make it look as if we're doing what they want, hadn't we?' He shouted some orders and the flotilla began to come about.

A little later, Nazeri sent messages to the other two boats and they turned away, leaving the *Dryad* to go on alone.

'What's happening?' Sayer asked.

'Akander and his men are going to burn the village,' Nazeri replied.

'Haven't these people suffered enough?' the seeker exclaimed in horror. 'Why—'

'This is a trap!' the captain snapped. 'If we're to retrieve the Eye, we have to create a little diversion. And Sayer, when I want your opinion, I'll ask for it. In the meantime, you'll do exactly what I tell you. If you lift a finger to help anyone – *anyone* – on the island, or even if you take longer than I like to obey an order, I'll kill you. Do you understand?'

CHAPTER THIRTY-SEVEN

'Seekers often come to feel that they "own" certain relics, once they have followed the stones' resonances and brought them back to their rightful place. Such proprietorial feelings are a natural part of a talent's involvement in the great task but, if taken to extremes, can engender jealousy and other destructive emotions. Care should be taken to ensure that, while a seeker receives the acknowledgement merited by his accomplishments, he does not become unduly attached to any particular stone, especially those of considerable significance. Such important relics are the spiritual property of all Tirokian citizens.'

Extract from *Yazd's Training Manual for Those Showing Magical Talent*

'I thought that might get their attention,' Nazeri said with evident satisfaction.

The first volley of fire-arrows from the *Saltrunner* had rained down on the huts with deadly accuracy. As several roofs burst into flame, there was suddenly movement onshore. People emerged from some of the huts and from other hiding places, some in the woods beyond. Concealment was no longer an option, and the island's inhabitants ran in all directions, looking like ants whose nest has been disturbed. The sound of their yelling and screaming carried faintly over the water, just audible above the noises of the wind and waves and the continuing howl of the sentinel.

Sayer watched the scene in horror. He knew that some of the plague victims were probably inside the burning huts. It was unlikely that the kyars would have been able to move them all when the rest of the islanders went to hide, and he could only imagine the panic among the healers. Even if he was wrong and the patients were safe, the loss of their shelters, with the worst of the winter still to come, would be disastrous enough. He felt helpless and sick with rage. Was Aphra among those people he could see scurrying to and fro? He was too far away to be able to recognize anyone and, in any case, everything was so confused that it would be easy to miss her. And where was Kailas? Was she in the middle of this terrible mess, or was she playing her part elsewhere? Sayer knew his wife well enough to be certain that, wherever she was, she would be taking an active role. However, the islanders' schemes might already be in disarray. Without having been party to the kyars' discussions, it was impossible to guess what their intentions had been, but Sayer doubted that they could have prepared for such a ruthless assault.

'There!' Nazeri said, pointing. 'It looks as though they're trying to get a message to the people in hiding. Follow them closely!' he called to the lookout.

A second wave of arrows added to the confusion of the scene on the shore, which was now wreathed in smoke. The messengers were heading west, towards the headland, but they soon vanished from sight. Nazeri sent signals for the *Dawn Flame* to accompany the *Dryad*, and for the *Saltrunner* to stay where it was and continue harrying the islanders by any means they saw fit.

'Now we can get on with the real job,' Nazeri said.

Sayer did not reply, partly because he had nothing to say, and partly because his mind was suddenly full of horrific images. Smoke burned his throat and lungs, screams filled his ears and flames leapt up all around. He was in the midst of the conflagration, but everything he saw and felt was coming from Kailas. The telepathic vision lasted only a few moments, and was overlaid by his wife's panic and guilt over what her actions had brought about; in that instant, Sayer knew that the kyars had not expected such a vicious response.

Kailas? Are you all right? He was desperate to try and contact her.

Sayer? Kailas's response was full of fear and sudden hope, but then the fleeting contact was lost, cut off by the intrusion of other thoughts, other pressing needs.

Although Sayer now knew where his wife was, the knowledge brought no comfort. He watched the village for as long as he could, hoping to see some sign that the islanders might be winning the unequal battle. Desperate efforts were being made to douse the fires and to help the remaining occupants to escape, but as the smoke thickened and the distance between the ship and the settlement grew, it was impossible to see whether they were having any success. Sayer could only hope that Akander would be content with this long-range attack. The thought of someone like Lieutenant Maier going ashore to create even greater carnage was too dreadful to contemplate.

The seeker was forced to abandon his speculation when Nazeri called for him to come to the foredeck. The two ships were rounding the point now, and Sayer was able to locate the spot where the Eye had been taken ashore in a small sandy cove. Theisen took his ship in towards the coast and dropped anchor, while everyone aboard the *Dryad* watched to see whether this provoked any response from the islanders. None came, and the first party of soldiers, all wearing face masks, went ashore – but not at the cove. Their objective, as Nazeri explained, was to establish a defensible position at the end of the headland, a base which would enable others to travel to and from the ships in relative safety. They would still be close enough to the starting point of the Eye's trail for Sayer to pick it up easily.

The advance party met with no opposition and had soon carried out their initial task, with archers stationed at vantage points and platoons of guards ready to move forward whenever necessary. More troops went ashore from the *Dawn Flame* then, accompanied by a man who wore a red headband. It was either another seeker, or someone pretending to be one. Either ploy might have made sense, but Sayer was taken aback nonetheless.

Noting Sayer's surprise, Nazeri smiled.

'That's Obra,' he said. 'We'll see how he fares, before you disembark.'

Sayer suddenly remembered that he was not the only seeker to have dealt with the Eye of Clouds. Obra had also been on that journey through the Rivash Canyon, albeit in a secondary role, and would be able to recognize the stone's unique resonance easily enough. This made Sayer wonder whether his own talent was really needed at all on the expedition, and also made him feel a little aggrieved. In spite of his current ambivalence, the Eye was *his* stone, and he was the one who should be going after it.

'If the kyars have any nasty surprises in store for us,' Nazeri explained, 'Obra would be a less significant loss to the great task, and we'll learn by his mistakes.'

Sayer understood then, and felt a measure of pity for his fellow seeker. Obra was expendable, as were the men who went with him.

'Take us in closer!' Nazeri called to the helmsman. 'We may need to move fast soon.'

As the ship moved slowly in the increasingly shallow water, they lost sight of the distant village. Sayer had already tried calling out to Kailas with his mind again, to no avail, but now he experienced another vivid telepathic flash. She was running – it was impossible to tell where – and gasping for breath.

Gods, Sayer. It's all going wrong.

He felt her distress as though it were his own.

What's happening? he asked, but there was no reply. She was gone again.

'There's movement inland!' one of the lookouts called. 'They're adjusting positions.'

Everyone watched closely, but there was no sign of any conflict. It seemed that the kyars were content simply to observe for the moment. Theisen was busy organizing a party to head inland, with Obra as their guide. He too was aware of the islanders' movements, and the soldiers all had their weapons drawn now.

'Can you tell where the Eye is?' Nazeri asked.

'A considerable distance from the coast,' Sayer replied, 'but I can't locate it exactly. I get the impression of height, though, so it's probably somewhere on the side of the volcano.'

Nazeri nodded.

'Logical enough,' he said. 'Assuming they want to draw us on.'

'I thought you were going to give them the opportunity to trade,' Sayer added bitterly.

'Keep your mouth shut, Seeker,' the captain growled, 'or I'll think you're a kyar sympathizer after all.'

'I'm not, but there are people I love out there.'

'Then you should have been more careful in choosing who to love,' Nazeri stated dismissively. He was still studying events on land as Theisen led his men north.

We didn't expect so many soldiers. Kailas's plaintive cry broke into Sayer's consciousness, without any visual images this time. *Can't you do anything?*

Once more he had no chance to reply before the contact vanished again. He felt wretched, but couldn't think of anything he *could* do.

The progress of the advance party was unhindered, although the route they were taking was hard to fathom, following a convoluted course that zigzagged across the headland and then into the broken terrain beyond. As before, a few kyars were seen moving in the surrounding areas, but they seemed to be keeping their distance and retreating as the soldiers advanced.

'That was their plan,' Nazeri stated confidently. 'To wait until our men were inland, then take those left on the shore and get to the ship. But I don't think they were expecting us to be here too. Let's go!'

The military forces and crew of the *Dryad* moved swiftly into operation, lowering small boats into the water and boarding them rapidly. One of the spare shriekers went with them to provide protection if necessary. As Sayer was about to go over the side he was offered a mask, but he shook his head and climbed down to the waiting skiff. Nazeri followed, and the oarsmen took them towards the shore at a good pace. Once these landings were complete, the camp at the tip of the headland was defended by a formidable force, but there was still no sign of any attack.

'All right, Sayer,' the captain said. 'Now it's your turn. They might have been able to confuse Obra, but you can see where he's heading now. Is he going in the right direction?'

The seeker nodded. He saw no point in lying. The kyars obviously expected them to follow the relic's trail, so trying to mislead Nazeri and his men would help no one. Perhaps he would get his chance to help Kailas later.

'Then we'll follow at a discreet distance,' Nazeri decided. He began shouting orders and a sizeable party set off, with the captain and Sayer in its centre.

'Just remember, Seeker, I'm right behind you,' Nazeri whispered. 'And my promise still stands.'

As they moved forward, scouts went out ahead and to either side of the main group, making sure they didn't walk into an ambush. Sayer could sense the Eye's trail like a tangled maze all around them, and he realized that the islanders must have taken it round in a tortuous route, to deliberately try to confuse and delay any seeker. However, Obra had already exposed that ruse, and because Sayer already knew the direction in which the relic lay, there was no need to follow the same twists and turns. Instead, they struck out directly along the spine of the promontory, gaining considerably on the earlier group.

They were soon crossing rough, sparsely wooded terrain that rose gently at first and then grew steeper. The soldiers were still wary of an ambush, but the area offered little scope for any sizeable group of attackers to hide. The relic's trail was clear now, and it was obvious that Obra was able to follow it with ease. Sayer began to think it was *too* easy, but said nothing, not wanting to wreck the kyars' plans if they really had any surprises in store.

The landscape became more barren and rugged as they climbed onto the lower slopes of the volcano. The rock here was rough and sharp edged, and brittle in places. It crunched underfoot, and the broken pieces chimed in an almost musical way. Stealth was almost impossible in these conditions, and they were forced to rely on their scouts to ensure their safety. They entered a series of ridges and gullies, running down from the mountain, and it became more and more difficult to keep Obra's group in sight. Runners reported back to Nazeri almost constantly, but there was still no sign of any opposition.

'Theisen and his men have entered a ravine,' one of the scouts said, somewhat breathlessly. 'They could lose touch with their own scouts.'

Nazeri nodded his acknowledgement but said nothing, and the man ran off again. The possible implications of the news were not lost on anyone.

There was an unpleasant smell of sulphur in the air, which grew stronger as they walked on. As they reached the entrance to the ravine, they saw that it turned to the right some distance ahead, and so they could see nothing of Theisen and his group.

'The Eye's trail leads in there?' Nazeri asked.

'Yes.' To Sayer it was as clear and bright as if it had been paved with gold.

'I don't like this,' the captain muttered, and called a halt. He sent several small groups of men to reconnoitre the land to either side of the gorge.

Don't go into the ravine! The words exploded in Sayer's head in tones of terrified panic. *Tyler was going to use it to trap the soldiers, but now he'll kill them if he can.*

How? Sayer asked, but Kailas did not reply. He had his answer a few moments later. From ahead came an ominous rumbling noise and the sound of distant screaming.

'Get clear! Get clear!' Nazeri yelled, waving his men away from the entrance to the canyon.

As they were scrambling to higher ground, a billow of steam filled the upper reaches of the ravine and the stench in the air became almost overpowering. Then a huge wave of boiling mud surged round the bend in the gorge with the force of an avalanche. Here and there in the bubbling brown mass Sayer could see a piece of clothing, a hand or some other unidentifiable remnant of the men who had been drowned by the scalding deluge. He felt sick, suddenly realizing that the soldiers were not the only ones capable of ruthlessness.

As many of the others around him watched in horror, Nazeri went into action, shouting out a stream of orders that gave his men no more time to think. They climbed rapidly away from the death-filled valley, and made their way along the ridge above. Ahead of them the scouts spotted some islanders, and Sayer saw a few of them fall as the archers found their targets. The soldiers would not hesitate to take whatever revenge they could for their dead comrades.

'Where's the Eye?' Nazeri demanded. 'Can you see it?'

'It's moving,' Sayer replied, before he could stop to think. 'Someone must be carrying it.'

'Which way?'

Sayer pointed and they set off again, clambering over the twisted boulders. More skirmishes were taking place ahead of them, accompanied by shouts and the clash of steel.

We failed. Kailas's voice sounded miserably in his head. *There's no way we can match them now. Lead them to it, Sayer, or they'll kill us all.*

I'm sorry, he replied. *There was nothing I could do.*

I'm sorry too. It's not your fault. I love you.

I love you too, he said, but he knew she could not hear him. The contact had been broken.

'It's stopped moving,' Sayer told Nazeri. 'This way.'

Once they had found the relic – it had been left lying in the open on top of a prominent boulder – Nazeri had called off the men who were pursuing the islanders, and headed back towards the shore. He did not bother looking for survivors in the flooded ravine.

Sayer felt terrible as he went with the soldiers. He wondered whether he would be able to escape, to stay on the island when the others left, but Nazeri's presence – he had never been more than a few paces from the seeker – made him think again. He told himself that he would be more use to the kyars if he remained in a position of some influence – albeit limited – in Qara, but the knowledge that he had been so close to Kailas, and possibly Aphra, and that he would now have to abandon them again, was devastating.

However, as they made their way down and the coastline came back into view, he began to wonder if Kailas's anguished admission of failure had not been premature. Something extraordinary was clearly happening offshore. Smoke was rising from the *Dawn Flame*, which seemed to be drifting out of control towards the bay to the west. What was more, several small boats were milling around in the water, together with a large number of men. The *Dryad* had not moved and the encampment on the headland was intact, but from this distance it was impossible to see exactly what was happening around the other ship.

Although Nazeri urged his men on, by the time they reached the coast the *Dawn Flame* appeared to have run aground near the small cove that Sayer had first seen, and there was less activity in the water. From the reports Nazeri received, it seemed that the ship had been attacked – exactly how was not known – and in the course of the battle most of her crew had gone overboard. The captain swore under his breath, then set about ferrying everyone back to the *Dryad* and the *Saltrunner*, which had just arrived from the east. Sayer went with him, feeling as bewildered as any of his companions, but hoping that the kyars might have salvaged something from the wreckage of their plans.

Once the evacuation was complete, Nazeri sought out one of the survivors from the *Dawn Flame* and demanded to know what had happened. Although the man was soaked to the skin and shaking with cold, he delivered his report with military thoroughness.

'They came at us underwater, sir. We think they must have used breathing tubes and covered themselves with drifts of seaweed, because by the time our lookouts spotted them they were all around us. We weren't able to defend the ship, but we put up a good fight,' he added defensively.

'What about the sentinels?' Nazeri asked urgently.

'All dead, sir.'

'You're absolutely sure of that?'

'Absolutely, sir. I slit one of their throats myself, and saw the other two die as well.'

'Good man,' the captain responded. 'We couldn't afford to have one of them captured while they were still able to work.'

Sayer guessed that the soldiers' orders had been very clear on this point, and wondered whether he would have met the same fate if he'd been in any danger of being captured.

'We tried to scuttle the ship,' the man went on. 'She's holed below the waterline and on fire.'

'Then why hasn't she sunk?'

'I don't know, sir.'

'Well, a burnt-out hulk won't be much use to them without a shrieker. Our job's done,' Nazeri concluded, holding up the Eye of Clouds for all to see. 'Let's go home.'

As the remaining two ships turned to head for Qara, Sayer looked back towards the island. Smoke was still rising from the village. Although he tried to listen for Kailas's telepathic voice, to tell her that this was not the end, that she must not give up hope, he did not really believe it himself. And all he heard was silence.

CHAPTER THIRTY-EIGHT

'On a personal note, I am bound to say that designing the comprehensive reference system for the archives of Qara has been both a pleasure and a privilege. Although the indexing is not complete (especially where the all important cross-references are concerned), every item we hold and each new artefact that is discovered can now be catalogued within the existing codex. Scholars will thus be able to proceed with their research in a much more precise and systematic manner, and I am confident that this will lead to many exciting revelations.'

From the annual report of the Chief Scribe to the
Council, in the 4th year of the great task

To his utter frustration, Sayer returned to a life that was even more cloistered than before; his efforts during the mission to regain the Eye of Clouds had evidently not been enough for him to be reinstated as a full-time seeker. Instead, he was taken back to his cramped apartment at the Hariolatorium and left to his own devices. For several days he saw no one except the guards who brought his meals, and his increasingly frequent requests to go out were all refused. He was not even invited to the second rededication of the

Eye which, as he subsequently learnt from one of the soldiers, had been a quiet, private ceremony, conducted with a minimum of fuss. Inevitably, rumours had circulated about the stone's disappearance but, for obvious reasons, this was not something Halion and the Council wished to emphasize. Now that the relic was back, they simply made certain that as many people as possible were aware of the fact. As far as the authorities were concerned, it was as though it had never gone missing.

Sayer was in effect a prisoner, and as a result he had plenty of time to reflect on what had happened on the Isle of the Dead. The more he thought about it, the more he believed that the plan hatched by Kailas and the kyars had been a good one. Luring a ship to the island, drawing the military inland to stretch their resources, and then approaching the ship underwater – taking advantage of the protection offered by its sentinel – so that they could capture it, must have seemed like the best opportunity they had ever had. That all their efforts had come to nought was due to their having underestimated the vigour with which their enemies would respond to the challenge. The fact that there had been three ships and a vast number of soldiers had made things difficult enough, but the diversion caused by the burning of the village and Nazeri's willingness to sacrifice Obra, Theisen and his men had meant that the kyars had stood no chance. In the end, all they had achieved was to intensify the deadly enmity between the islanders and the military forces of the Council.

Kailas's role in all of this was the hardest thing of all for Sayer to accept. Had her conversion to the kyars' cause been a gradual process, or a spur of the moment decision? He still found it hard to picture his wife climbing up inside the uppermost spire of the Tower of Clouds in order to steal the Eye, and yet that was just what she had done. And while her motives had no doubt been honourable, her actions had forced the islanders into their ill-fated bid to escape. Now that it had failed, how would the kyars regard her intervention? Kailas could not have foreseen the devastation she had unwittingly brought down upon Jazireh, but she had given them no choice in the matter. Once the Eye was on the island, confrontation was inevitable – and the consequences had been dire.

From a personal point of view, Sayer had lost his wife and his unborn child, and there now seemed little prospect of ever seeing them again. Their telepathic link had only emphasized just how much he missed her, and he brooded about this too. The bond between them was obviously still developing; it had been intermittent and uncontrolled, but it had been a more direct form of communication, over longer distances, than ever before. He sometimes fantasized about being able to talk to her, no matter how far apart they were, and he had even tried to do so from Qara. His lack of success had left him more depressed than ever.

The final reason for his mounting frustration was that he was quite unable to discover anything about the kyars' progress on the mainland. He could only assume that they had been able to find out what had happened on the island, but he would have liked to be able to tell Bylar the whole story and get his reactions. He would also have liked to know what messages the crow had brought with it. He could not help wondering whether any of the information it had carried might have made a difference to the outcome of the conflict, and he tortured himself with a variety of far-fetched imaginings.

Eventually, just when he was thinking that he could stand his confinement no longer, he was granted some respite, and summoned to see Halion at the Council meeting house near Dominion Square. It was a pleasure just to be out on the streets again, even if the prospect of the interview was less than enticing.

'Come in and sit down, Sayer,' the archivect said briskly when he arrived. 'I thought it was about time we had a talk.'

Sayer did as he was told, wondering what was coming next.

'I realize this is a difficult time for you,' Halion went on, 'and I feel partly responsible. Kailas was my choice for you, after all, and it is her misguided actions, more than anything, that have raised the doubts over your future. Incidentally, I've had the marriage formally annulled, so she's not your responsibility any more. We'll find you a new wife in due course.'

Sayer stared at him in disbelief. *Annulled?* Just like that? He was stunned, speechless – and waited in silent rage to see what further surprises Halion had in store.

'That part of your life is over,' his master continued. 'It's your future we have to consider now. I've thought about this a good deal, and have decided that it would be best if you did not travel at present.'

Sayer was about to protest that he was a seeker, that travelling was an essential part of what he did, but the implications of Halion's words sank in and he held his tongue. It was obvious that he was still not trusted, and probably would not be trusted again until the kyar problem was solved once and for all. While the rebels posed any kind of threat, he would remain suspect.

'We'll keep this under review, of course, but for now it seems best to utilize your talents in research. The invigilators tell me that you show a great deal of promise in that respect. There are a huge number of documents and other records that are connected with The Plan which have never been investigated properly, and certainly not by someone as gifted as you.'

'I will play whatever part is assigned to me in the great task,' Sayer responded, trying to sound humble and sincere, even though all his hopes were sinking. His future was mapped out in his mind; endless, meaningless toil, locked away in the dusty archives of the Hariolatorium. It was dispiriting and demeaning, but he was in no position to refuse.

And so the nightmare began. After a single day he knew that his new task would be even worse than he had imagined, and he wondered whether this was not another subtle form of torture. Every hour spent in the airless, windowless chambers seemed to last an eternity and, for all he achieved, he might as well have been asleep in his apartment.

He worked with two scribes and a variety of junior assistants, who all approached what they did with a degree of seriousness that bordered on the obsessive. This particular team had been asked to assess an obscure section of the archives – a section that contained a great number of fragmentary stone tablets. Many of the earliest records of the Temple, which were collectively known as The Plan, had been etched in stone, rather than written down on paper, and it was felt that Sayer's previous experience with relics made him suitable for this particular investigation. His job was to handle the fragments, read what was inscribed upon them and then try to interpret the messages, using whatever he could glean from the internal resonances of the stone itself. The scribes eagerly wrote down everything he said, and cross-referenced their findings with earlier records. The assistants were charged with the task of carrying the tablets to and fro, locating specific items requested by the scribes, and then replacing them in the long racks on which they were stored.

None of these investigations produced anything that seemed remotely interesting or useful to Sayer, although he did catch several curious glimpses of the distant past, but his colleagues appeared delighted by even the most inconsequential of his utterances. When he realized that two fragments previously thought to be unconnected were actually part of the same original tablet, the scribes' excitement was boundless – so much so that they insisted on studying the two pieces for several more hours.

At the end of the second day Sayer was actually looking forward to the lonely misery of his apartment, and after the third he was seriously considering murder – or suicide. It was only his all-consuming need to discover what was going on in the world outside his dungeon that kept him from acting on these impulses. Although he tried to engage his guards in conversation whenever he could, they remained tight-lipped for the most part, and he could see no end to his isolation. His spirit grew smaller, until he began to feel that he was almost invisible; even his dreams were plagued by disquieting images. He was drowning in his own sense of futility.

It was on the fourth day that he found a reason to go on living.

'Archive reference MS5352,' Nuhin confirmed happily. The senior scribe nodded to the assistant who had placed the thin sliver of stone on the table in front of them. 'See what you make of this, Sayer.'

The seeker picked up the jagged fragment. He felt no immediate spark, no rush of history, and resigned himself to another fruitless hour of probing for non-existent secrets. Automatically he began to read the words that were etched into its surface, studying the delicate letters that had faded to almost nothing. Some of it was illegible and, as both sides had been broken away, none of the sentences he could decipher were complete. As a result what he was able to read made little sense.

'We could do a charcoal tracing,' the other scribe, whose name was Troyna, suggested. 'If the lettering is too faint.'

'Maybe later,' Sayer replied. 'Let me look first.'

Both scribes sat waiting eagerly, their pens poised to record any pearls of wisdom that dropped from his lips, and Sayer wanted to laugh at the absurdity of it all. He was tempted to make up something outrageous, but resisted, knowing that his reputation was uncertain enough as it was. He ran his fingers over the words like a blind man, trying to confirm the evidence of his eyes, then read out his findings. These had no doubt been catalogued earlier, within the original archive reference system, but he was aware that the scribes liked confirmation of what they already knew. It lent whatever followed an air of authenticity.

'"they lead us dow",' he began.

The scribes' pens scratched away.

'"it of fire and scorp",' Sayer went on. '"may be curved or", "Beware the dark mir", "on the ghost road".'

That was all there was. Although at first sight he could make neither head nor tail of it, there was something familiar about some of the phrases – and it took him only a few moments to work out why.

'This is from *The Oracles of Zavanaiu*.' He paused, looking puzzled, aware that the scribes were regarding him expectantly. 'But surely this predates the oracles?'

'Can you confirm that?' Nuhin asked.

'Yes.' Although Sayer had been able to sense little from the resonance of the stone, he could at least tell that it was ancient. If this really *was* part of The Plan, then it dated from the time of the Temple's original construction – long before the legendary mad prophet had decreed that it should be rebuilt.

His companions remained silent now, waiting for him to go on. Evidently they too recognized the resemblance, but wanted Sayer to work it out for himself.

'So Zavanaiu was quoting from this. Do you have the full text of the oracles here?'

'We have a transcription, yes,' Troyna replied. He consulted another battered ledger, then called to one of the assistants and issued precise instructions.

'I remember the bit about fire and scorpions,' Sayer commented.

'It's hard to forget that passage,' Nuhin agreed, affording the seeker a rare glimpse of his sense of humour.

The assistant returned, and set a leather-bound tome in front of Troyna. He opened it, found the page he wanted, then slid it over to his senior colleague. Nuhin glanced at it, nodded, and passed it on to Sayer.

'"Not all omens are what they seem",' the seeker read, '"and the paths they lead us down may end in the pit of fire and scorpions. So tread lightly on the ghost road, and remember that the gods use strange messengers".'

He picked up the fragment and peered at it again.

'That fits,' he said. 'This is definitely Zavanaiu's source, but he missed part of it out. I wonder why.'

Again the scribes said nothing, concentrating first on their own writing, then looking up at him expectantly.

'What "may be curved"?' Sayer wondered aloud. 'And why should we "beware the dark mir", whatever that is?' He frowned at the incomplete word.

'Mirage?' Troyna suggested. 'Miracle? Mirror?'

'Mirrors were once used for the purposes of scrying,' Nuhin observed. 'Given the earlier reference to omens, that seems a possibility. Does the resonance of the stone give you any clues?'

Sayer shook his head. Although he had no idea what the missing words were, the phrase 'the dark mirror' echoed in his brain. He had seen it somewhere before, but he couldn't remember where.

'Do the oracles often quote from earlier sources?' he asked curiously.

'There are several known instances,' Nuhin replied.

'I thought they were supposed to be divinely inspired.'

'Even when messages come from the gods, they are often couched in familiar terms,' the scribe explained. 'Zavanaiu may have seen this tablet before he experienced his visions, and when he needed to write them down he simply used phrases from his own memory to express the will of the pantheon.'

Sayer read the relevant section of the oracles once more. It seemed now to be a warning rather than an instruction, which was consistent with the tone implied by the words from the missing sentences.

'Is this an accurate transcript?' he asked. 'The full text?'

'Of course,' Nuhin answered, sounding mildly offended.

'Can I see the original?'

'Of course not!' Troyna gasped.

'Zavanaiu's original writings are kept in the vaults of the Treasury,' Nuhin said. 'No one is allowed to touch them.'

'Why not?'

'They're too precious, too fragile. Handling would destroy them and transcriptions are widely available, so it is unnecessary.'

'Aren't you curious to see if the original contains the part that's missing here?' Sayer persisted.

'It does not,' Nuhin stated firmly. 'If it did, then it would be on our copy.'

Sayer could tell he was not going to get anywhere in this argument, so switched to another line of enquiry.

'How can a mirror be dark?'

'Only if it reflects darkness,' Troyna replied thoughtfully.

'But . . .' Sayer hesitated as new thoughts sprang into his mind, thoughts he could not reveal in his present company. 'We're wasting time here,' he said. 'I can't read anything more in this stone.'

Although the scribes looked disappointed, they accepted his verdict and, after making the appropriate entries in their records, moved on to other work. However, they achieved little for the rest of that day because, unknown to them, Sayer's concentration was now distracted by speculation of his own. The reference to 'a dark mirror' had been nagging away at the back of his mind, and the memory had finally surfaced. He now knew where he had seen it before – and the possible implications were staggering.

CHAPTER THIRTY-NINE

'A mirror, black and full of light,
A mirror that assigns our roles,
Reflects the yellow flame of might,
False suns illuminate the scrolls.

'Blind Yma turns her face aside,
And the scryer's madness ceases.
Her fire is doused, his masters hide,
The dark mirror lies in pieces.'

From *A True History of Tirok*

One of the few indulgences Sayer had been allowed in his hermit-like existence was access to writing materials. He had requested these on the pretext of needing them to continue his work, although he really wanted them as a possible means of communication with the outside world. In the event there had been no opportunity for this, and so he had barely used them at all. This evening, however, the first thing he did on his return to his quarters was to write out from memory the two verses Hurghad had left for him. It was there, of course, that he had first come across the reference to a 'dark mirror'. Reading the lines again now, he felt the stirrings of genuine excitement and a growing certainty.

Nuhin's remark about mirrors having once been used for scrying had given Sayer the crucial clue to interpreting the verse. What if, for the purposes of the poem, a 'mirror' actually meant scrying or prophecy? He realized that this was all speculation, but once that first assumption was made, everything else flowed from it. After the enigmatic first line, the second translated as 'A prophecy that assigns our roles' – a perfect description of *The Oracles of Zavanaiu*. If that premise was accepted, then the rest of the verse implied a very jaundiced view of the documents that had become central to Tirok's way of life. Could it really be a simple coincidence that the archivects – people who could reasonably be described as mighty – wore *yellow* robes and headbands? And did their 'false suns' exert an undue influence over the contents of the oracles?

The second verse added further weight to Sayer's argument. Yma was the goddess of prophecy and fire, and if she had turned her face aside, then the implication was that these prophetic visions were not genuine. If the 'scryer' was Zavanaiu, then the fact that his 'madness' had ceased could refer to the end of his revelatory trance. Zavanaiu was known as the 'Mad Prophet of Qara', but it was possible that he had been more rational and pragmatic than anyone guessed. His hidden masters – the Council? – might have forced him to write what they wanted, thus effectively dousing Yma's fire of truth. And when that assumption was made, the last line of Hurghad's message took on a new meaning altogether. When he had first read it, Sayer had naturally taken it to refer to the pieces of a broken mirror lying on the ground. Now its real significance seemed as clear as day. The dark mirror *lies* in pieces. In other words, the prophecy contained no truth. Zavanaiu had been made to write whatever the archivects wanted. The oracles, on which the entire society of the nation was based, were fakes!

Sayer realized now that Hurghad had tried to tell him this before his death. When the seeker had claimed that the oracles came from the gods, the hermit had replied, 'But they still had to be written down by a man. It would not be the first time men used religion for their own ends.'

Sayer could hear the old man's voice now, and wished he had not been so incredulous at the time. Much had changed since then, of course. He had learnt a great deal about the hidden forces that ruled his homeland, and was now prepared to believe almost anything. Although he might once have been tempted to think that the verses were the deranged ramblings of an insane old man, that time was past. His experience with the fragment earlier that day had been the turning point. The fact that some parts of the oracles had been quoted – and quoted inaccurately – from earlier sources, made them seem decidedly unmystical. And if there was nothing to hide, then why were the original documents kept locked away in the Treasury vaults when transcriptions were freely and widely available? Sayer realized that he knew no one who had even seen them, let alone touched these precious records – and the reason for that now seemed obvious. Either they did not exist, or they did not say what everyone had been led to believe. Or, if they appeared genuine on the surface, their real origins would be betrayed if anyone with the necessary talent was able to gain access to them.

The explosive nature of this secret was abundantly clear. Even Hurghad, whose writings had normally been so straightforward, had felt the need to couch his theory in obscure, poetic terms. This was the knowledge that would make the kyars' arguments for change unanswerable, which would expose the self-serving hypocrisy of the Council – and which would allow the country's resources to be concentrated on something more worthwhile than rebuilding an anachronistic, irrelevant shrine.

Sayer felt rage swell up within him. His life, and the lives of thousands of others, had been shaped by a lie. The staggering waste appalled him. He knew he had to do something about it – but he was only one man. He had no proof, only supposition. Although it was enough for him, the people of Tirok were so inured to their subservient way of life that it would take more than one lone voice crying in the wilderness to bring about a revolution. He had to get into the Treasury vaults, to obtain incontrovertible proof that he could show first to the kyars and then to the rest of Qara. Yet how was he to do this? He couldn't even escape from his own lodgings, let alone gain access to the most heavily protected building in the city. He was desperate to act, to smash his way through stone walls with his bare fists, to scream his defiance of Halion and all his contemptible allies. But he had to wait, to bide his time and plan his next steps carefully.

One thing was certain, however. Whatever the cost to himself, it would not be too long before he did *something*.

'All right, Sayer. Get those clothes off. All of them!'

After a single peremptory knock, Galieva had flung open the door and barged into his room. Now she stood with her hands on her hips and a mischievous grin on her face. He stared at her as though she were an apparition.

'Come on. I haven't got all day.'

'What?' Sayer was quite unable to grasp what was going on. He had hardly slept that night, and the sight of one of the people he had longed to see had come as a shock. He knew vaguely that he ought to be taking advantage of this unexpected opportunity, but he could not think how, and Galieva's order for him to strip had only confused him even more.

'Shall I undo the buttons for you?' she asked sarcastically.

'I have . . . I have something important . . .' he began,

then noticed the guards, who were just outside the door, listening to the exchange, and fell silent.

'I'm sure you have,' Galieva replied tartly. 'I can turn my back if you're too shy to show me, but I need the clothes, so get undressed now!'

'Why?'

'Do you realize you've been wearing those same things for several days now?' she said. 'And you look as if you've been sleeping in them too. There have been complaints, Seeker, and I'm not surprised. Frankly, you stink!'

Behind her the guards were smirking, enjoying this early-morning interruption of their tedious routine. Sayer began to remove his garments and, at Galieva's request, tossed them onto the floor between them. She watched him, making no move to turn her back and ignoring the soldiers' laughter, and did not speak again until he was naked.

'I'll wash these and return them tomorrow,' she said as she scooped up the pile and turned to leave. 'Didn't look that important to me,' she remarked to the guards as she swept past them.

Sayer, feeling stupid and embarrassed, wanted to say something more, but did not dare. She had already given him the lifeline he needed. Tomorrow he would be ready.

Sayer was too distracted to work properly that day, and the scribes found him to be unusually ineffectual. His thoughts were preoccupied with how he should communicate with Galieva – with words, signs, written messages? – and what he should say. He must tell her about the oracles, but it wasn't something he could just blurt out without explanation. There was also the question what he should *ask* her. There were so many things he wanted to know.

He fretted over these problems all evening and most of the night, without reaching any useful conclusions, and eventually fell into an exhausted sleep. The next morning he awoke in a panic, expecting Galieva to arrive at any moment and knowing that he was not properly prepared. As it turned out, there had been no sign of her by the time he was escorted to the archives to begin work at the normal hour, and he spent the day worrying about what had gone wrong.

When he got back to his quarters that evening, he was dismayed to see that his clothes, now clean and neatly folded, were lying on his bed. Galieva had returned, but he had not been there to see her. He groaned and cursed her silently. Surely she knew he'd be absent if she came in the middle of the day? Then it occurred to him that a meeting in his apartment – with curious guards watching over them – would not allow them to talk openly. He realized suddenly that Galieva must have used his clothes to conceal a message. Eager now, he searched them, looking for a note or any sign, but found nothing. His frustration grew until at last he felt a tiny brooch that had been pinned to the underside of his tunic collar. It had not been there before, and he unclasped it in order to examine it more closely.

Midnight. Be ready.

The words formed in his head of their own volition. He did not recognize the 'voice', but he had no doubt that this was the message he was looking for. And yet it told him next to nothing. What should he be ready for? He tried to read more from the resonance of the small, dark-red gemstone that was set into the metal, but only heard the same message repeated several times, growing fainter every time like an echo. He eventually decided that if the kyars were involved, whatever happened could only be to his benefit – and he would be as ready as he could be. The very fact that the rebels had someone capable of impressing a message like this on an inanimate object – even if it had been very simple compared to the one Aphra had sent – was reassuring in itself. Sayer settled down to wait quietly, barely able to suppress his agitation.

The longest night of the year was only a few days away now, and it seemed to Sayer that the hours of darkness crept by until he began to think that midnight would never arrive. He paced the room, then forced himself to sit quietly, in case his incessant movement made the guards suspicious. Everything in the building grew silent as the city slept.

When he heard the key turn in the lock, he jumped to his feet, ready – he hoped – for anything. Galieva stepped inside and closed the door quietly behind her. She smiled, glad to see that he was awake and dressed.

'You got the message, then?' she whispered.

Sayer nodded.

'Put this on,' she said, tossing him a black, hooded cape. He did as he was told, knowing that the cloak would be an effective disguise and thrilled at the prospect of escape.

'Where are we going?'

'Where would you like to go?' she asked, grinning.

'Anywhere! Just get me out of here.'

'We've been thinking the same thing for some time,' she told him. 'Follow me and don't talk unless you have to. Let's go.'

She opened the door again and checked the corridor before stepping outside. Sayer followed, his eyes straining in the dim lamplight. He glanced anxiously at the two sentries, who were sprawled at their post, but they were paying him no attention. In fact they lay so still that he thought at first they might be dead, but as he came closer he realized that they were breathing slowly.

'Don't worry about them,' Galieva whispered. 'They won't wake up until morning.'

They went on, Galieva moving with the stealth and grace

of a kyar, which Sayer decided was only appropriate. He realized that he was close to hysteria and tried to calm himself down, even though his heart was racing so fast he thought it would explode. They went down two flights of stairs to the ground floor but then, instead of heading for one of the entrances, Galieva led him down again, towards the basement where the archives were stored. He wanted to ask why they were going this way but, mindful of her earlier advice, he kept quiet and simply followed. The familiar musty smell of his workplace enveloped them. Their progress became slower still here, because navigation was difficult in the almost total darkness. In the end Sayer had no idea where they were, and he became even more bemused when Galieva squatted down in a corner and beckoned him to join her.

'Wait here. Whatever happens, don't move until I get back. All right?'

Sayer nodded, and she vanished into the shadows. A short time later he heard several distant crashes, then some shouting and the sound of running feet. Moments after that he was astonished to find that the far end of the basement was ablaze. The flickering light of the flames made the place seem to jump and sway, and his nostrils caught the first acrid whiff of smoke. As far as he could tell he was now trapped inside a potential inferno, and he was terrified. Was this some sort of trick? Had the kyars rescued him only to let him be killed? He was about to try to escape when a breathless Galieva was suddenly at his side.

'What's going on?' he whispered urgently.

Galieva held a finger to her lips, and put a restraining hand on his shoulder as she watched the progress of the fire at the far end of the archives. Coils of smoke were now creeping along the ceiling, billowing down in places as the currents of air shifted. The shouting Sayer had heard earlier came closer, and he became aware of half-seen figures milling about amid the smoke and flames.

'Now,' Galieva decided, pulling Sayer's hood over his head. 'Let's go.' She grabbed a couple of books from the nearest shelf and thrust them into his hands as he stood up, took some for herself, then ran towards the conflagration. Sayer followed as best he could, coughing as the smoke caught his throat and the heat of the fire beat upon them. They were soon in the middle of a scene of utter confusion. The blaze had taken a firm grip on several sections of the shelving, and a large number of guards and invigilators – who had obviously been rudely awakened from their beds – were trying either to put out the flames or rescue the precious relics. They did not appear to be succeeding in either task, and no one paid Galieva and Sayer any attention as they ran through them and up the steps.

The scene at the top was almost as chaotic. Much of the corridor was ablaze, the wooden panelling and banisters covered in flame, and men were running to and fro as smoke obscured almost everything. Galieva and Sayer made straight for the main entrance, and stumbled out onto the street to join a throng of people who had either escaped from the fire or were arriving to help fight it. The general pandemonium, the darkness and the drifting clouds of smoke meant that they were able to slip unnoticed to the edge of the crowd and then into a side alley, where they discarded their books. They ducked into a doorway and waited, but no one followed them. Galieva took a deep breath, started coughing and ended up laughing.

'Gods, that was fun,' she spluttered. 'It's amazing what you can do with a little oil and a few lamps.'

'You did all that yourself?' Sayer asked in open admiration.

'Oh, no. I had a little help. And we're not done yet. We still have to get you out of the city. They can't enforce the curfew once we're outside the walls. Come on.'

'Where are we going?' he asked as she led the way into the back streets.

'To Souls' Gate. We have to get to the docks.'

'Why?'

'There's a ship coming in from the Isle of the Dead,' Galieva replied. 'We thought you might like to be there to meet it.'

CHAPTER FORTY

'Blood is sacred.'
Inscription at the base of Durak's Altar,
within The Sanctuary

Sayer was astounded by Galieva's news, and his mind teemed
with questions. However, he could not begin to ask them
until they had made the long journey across the city, and
completed their escape by slipping through a narrow tunnel
to the side of Souls' Gate – which Sayer had not even known
existed. He wondered briefly how the kyars had managed to
make sure it was left unguarded. Once they were outside the
walls, however, he had more important things on his mind.

'How do you know there's a boat coming?' he asked
Galieva as she led him on into the ramshackle town that had
grown up between the city and the lake.

'The third crow came back the day before yesterday,' she
replied.

'Will Kailas and Aphra be on board?'

'I don't know for sure, but it's very likely.'

Sayer's heart lifted at her words, and the immense yearning he had endured for so long spilt over into an almost
unbearable flood of anticipation. He also felt an unprece-
dented sense of freedom, not just because of his own escape

369

from confinement, but because there was no going back now. After tonight there could be no more pretence; his allegiance had been publicly declared. He was a kyar.

'How will they get the boat past the monsters?' he asked, returning to present matters.

'Your guess is as good as mine,' Galieva replied, 'but this is it, Sayer. If they make it, there'll be no turning back.'

She sounded ecstatic, and the echo of his own thoughts was uncanny, but the element of doubt implicit in her words sent a sudden chill through the seeker. *If* they make it? He was about to ask what she meant when he suddenly lost all sense of time and place.

He staggered, and fell to his knees as the inside of his head exploded. He was blind and deaf, and the pain was so great he thought he was going to die. His whole world became a hurricane of garish colours and anguished howling. Voices struggled to make themselves heard amid the storm and he clung to them tenaciously, hoping they might explain what was happening to him, but the roaring drowned out their words.

'Sayer, what's happening? What's the matter?'

An alien presence drifted into his tormented consciousness. Although he could not see her, he knew it was Galieva, knew vaguely that she had wrapped her arms around him in a futile attempt to protect him from the assault that came from within. And from far away.

He tried to speak, and failed.

Dreadful visions intruded upon the tempest, images of violence, of razor-sharp teeth and nightmarish tentacles, of blood and rage. Streaks of livid colour splattered across his thoughts, accompanied by wordless screams. He felt their fury, their need for vengeance, their ravening. And, buried deep beneath the more violent emotions, he felt their sadness. He cried out in pity and remorse, weeping now.

I can't do this. I'm not strong enough.

Kailas's voice was full of despair, but to Sayer it was a beacon of hope. She was in the midst of this terrible dream and now, at last, he was no longer simply a victim. He had a purpose.

You are stronger than you know.

Sayer? The wonderment in her voice filled him with love, and lent him his own strength. *Where are you?*

I'm here, he replied. *With you. Always.* He was calm now, beyond the pain.

She did not need to ask for his help. He was giving it already.

'Gods, you scared me!' Galieva exclaimed as Sayer's sight returned and he looked up at her. 'Are you all right?'

The seeker felt as though his entire body had been battered by wooden clubs. His head ached abominably, and almost every muscle was afflicted by cramps. When he opened his mouth to speak, blood ran down his chin and he spat on the ground, realizing that he had bitten his tongue.

'I'm fine,' he said, and tried to smile.

'You don't look it,' she replied, but he could tell that she was greatly relieved.

'It's over,' he told her quietly.

They were sitting together, huddled in the doorway of a squalid wooden hut beside a muddy alleyway. The scene was illuminated by a full moon directly overhead, and Sayer realized he had no idea how long they had been there. He sat up carefully.

'What happened?' Galieva asked.

'I don't really know.' He could have said more, but he was still trying to work it all out for himself. Although the link was still there, it was silent now and oddly serene, a single colour that overlaid his thoughts.

Galieva did not press him for details, knowing that he would explain eventually – if he could.

'Do you still want to go to the docks?'

'Yes. They've got away from the monsters, so they shouldn't be too long now.'

Galieva had the good sense not to ask him how he knew this, and merely helped him to his feet. Although his progress was unsteady at first, his determination drove him on. They soon found that they were far from being alone; a large number of people were converging on the docks, and there was a feeling of curious expectancy in the air.

'The grapevine's done its job,' Galieva commented with obvious satisfaction. 'But that means the garrison will have been alerted too, so keep your hood up for now.'

At first not even Sayer could believe what he was seeing. The kyars could not have wished for a more spectacular entrance. The *Dawn Flame* shone like a violet beacon in the night, the entire ship enclosed in a radiant aura that extended like a tent over the hull, deck and rigging. Even though he had been a part of it, Sayer was still in awe of what Kailas had achieved. The ship was immeasurably larger than anything that had been protected before – by any silk – and yet she had succeeded. What was more, she had evidently maintained the shield for several hours, a feat that was unheard of, even when dealing with a small relic. Sayer felt pride as well as wonder at his wife's accomplishment. He knew that other talents had played a part, but Kailas had shaped all their efforts. He longed to hear her voice again. She had been silent for a long time now, and he dared not try to renew the contact in case he disturbed her concentration for this final, vital part of the journey.

Sayer and Galieva had been lucky enough to find a vantage point on an outside staircase, and watched the ship's approach from there. The docks were now filled with a jostling throng, and everyone gazed out over the black water. The harbour itself was also getting crowded. A number of small boats had set sail, wanting to get a closer look at the miraculous apparition. Everyone concerned with the business of the port recognized the *Dawn Flame* as the vessel that had reportedly been sunk, and its unexpected reappearance – especially in these extraordinary circumstances – had roused enormous curiosity. Other boats set forth, driven by more substantial motives. Some went to offer assistance, but when they found that none was required they withdrew and escorted the ship into the port from a distance. At the same time, vessels manned by soldiers from the harbour garrison were trying to prevent the *Dawn Flame* from docking. However, their orders and threats were simply ignored. The ship and its passengers were invulnerable within the violet shield, and the few half-hearted attacks came to nothing. The military forces withdrew in consternation, trying to disregard the jeering of the crowd.

The *Dawn Flame* came on, slowly but steadily, and as she drew closer to the shore it was possible to make out the people aboard, moving about and watching from inside the all-encompassing aura. At last she slid alongside one of the jetties and came to a halt. Ropes were thrown ashore, and these too were enveloped in an unnatural violet glow. This caused the people waiting on the dock some concern, but as soon as one of their number grasped a rope and came to no harm, the others were seized and the mooring secured.

At this point, there was a sudden commotion at the harbour end of the jetty. Amid much heckling and angry protests, a sizeable force of soldiers from the local garrison swept down towards the newcomers. However, no one had yet tried to come ashore from the *Dawn Flame*, and its protective shield remained in place. A group of people had gathered on the raised foredeck, and a murmuring spread through the crowd as one of them stepped forward. Even through the coloured haze, he was instantly recognizable to most of those watching. It was Rivolier, the people's poet. The onlookers grew quiet in anticipation.

'You know me!' he called, his resonant voice seeming to fill the entire harbour. 'I—'

'You are under arrest!' the captain of the guard shouted. 'For violating—'

The rest of his words were lost in a storm of protest and abuse, followed by an insistent chant of 'Rivo, Rivo, Rivo!' from the surrounding multitude. The soldiers seemed only then to realize that they were cut off at the end of a pier by a hostile crowd. The captain fell silent, no doubt shocked by the disregard of his authority, and looked around hopefully for signs of reinforcements. When some semblance of quiet had been restored, Rivolier spoke again.

'I had the plague, but now I am well. I am cured!' He spread his arms wide and, even in that peculiar light, he did indeed look robust and healthy. The crowd's murmurings grew to a roar, then fell away again as the storyteller held up his hands and cried out once more.

'The kyars have been telling you the truth! The plague is not always deadly. I am the living proof.'

'You're lying,' the captain yelled back. 'You were never ill.'

'Then why was he exiled?' someone in the crowd shouted, and others joined in, drowning out any possible reply.

'There are others on this ship who will tell you the same story,' Rivolier continued. He turned and beckoned to someone behind him, and an old woman stepped forward readily. 'This is Kelara. She suffered far more than I, and yet look at her now!'

There were evidently some among the spectators who

knew the old woman, and their shouts of joy and amazement spread through the crowd like wildfire. For her own
part, Kelara stood erect and smiling, self-consciously enjoying her moment in the limelight until another man stepped
forward. Sayer recognized him as Skehan, one of Aphra's
apprentices.

'I have not suffered from the plague,' he shouted. 'But I
have worked among those who have been its victims. My
colleagues and I are healers, and we bring with us herbs that
can help cure the contagion. We may not be able to save
everyone who gets the plague, but we pledge ourselves to
try. No one need suffer exile simply because they fall ill.'

'You are a liar and a criminal!' the captain yelled, trying
once more to make himself heard.

'My only crime is that I dared oppose the Council,'
Skehan declared passionately. 'I am a kyar – and proud of it.'

The captain turned then, and signalled to some of his men.
Two archers reacted almost instantly, each arrow speeding
directly towards the healer's chest. He flinched instinctively,
but neither shaft reached its target. The shield deflected
them both so that they fell harmlessly into the dock.

'We are no criminals!' Rivolier cried over the rising wave of
protest. 'The wrongdoing has been committed by the archivects and their servants who enforced this evil deception.'

By now the mood of the crowd was turning ugly and,
with more people arriving all the time as news of the *Dawn
Flame*'s homecoming spread, the atmosphere was swinging
decisively in the kyars' favour. Other military units, on the
fringes of the mob and aboard their vessels, were more or less
helpless against the angry press of people. Many of them
found themselves being pelted with stones and other debris
and prudently withdrew to safer positions – leaving the
troop at the end of the pier isolated and vulnerable as the
gathering threatened to turn into a full-scale riot. Too late,

their captain realized their predicament and ordered his men to retreat – but they had nowhere to go. A great crush of people descended on them and not even their swords could prevent them from being swept back. Most of them ended up in the water, swimming for their lives as the citizens of Qara celebrated their victory. Only then did the magical shield slowly fade. The newcomers were now able to go ashore, and were soon absorbed into the welcoming throng.

It took Sayer and Galieva some time to reach the ship, because they had to struggle against a human tide that was now flowing jubilantly away from the pier, but they made it at last and clambered aboard. By then there were only two people left on the *Dawn Flame*, and Sayer ran to them at once. Kailas was lying on the deck next to the base of the mainmast, with one of the healers kneeling next to her. His wife was unconscious, and did not respond when Sayer took her in his arms.

'I can't rouse her,' her companion said. Sayer recognized her as the woman called Cainas.

'She's exhausted,' he replied. 'It's hardly surprising, after an effort like that.'

'She was amazing,' Cainas agreed. 'I can't believe we're actually here.'

'A few days' rest and she'll be fine,' Sayer added, hoping this was true but knowing in his heart that it might not be as simple as that. He could sense the dark abyss of silence into which Kailas had plunged, and he was not sure she would ever be able to climb up from such a fathomless depth. He held her tenderly, praying that she would come back to him.

'You're Sayer, aren't you?' Cainas said.

He nodded.

'Did Aphra come with you?' he asked, wondering whether he might have missed his sister in the turmoil.

'She wouldn't come,' the healer replied. 'We tried to argue with her, but you know what she's like.'

Sayer's heart sank again. He wasn't sure he knew his sister at all.

'I hate to bring this up,' Galieva put in, 'but we ought to get Kailas off the ship. It's sinking.'

Sayer glanced around in alarm and saw that she was right. The gunnels were already below the level of the jetty, and the mooring ropes were creaking ominously. Together they carried his wife over to the side and onto the pier.

'Tyler said the repairs were only temporary,' Cainas said, as they watched the *Dawn Flame* sink lower into the water. 'Her shield must have been the only thing that kept us afloat.'

'We'd better go,' Galieva said. 'Sooner or later the military are going to try and regain control of the harbour, and I'd rather not be here when they do.'

Sayer glanced at her, understanding, but not caring where they went. Aphra had not been on board as he had hoped, and Kailas was in a deep coma. In the midst of what had been a massive triumph for the kyars, he alone was bereft.

CHAPTER FORTY-ONE

'Magic that has a measurable effect upon the physical world, as opposed to the intangible realm of men's thoughts, exacts a proportionately greater toll upon the talent involved. For this reason the recovery time of a silk after any action will depend upon the size, duration and complexity of the task that has been undertaken.'

Extract from *Yazd's Training Manual for Those Showing Magical Talent*

'Kailas told us this might happen,' Jase said, and glanced apologetically at Sayer. 'I can't reach her.'

Two days had passed since the return of the *Dawn Flame*, and in that time Kailas had not stirred. Her breathing and pulse were so slow that they were almost imperceptible. Sayer had stayed by her side the whole time, tending to her, begging her with words and thoughts to come back to him. But she remained out of reach, engulfed in silence.

'At first we thought she'd stop and rest when we were beyond the ring of buoys,' Skehan explained, 'but she was either unable or unwilling to stop. Anyone who tried to go near her was literally thrown back by the force of her effort.'

'I think she knew we'd sink if she let go,' Cainas said.

Since Sayer and Kailas had been installed in the dingy wooden house in the midst of the shantytown, there had been a constant flow of visitors, but this was the first time that all three of Aphra's apprentice healers had been there together. They had all tried individually to 'look inside' Kailas, and had met with a similar lack of success. Cainas, whose talent was the strongest – even though her mind was less focused – had clearly been shocked by the impression left by the coma; although the reactions of the other two had been more guarded, they were obviously worried too.

Now that he knew his own telepathic link was of no use, the healers had been Sayer's best hope of helping his wife to recover, but this profound emptiness was beyond their experience. They were all very tired, having been working more or less continuously since their arrival. Although their dramatic entrance had made a considerable impact, many people were still sceptical, and the healers had been determined to demonstrate their skills as widely as possible. In the past the tendency had been for the families of anyone who showed any sign of the plague to hide the fact, in case they lost them unnecessarily, so there were entrenched attitudes to overcome as well as the disease itself. However, progress was being made, especially as the medicines made from aphran were most effective during the early stages of the illness. If it had not been for his personal concerns, Sayer would have been delighted by the healers' achievements, not least because he knew his sister had been responsible for developing their methods of treatment.

'We all owe Kailas our lives,' Jase said now. 'We'll keep trying to help her.'

'Thank you.'

'It's the least we can do,' Skehan said. 'Kailas was the only reason we were able to escape. We know how much she sacrificed in order to try and rescue us. When the first plan failed, some people blamed her, and I think she felt she needed to prove herself.'

'She's certainly done that,' Cainas said.

'Did Aphra blame her?' Sayer asked, remembering the strained relationship between the two women.

'At first, yes,' Jase replied. 'The scale of the attack was a terrible shock, and left us in a real mess. A lot of Aphra's patients died in the fire.'

'But that wasn't Kailas's fault,' Sayer protested.

'Aphra realized that eventually,' Skehan said. 'And she was as astonished as any of us when Kailas offered to try and protect an entire ship.'

'The *Dawn Flame* had been badly damaged,' Cainas added, 'but we managed to patch her up, so something good did come out of the attack.'

'I wish I could have done something—' Sayer began, still feeling guilty about his own passive role in the raid.

'We know you had no choice,' Skehan cut in. 'Kailas told us.'

'Why didn't Aphra come with you?'

The three healers glanced at each other. It was a momentary hesitation, but a telling one.

'She chose not to,' Jase answered. 'Someone had to stay behind and look after those who were still sick.'

'She had to tend the herb gardens too,' Cainas added, 'and train more healers to take over from us.'

'The people who went on the ship were chosen either because they'd recovered from the plague, because they were healers, or because they could help Kailas with the shield,' Skehan explained. 'But we couldn't take everybody. This was our one chance to make an impression on the mainland. Volunteering to stay behind was as brave as wanting to go.'

Sayer looked at each of them in turn, his gaze finally coming to rest on Cainas, the weakest point in their defences.

'Aphra's ill, isn't she?' he said.

Although Cainas did not answer, her expression told him all he needed to know. The silence of the others confirmed it.

'There's every reason to believe she'll recover,' Jase said eventually. 'If anyone can beat it, Aphra can.'

'She told us not to tell you,' Skehan said. 'She didn't want you worrying about her when you need all your energy to help us here.'

'And to help Kailas,' Cainas added. 'She wanted you to be happy with her, Sayer.' The healer's eyes were brimming with tears now, and she turned away as Sayer looked down at the unmoving figure of his wife. No one spoke for a while.

'I saw another silk at work once,' Jase said, breaking the uncomfortable silence. 'That was incredible enough, but what Kailas did was beyond anything I could have imagined.'

'There were others on board who lent her some support,' Skehan added. 'No one else on the island had trained as a silk, but she identified a few who had some latent ability and they came with us. Kailas made herself the focus of all their efforts so they could work together.'

'I know,' Sayer said, recalling his own remote involvement. 'I'd like to talk to some of them.'

'Sayer?'

The seeker turned to face the newcomers. Although he did not recognize them, the presence of strangers caused him no alarm. The kyars were keeping an unobtrusive watch over his hiding place, and would not have let anyone enter unless they were friends.

'Come in.'

'My name is Maehl, and this is my daughter, Faia. Skehan said you wanted to talk to us.'

The man limped slightly as he came forward, and his face

and arms were badly scarred, but the girl, who could have
been no more than six years old, was dark and beautiful.
Unlike her father, she did not seem at all nervous.

'Hello,' she said, her wide eyes staring, not at Sayer, but
at the pale figure of his wife where she lay on her pallet.

'Hello,' he replied. 'You both helped Kailas protect the
ship, didn't you?'

Maehl nodded.

'Among others,' he agreed.

'It was hard,' Faia said. 'I've only just woken up. Isn't
Kailas awake?'

'Not yet,' Sayer replied heavily.

'You were there too,' Maehl said. 'We all felt your presence, though we didn't know who it was at the time.'

'Did you sense the monsters when you were leaving the
island?'

'Don't call them that,' the girl said. 'They don't like it.'

'How do you know?' Sayer asked, immediately intrigued.

Faia looked confused, and glanced at her father.

'I just know,' she said eventually.

'Did they frighten you?'

'A little. They came to look at us, but they knew they
couldn't hurt us in the shield.'

'They scared me to Khorasan and back,' Maehl admitted.

'There were stories in their minds,' Faia volunteered.
'They made me cry.'

'Sad stories?'

'Yes.'

'Do you remember what the stories were about?'

'It's all mixed up.' She paused, looking uncertain again.
'They were burying big eggs in the sand, and then a man
came and broke them. There was a fire too, and things fell
off the ships that they didn't like. That's when they started
to fight, but they were only trying to save their babies.' Her

voice had risen and she was visibly upset now.

Her father moved to comfort her, and glanced at Sayer with pleading in his eyes.

'It's all right, Faia,' the seeker said. 'They were just stories.' It was a lie and he knew it, but the child had been through enough. 'Did you feel any of this, Maehl?'

'Only in the vaguest sense,' he replied. 'Nothing specific. I know the creatures were sad as well as angry, and that they're very old, but that's all really.'

'Was Faia born on the island?'

'Yes. Why?' He was still holding his daughter close.

'She's obviously more sensitive than either of us. I was just looking for a reason. Thank you, Faia. You've been a great help.'

The girl turned to face him again, wiping her eyes.

'I hope Kailas wakes up soon,' she said.

So do I, Sayer thought. So do I.

Later that evening, Sayer was still mulling over the conversation. Could it really be that simple? Jazireh, it seemed, had once been the breeding ground of an ancient species of amphibious creatures, probably dating back to a time long before mankind ever came to the land. A single man had stumbled onto the site, causing untold damage either through ignorance or malice, and the creatures – not unnaturally – had reacted by defending their young. As the encroachment of men and their ships corrupted the age-old habitat, the creatures assumed that all sailors were intent on destruction and so retaliated with increasing ferocity. When the colony had been set up, it confirmed the implacable enmity between the two races, and the conflict became – for the creatures at least – a battle for survival itself.

It all made perfect sense. The problem was, what could be done to rectify the situation now?

* * *

'Look who I've found!' Galieva remarked as she came in from the street.

Bylar followed her. He was one of the people Sayer had most wanted to see, but now, in the third day of Kailas's death-like sleep, he found it difficult to raise much enthusiasm.

'How is she?' the kyars' leader asked gravely.

'No change.'

'Give it time. The healers tell me there's nothing wrong physically.'

Sayer nodded. He had been told the same thing, but how long could that last? Sooner or later the coma must take its toll, and the gods alone knew what effect it would be having on the baby inside her.

'Your wife is a remarkable woman,' Bylar added. 'We all have much to thank her for.'

Sayer still could not think of anything to say.

'Can we talk?' the kyar asked.

'Of course.'

'Galieva tells me you have an interesting theory about *The Oracles of Zavanaiu*.'

'It's more than a theory. I'm sure they're fakes.' Sayer went on to explain about Hurghad's poem, and about his own findings. 'I can prove it,' he concluded, 'if we can get inside the Treasury.'

'That could be a bit difficult just now,' Bylar replied. 'Security in the city has been tightened up, and especially so in places like the Treasury. We've no access to anyone of sufficient authority to get us in or the oracles out. The few sympathizers we *do* have are too low in the pecking order, and they're having to keep their heads down at the moment anyway.'

'But don't you see—' Sayer began.

'Of course. I understand, and nothing would please me more than to expose the Council's lies, but it's just not possible.'

'There must be *something* we can do.' Sayer found that he needed this revenge, and he was not prepared to give up yet.

'We'll keep working on it,' Bylar assured him. 'In the meantime, we have to look at other options.'

'Such as?'

'This, for a start.' The kyar took something from his pocket and held it out to Sayer. It was Hurghad's message stone.

The seeker took it gingerly, not allowing the images to form, but knowing they were there.

'That's proof of Halion's dishonesty,' Bylar said. 'A lot of people already know he's lied about the plague and the Isle of the Dead, and if we can present them with this evidence they may believe us about the oracles too.'

'How do we do that?' Sayer asked. 'You've got to have talent and touch the stone to see what's there.'

'I've got an idea about that,' the kyar said. 'How much do you know about what's going on out there now?'

'Not much.' Some of his visitors had given Sayer a few reports, but he hadn't paid them much attention.

'Well, the city is pretty much sealed off,' Bylar said. 'They're only letting certain people in and out of the gates. That's why it's taken me so long to get here. The entire army is on full alert, and all the archivects' estates are heavily guarded. Even here, the port's under martial law and the trade routes are being patrolled by military units. There have been some skirmishes and raids, and a few arrests, but Halion knows he's treading on thin ice out here. We've many converts among the people who saw the *Dawn Flame* arrive, but inside the walls it's different. People there have a lot more to lose, and we have to overcome uncertainty and scepticism. The latest thing is a new decree stating that anyone who breaks the law – any law – is liable to lose their citizenship on the spot. Which means that the soldiers can do more or less what they like.'

'We're all outlaws now,' Galieva put in.

The situation sounded grim to Sayer, but Bylar was not finished.

'The one place Halion can't isolate entirely is the Temple,' he went on. 'To do that would give the lie to everything he's been claiming.'

'So is that where we strike back?' Sayer guessed.

'Yes. Halion's planning something big for the midwinter festival. Apparently the very last piece of the Tower of Clouds has been recovered, and he's going to use the occasion to make a major public announcement. Rumour has it he's going to proclaim himself as Tirok's sole overlord.'

'And disband the Council?'

'Looks like it. Some of the other archivects haven't been seen for a while. It seems that Halion's taking advantage of the situation to get rid of rivals as well as enemies.'

'How will he justify that?'

'No doubt he'll have arranged for the gods to give him their blessing,' Galieva remarked.

'You may be right,' Bylar said seriously. 'Remember when Durak's head appeared in the smoke in Dominion Square? It doesn't take much imagination to see that Halion could present another, even more impressive demonstration at the Temple. He's got vast magical resources to call upon.'

'But to do that,' Galieva reasoned, 'to make it effective, he needs a lot of people there to witness his triumph.'

'Exactly,' Bylar agreed. 'However many guards he has there, they won't be able to stop some of us getting in as well. And we have magicians of our own.'

'When is midwinter's day?' Sayer asked.

'Two days from now,' Galieva replied.

'That doesn't give us much time.'

'No, it doesn't,' Bylar admitted. 'So if you've got any ideas, let's hear them.'

Sayer's mind went blank.

'All right,' Bylar said, seeing his bemusement. 'Here's what I think we should do.'

That evening, Sayer returned to his bedside vigil, holding Kailas's hand and talking to her, with both words and thoughts, in the forlorn hope of some response. At the end of his discussion with Bylar he had been almost over-whelmed by the responsibility that had been placed on his shoulders, but looking at his wife now, he was determined to succeed. Her monumental effort deserved no less a response from him. The sheer scale of what had been proposed had left Sayer breathless, but he would not be alone and – with others to help – there was no reason why he could not achieve as much as Kailas had. He just wished that she could be there to share it with him.

It now seemed increasingly unlikely that he would ever see Aphra again. If Kailas was also lost to him, then his own life would have little meaning, whatever the outcome of the imminent confrontation. Before Bylar had left, Sayer had remembered to tell him his theory about the creatures around the Isle of the Dead. The kyars' leader had promised to send word to those left on Jazireh when the crows next returned there. However, it was events on the mainland that preoccupied both men now.

'I wish I had your strength, your courage,' Sayer whispered, looking at his wife's beautiful, yet inanimate face. 'I love you, Kailas. Wherever you are, I hope you know that.'

He was startled by a soft cough behind him, and looked round to see that Cainas had crept into the room unnoticed.

'I'm sorry,' she mumbled in embarrassment. 'I didn't mean . . .'

'It's all right. Come in.'

'Can I try again?'

'If you're sure you want to. I know how hard you've been working.'

'It's the least we can do,' Cainas replied, repeating her colleague's earlier words.

She came to kneel beside the pallet, placed her fingertips on either side of Kailas's head, and closed her eyes. Sayer had some idea of what she was experiencing because of Aphra's message stone, but he had little hope of any positive results now. Cainas and the others had each tried several times to heal his wife's condition, but it had proved to be beyond their skill. As before, Cainas withdrew, breathless and pale-faced.

'I can't—' she gasped. 'She's so . . . far away still.'

'And the baby?'

Cainas managed a weak smile.

'She's fine. Kailas's body is protecting her.'

Sayer took what comfort he could from that.

Later, when they were alone once more, he touched her head himself and tried to see into her thoughts, but the Kailas he knew had vanished. There was only the silent abyss, and darkness.

CHAPTER FORTY-TWO

'Midwinter's day is sacred to Ailor, the breath of
clouds. Rainwater collected on this day is considered
to be particularly efficacious.'

From *Balak's Codex of Water Rituals*

At noon on the shortest day of the year, the Great Temple of
Qara was filled to bursting point. Naturally enough the
centre of all attention was the Tower of Clouds, the magnificent structure dedicated to Ailor. Its cavernous interior
was packed with dignitaries, while the road around it was
guarded by a solid ring of soldiers holding back the crowds.
The streets and alleyways that radiated out from the tower
were also thronged with people, and the Penitents' Way was
one long mass of humanity stretching all the way to the
Kyar Arch and beyond. Every vantage point had been
claimed long ago; many walls and roofs were covered with
spectators and, for once, the omnipresent soldiers made no
attempt to stop such irreverent behaviour. Everyone wanted
to catch a glimpse of Halion when he made his promised
appearance – on the balcony situated a third of the way up
the Tower of Clouds, overlooking the Penitents' Way.

The sky was overcast – appropriately enough – but there
was still a feverish excitement in the air. There had never

been a midwinter festival like this before, and no one knew exactly what to expect. There were silver and white banners everywhere, and many of the crowd were dressed in their finery. Countless conversations formed a ceaseless ebb and flow of sound, like the voice of a human sea.

Sayer was aware of all this only in his mind's eye, his imagination compensating for the darkness in which he lay, cramped and breathless, awaiting his moment. All the resources of the kyars had been used to find him this hiding place the previous day, and he had waited throughout the night and morning, fearing detection at any moment. He had heard the soldiers as they made several security checks; at one point two of them had stopped so close by that he had been able to hear their desultory conversation. However, no one had even suspected his presence and now the only thing he heard was the distant murmur of the crowds.

A sudden burst of triumphant music was followed by the echoing sounds of movement from far below, and Sayer knew it was time. He took a deep breath, trying to steady his nerves, then reached up and pushed with all his might. The stone did not move at first, and he came close to panic, but then – with a grating sound that made his heart race – the lid of the sarcophagus shifted. A few moments later Sayer was able to get his fingers round the edge of the stone, and with the extra leverage he managed to move it aside and clamber out.

He glanced around quickly, but there was no one else on the balcony inside the tallest spire of the Tower of Clouds. He apologized silently once more to the long dead priest whose dusty bones had been moved to provide Sayer with a hiding place, and stretched knotted muscles. Peering over the edge of the balustrade, he saw the last of the dignitaries making their way towards the main entrance to join the crowds on the Penitents' Way. That meant it was almost midday, and Halion and his entourage would be on their way to the exterior balcony several levels below where Sayer now stood. He still had some climbing to do and so, ignoring the protests of his stiff limbs, he made his way to the next section of the spiral staircase. The desecrated tomb now contained only the clothes and false hair that had been his disguise the previous day, and he left it open, knowing it would make no difference. He began to breathe more easily, sure of his own role in what was to follow, and hoping that those he was depending on would also be in position.

The last part of his journey was up a long wooden ladder to the final, tiny circular parapet just under the summit of the tower. When he reached the top, Sayer yanked at the wooden struts and pulled the ladder from its brackets. Then he pushed it away from the wall so that it fell outwards and into open space. The lower end came away too, and the whole thing toppled out into thin air. It plummeted, seeming to take an age before it smashed onto the floor far below and shattered into a hundred pieces. Even if anyone had noticed the noise of the ladder's fall, it could make little difference now. Sayer no longer had any way down and, more importantly, there was no way up for anyone else.

The seeker heard a muted cheer as he reached the uppermost skylight in the tower, and he guessed that Halion must have made his appearance on the lower balcony. Sayer was now only a short distance below the tip of the spire, almost within touching distance of the Eye. He glanced at it now, then levered himself up to look out of the window. The panorama from this dizzying height was breathtaking, with the entire northeast end of the Temple laid out before him like a miniature town. Beyond that he could see the walled city, the lake and, at the limit of visibility, the Isle of the Dead. His gaze lingered there for a moment, but then his attention was drawn back to events much closer at hand as

Halion began to speak. Leaning forward so that he could look down, Sayer could just see the balcony on which the archivect stood, his bright yellow robes making him easy to spot.

'Fellow citizens of Tirok, my friends. Welcome!'

Halion's words boomed out at a volume that no ordinary voice could have achieved, carrying over the vast expanse of the Temple site. The crowds reacted with a rustling surge of astonishment and then an almost reverent hush. Sayer knew that this was the first – and probably the least – of his enemy's magical tricks. That was as expected. Let them use all their talent, he thought, all their strength. The kyars had to be patient, and he would choose the time when they would strike. As Bylar had said, there would probably be an obvious moment when they could turn the tide, when their own resources would be capable of matching the archivect's.

'This is a day of renewal,' Halion went on. 'Of celebration! With Ailor's grace, we have braved another winter. From now on the days grow longer once more. But that is not the only reason to rejoice. The Tower of Clouds is complete at last!'

The applause that greeted this announcement was begun by the group immediately below the balcony. These were the people who had been inside the tower, and a space had been cleared for them by the guards. The wave of approval spread outwards until it became a full-throated roar that took some time to die away.

'One stage of the great task is finished!' Halion cried. 'One part of The Plan is now fulfilled in every detail, and we must use this to inspire our future efforts. The very last relic from the Tower was retrieved by the seeker Mayumi, and has now been replaced.' The archivect gestured towards another person on the balcony, but Sayer was unable to see him until he stepped forward and bowed, accepting another enthusiastic round of applause. 'In these troubled times,' Halion went on, 'such loyalty from servants of the great task is doubly welcome.'

Mayumi's loyalty to Seigui didn't last long, Sayer thought sourly.

'I regret that not everyone has been so true to their faith,' Halion said, in tones of heartfelt regret. 'And the malaise is not confined to the kyars, those contemptible outlaws who have been spreading such outrageous lies. There are even some in high places who have succumbed to the temptations of jealousy, greed and blasphemy. It is my sacred duty to rectify this lamentable situation, and it is a duty I do not take lightly. It is therefore decreed that I alone shall speak for the governance of Tirok.'

This declaration, while not entirely unexpected, raised another storm of sound, although not of a wholly positive nature.

'The Council has been disbanded,' Halion continued, 'and I will now assume command of the entire army, as well as taking responsibility for the talents who formerly owed their allegiance to my fellow archivects.' He paused to let this sink in, then raised his voice again. 'I proclaim all this in due humility, knowing that I have been chosen by the gods for this task, and I pray now for a sign from the pantheon to mark their approval.'

Here it comes, Sayer thought, subliminally aware of the rising tide of sorcery that was focused on the archivect.

The air in front of the Tower of Clouds began to shiver and twist, and sparks of light flashed and coalesced in an oddly dancelike motion as a massive image formed before the crowd. Watching from his eyrie, Sayer could only gasp as loudly as any of the spectators. He had expected a formidable display of power from Halion, but this was beyond anything he could have imagined.

Although the phantasm did not appear entirely solid, it was an exact replica of Halion, complete in every detail. The only difference was that this version was taller than fifty men.

The archivect raised his arms, and as he did so the giant also moved, duplicating the motion exactly. The crowd were silent now, awe-struck and afraid. The gigantic mouth moved as Halion spoke again, and his voice was loud enough to shake the earth beneath their feet.

'The gods have sent a sign. I have been blessed.'

Sayer recognized the quotation from *The Oracles of Zavanaiu*, and it was obvious from the murmur from the crowd that others did too.

'To demonstrate my resolve to honour my pledge, my first act as Tirok's Overlord is to offer the pantheon a sacrifice.' As Halion pointed towards a group of soldiers waiting in one of the nearby ruins, the giant image echoed his gesture – making it seem as though the gods themselves were issuing an order. 'Bring forth the prisoners!'

The guards forced a way through the crowds and climbed up onto a raised platform, set at the junction of the Penitents' Way where it looped around the tower. The six prisoners were forced to kneel, their hands tied behind their backs and, even though he was far away, Sayer recognized at least two of them. The first was Becerra, the other member of the Council who – like Seigui – had been outspoken in his criticism of Halion. The second was Bylar.

'Blood is sacred!' Halion roared. 'By their various treacheries these men have forfeited the right to live. I invoke all the gods of the pantheon to witness their deaths. Accept our offering.'

The soldiers drew their swords as the crowd, torn between the giant and the spectacle below, muttered uneasily. Halion's claiming of supreme power was being followed by an all too dramatic demonstration of the way in which he intended to use it.

Sayer had been so horrified by what was happening that he almost failed to act. But as he recognized that the crucial moment had arrived, both mind and body sprang into action.

Now!

As he scrambled out of the skylight and balanced precariously on the sill, he felt all the others join him, their thoughts linked with one purpose. Sayer took that astonishing new power and shaped it, throwing it back into the world. Magic had a second focus now, and the conflict between the two was immediately apparent. The outlines of the giant blurred and wavered. The crowd's muttering grew louder, and Halion looked round in alarm.

'Wait!' Sayer cried, and his voice, while not matching the archivect's, was far louder than he could have managed alone. 'This is not a sign from the gods, only an abuse of magic. Will you stand and watch while murder is committed?'

The giant was turning now, causing untold alarm in the crowd near its spectral feet. It waved its arms as Halion issued urgent instructions, the enormous face a mask of fury. Sayer knew that soldiers were being despatched to silence him, but for a time at least his position was impregnable.

'Another traitor!' Halion screamed, but the voice, which had once been overwhelming, cracked and faltered, and his next few words went unheard. The talents who were maintaining the giant image were evidently growing weary now, and the unexpected interference was causing them problems.

Sayer recognized what was happening, wrapped himself round with the thoughts and strength of his allies – just as Kailas had done on the *Dawn Flame* – and pressed home his temporary advantage.

'Is this the man you want as Overlord of Tirok?' he asked,

aware now that tiny bolts of lightning were detonating all around him. Many of the people below had spotted him and were pointing up at the tiny figure on the spire. The executioners hesitated, not sure what they should do.

'You know Halion lied to you about the cure for the plague!' Sayer cried. 'The kyars told you the truth about that.'

The archivect's image, which had been growing fainter and more blurred, vanished altogether now, and Halion spoke again with renewed power.

'Will you believe a common criminal?'

'He also lied about the death of Archivect Seigui,' Sayer continued. 'The kyars did not kill him. Watch and see what really happened!'

Halion began to laugh, but he was powerless to prevent what happened next and his derision faded into silence. Although Sayer had less talent at his disposal, he was able to shape it for himself, whereas the archivect was dependent on others, on prearranged plans.

As Sayer held Hurghad's stone tightly in his outstretched fist, a new vision appeared. Horses galloped in the air above the crowd, the white robes of the riders flapping in the wind. A ragged figure darted out, and the leading mounts shied and swerved. Sayer was in a trance, feeding his own memories of the murder into the scene, but relying on the stone to give it form. The black soldiers emerged, and moments later Seigui lay dead on the ground, his neck broken by Nazeri's sword. The record was complete and the images disappeared, but the point had been made. Halion protested loudly that this was more falsehood, and then that the attackers had been kyars dressed to look like guards, but few people paid his ravings any attention. The tide was beginning to turn.

Sayer awoke as from a dream, almost overbalancing, and

heard shouts echoing inside the spire. He recognized one of the voices as Nazeri's, and knew that his time was limited. He drew himself up to speak again, diverting the power of the magic back into his own voice.

'But the greatest lie of all has been hidden for thirty years,' he shouted. '*The Oracles of Zavanaiu* are fakes!'

'Blasphemy!' Halion retorted. 'Where is your proof?'

Sayer had none to offer and the crowd, who had been reacting to each turn of the supernatural debate, growled like a gigantic animal. Their indecision hung in the air.

Something happened to Sayer then, something he could not explain. Whether it was guidance from the gods, or prompted by a more mundane instinct, he chose to alter the plans that had been laid so meticulously over the last two days.

Look inside Halion! he told his allies. *Look inside!*

He felt them respond, not understanding at first, and then more willingly as the seeker's purpose became clear.

'Will you look into Halion's thoughts?' Sayer shouted to the throng. 'To see *his* truth?'

'What are you . . . ?' the archivect began, then screamed, clutching his head as if it were about to explode.

Halion was now the focus of *all* the magic in the Temple – and its conflicting demands were tearing him apart.

The air around him grew bright with transient images, ephemeral flashes of colour and the fleeting shapes of a dream. The ground shook, and the Tower of Clouds trembled. Until that moment Halion had accepted the power of all the talents at his command, and used it to further his own ends; now the magic was using *him*. Sayer's colleagues had begun the reversal, but the process soon became a cascade, an unstoppable force. At the epicentre of a double magical storm, Halion was helpless. His mind was exposed and he could hide nothing, not even his memories.

With the strongest magical force ever seen in Tirok filling the air, every person there looked into Halion's past. Everyone, even those with no discernible talent, saw exactly how he had affected their lives. Sayer relived his childhood abduction, the rape of Aphra and all the other wrongs he had endured, but he did so gladly, embracing the pain. He knew that everyone in the Temple saw something different from their own history — all the hypocrisy and injustice, the lies and deceit — and Sayer also knew that for Halion this exposure was the most painful form of torture imaginable. The seeker had claimed his revenge.

Best of all, one of the betrayals laid bare was the very thing that Sayer had been unable to prove. Everyone whose life had been ruled in some way by *The Oracles of Zavanaiu* saw Meydan explain to his son that the prophecies were indeed false, invented to give the Council control over the people.

In the midst of his mental torment, all Halion's sins were revisited upon him and even his followers turned away from him in horror and disgust. He was soon left alone on the balcony, his body rigid in agony.

The magic was an elemental force now, beyond the control of any of those who had instigated it, including Sayer. As all the different disciplines combined in chaotic and quite unpredictable ways, it started to affect the physical world, making the very fabric of the world unstable. The Tower of Clouds shook again, and a few stones fell from its outer turrets. Panic seized the mesmerized crowds and they began to turn and flee. The crush was so great that many were trampled underfoot, but the area around the tower nonetheless cleared quite quickly.

Ironically, the kyars had planned to destroy the upper part of the Tower of Clouds as proof of their serious intentions. Sayer was to have asked the onlookers whether the gods would allow them to do this if the Temple was really so important to them. In so doing, he would prove that the oracles had indeed been forgeries. That was no longer necessary, but the preparations had already been made, with artisans having secretly weakened key points in the structure, ready to bring about the largest demolition any of them had ever attempted. Now it seemed that the tower was going to collapse whether they did anything about it or not.

Sayer should have been protected by a group of the kyars who had been trained as silks, together with others like Maehl and Faia who had some natural ability in the field. Their intention was to envelop him like a relic, so that when he fell, with the spire crashing down all around him, he would survive. Nothing like that had ever been done before, but if it worked it would seem as if it were a miracle, another sign from the gods to convince the people of Qara that Sayer and the kyars were right.

However, no one had foreseen the extent to which the magic itself would take over, spiralling out of control. Sayer, who was now desperately hanging on to his perch, tried to make telepathic contact with the silks, with anyone who might help him, but they were all lost in the psychic hurricane. No one was going to save him when the tower fell. The entire structure creaked and groaned as it shook in the grip of a supernatural earthquake.

He had no way out, no hope, no longer even any fear. Sayer knew he was going to die, and in his final moments his achievement in having destroyed Halion meant nothing. He felt only regret that he would never know what became of Aphra, or of his unborn daughter, or Kailas.

With a huge roar, one of the lower walls of the Tower of Clouds imploded. The entire structure began to fold in on itself, and the spire that Sayer had been clinging to was suddenly no longer a perfect arrow pointed at the sky, but a jumble of its component shapes. He began to fall.

Give me your shape.

Kailas's quiet voice sounded calmly over the roaring of stone, and Sayer responded instinctively. The violet glow formed around him like a second skin, and he stared at his hands in wonder. He was still falling, but now he had no fear of the masonry that tumbled all about him, and he laughed aloud, still not quite believing what was happening. It was the most extraordinary experience of his life. He was cocooned in a shield built of talent and love by the one silk who was outside the storm. Kailas did not speak again, but they had no need of words. The bond between them was complete.

He worried then that, even though he would not be crushed, he might be buried, trapped beneath the rubble. But when he finally came to rest, and the last of the boulders either missed him or bounced away, he was safely on top of a vast heap of milk-white stone. As the dust settled, he stood up and clambered down to the ground, where those close enough to witness his emergence stared incredulously at a man, encased in violet light, who had come back from the dead.

Far above thunder rolled, and it began to rain.

The seeker did not even notice, nor did he have any time for the people who came to greet him. There was only one person he wanted to see.

Sayer began to run.

CHAPTER FORTY-THREE

'False promises from poisoned lips,
And magic signs of blackened hearts,
The law of death that evil grips,
By hollow threats a tyrant starts,
And Qara hoped for freedom.

'His giant crumbled into dust,
The tower fell to crush his plan,
And heroes did what heroes must.
In silk arrayed, the seeker ran,
And Qara sang of freedom.'
                From Rivolier's *The Song of Qara*

The violet aura had faded long before Sayer burst in the door. The kyar who had stayed with Kailas looked up, first in alarm and then in confusion.

'She woke up and said something, but I couldn't understand her,' the woman said, as Sayer knelt by the bedside. 'Then she closed her eyes again and I've not been able to rouse her since.' The disappointment was plain in her voice, and Sayer realized that she could have no idea about what had happened at the tower.

'Don't worry,' he said, confident that he would be

proved right this time. 'She'll wake up soon.'

As he took his wife's hand in his own, she opened her eyes briefly, and smiled.

The following morning, Kailas was able to stay awake a little longer. Cainas had been to see them, and had pronounced both mother and baby to be in good health, but it was a later visitor who brought yet more welcome news.

'There's been a mass exodus from the Isle of the Dead!' Galieva exclaimed, and for a few moments Sayer was too astonished to speak. It was left to Kailas to respond.

'Who escaped?'

'We're not completely sure,' Galieva replied, 'but we think it was everyone!'

Sayer's joy at this news was tempered by an instinctive caution, and his doubts grew as the day went on. In spite of the kyars' determined efforts, no one had been able to find Aphra by the time night had fallen.

Bylar was the next person to bring more visitors. The kyars' leader had managed to escape during the chaos in the Temple. Although many people had been killed that day, none had died at the hands of the executioners.

Bylar beckoned to someone waiting outside and Graovac came in, leading a small girl by the hand.

'This is Elli,' he said. 'She was on Jazireh. My crows like her, but she's a bit shy with people. Go on then, sweetheart, tell the seeker what you wanted to say.'

The girl, who had been determinedly looking down at her feet, glanced up.

'Do you know Aphra?' she whispered.

'She's my sister,' Sayer replied, as foreboding cast a shadow over his heart.

'She looked after me when my mother died,' Elli said,

overcoming her nervousness. 'She said to tell you we talked to the loopoes.'

'The loopoes? Who are they?'

'The creatures in the lake. That's what they're called.'

'And you talked to them?'

Yes. Like this.

As the words sounded telepathically in Sayer's head he glanced at Kailas, and knew by her expression that she had 'heard' them too.

'What did you talk to them about?'

'They told me stories,' Elli explained. 'I didn't under-stand them, but Aphra did. Then we told them we were going away, and we wouldn't hurt them like the shriekers do if they promised not to hurt us. Aphra told me to say the island would be theirs again.'

'And that's why they let you all get away?' Sayer asked, amazed by what had been achieved through the innocence of a child's mind.

Elli nodded solemnly.

'One of my birds brought a message, telling us about the creatures' history,' Graovac explained. 'Aphra was the one who worked out what we had to do, and she helped Elli talk to them.'

'And did Aphra come with you?' Sayer asked, though he feared he already knew the answer.

'She wanted to stay with Tyler,' Elli said.

'Your sister refused to leave,' Graovac amended. 'And Tyler chose to stay with her. The only people left on the island were too sick to travel, and Aphra wouldn't let them die alone.'

'Then she may still come home?' Sayer asked hopefully.

'I don't know,' Graovac replied gravely.

'She was ill too,' Elli added, looking at Sayer with eyes that had already known too much sorrow.

* * *

It took Sayer a few days to find a ship's captain willing to take him and Kailas to Jazireh. Business in the port was understandably chaotic as Qara came to terms with the overthrow of Halion and the Council, and Sayer's problems were exacerbated by his refusal to allow a sentinel on board.

They finally sailed on a small fishing boat, with a crew consisting only of kyars. Graovac and Elli went with them, and the little girl was the only one who was quite unafraid when one of the monsters swam alongside. The creature merely observed their progress for a while, then vanished into the depths.

'I told her what we were doing,' Elli remarked, as if this were nothing special.

'She has a remarkable gift with all animals,' Graovac told Sayer, with a touch of pride that made it obvious the young orphan would not lack for a home or affection.

They anchored just offshore, and Sayer and Kailas went on alone in a rowing boat. There were no signs of life anywhere. Much of the usable wood had been taken to build rafts, and the blackened remains of the village were forlorn and silent.

They widened their search and eventually found Tyler on the headland, leaning against the trunk of a tree. Aphra lay cradled in his arms, like a child. She did not stir as they approached and, from the tears that coursed down Tyler's weather-beaten cheeks, Sayer knew he had come too late.

He knelt before them, unable to hide his own grief, while Kailas, helpless for once, stood a little way off.

'I loved her,' Tyler whispered hoarsely, glancing up at Sayer with such pain in his eyes that it was all the seeker could do not to look away.

'I loved her too,' he managed to say.

'When she first came here, she would let no man near

her,' Tyler went on. 'When I finally won her over, it was too late.'

'Was it the plague?'

Aphra's head was resting peacefully against Tyler's chest, but from what Sayer could see she was not marked, just painfully thin, her face drained of all colour.

'Her experiments weakened her,' Tyler explained. 'She used to say, how can I test medicines on anyone else if I'm not willing to try them myself? That, and working till she was exhausted, took all her strength. Even when she knew someone was dying, she would never stop . . .' He broke off, and glanced despairingly at the sky. 'I loved her,' he repeated in a choked voice.

'And she loved you,' Kailas said, her own voice firm and sure.

Tyler did not respond at first, but then he nodded gratefully.

Sayer wanted to say something too, but he could not speak. He knew his sister had given her life for what she believed in, and had done so gladly, but the injustice of her fate made him feel as though his heart would break. He could only hope that Tyler's love had made her last days a little more joyful.

Aphra was buried next to those she had not been able to save, at the end of the last row of graves. Each of her three mourners said their farewells in their own way, and then they sailed away for the last time, leaving the island to the creatures whose ancient home it was.

EPILOGUE

''Gain, 'gain!'

'I've read you that story three times already,' Sayer protested, but he couldn't help smiling.

'It's time for you to go to bed, young lady,' Kailas added.

Their daughter remained adamant, stabbing at the book with an imperious finger.

''Gain!'

'All right,' Sayer agreed, capitulating. 'Once more, then no more.'

Aphra subsided contentedly, but watched her father closely in case he tried to trick her by skipping any part of her favourite tale.

It had been Kailas's idea to name their child after the aunt she would never know, and it seemed to Sayer now that the decision had been prophetic. His daughter was only two years old, and yet she already reminded him of the twin sister he had loved so much and known so little. Of course, part of that was because of her deep blue eyes, that matched his own, but more than anything else it was her defiant personality that made him remember times past. On several occasions the expression on her small face had been the same as that on Aphra's when, as an eight-year-old, she had faced the soldiers and declared, 'I'm not afraid of you.' At other times the little girl was given to long thoughtful silences in which she appeared to be guarding her own secrets, just as her namesake had done for so long.

In other respects Aphra naturally resembled her mother. She had inherited Kailas's golden hair and fair skin, and it was already possible to see that she would retain the same elfin beauty as she grew older. It was too early to tell whether she possessed any appreciable talent, but their friends all assumed that it was simply a matter of time, and Sayer was in no rush to find out. The healers who had helped Kailas at the birth reported a sense of almost radiant happiness when Aphra had come into the world, and since then she had continued to bring a special joy to all those whose lives she touched. Like all babies, she took it for granted that the entire universe revolved around her, but she repaid her parents' devotion with a fierce, unshakeable love – and a smile that made the midday sun seem dull.

Aphra's first two years of life had seen much change throughout Tirok. The country's borders were open now and – even though only a handful of foreigners ventured as far as Qara – merchants and envoys from other lands regularly visited the outlying regions, drawn by the prospect of increased trade and the opportunities to exchange knowledge.

A new form of government was evolving slowly from the aftermath of Halion's fall. The kyars and the most influential families of Tirok had managed to put old differences behind them – although not without many difficulties – and the uneasy coalition had grown in confidence as time passed. It had been a dangerous and uncomfortable period for many people, and there had been some fighting and destruction, but thankfully, that phase had passed fairly quickly. Even so, a huge number of people had been cast adrift, and found it hard to come to terms with the loss of their old way of life.

Things became somewhat easier as it was made clear that the new authorities – such as they were – genuinely wanted to work for the common good.

The most obvious result of this was that all work on the rebuilding of the Temple had been stopped, leaving it as a half-built but perfectly sufficient monument to the gods, and the resources switched to other projects. New houses, hospitals and other substantial buildings had been constructed in and around Qara, and the food supplies had been reorganized on a more equitable basis. The aim was to prevent anyone in the city suffering for want of a sound roof over their heads or food on their table. Not all these plans went smoothly, of course, but enough progress was made to ensure that no one lost heart. For the vast majority of the population, life was definitely improving. They now had a say in the way their country was being run, and most of them also recognized that the revolution had not just been a material one. A new spirit pervaded Tirok as, for the first time in many years, people who had lived in complete subjugation regained their self-belief and were able to see their way to a new future.

Sayer was also able to look forward rather than back. Although he was still saddened by the loss of his sister, the worst of the grief had passed. He regretted many of his own actions, his missed opportunities, but there was nothing he could do about that now. His only recourse was to make what he could of his own life, and try to make her dreams come true. Without his twin he would never be complete, but he had discovered that he could be happy. Kailas and the younger Aphra had made him whole again.

'"You wouldn't believe me if I told you",' Sayer read, finishing the story once more.

Aphra looked at each of her parents in turn, obviously wondering whether she could get away with asking for another repeat.

'Time for bed,' Kailas said firmly, but Sayer seemed to be in no hurry now and his daughter was happy to stay snuggled close to him.

'Are you ready for our big adventure?' he asked.

'Ship!' Aphra said delightedly.

'That's right. The first part of our journey will be on a ship.'

Kailas watched her husband fondly, recognizing the signs. His thoughts were already far away.

'Do you remember the name of the man who gave me this book?' he asked.

Aphra shook her head.

'He was called Mehran-Dar, and we're going to see if we can find him.'

This was something Sayer had been wanting to do for a long time, and now that he and Kailas had agreed that Aphra was old enough to travel, they would be leaving for Mazandaran within the next few days.

Thanks to the pioneering efforts of the kyars, the plague was no longer spreading as fast, but it remained a serious problem. Sayer's attempts to adapt his own talents and become a healer had been only partially successful. As a result he had decided that the best use of his particular skill would be to find Mehran-Dar – who was not only a master healer but a teacher as well – and hope to persuade him to return to Qara with them. Using the multiple resonances of the book he had been given, Sayer believed that he would be able to follow his trail into Mazandaran.

'It'll mean leaving our home for a long time,' he said now, 'but Mama and I will always be with you, so that will be all right, won't it?'

Aphra nodded, but her eyelids were drooping now, and Kailas wondered how much of the one-sided conversation her daughter had actually taken in.

'Come on, little one,' she said, and stooped to pick her up.

Sayer watched them go to the bedroom, thankful that their world was one in which this Aphra might have a chance of lasting happiness. It was a world that he and Kailas had helped to shape, and their marriage was now the most important aspect of his life. A long forgotten memory intruded suddenly upon his thoughts then, and he leapt to his feet.

'What's the matter?' Kailas asked as she came back into the room.

'There's something we have to do before we leave Qara.'

'What's that?'

'Halion had our marriage annulled before . . .'

'Annulled?' Kailas asked in surprise.

'Yes.'

She began to laugh then, wondering why he hadn't thought to mention this before.

'Does it really matter?' she asked.

For answer, Sayer knelt down on one knee and took her hand in his.

'Will you marry me?' he said.